Debra Clopton

HER FOREVER COWBOY

and

YULETIDE COWBOY

HARLEQUIN® LOVE INSPIRED®CLASSICS

Recycling programs
for this product may
not exist in your area.

ISBN-13: 978-0-373-60182-0

Her Forever Cowboy & Yuletide Cowboy

Copyright © 2015 by Harlequin Books S.A.

The publisher acknowledges the copyright holder
of the individual works as follows:

Her Forever Cowboy
Copyright © 2010 by Debra Clopton

Yuletide Cowboy
Copyright © 2010 by Debra Clopton

HARLEQUIN®

www.Harlequin.com

Printed in U.S.A.

CONTENTS

Award-winning author **Debra Clopton** lives in Texas with her husband, Chuck—whom she met on a blind date. She enjoys touching readers' hearts, making them laugh and entertaining them with her stories—sometimes using the real-life escapades that happen on her ranch. She likes to travel and loves spending time with her family, including her beautiful baby granddaughters. Visit her at debraclopton.com and sign up for her newsletter.

HER FOREVER COWBOY

When my spirit grows faint within me, it is you,
O Lord, who know my way.
—*Psalms* 142:3

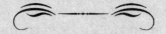

This book is dedicated with much love and appreciation to my new friends Sharon Howell and Jo Anne Faerber. Jo Anne, I'm so glad you came to my book signing and brought Sharon to meet me. God blessed me that day—you gals have inspired me to step out of my comfort zone this year and let God lead me forward.
Bless you both for listening to His voice!

Chapter One

Susan Worth rubbed her eyes, fighting the exhaustion threatening to overtake her. She'd spent most of the night saving the life of an unborn calf and mother and her adrenaline had kept her moving. Emergency calls had kept her out three nights in a row and she was dead on her feet—the drone of her truck's engine and the dark, deserted road were working against her. Tightening her fingers around the steering wheel, she dug deep, sat up straight and concentrated on keeping her eyes open.

She still had an hour's drive to make it home. Once again she was alone in the middle of the night on a deserted road, halfway along the seventy-mile stretch between the tiny ranching town of Mule Hollow and the larger town of Ranger, where her clinic and apartment were—for the time being.

She loved her job and had worked hard to have her career as a small-town vet. But the exhausting pace was sometimes too much to take. The threat of falling asleep at the wheel was a risk for anyone who covered a full day's schedule and handled all emergency calls.

More so for her, since her large-animal business had grown so big over in the Mule Hollow area—great for the bottom line, but bad on the body.

And bad on her personal life. With her hours growing longer and longer, quality life after work had become almost nonexistent.

She blinked hard and glanced at the clock—2:00 a.m. This was the third night in a row she'd been out this late. Third day in a row she'd not had time to catch up on lost sleep. Daytime emergencies and scheduled small-animal appointments had her hands tied, but she'd been warned it would be this way. The retiring older vet, a male, had told her that since she was a woman she should concentrate on small animals and leave the big stuff to a man. That advice hadn't sat well with her.

She smiled, tiredly remembering how insulted she'd been. But her dad always said, "Susan, take advice, then do it your way." And that was what she'd done.

She'd bought her clinic and embraced the loyal, small-animal clientele that came with it. But though she dearly loved and adored dogs and cats, her passion was working with large stock. She'd gone after that clientele with a vengeance and proved to the men who'd give her a chance that she knew what she was doing. She loved horses and cattle and as her reputation grew, so had the business. Now she was burning the candle at both ends and in between, too.

She loved her life. She really did…but something had to give, and she understood this clearly. Either that or she was going to crash and burn. *Maybe right now if you don't snap to!*

She rubbed her neck and watched the road. A few weeks ago she'd finally forced herself to come to the conclusion that she wanted a change…a family. She'd lost her mother during childbirth and had been raised by her dad. Since his death she'd felt so alone, and no amount of work could fix that. Her dad had filled his life with work and she'd striven all her life to please him, but she needed more. He'd had her…she had no one now.

As if God was giving her the nod, she'd gotten an offer for her small-animal clinic almost the instant she'd come to the realization that she wanted to make a change. God's timing—what an amazing thing.

Sighing, she shook her head to wake herself up—this week was proving to her that she'd made the right decision. She hoped relocating her large-animal clinic to Mule Hollow, to the heart of her business, would give the heart of her love life a boost, too. Only time would tell.

Susan shook her head, her chin dipped and she realized she'd closed her eyes momentarily. She still had fifty miles to go.

Focus, Susan. She took a deep breath and pressed the button to roll down her window. She inhaled the fresh air. She thought about hanging her head out the window, but didn't. Instead she let her thoughts churn. It wasn't that she couldn't find a date. She managed short relationships from time to time. Short being the keynote, because either the guys ended up being big losers or the ones who were nice were interested in a woman who wasn't so focused on her work. As most of them put it, "a woman who isn't owned by her work." Who could blame them? Really, a man wanted a woman to be there for him. A woman who worked a hundred or more hours, on a normal week, wasn't exactly what a man would consider marriage material....

Susan's eyes closed.

A flash of light had her jerking awake to see a motorcycle in the beam of her headlights just as her truck swerved off the road. And straight for a stand of trees!

"Oh, my goodness!" she exclaimed as the truck bounded over the rough ground and the back end fishtailed and swerved around. Susan fought for control as the truck slid broadside toward the large solid trees— but it was useless. One thought hit her as she held on tight and everything started to spin—she'd made the decision to change up her life, but maybe she'd made the call a little too late.

The driver was a woman.

Her arms were crossed over the top of the steering wheel and her forehead was resting on them. She wasn't moving.

Cole Turner's heart thundered against his ribs. Playing chicken on his Harley at two in the morning with an oversize hunk of truck hadn't been his idea of a great welcome home.

But it was exactly what had just happened.

His motorcycle helmet fell unheeded to the ground as he placed a hand on the open window. "Ma'am. Are you okay?" His gut tightened with tension when she didn't answer and the hair on the back of his neck stood up. "Ma'am," he asked again, with more force. His adrenaline kicked into high gear and he spoke louder. "Can you hear me?" When she still didn't respond, he reached through the open window to check for a pulse. Her skin was warm, but at his touch she lifted her head. Relief washed through him as she eyed him groggily.

Susan Worth.

He recognized her—she was the vet his brother Seth used at their ranch in Mule Hollow. Seth seemed overly impressed by her and often sang her praises when they talked on the phone.

But Cole hadn't been nearly so impressed when Seth had introduced them at his wedding six months ago—the woman hadn't given Cole the time of day.

"Cole—" she said, her voice wobbling.

The wobble got him, and despite her snub before, he felt for her. "Cole Turner, at your service," he drawled, tugging open her door and offering her a grin and a hand. Getting her out of the truck would help put some color back into her face. She was as pale as the shimmery moonlight cascading over her. "Are you okay?"

"I fell asleep…" she said, her stunned eyes holding his. "I can't believe I fell asleep." Disbelief turned to disgust.

Scowling, she slid from the seat, ignoring his offered hand. He reached to help her anyway. All long-legged and lanky in her jeans and boots, she was almost as tall as he was. He'd forgotten how beautiful she was, even with weariness and anger etching her face.

"Well, you've been working hard," he said, trying to make her feel better. He was assuming her being out this late was work-related, since she was a vet.

"No excuse," she snapped. "I shouldn't have fallen asleep."

So the doc wasn't going to give herself a break. "You're right, you shouldn't have. But you did." That got him a startled glare. "Fact is, you look like you're about to drop on your feet. That bein' the case, what are you doin' out here in the middle of nowhere at *two* in the morning when you are so worn out?" And what was he doing sticking his nose where it didn't belong?

"I am a *vet*. I was heading home to Ranger after running an emergency call—for your brother, actually. We almost lost a momma and her unborn calf."

"You were at *our* place? Seth let you head back to Ranger in this condition?" Cole's temper shot sky-high. Bone weariness hung over her like a cloak—Seth had to have seen that. "What was my brother thinking? One glance at you and anyone can see you're in no shape to travel. Look in the mirror—you look like you haven't slept in days."

Her shoulders squared. "I beg your pardon. Seth didn't *let* me do anything. I did my job, saved that calf, then left—it wasn't any of Seth's business what I did after that. And it sure isn't your business—"

That did it. "Lady, it's two stinkin' a.m. When you almost ran me down with your truck it sorta *made* it my business. So don't even think about getting defensive. Four seconds farther along the road and you'd have been topping that hill the same time I was. You'd have wiped me out with your big truck while you were taking your little nap."

He was stepping across boundaries and he knew it. But he'd been involved in far too many rescues and recoveries that had nothing to do with careless acts on the part of the victims…good people died from no fault of their own every day. *This* was carelessness on the doc's part and he'd witnessed it—that made it his business. Whether she wanted it to be or not.

He hadn't asked for it, but he wasn't the kind to back

off from what was right if it would save a life. Even that of a gal who'd taken one look at him six months ago and stuck her pretty nose so high in the air that if it had started to rain she'd have drowned on the spot.

Nope, if there was one thing he had no use for, it was a stuck-up woman. But he couldn't, in all good conscience, just walk off, either.

Being nearly run down by Susan was the last thing he'd expected when his brother Wyatt had basically blackmailed him into coming home for a visit. It would have suited him fine not to have seen her again while he was in town.

Susan suddenly lifted fingers to her temple and, looking at her, he thought his words might have hit home.

"If you must know I've had emergency runs three nights in a row," she said. "Plus I've had packed schedules during the day, so that doesn't leave much time to sleep."

Her excuse slid off Cole like water off a duck's back. "Some things you make time for. A dead vet doesn't keep appointments—no matter how important they may seem. Do you not realize what a narrow escape you just had?"

She flinched. "It didn't happen, though—"

"Hardheaded woman!" Cole shook his head, realizing this was going nowhere. "This is a waste of time. Come on, I'll take you home. We'll worry about your truck in the morning."

Susan felt as if she was in a big tunnel full of thick fog as she stared at Cole. She was still trying to process everything that had just happened. Falling asleep at the wheel was horrible; nearly running over a motorcycle rider was horrific; nearly killing herself was terrible. But looking up after all of it to find drop-dead gorgeous, fly-by-the-seat-of-his-pants Cole Turner leaning in her window was her payback for all of it. *She'd almost run the poor man down!*

She could only stare at him as he jumped all over her. His T-shirt-clad chest was bowed out and his eyes were clashing with hers, and like the cold waves of an angry ocean he took her breath away. It had been the same way at his brother's wedding when she'd first met him.

"Well," he drawled, lifting a ridiculously attractive eyebrow—*oh, for cryin' out loud!* She was so tired she was now noticing how attractive his eyebrows were.

"Look, I'm sorry," she said, struggling to get her head back on straight. "I'm doing the best I can at the moment."

"It's not good enough."

"Excuse me." She might feel guilty, but if he thought he was going to stand there making her feel worse with all his high-handed tactics he was wrong—matter of fact, he was starting to irritate her. "I'm not going anywhere with you. My truck is fine—"

"You're not fine."

"I am, too," she argued. "So what are *you* doing out here at two in the morning? I thought you were rescuing people on the coast."

"I decided it was time to come home for a visit. Somewhere around Waco, I decided to drive on through the night. Good thing, too, since you were the one in need of being rescued...which sort of puts a spin on you being fine." He cocked his head to the side, sending a thick lock of hair sliding forward across his forehead.

Susan rubbed her temple and stared at the man Mule Hollow folks called the rolling stone. He'd left town straight out of high school and rarely came home to visit. He was probably wishing he'd stayed away tonight.

She knew she sounded ridiculous every time she denied being worn-out. The look in his eyes told her he knew that if he blew hard enough she'd topple over.

"You're right," she said reluctantly. "I did need your help. But now I'm fine. Really. I almost ran you over. The last thing I'm going to do is make you take me the hour back to Ranger." Especially on a motorcycle… she was terrified of the things. Not that she'd dare tell him that, she thought as she turned back to her truck.

"Whoa, there. Look at it from my point of view." He placed a hand on her arm to halt her. "I can't let you get back in that truck. What kind of man would I be to do that?"

His hand was warm and the pads of his fingers were rough against her skin—a tingle of awareness waltzed slowly through her. Whoa—the man was trying to take charge of her business and she was thinking about tingling skin! What was wrong with her? This would not do. "Cole, I don't need you—I can take care of myself," she said, locking firm eyes on him. She'd spent her life learning to stand on her own two feet. She didn't need a virtual stranger telling her what to do. The last thing she expected was for him to reach past her and snag her keys from the ignition.

"Obviously there's no reasoning with you," Cole said. "I hate to break it to you, but you're comin' with me. End of story."

"Cole Turner, give me those keys!" she exclaimed. "Right this minute."

"I like that fire you got goin' on there, darlin'. But no can do. See, a friend wouldn't let a friend drink and drive, and I won't let you sleep and drive."

Glowering at him in the moonlight, she plopped one hand palm out. "Then I'll sleep in my truck. Hand over my keys. Now."

"Not happening." He proceeded to step around her, blocking her from the inside of the truck as he slipped the key back in the ignition, pressed the automatic button and waited as the window rolled closed.

"Cole Turner," Susan gritted out from behind him.

His back burned from the heat of her wrath. Ignoring it, he slipped the key safely into his pocket, locked the truck door then slammed it firmly shut. When he turned around she had her hands on her hips shooting daggers at him with those amazing electric-blue eyes. He did like her eyes.

"You are not funny, Cole. I want my keys."

She was tenacious. "You might as well give it up, Doc. I'm more stubborn than you, and you're going for a ride with me and that's it." Snagging his helmet from the ground, he strode up the embankment toward his ride. "Come on, Doc," he called over his shoulder. "We're burning up precious darkness standing here arguing. There is nothing more you can do."

A loud huff said what she thought of him.

No surprise there…he wasn't exactly impressed with her, either. Still, her footsteps, make that stomps, behind him brought a smile to his lips.

Chapter Two

Maybe sleep would help.

Everything was sort of mingled and mixed in a confusing way in her fuddled brain. It was hard to separate them. She was definitely going to need a few hours of sleep to ensure she didn't make some crazy mistake—like making goo-goo eyes at the man. *So* not happening.

Of course him acting all me-man-you-woman on her was helping toss some cold ice on the situation. Taking her keys like he did—out of concern or whatever—didn't sit well. She was embarrassed beyond belief that she'd nearly run him down. She was reacting badly—in part because of the fact that she found the man unnervingly attractive. Cole was tall at about six-three, which for a gal of five foot ten inches, like her, made for a nice combination. He was lanky lean, with an athletic grace about him. She had a feeling he was a jogger…but she wasn't about to ask him.

"Put this on," Cole demanded, swinging around so quickly she practically ran him over. He steadied her with his hand then held his helmet out to her.

"What about you?" she asked, holding the slick red helmet away from her.

He took it back and settled it on her head. "You wear the helmet." He stared hard at her as he pushed her hair out of her face and, oddly, his actions touched her.

Totally out of her comfort zone, she stood like a deer in headlights as he tugged the strap snug. She fought to seem calm.

"It's a bit large, but better than nothing," he continued, thankfully not picking up on the battle that was waging in her head. "Not that I plan on letting anything happen to you."

His gentle words caused a rush of butterflies to settle in her stomach. Not good at all. Cole Turner was a restless spirit. A wandering man.

She backed away from his touch, feeling foolish, especially when his own expression said nothing at all about returning her infatuation.

Oh, no, instead he threw a leg over the big machine, glanced over his shoulder and gave her a lopsided grin. "Hop on."

She swallowed hard, reminded herself this was her only option for getting home then climbed on behind him. She sat stiffly, really not wanting to stretch her arms around his waist.

"How, um, long are you in town for your visit?" she asked, needing something to fill the moment. She hoped he was leaving the next day.

Instead of answering, he cranked up the bike and the engine burst to life. He glanced her way and his eyes glinted in the moonlight. "Depends on a few things, but I might be here for a few weeks."

A few weeks! "That long?" she squeaked the words

out. Thankfully they were drowned out by the roar of the motorcycle.

Or so she thought.

"Yeah," Cole said with a grin. "That long. Now hang on. It's time to get you home so you can get some rest."

Like that's going to happen. She was wide-awake; her arms were wrapped around Cole Turner—the handsome nomad.

The rolling stone. From what she knew of him he would never be happy unless he was roaming the country. She'd never be satisfied until she was settled and had a family, so this infatuation was ridiculous. Sleep. She needed it! If she wasn't so tired she wouldn't be engaging in this weird assortment of thoughts.

A very long time ago she hadn't thought she wanted a family, either, but…things changed. She sighed and tried again to quiet her mind.

"You okay back there?" Cole called over his shoulder a few miles down the road. His words were almost lost in the night as the air rushed over them. She gave up and settled closer to him, nodding her helmeted head against his shoulder. Weariness sank over her as they rode and thankfully overcame most of her wayward thoughts.

He didn't try to talk to her over the drone of the engine, blessedly. He made sure she hadn't fallen asleep every once in a while but other than that he left her alone. She had to admit that he might have been right about her not having any business driving herself.

"That's it," she said almost an hour later when her clinic's small lighted sign came into view on the outskirts of Ranger. "My apartment is out back." She pointed out the drive around the far side of the metal building and then past the holding pens.

"You live back here by yourself?"

The censure in his voice was unmistakable and it sent her an immediate reality check. "It's small, but it worked for me," she said when the little apartment that had been built onto the back of the barn area came into view. She didn't tell him that soon it would no longer be her home.

"No one has ever tried to bother you back here?" He turned the engine off.

Susan wasted no time getting off the machine and removing the helmet—she didn't plan on giving him the chance to do it for her. "No, they haven't," she said, holding out her hand. "Thanks for everything. Now may I have my keys."

He got off the bike and dug her keys out of his pocket. But instead of handing the keys to her he began taking her truck key from the ring. "What are you doing?"

"I'm taking this. As soon as it's daylight—in about three hours—I'll crawl up under it and make sure you didn't tear anything up while you were plowing up turf. If everything checks out, I'll have your truck here by seven or eight. You won't be doing calls before then I hope."

She didn't like him taking control like this. But since she could tell there was no sense arguing, she didn't. She was too tired. She took the rest of the keys from him. "Eight will be fine. Thank you," she managed, though her jaw ached from clenching it.

He smiled and she could practically hear him thinking "checkmate."

Maybe not, though, she thought a few minutes later as she closed the door to her apartment and listened to the motorcycle purr its way back toward the pavement.

The man was used to sweeping into emergency situations and taking charge. That was what he did for a living—helped in rescues, then remodeled and rebuilt after hurricanes and other disasters. So maybe there wasn't anything personal about how he was treating her.

Maybe. But as she took a quick shower and then fell into her bed—basically passing out from exhaustion—she knew she wasn't buying that notion by a long shot. Cole had pretty much made it clear that he thought she was an irresponsible fool for letting herself get so tired. He'd been doing his civic duty by keeping "the fool woman" off the streets—that was *pretty* personal. Of course, nearly running him down was, too.

"I'm just sayin' it's a fine thang you came along when ya did last night," Applegate Thornton said, his voice booming in the early morning quiet.

Cole had just crawled out from under the truck when the older man and his buddy, Stanley Orr, pulled up in their trucks, one behind the other. They'd wasted no time trotting down the incline to see what was going on with the lame truck. It shouldn't have been a surprise to see the two old friends out and about so early, since they always met at Sam's diner for coffee at sunup then played checkers all morning. Today they'd be late; Susan's mishap was of more interest to them than today's checkers game.

The seventysomething older men had been great friends of his grandfather and Cole always enjoyed seeing them on his quick trips through town. Now, he wiped his hands on his work rag and nodded. "Yes, sir," he said. "I'm not disagreeing with you. I'm glad I was out here when I was or else Susan would still have been sitting here when you fellas drove up this morning.

"What I'm wondering is what in the world everyone is thinking when they call that woman out on the road at all hours of the night? There are other vets to call, you know." He planned to let everyone know he was unhappy about that situation and there was no better place to start than with these two. Talk about a grapevine. It didn't get any quicker than them when it came to spreading information.

Instead of answering him they looked at each other and raised their bushy brows. "Am I missing something here?" Cole asked. "You can bet I'm having a talk with my brother when I get back to the house." Oh, yeah, Seth was about to get a royal chewing out for letting Susan leave the ranch when clearly she was ready to drop. He'd told Cole once that she needed help, so why didn't she have it?

Stanley, affable, slightly plump and balding looked perplexed. "You ain't been around Susan much, have ya?"

Applegate, taller and thin as a fence post, wore his signature frown as he grunted. *"Obviously."*

Both men wore hearing aids and still their words cracked like thunder, even App's grunt stirred up the cattle milling in the pastures behind the barbed wire.

"So what does that mean?" Cole asked.

Applegate grunted again. "It means that Susan does what she wants. That gal is all-fired determined to be accepted on a man's terms. If any of us was ta tell her she ought'n ta be out that late—or *worse,* if we had livestock that needed tending and we didn't call her—" He whistled long and slow, while wagging his head.

"That's right," Stanley continued. "She'd let us have it with both barrels."

"After what I saw last night, I can believe that."

"Yup, I'm shor you did. That little gal kin be real hard-nosed when it comes to her job," Applegate said. "She don't take kindly ta bein' treated like a lady. And she's real good at what she does."

"Ain't that the truth," Stanley said.

She'd made it clear last night that she hadn't liked him taking charge. "Maybe so," he said, at last. "But I don't like it. It doesn't feel right. And it sure doesn't feel safe."

App tugged on his hat brim as the sun shifted a bit higher over the horizon. "It'll be a little easier when she gets her office relocated here in town."

That got Cole's attention. "What do you mean?"

Stanley and Applegate grinned at each other then gave him the we-know-something-you-don't-know look. Cole knew they were also speculating at his interest in Susan. But he couldn't help that. He leaned against the truck and crossed his arms waiting for them to elaborate. He was going to have to get on the road in a few minutes but he wanted the lowdown on this.

"So…" Applegate took his time, rubbed his narrow jaw. "She didn't tell you she's bought a place on the west side of town about four miles out."

"It was two in the morning when I came across her. We weren't engaging in conversation beyond me telling her I was taking her home—" No sense elaborating on the tone of that conversation.

"Guess that went over like a basket of mad cats." Stanley chuckled. "You don't 'tell' our Susan anythang where her business is concerned. That's what we been tryin' ta tell ya."

He shouldn't have let it slip that he'd "told" her he was taking her home. No one needed to know he'd had to hijack her keys to get her to cooperate. *Hardheaded woman.*

"So where is this place?" he asked.

"It's a small property—little house and a large metal building." Applegate was more than happy to fill him in. "It used to be that oil supply company. You remember the place? Back b'fore the oil boom busted in the eighties. B'fore ever'body moved off."

Cole nodded. "I remember." It was the beginning of the town's slow death.

"She's got some contractor comin' outta Ranger in a couple of days ta start turnin' it into her new office."

"You don't say." She was moving to Mule Hollow and hadn't mentioned it. "Is she going to live here?" he asked to clarify his assumption.

"Yup," Stanley said. "In the house on the property. I even thank she done put some stuff in thar."

When he'd made that comment about where she lived now, she'd had the opportunity to tell him and hadn't. She kept her business close to the cuff. Or she knew he'd soon find out and this was her way of telling him to mind his own business. He smiled at that. She had spunk. He pushed away from the truck.

"Well, thanks for the info, fellas. Now I better get this to her so she'll have wheels when she needs them. Wouldn't want to make her mad." That got him some slaps on the back and hoots of agreement.

Earlier, after taking her home, he'd driven the hour

and a half back to the ranch and hadn't been able to stop thinking about their encounter.

He didn't stay at the ranch house when home, but down at the old stagecoach house that was the original homestead on their ranch. He always enjoyed the old house and had felt that same ole tug of nostalgia as he'd driven down the dirt road toward it. The moon had highlighted the rocky road as it wound across the pastures and as it always had, he couldn't help thinking about the others who'd traveled this same road over a hundred years ago. Men such as Doc Holliday and outlaw Sam Bass had passed by either on horseback or by stage. As a kid he'd thought it was cool and that hadn't changed as he'd aged. His great-great-great-great-grandpa Oakley had won the place in a poker game more than a century ago.

Now Applegate looked from him to his truck. "We kin follow you ta Susan's and brang you back if ya need us to."

Cole shook his head and packed up his last few things. "Thanks, but no need. I've got it covered." He figured if Susan wasn't making any calls out this direction, he'd have Seth drive to Ranger and pick him up.

After only a bit of cajoling, the tires found grip and he drove out of the ditch. App and Stanley waved him on as he headed toward Ranger—looking in his rearview, he saw them hop in their trucks and head toward town. They were driving at a fast clip; no doubt about it, everyone was about to know about last night....

Susan didn't like to show weakness, it was obvious. Was that what was driving her crazy attitude last night?

Not that he thought some determination in a woman wasn't a good thing. Before he could pull back, his thoughts went to Lori. She'd been full of determination, too; if it hadn't been for that grit she wouldn't have made it as long as she had… Six years and he still couldn't think about that sweet girl without his gut twisting up like a bull had stomped him. And just like he always did, he shoved the thoughts of her back into the dark shadows and forced all the trapped emotions down with them.

He focused instead on Susan Worth.

The woman had been careless last night and almost killed herself. It bothered him that she was so obsessed with her job that she'd take her life for granted…when others fought so hard for one more breath.

Stop it. It usually took at least a couple of weeks in one spot before restless memories drove him to move on. He'd been home less than five hours and already he was fighting with the past. Home was always the worst. It was easier to pretend things like home and hearth didn't matter when you didn't have them staring you in the face.

Wyatt better show up soon or Cole was out of here. His brothers knew he'd fallen in love with a terminally ill barrel racer.

But they'd never met Lori. She'd been more ill than he'd realized when he first met her and that had prevented any travel. She had tried hard not to fall for him—to prevent the hurt something like that could cause. She'd tried hard to ignore what he'd known from the moment he'd laid eyes on her sweet face…love didn't have a perfect timetable. It happened even while a person was dying…love was brutal that way. And special.

As long as he was on the road, working to help folks, he did all right and actually enjoyed his life. When the restless memories threatened, he finished up what he was doing and headed out to find a new job—a new project.

And the recent turn of bad luck on the Gulf of Mexico had given him plenty of choices. Helping rebuild something a hurricane or a tornado had taken away from a family gave him a good feeling. It also helped the anger at God that plagued him…he tried not to dwell on it, and he wasn't going to now. Only, coming back to Mule Hollow was coming home…the place he'd longed to bring Lori. Home reminded him too much of how bad God's timing was and how He seemed to pick and choose who He deemed good enough to get a miracle. Or who didn't.

Who got their prayers answered…and who didn't.

Home was where you brought the one you loved… unless you weren't one of the special ones who God shined His light on and listened to.

Chapter Three

Susan was standing out front with a tiny, blue-haired woman and a large dog that resembled a chocolate Lab but was shaped more like a big, brown, chocolate kiss… or a gigantic tick.

Susan was far more attention-worthy than the dog, with the morning sun glinting off her corn-silk hair. But even her beautiful hair didn't compare to the smile on her face—that smile startled him so bad he ran over a curb while pulling into the parking lot.

Yup, he was the one who needed rest now. It would help him get his head back on straight—a few hours of shut-eye had sure helped the prickly vet. No doubt about that…no doubt at all.

It wasn't just the softening of the dark circles, but she was smiling—he hadn't even got a hint of one of those last night. Though he didn't figure that was totally due to lack of sleep.

"Good morning." He got out of the truck and moved toward the women, who had been staring at him ever since he'd jumped the curb.

Susan crossed her arms and nodded—the smile gone in a flash.

But the little old lady had one big enough for the both of them. "Well, one thing's the truth, my mornin' just got better thanks to you, young man." She gave him the once-over. "My goodness, but you are a handsome fellow. Just in the nick of time, too. Bein' timely is important. Don't you think?"

"Yes, ma'am, real important—"

"Good. Good." She broke him off with a wave of her cane. "I like you—I like this one, Susan." She shot Susan a sharp eye then gave him a soft smile. "Would you mind terribly, helping Catherine Elizabeth into her car seat? Arthur, the scamp, is acting up today—been giving me and my Catherine Elizabeth both a run for our money. But *you*—" she smiled up at him, her cloudy blue eyes shining as she grabbed hold of his bicep and squeezed like she might check the ripeness of a grapefruit "—you look like you're in plenty good shape, so the old bully won't bother you. No *sirree,* he won't."

Cole looked around for Arthur with every intention of setting the so-called bully straight. He wouldn't stand by and let a man mistreat the little lady. But there wasn't anyone else around. He glanced at Susan for some kind of hint and saw that she was biting back a smile. And amazing enough her eyes were twinkling—he lost his train of thought.

"Mrs. Abernathy, may I introduce Cole Turner," she said rather loudly. "He's the one who came to my rescue last night. Cole, this is Mrs. Abernathy and *this* is the one and only Catherine Elizabeth."

Mrs. Abernathy was still holding on to his bicep with her tiny hand and gazing up at him sweetly. Catherine

Elizabeth had managed to lift to her feet and lumbered over to him. She sank onto his boot like a melting blob of ice cream.

"Glad to make your acquaintance, ma'am," Cole said. "And Catherine Elizabeth, too." He glanced around again for Arthur but no man had come out of the building. They all were looking at him expectantly—waiting. "Oh, sorry, you want me to load the dog into the car?"

"Thank you. She's just too much for me. But not you." She rubbed his arm. "You remind me of my Herman—God rest his soul. He was tall and strong, too. I'm glad Susan's found a young man like you."

"Mrs. Abernathy," Susan interjected, "he's not my, um, young man."

Mrs. Abernathy patted his arm. "Well, he should be, dear. You need a strong man, since you're such a darling, strong woman yourself. I, too, was a strong woman."

It was Cole's turn to bite back a smile. The woman wasn't even five foot and probably had never weighed a hundred pounds soaking wet in her entire life.

She gave him a knowing look. "There's more to being strong than size, young man. Arthur's just beat me down a bit through the years and I have to admit it weighs on me…makes even my strong spirit weak at times."

Cole shot Susan an inquiring glance. "Who is that?" he mouthed over the little lady's head.

"Ohh," Susan gasped. "Sorry. Mrs. A., as we affectionately call her, and Catherine Elizabeth both suffer from Arthur-itis."

Mrs. A. shook her head. "He's a mean one, that Arthur. But the good Lord puts such nice men in my path to help out in times such as these." She let go of his arm and, leaning on her cane, she walked carefully to her car.

Watching her slow progress, Cole agreed that Arthur was a real bummer. "Will it hurt when I pick her up?" he asked Susan, staring down at the dog.

"Just be careful and she'll be okay. But don't throw your back out or anything." The last part was soft so that Mrs. Abernathy couldn't hear.

He almost laughed as he leaned down for the dog. Who did she think he was? Some kind of wimp?

"I mean it—lift from the knees," Susan said, bending over to whisper the words close to his ear.

The warmth of her breath tickled his skin and sent a shiver of awareness rippling over him. He chuckled, both from the humor in the warning and the shock of her warm breath on his skin, then he lifted—*whhoa!* The dog was deadweight.

Susan slapped him on the back. "Told you lift with the knees."

"No kiddin'." Sending her a good-natured scowl, he then gave it a fortified effort. It felt as if he was hauling a bag of lard into his arms. "*What* does she feed this horse?" he muttered for Susan's ears only. She chuckled and Catherine Elizabeth promptly gave him a big ole lick across the jaw, as if telling him not to worry.

"Oh, look, my baby likes you," Mrs. Abernathy called as she swung the door open wide.

"Seems that way," he grunted. Reaching the car, he leaned in and placed the dog gently into the backseat. She immediately settled into a spot worn into the imprint of her body.

"Can I help you?" He held out one hand to Mrs. Abernathy after gently closing the door on that...dog.

Mrs. Abernathy batted her eyes at him and blushed. "You are such a catch, young man." She slipped her hand into his. She looked at Susan. "If you were smart you'd snatch this one up before someone else puts a ring on that blank finger of his."

Susan surprised him by not looking insulted at the notion. Instead she smiled patiently at her client. "You take care now. And call me if Catherine Elizabeth gets uncomfortable. That extra dose of meds should help her."

"Thank you, dear," the tiny lady said and eased behind the steering wheel. "You," she said, squeezing his hand before releasing it, "have made my old heart's day!"

"And you have made mine," he said. "You be careful."

She gave him a mischievous smirk. "What fun would that be? Bye now."

He laughed and moved out of her way to stand beside Susan. They watched as the big Crown Victoria eased out of the drive. Mrs. Abernathy's little blue head could barely be seen over the dash and was totally hidden from behind.

"How does she drive a car that big?"

Susan laughed. "Carefully."

"Thank goodness. I half expected her to blast out of here on two wheels."

Susan beamed. "There was probably a day when she did exactly that. Arthur's put a damper on that, I'm afraid."

"Not on her spirit, though, I can see," he said, suddenly feeling rascally himself. "So, you gonna take her advice and marry me before someone else does?"

He was kidding. Susan knew he was, but the question took her completely by surprise. "Of course," she said, turning to face him. "I've been waiting on you my whole life," she teased back, momentarily letting her guard down.

A slow, dangerous smile spread across his no-way-should-he-be-so-handsome face and his eyes lit with mischief. "You did a joke. Sleep agrees with you, Miss Worth."

She laughed. "I guess it does. But don't go rubbing it in or I'll have to hurt you," she said, before she thought about what a bad idea it was. And it was. She glanced away, toward her truck, taking a breath to settle the strumming of her heart. "Thanks for bringing my truck back." She headed inside the clinic before she got herself into trouble. The scrape of his boots on the wooden porch said he was following her. "I'm assuming you aren't still holding it hostage and you're actually going to hand the keys over to me."

His low rumble of laughter had her moving faster to get inside and behind the counter. She needed a barrier between them—she'd enjoyed watching him with Mrs. Abernathy and Catherine Elizabeth a little too much. The man was a charmer.

And *bossy,* she reminded herself.

And a rover with no concept of responsibility...*not a man for her.*

"Truck's all yours," he said, leaning a hip against the counter. "It checked out good. No undercarriage damage at all. Just a whole herd of dirt clods. The only bad working part it had last night was a worn-out driver who needs to take better care of herself."

And here we go again! "I was tired," she snapped, letting the pencil she'd picked up fall to the desk. "It happens. Can we drop that?" Of course her anger was welcome because it helped put that much-needed barrier back up.

He cocked a brow and his gaze dropped to the pencil she'd just dropped. He picked it up, then as he studied her, balanced it on his upper lip as a schoolboy might do. *Sigh.* The man looked entirely too cute...and was probably well aware of it. She tapped her boot.

"Well," she snapped again, "are you going to drop it?"

"Nope," he said, causing the pencil to fall. He caught it without looking. "Not unless you admit that you should have taken your safety into consideration. That sleep you got last night did you a world of good, didn't it?"

She'd slept like a rock for four hours, but boy, she hated admitting it to him. "If you must know," she huffed, "Mrs. A. had to knock on my door and wake me up this morning."

"All right! Hit me with five," he whooped and held up his palm. "That's good."

She ignored the invitation. "I don't like oversleeping."

He wiggled his fingers. "C'mon. Hit me with some love."

Huh? "No! Would you stop?"

He shook his head, reached across the counter and wrapped his fingers around her wrist. His touch was gentle and as the slightly rough pads of his fingers slid across her skin she shivered. Startled by his actions and her reaction she started to pull away, but he held firm and laid her palm against his.

"There, that wasn't so hard," he said. "You need to loosen up, Susan Worth."

Tugging free of his grasp, she hoped she wasn't pink and that she didn't look as shaken as she felt. "You need to mind your own business," she ordered.

He slapped his hand to his chest. "Wow, what a blow. And after all I've done for you."

"Look," she offered, needing to get him gone. The sooner he was out of her hair the better off she'd be. "I've got a couple more patients to see this morning and then I'm heading out to Clint Matlock's ranch for the rest of the afternoon. I could give you a ride back, but not before then. Unless, of course, you've already arranged a ride." Something told her she wouldn't be so lucky.

"Thanks. I'll wait for you. Unless you need me to hoist more obese dogs into cars—I hope all your clients aren't that large."

Despite herself, a smile tugged at her lips. "I've given up trying to get Catherine Elizabeth on a diet. Mrs. A. has no one else to cook for, and from what I understand, Herman loved to eat. So she can't help but spoil poor Catherine Elizabeth."

Cole did a biceps curl, flexing his muscle for her. "She liked my guns. How about you? I mean, since you have agreed to marry me, what do you think?"

She grunted. "I think you need to go sit down and read a magazine."

"Yup. Just as I thought. You are side-stepping the question because you agree with Mrs. A."

Oh, she agreed—the man had some muscles. Probably from all that construction work he did. But she wasn't about to tell him.

She was relieved when the sound of a motor drew her to glance out the window at the truck pulling up outside. She sent up a silent word of thanks that she could get to work and hopefully get her head straightened out…because it was playing in dangerous waters at the moment. She was moving to Mule Hollow for more reasons than her work. She was moving there with the intention of making room in her life for a husband. That meant flirting with inappropriate men, like Cole, was out of the question.

Now, she thought as she met Cole's watchful stare, if only God would suddenly zap the handsome rover back to wherever it was he'd been before he'd ridden into town last night, she'd be one happy gal.

A man like Cole was not hard to read. He had no plans to settle down; it was all about his job—a job he loved. The ranch he owned with his two brothers had started out as a stagecoach stop—Cole's roots ran six generations deep and yet of the Turner men, including a first cousin who had also been a groomsman in Seth's wedding, Seth was the only one who'd actually stayed true to those roots by keeping the ranch going.

Susan wanted a family. Her mind was focused on that, and yet she still had to keep her business running. Her dad had cared so much about her having a career, wanting his little girl to be able to take care of herself. She'd done that, but now she had to find a way of balancing family with her work. She knew that meant she had to find a man who would complement her life. So even looking at a rover like Cole was out of the question.

She walked around the edge of the counter and forced herself not to make a wide arc around him. Instead she stopped beside him and glanced at his "guns."

"Actually, Mrs. A. has a great point. But in reality it'll take a bunch more than that to interest me."

The door opened and she hurried to usher the prancing pack of toy poodles into the exam room. The owner was so flustered trying to hang on to four leashes at once that she didn't even give Cole a glance. Susan, however, paused to note Cole had taken the first seat in the small waiting area.

"Whatever you say, but I'm here," he said, flexing his muscle for her. "If you need me, you just call."

She shook her head and closed the door with a resounding thud. She needed Cole Turner the way she needed a hole in the head!

Chapter Four

"So what's up, brother?"

Cole opened his eyes and found his brother Seth leaning against the door, grinning.

"Thought I'd swing by and welcome you home, since I heard through the grapevine you'd arrived."

After Susan had dropped him off at his truck, Cole drove back to the stagecoach house, walked inside and crashed on the couch. It had been a long time since he'd slept. "Sorry I didn't come by. What time is it?" he asked, rubbing his jaw as he swung his legs around and plopped his feet to the ground. He felt like he'd been run over by a truck. This was most likely how Susan had been feeling last night when she'd run off the road.

"It's five. And from App and Stanley's account it sounds like you've been busy since arriving last night."

Cole gave him a groggy nod. Good ole Applegate and Stanley. "Yeah, you could say so. Susan's going to love knowing everyone in town knows she fell asleep at the wheel."

"That's the honest truth," Seth grunted. "You look like the dickens, bro." Seth strode into the kitchen, separated from the living room by only an ancient dining table.

"Feel like it, too."

"You could have given me a call. I would have come and helped out." He grabbed the coffeepot and began filling it with water.

"Yeah, with the cell-phone coverage Mule Hollow has I'd have been wasting my time."

"True, but the phone here works and I could have at least picked you up after you drove Susan's truck to the clinic."

"Believe me, as hot as I was at you this morning— you wanted me to get some shut-eye before you saw me." That drew Seth's attention. "What were you thinking letting that woman leave your barn in the shape she was in last night?" Cole stood up and felt his blood pressure rise thinking about Susan barreling toward those trees as he'd topped the hill. "She was so tired she very nearly got herself killed falling asleep at the wheel."

"For starters, one doesn't tell a man how to run his business. Same goes for Susan. She's worked hard to get where she is with her business and she doesn't take kindly to being separated out. She assured me she was fine—"

It was the same thing App and Stanley said. Still, Cole pointed out, "She looked like death warmed over—"

"Hey, I took her at her word. Like I would have a man in that situation. Didn't say I liked it, but that's the way she wants it."

Cole padded angrily into the kitchen, not willing to take that as an excuse. "She wasn't fine. She was dead on her feet. She'd been up three nights in a row. Did you know that?"

"Yeah, I did," Seth snapped, jabbing the on button to the coffeepot before swinging to face him.

"Then what were you thinking? You would have been responsible if—"

"Now just hold on, Cole. I hate that she had to work that much, but it couldn't be helped. None of us call her out like that unless absolutely necessary. I'd have had a dead cow and calf this morning if not for her efforts last night. If I'd let them die so she could get some sleep, Susan would have taken it as a slap in the face. You know good and well she's my friend, but we tread a fine line where Susan is concerned."

Cole rubbed his aching neck and told himself to back down. He didn't like it, but he also knew his brother. Seth was levelheaded and kind, and Susan really was his friend. "Sorry, I get your drift," he grumbled, still frustrated. "But it'd sure be a shame if something happened to her."

Seth nodded and his serious expression said he was sincere. "We'll all rest easier when Susan gets moved into town. Did she tell you about all that?"

"Yeah, she told me. *Only* after I asked her. Applegate told me she was moving into town this morning—or Stanley. One of the fellas did—their conversation ran together in my brain."

Seth looked amused. "App and Stanley's conversations tend to run together even on a good night's sleep."

"You have a point." They both chuckled, easing the tension.

"So how long are you here for? I'm here to wake you up and haul your sorry hide back over to the house so Melody can interrogate you. But it should be a fair trade since she's hard at work cookin' up a meal fit for a king."

Cole took the cup of coffee Seth handed him and held it aloft. "Then let me drink this, and then I'll hop in the shower so I'm presentable to my new sister-in-law. I already have one hometown gal irritated with me, I wouldn't want to make that sweet bride of yours unhappy with me, too. How'd you get so lucky anyway?"

"Not lucky, but blessed, thanks to the good Lord and Wyatt."

Cole took a swig of coffee. "Our big bro the matchmaker. Never in a thousand years would I have expected that six-foot-four-inch hunk of hot air to be a little Cupid!"

That got a big laugh from Seth. "Boy, does that paint some kind of picture!"

Cole grimaced. "True. Still, it is amazing that he met Melody one day and knew she was the match for you." He cocked a brow at Seth, who reciprocated. It had been a weird thing when Wyatt met Melody and decided instantly to have her do some research on the family history. History that Seth hadn't wanted researched. It had thrown the two of them into a battle of wills and then into a hunt for long-lost treasure.

"Wyatt wouldn't be such a great lawyer unless he was good at reading people," Seth mused. "Maybe that was it."

Cole didn't know what it was, but serious, level-headed Seth was happier and more relaxed than Cole had thought possible. He deserved it. "You look good, Seth," he said, drawing his own thoughts away from Lori. Thoughts of how happy they could have been if things hadn't been…the way they'd been.

"I am happy. Melody—"

"Completes you," Cole teased with the famous movie line, forcing the door to his past shut.

"You laugh, but it's so true."

"I'm not laughing. I like it. Wyatt might have missed his calling."

"Maybe he'll do the same for you."

"Oh, no," Cole said. "I've got places to be and things to see. I'm not settling down—but it sure looks good on you."

"So, any clues why Wyatt wanted you home or what he had to do to get you here? What's up with that?"

"He said he'd tell me when he showed up tomorrow." Cole set his coffee down and headed toward the hall, tugging his shirt up over his head as he went. "But *I* came because I decided it was time to come see how married life was treatin' you."

"Well, in that case it should be clear that I'm doin' well."

Cole halted at the doorway to the hall. "I can see that, but I want to get a gander at Melody and make sure she's got the same goofy grin on her face. I'll be out in a minute."

"Cole, hold up a minute. About Susan."

"What about her?"

"I'm guessing you're in town for a short visit and, well, you should know Susan is looking for a real relationship. One that includes a future and a family. I hope you keep that in mind while you're here."

Cole shot Seth a warning look. "I didn't come back here to break any hearts, if that's what you're worried about. I'm here and then I'm back on the road. I've got places to be."

"Look, Cole, I didn't mean it like that. It's been six years. I'm actually hoping you're ready to settle down and think—"

"Don't go there, Seth," Cole warned, an edge to his voice that had Seth setting his coffee down and frowning at him in disappointment. He pushed away from the counter and stood staring at Cole. The tension between them was born of love and concern. Still, Cole hadn't come home for more lectures on the life he'd chosen.

He turned and headed to the bathroom. Truth was, he didn't really have a clue why he'd come home. Sure Wyatt had forced him in a way Seth would never know about…but even with that, Cole hadn't had to come. So why had he?

Okay, just calm down! "What do you mean you're going on an extended hunt in Alaska?"

Susan was behind the counter at Sam's diner talking on the diner phone. The cell reception in Mule Hollow was extremely scarce so she often had to use client landlines to keep in touch with Betty, her part-time receptionist, back at the office. Today she'd expected to meet her contractor out at the new property so they could go over plans before he started working. He hadn't shown. After waiting an hour she'd driven into town to use Sam's phone.

Betty had given her the distressing news that her contractor had quit. *Quit!* He couldn't quit. She'd immediately dialed him up.

"Just what I said," the louse drawled. "I'm *goin'* to Alaska."

Susan turned her back to the diner, lowering her voice so as not to shout to the small crowd in the diner.

She didn't want everyone to know she had trouble. "You said I was next in line," she said, using great restraint. Her daddy always told her to keep a lid on her temper, that a ranting woman didn't get any respect from a man, but…she was so mad she could spit nails! "We had a deal."

"Look, lady, I got a better deal. An offer I couldn't refuse, so to speak. I'm outta here on the fishing trip of a lifetime."

An offer he couldn't refuse. Where did he get such an offer? "So, let me get this straight. Your word means nothing."

His next words were not nice. And being told in no uncertain terms that she was "up a creek without a paddle" did not help her mood.

If the guy quit for a better job she might not be so furious. But, no, the man was going fishing. *Fishing!*

Fighting down the urge to kick something, Susan carefully hung the wall phone in its cradle. It took all she had not to slam it down.

Now what?

She bit her lip and stared hard at the phone. What was she going to do? The interior of her new office space needed walls torn out and new ones built. Counters and shelves, not to mention the electric wiring and plumbing required updates, too. And it all had to be done by the end of the month. She could hear her dad's calm voice reminding her to keep her cool, buckle down, and get the job done. "Getting the job done was what mattered," he'd say, in that Texas twang that still made her smile to think of it. Still made her miss him like crazy. Still made her want to please him. And she would. She'd had setbacks before and his words always drove her to get it done.

Right now she had to get her appointments finished for the day and get home. If she was lucky tonight, she'd get a full night's sleep and be ready to tackle finding a new contractor tomorrow. She was still working on fumes from exhaustion. If tonight went without an emergency call she'd get the much-needed sleep and wipe out the fog of exhaustion clouding her head. But lately it seemed like emergency calls were non-stop.

"Here's your burger, Doc," Sam said, coming out of the back with a paper bag in his hand. His sharp old eyes seemed to look through her. "Every thang okay? You look kinda pink."

"Everything's fine, Sam—" She bit her lip. "Actually that's not true. You wouldn't happen to know a good contractor, would you?"

Sam was a tiny man in his mid-to late-sixties with the boundless energy of a man much younger. He was a hard worker like her dad had been and she respected him greatly. He also knew everyone within a hundred-mile radius of town.

He scrubbed his chin. "Contractors. You got trouble?"

"Looks that way. I need to get moved in before my contract deadline gets here in three weeks. But," she practically growled the word, "my guy just hung me out to dry. He said he got offered a fishing trip. *A fishing trip.* And is going fishing in Alaska."

Sam grimaced, his weathered face wrinkling. "Tank Clawson always was one ta put play b'fore work. It's a wonder the man kin afford ta finance all his vacations."

Susan knew what it was. Supply and demand paid

well. The man did good work when he did it and people were willing to pay him top dollar. She'd hired him because he'd said he could fit her in between two big jobs that were scheduled. "I didn't get the impression that he was paying for this trip."

Sam tugged on his ear. "That's purdy odd."

"Yes, sir, it is. Thanks for the lunch, Sam. What would I do without you?"

His brows dipped. "You'd dry up and wither away. You need ta slow down, sit in one of them thar booths and eat that burger on the sit-down rather than on the blamed run. If you did that, one of them cowboys might sit down with you and who knows where that would lead."

She glanced toward the tables and the three different tables full of cowboys. She was going to do that soon as she got settled. "No time today. I've wasted more time than I had to give. I still have a load of cattle to see at Clint's place and that's going to take all afternoon." She grabbed the bag and waggled it at him. "Thanks again."

He scowled. "It ain't no wonder Cole Turner had to rescue ya out of that ditch. It's a wonder you didn't fall asleep sooner and get yorself killed."

"Sam, I'm trying to slow down. If I can get a contractor out there working, the sooner I'll get to sleep more."

"I'm on it."

"Thanks. I'm sure if there is a contractor out there to be found, you'll find him—or you'll help me find someone who knows one."

"Yup. I might jest have a good 'un in mind already."

"Really?" Susan's hopes shot up. "Who?"

"Can't say just yet. You comin' to the barbecue tomorrow night at Clint and Lacy's ranch, aren't you?"

"Yes," Susan said, wondering who he had in mind. "Are you?"

"Yup. Got my relief cook lined up fer this place. Me and Adela will see you thar." He nodded. "Probably gonna be an interesting night since Cole will be thar, too."

Just what she'd been afraid of—the man was going to start turning up all over the place. There would be nowhere to hide until he got bored and left. "He won't be around long from what I've heard about him," she said, and then wished she'd just taken her burger and hit the road as planned.

"Maybe." Sam slapped his ever-present dish towel over his shoulder with a grin. "And maybe not."

Chapter Five

Cole's gaze swept over the gathering as he trailed behind Seth and Melody toward the backyard barbecue. Clint and Lacy Matlock had a beautiful ranch. The main house sat on a hill and overlooked a stunning valley.

It wasn't the view that had Cole's attention, however, it was the tall beauty leaning against the deck banister watching him.

He'd wondered if she was going to be here. As much as they had a weird kind of thing going on, he realized the minute he saw her that he'd been hoping to see her.

As he passed a tub of iced-down sodas he grabbed two and headed her way. Maybe he should have stayed back, but that wasn't part of his makeup. Even if she didn't look happy to see him.

He mounted the steps. "Don't look so hostile, Doc. I come with soda." He popped the top of a can and handed it to her; she didn't take it. "Come on now, it would be rude to snub your handsome rescuer."

She reluctantly accepted the drink. "You are going to milk that accident for all it's worth, aren't you?"

"Maybe." He opened his drink and took a swig. "I

have to say, I'm pretty good at reading people, but you are a puzzle."

"How so?"

"Despite my being your knight in shining armor, I continually get the feeling that you'd as soon see me run over by wild horses."

Susan almost choked on her soda. "I do not."

She had added a touch of shimmer to her lips and now she clamped those pretty lips together. It was a warm day for April but the temperature edged up a few more degrees as they stared at each other. "Oh, you know it's true."

"For your information, I know you aren't going to be in town long. So, I—"

"How do you know?"

"Well, um…you never come home much."

The good doctor was flustered. "Have you been checking up on me, Doc?"

"No. Of course not."

Call him crazy for flirting—and he was, but he was enjoying himself. He was about to press further when Norma Sue Jenkins rounded the corner of the house and spotted him.

"Cole Turner," she bellowed and engulfed him in a bear hug. The short, stout woman practically lifted him from the deck in her enthusiasm.

"You are a sight for sore eyes!" Norma Sue declared. She was married to Clint Matlock's foreman, Roy Don. She and Roy Don had been friends of his grandparents and his parents. As a boy he and his brothers had spent almost as many evenings at Roy Don and Norma Sue's house as their own. Norma was pure robust Texas cattle-woman from the tip of her boots to the top of her white

Stetson. She'd always worn jeans and pearl-button, Western shirts or blue bibbed overalls—except on Sunday when she was partial to striped dresses. Tonight she'd chosen jeans and a pale blue, pearl-button shirt. Her kinky gray hair poked out from beneath the Stetson and tickled his jaw when she yanked his head to her shoulder and smothered him as if she hadn't seen him in years.

Norma Sue had always been a big hugger and he'd hated it as a kid. But as a man who often missed his parents and grandparents, he enjoyed the comfort her hugs always gave him. "I missed you, boy," she said, finally releasing him.

"Norma Sue, I saw you at the wedding, so if you keep this up folks are gonna start talking."

She slapped him on the arm and frowned. "I'm gearing up for when you leave town and don't come back again for years. Like *before Seth's wedding*," she said accusingly. "I can't believe you came home twice in the same year."

Roy Don had come over and now reached in for a quick fatherly hug of his own. "Welcome home, son. She gets plumb mad when she thinks about you off running the roads and not having enough time to come home. I didn't hardly have any peace after you rode off into the sunset only hours after the reception."

"Sorry about that." Cole had planned on staying around longer after the wedding, but as happy as he'd been for Seth and Melody, emotions he hadn't expected had slammed into him during the evening. He'd had no choice but to leave. He'd been in a blue mood for weeks afterward.

He'd been furious with God after Lori, and it had taken him a long time to regain some kind of relationship with his God. Just like the relationship between father and son can be strained, so had his become with his heavenly Father. But as a father and son reconciled so he had been trying. Unexpectedly Seth's wedding had almost taken him back to square one.

There was no way he'd ever want Seth or Melody to know that… Wyatt, on the other hand had figured it out—not that he'd figured it out completely, but still… that was Cole's reason for being here now. His big brother had decided it was time for Cole to come home for an extended visit and had threatened to tell Seth all if he didn't cooperate and return. Wyatt reasoned that if Cole came home and spent time with the newlyweds it would help him get over his past. Cole didn't want to get over his past…and that, Wyatt had argued, was the problem.

"Now—" Roy Don grinned beneath his wide mustache "—you can well imagine my *delight* to hear you were coming back for a visit so soon."

Cole chuckled at the old cowboy's use of the word *delight*. "I'm glad it's helped you out."

Norma Sue beamed, her round cheeks so tight they shined in the dwindling sunlight. "Two times in one year, that's a record. And a long time coming." She glanced at Susan. "We're hoping maybe he'll stay."

"I see." Susan's skeptical, blue gaze hit him full force before dropping to the can of soda.

Something about the look he'd just seen had Cole stumbling over a reply. "I've been real busy," he said, yanking his gaze from Susan's and meeting Norma's hawk eyes. The woman's brain was clicking along as she studied him and Susan. "Unfortunately there's been lots of rebuilding needed along the Gulf Coast." He needed to get this conversation back on track and fast.

"We know you've been doing great things," Norma Sue said, jumping on board.

"You represent your hometown very well," Roy Don chimed in. "Don't you ever forget how proud we are to call you our own."

"That's right," Norma Sue agreed. "We're just glad to get to see you. We can't help but hope you settle down here with a nice girl who'll give you lots of babies." Her gaze slid toward Susan and his followed—like an idiot. Susan's eyes flared but she did a great job holding her expression neutral.

He swallowed hard and hoped he did as good a job. "I'm not really lookin—"

Norma broke in and slapped him on the back. "We're sure glad you were there for our Susan. God knew what He was doing when He had you there to help her. At exactly the right moment—isn't that something. I tell you, I *do* believe in God's timing."

Susan's eyes widened. If it hadn't been so off base for him he might have found her reaction funny. Norma Sue never had been one for beating around the bush.

"Now, Norma, don't go thinking of matchmaking me," he warned. Norma Sue and her two best friends, Esther Mae Wilcox and Sam's wife, Adela, were eaten up with matchmaking. They'd saved the town from drying up and blowing away by coming up with the idea to advertise for wives. They'd found their calling, that was for sure. The proof stood around the yard—most all of the couples at the ranch tonight had been matched up by them in some way.

"Cole!"

The shriek came from Esther Mae Wilcox as she emerged from the house carrying a big bowl of fruit. She plopped it down on the long table then hustled his way. Esther was as loud in person as she was in attire. She wore purple-and-pink-striped calf-length pants and a purple shirt with a humongous pink rose across one entire side. It was as bright pink as her hair was brilliant red. Her personality was just as vibrant.

"About time I got a hug. I heard you were back in town." She threw her arms around him.

"Esther Mae, how in the world are you?" he asked. When he was five he'd been squirming to get away at this point. "Is that Hank still treatin' you right or are you ready to run away with me?"

Esther Mae giggled and stepped away. She was a tinge of pink herself. "You always were a charmer— you and Wyatt got that direct from the Turner side."

"True, but the offer stands."

She elbowed him. "My Hank wouldn't know what to do if I ran away."

"I know that's the truth." He laughed.

"Our forty-year wedding anniversary is tomorrow."

Norma Sue gave everyone a comical grimace. "You two are sure getting old, Esther Mae."

"Hey, don't try that. You and Roy Don are coming up on forty-three years."

"True, but I was a baby when we got married."

"So was I." Esther Mae giggled. "That's my story and I'm sticking to it."

Cole chuckled and his gaze slid toward Susan. He was startled at the wistful look in her eyes as she stared at Esther Mae.

"That's wonderful, Esther Mae. I'm so happy for

you two," she said. "Um, I need to head inside. I told Lacy I'd help her."

Cole watched her leave. This evening was good for her. She wasn't working; she didn't look tired. On the contrary, she looked fantastic. Yet there was something about her that didn't seem right. And he couldn't help but wonder what that something was.

"Lacy!" Susan entered the kitchen and was relieved to find her friend alone. She'd just finished icing a cake and was running her finger along the rim of the bowl of leftover icing.

"What's up, girlfriend? You look like you've seen Elvis or something."

"I wish! It's Norma Sue and Esther Mae. I think they're up to something. I see it in their eyes."

Lacy plopped her icing-covered finger into her mouth on her way to the sink with the knife and bowl. "I hate to break it to you, but you're right on target with that. This afternoon they came into the salon buzzing like bees," she confided, grimacing. "Cole's coming home has put a sparkle in their eyes and you know what that means. Adela's in the back room rocking Dottie's baby to sleep, but believe me, she's on the same page with her cohorts. The matchmaking posse is locked and loaded."

Susan bit her lip. "Any idea what they're locked on to?"

"They're determined to get Cole to stay home. They're looking for a match for that hunk of hometown cowboy, convinced falling in love will do the deed."

Dread filled Susan. "But he's not looking to stay."

"A man can change his mind."

"Well, yes, but he just seems like he loves the road."

"The road gets old. Or so they say." Lacy picked up

the cake and beamed at her. The petite blonde's blue eyes sparkled with mischief. "You worried about something?"

"N-no. I mean, the man doesn't mean anything to me." Susan meant it, too.

"You two sure sound like y'all have hit it off."

"Oh, no, we haven't."

Lacy laughed. "That cowboy had you in his sights the minute he got out of his truck and headed toward this house. And you zeroed in on him just as quickly."

"That is so not true. And besides, you weren't even outside."

"Ha! I was looking out the window. The temperature went up twenty degrees."

"Lacy Matlock, you better back up right now. Do not put any ideas in the matchmakers' heads. I'm your basic homebody tied to my job and he lives on a Harley. He and I just don't compute as a match."

"That is just typical Susan Work-and-No-Play Worth," Lacy practically sang. "I thought you were moving here to have a social life. The gals have that in mind for you, so relax, get to know the guy. Have a little faith."

Susan felt hot. Hot as in get-sick hot. *Cole Turner—* no way.

No matter how attractive she found Cole Turner he wasn't the one for her. The risk was too great where he was concerned.

Faith was good to have, but God didn't just give people good heads on their shoulders. He put a brain inside, too. If she threw caution to the wind and let the ladies match her with a rolling stone, she'd be crazy.

She was startled when Lacy sobered and suddenly hugged her.

"It's okay," she said. "You know the gals well enough to know they only want the best for you, right?"

"I know what's best for me and it isn't Cole Turner."

Lacy hooted at that and it didn't make Susan feel very confident as Lacy tugged her toward the door. "You are about the wariest gal I ever saw. It's time to eat, Susan. But remember that sometimes God does open others' eyes to things to give us little nudges in the right direction."

"I've got a great sense of direction and that's why I'm staying as far away from Cole as I can get while he's in town."

Lacy glanced over her shoulder as she led the way outside. "Whatever you say. But I've got a feeling it won't be that easy."

Oh, yes, it would be, Susan thought as she stepped out onto the deck and practically ran into Sam.

"Just the woman I been lookin' fer," he said, grabbing her by the arm. "You still needin' a contractor?"

"Yes," she said, feeling relief just from the enthusiasm she heard in his voice. Getting the work started on her clinic would take some of the pressure off her. "Did you find someone already?"

"Yup, shor did. Come with me." He tucked her arm into the crook of his wiry arm and headed across the deck.

The crowd around Cole had grown and that was the direction Sam was taking her. She studied the group and knew none of them were contractors. *"Sam,"* she said, slowing her steps.

"Now, don't go gettin' cold feet," he said, coming to a halt in front of Cole. Cole looked from her to Sam.

"Cole." Sam grinned. "Susan has a proposal for ya."

Chapter Six

"A proposal?"

Cole's smoky-blue eyes deepened with warm curiosity as he crossed his arms and studied Susan. Unbelievably, for that moment she felt as if she was the only person standing near him. It was as disturbing as the past three minutes had been.

"Yup," Sam quipped, pushing Susan forward a step. "Susan's got the perfect job for you while yor home."

Susan wanted to crawl under a rock, but everyone was looking at her. She fought to look calm and collected.

"And what would that be?" Cole drawled, shifting his weight against the deck railing he was leaning against.

"Yesterday her contractor left her high and dry when he quit on her. She's in a bind and needs a good contractor—you'd be perfect for the job."

Perfect for the job! Oh, what a nightmare.

Cole straightened, looking as startled as she felt. "Do you really need some help?" he asked, sounding as if he'd like her to say no.

She couldn't say no, not with the whole town listening. "Yes, but I'm sure you wouldn't have time for something like that. This was Sam's idea. Sam," she said, turning her attention to the older man, "he's here to visit with Seth and Melody before he goes back to work." There, she'd given him the perfect out. Maybe he'd take the hint and hit the road sooner.

"Actually—"

Just the way he drew the word out had her every nerve on full alert as her gaze shot back to meet his.

"I could come out and take a look."

Talk about blowing her plan to stay away from him to smithereens. She couldn't allow this to happen…and yet she was needed in her clinic.

"But only if you wanted me to," he added when she said nothing.

"That is a great idea," Lacy called from the back of the crowd. Susan shot her a glare and caught the twinkle of laughter in her eyes.

"So perfect!" exclaimed Esther Mae.

"No," Susan blurted out. She couldn't even consider this. No matter how desperate she was.

"But it is the perfect solution," Norma Sue admonished, looking at her as though she was crazy for even considering saying no to the darling of Mule Hollow.

This was absolutely unbelievable. Her only consolation was that she realized Cole looked as conflicted as she was. That was slightly comforting in an odd sort of way. *Slightly.*

"Let him take a look," Applegate said, stepping out from somewhere in the crowd. She hadn't even seen him until that moment. "You ain't never been a fool where business was concerned, so don't start now."

She shot him an indignant glare, no longer able to control her displeasure at this entire idea.

Cole cocked his head to the side. "You want me to take a look?"

Boy, was this crazy. "Sure," she snapped, feeling out-numbered. "If you've got the time that would be…fine."

"He's got the time," Seth said from beside Applegate. "Me and Melody will be glad for him to do anything that will prolong his visit."

It was Cole's turn to aim a quizzical expression at his brother. "You just tell me when and where and I'll be there to take a gander at what you've got."

Susan's heart sank. She took a deep breath and gave a tiny nod. It took all she had to make her chin move down and up.

"Take him over thar now," Sam declared. "You don't need to be hem-hawin' around. This clinic business needs ta get goin' as soon as possible and this here bar-becue will still be here when y'all get back."

"Now?" Susan gasped before she caught herself.

Cole chuckled. "Sure. Now sounds good to me. Lacy, we'll be back before the hour is up. Is that okay?"

"Yep, yep, yep," she sang in true Lacy fashion. "Take all the time you need. You know my parties just keep going."

Susan could only hold in her dismay as Cole stepped forward and took her arm. His fingers were warm and sent tingles dancing across skin as he guided her toward his truck. Suddenly she found herself in the same situation as the night of the accident when he'd taken over… railroaded once more.

"This is ridicul—"

"Hold on," Cole murmured close to her ear as they

walked. "This is the easiest way. If you don't go with the flow, you won't hear the end of it all night."

He was right and she knew it.

Yes, she was being railroaded all right. But this time it was by the entire town! What in the world was she going to do?

Cole was trying to ignore the obvious matchmaking endeavor they'd just witnessed as he closed the passenger door to his truck and headed around to his side.

He climbed in with a quick glance at his passenger then concentrated on getting them on the road and away from prying eyes and calculating minds!

His friends wanted him back home and it was obvious that this was how they planned to do it. He'd expected to stay in town long enough to make Wyatt drop this sudden interest in his life and well-being. He hadn't expected this.

A couple of days was what he'd hoped it would take. Wyatt had said he was going to join him here and he'd planned to leave soon after. But his big brother, in true Wyatt form, had called this afternoon and said it would be Wednesday or Thursday before he could make it to town. His caseload was too full and he couldn't get away. That was almost a week away. So Cole had agreed to stay until then.

Now oddly enough he was intrigued by the whole aspect of what had just transpired. The fact that he was intrigued and not mad about it was weird. But if Susan was worried about him getting the wrong idea then she didn't have anything to be concerned about. Nope, intrigued or not, he wasn't here to fall in love—as it was so obvious his little matchmaking hometown friends were envisioning. Susan could rest easy on that point. He wasn't lookin' for love.

"So your contractor left you hanging?" he asked finally, when she made no attempt at conversation.

"Yes. He got an offer he couldn't refuse. Chose to go fishing in Alaska. Some people's work ethic amazes me."

"On that we agree." Cole shot her an agreeable glance. Even in disasters he was amazed at how men would walk off from jobs and leave folks in the lurch. Folks who'd already suffered enough pain when their houses had been destroyed by acts of God... He knew how they felt in a way. He'd lost Lori due to a lack of action on God's part—he pushed that out of his head. "Someone with a work ethic like yours *would* feel that way." Instantly he felt her eyes drill into him and he decided keeping his eyes on the road was the smart thing.

"I believe in working hard," she said. There was a defensive edge in her words. "Being dedicated to what I do. And being there when my clients—who *rely* on me—need me."

"Calm down," he urged, meeting her glare. "I didn't say it was a bad thing. I admire your dedication."

Two bright spots of pink appeared on her cheeks. "Oh, sorry. I didn't mean to be so touchy. It's just, well, not everyone feels that way."

They'd reached the crossroads and he pulled the truck to a halt before turning the direction of the clinic. "I'm sure in your business being a bit touchy comes in handy. You probably have to stand your ground." He caught a flicker of emotion in her eyes that he'd glimpsed momentarily when she'd been exhausted. Vulnerability wasn't her style but it was there and he knew instinctively that she hated it. Saw it as weakness.

"Yes, I do," she said, rubbing her thigh as if the idea worried her.

The deep sigh that followed the statement seemed to go unnoticed by her and he wondered if she'd even realized she'd done it. He couldn't help being curious about her. Wondered if there was something in particular that drove her. "It's this way, right?" he asked, knowing it was, but wanting to give her something else to think about.

"Yes, about five miles out."

He drove as she gave him more detailed directions and related who it had belonged to. All stuff he'd already garnered from Applegate and Stanley. "That'll be a perfect spot for your business. I guess that place has sat empty for years now?"

"Yes. I'm excited. But you don't have to do this."

He smiled and meant it. "I know. But I can at least take a look for you."

An uncomfortable silence settled between them. He chose not to press. He was a quick study, and it didn't take a genius to figure out that Susan hated to be pressed.

Tonight he didn't want to fight. Glancing at her, he realized he wanted to get to know her better. Despite their ability to rub each other the wrong way, they did have a few things in common.

"There it is," she said the instant it came into view.

It had weathered well on the outside; since it was a metal building he'd expected as much. But the rutted drive would need some attention before horse trailers and an abundance of traffic started in on it. "You picked a good spot," he commented as he pulled to a stop.

"Thanks. It's a bit off the beaten path, but so is everything else around here."

She opened her door and hopped from the truck before he could say more. He watched her stride to the front door first, then he followed. It was easy to tell she was uncomfortable being in close proximity to him. But she was excited about her place, though she seemed to be downplaying it a bit.

A sense of challenge overtook him as he moved toward her. Who was Susan Worth? All kinds of questions had been popping up in his head about her lately. What drove her? Why was she so determined to hide the flicker of softness he'd glimpsed briefly both today and the other night? Those and other questions surged, but he pushed them away as he followed. He was here to look at her building...not play fill in the blank with the doc.

The building was like most of the older metal buildings—white corrugated sheet metal with faded blue trim around the windows and along the roofline. The metal front door was dull gray with no window and a large dent at the bottom as if it had been kicked.

There were two large windows on either side of the door, so that would at least let light into what he assumed would be the waiting area. She unlocked the door and led the way into the large open room. In the business of assessing damage and fixing it, for insurance claims or for emergency situations, he was used to walking into buildings and automatically evaluating the situation.

"Not too bad," he said, as his gaze took in the cheap paneling in the room. He glanced out the door that led into the back area where oil rig fittings and pipes had once been kept. "At least it has good bones."

She tucked her fingers into the fronts of her jeans and rocked onto her toes. "It does, doesn't it?"

The excitement in her voice was unmistakable. What was up with that? Was it just to him that she was trying to appear subdued?

"So what do you want to do in here?"

"As you can tell, this room is too small and that back area is too big. I need a reception area built and then exam rooms. Also an office and a records area. Plus holding area and surgery. And a dispensary. Something similar to what I have in Ranger."

"Good idea. How many exam rooms?"

"At least two. And I'll want the surgery to be larger than what I have now."

As he'd hoped she would, she began to loosen up, tugging her fingers from her pockets she began using her hands to help describe where and how she wanted things constructed. Moving about the room and out into the back area she elaborated on her vision for the space. He kept his comments to a minimum, only offering suggestions occasionally.

When she finally finished she spun toward him. "So, that's about it. I know it's a lot and my problem is I need it done by the end of the month. My buyer at the Ranger clinic wants to take over the first day of May. I had agreed originally because my contractor assured me it could be done—there was no fishing trip in the picture. Now, I'm not sure. What do you think? Could it be done?"

"Yes."

"Is this something you might really be interested in

taking on?" she asked with a mixture of uncertainty and wistfulness all rolled into one sweet expression. His heart twisted remembering a similar expression.

"He was right. It is doable," he said, modulating his tone to hold steady. This was about Susan. "Given, the amount of work we're looking at it might be tight. I wouldn't delay getting started for much longer." He hadn't answered her question. Did he want to tackle it?

She frowned. "That's what I'm afraid of. And there just aren't that many contractors who want to drive all the way out here to the middle of nowhere. This is cattle country, but there's not a lot of building going on."

Cole had a feeling he was going to live to regret this but he couldn't leave her hanging. He hadn't planned on working construction while he was home. Hadn't planned on staying the four weeks it would take to do this job. "I know I'm the last man you'd want to work with." Might as well put the truth on the table.

"Yes."

He grinned; he couldn't stop it. "Most women would have lied on that one."

"What would be the use in our situation?" she said. "Be honest, this is the last job you'd want. Working for me, while the town tries to figure out how to keep you here."

"Yes," he answered as bluntly as she had. "That said, I'm still offering my services if you want to take me up on the offer." There were all kinds of reasons why he wanted to turn tail and hit the road. But he could help her. He could get her into this building on time and get her dreams heading in the right direction.

The fulfillment of some dreams—other people's dreams—drove him. God hadn't given him the chance or the ability to make his own dream come true. His dream of a life with Lori—of seeing Lori survive her cancer—that had all been out of his hands. But other dreams…dreams that had been dashed through the wrath of Mother Nature—God had granted him the ability to revive.

In doing so, He'd given Cole a reason to keep going. A reason to get up in the mornings.

Susan looked slightly pensive, unsure about him. He didn't have to convey to her that the folks of Mule Hollow would be on a matchmaking tear once she agreed.

She took a deep breath, turned on her heel in a slow swivel as her gaze roamed the office of her dreams. Suddenly she spun back. "When can you start?"

Chapter Seven

"**P**raise the Lord!" Betty exclaimed on Saturday morning. Susan's receptionist let her half-eaten doughnut hover in front of her mouth as Susan entered the clinic. "You look like you're back in the land of the living. Got some sleep the past couple of nights?"

"Sure did," Susan said, watching as Betty stuffed the rest of the doughnut into her mouth. "You sure you even taste what you're chewing so fast?"

Swiping sugar particles from her lips, Betty grinned. "You should be cramming down a few with the crazy busy day you've got ahead of you. And I do mean crazy! Your tongue's goin' to be dragging before noon!"

Susan glanced down at the book. It had every slot filled in and then more scribbled into the margins. Betty still insisted on using a paper schedule instead of the computer because she couldn't fit folks in—and she always had to fit folks in. "Wow, I tell you, Betty. I'm ready for a rest."

"I've been telling you that you need to slow down. I know your daddy meant well driving you to be a success, but surely he didn't mean for you to be old before your time. And I know your momma wouldn't have wanted this. No mother would want her daughter so caught up in work she couldn't enjoy life."

Susan didn't talk about her mother much, but she had talked with Betty about growing up without a mother. She and her dad had made it, but there had always been that void left by her absence. Knowing her mother had died giving birth to her had made Susan feel horrible growing up. But she'd known her mother loved her dearly. "I know you're right. Since Dad's death I've been thinking about that a lot."

"Good. You need to think about what she'd want and find a husband who'll give you babies and help you in your business."

Susan nodded, hoping such a man was out there for her.

"So what's this I hear about the hunky Cole Turner? I take my three days off and come back to a very disturbing situation."

"How did you know about Cole?"

"Me'n George drove to Mule Hollow on Thursday night for all-you-can-eat catfish at Sam's. Believe me when I say I heard all about your falling asleep and the white-knight rescue. Why, to hear them talk it was straight out of one of them romance novels I read."

Susan cringed at being the talk of the town. It came with the territory when one lived in a small town, but to have everything blown out of proportion like this wasn't good. The reality had hit home at Lacy's when she'd realized she was now the target of the matchmaking posse. And then, she'd made things worse by giving in to their plans.

Things could only get worse on that front now that

she'd done it. Needing sugar, she picked up a dough-nut, but put it back down. "Don't believe everything you hear," she said, snatching up the stack of mail and thumbing through it.

"So what is going on? I heard he's the wandering brother. Not the lawyer, though from what I hear he flies all over the place, too. What is it with these Turner men?" Betty was talking at the speed of light and didn't pause after the question. "Only one that knows how to stay put is Seth… You should have snatched that one up but quick," she huffed. "Not go gettin' on the back of this Cole's Harley. Is it true you did that?"

Susan nodded. "Believe me, I didn't want to get on the back of that thing, either."

The mother hen in Betty was out as she crossed her arms and met Susan's gaze. She took this job seriously. "Flirting around with a man like that isn't gonna help you find yourself a husband. That's why you're mov-ing to Mule Hollow in the first place. You don't need to be messing around with someone like this dude. You need a cowboy who is going to hang around. A Harley," she harrumphed.

"Boy, aren't you wound up this morning?" Susan wondered where her first appointment was. It would help everything if they'd arrive and she could get to work.

"Hey, I'm all for you moving your practice so you can have time to find a husband. But from all accounts this Cole is a good man, but he's a rover. You need a man who will help you in this business where possible. *Someone who will be there for you*. You don't need one off saving the world."

Saving the world. Was that what Cole was doing? "You're right. I agree totally." True.

"Then set your priorities right. You have more dating trouble than anyone I've ever seen. I love you like a daughter, but we both know you haven't had much luck picking the right men. It's time for you to use your head and find someone right."

Susan knew she'd made mistakes where men were concerned—the few she'd tried dating. They always never lasted because she had to put her work first. Building a business wasn't easy. Especially in a man's world. It caused them to think she was bossy. *Bossy!* That word ate at her. But it was the fact that she always picked men who couldn't appreciate her for the person she was or what she did for a living.

"I'm not falling for the guy, Betty. I didn't ask him to come back to town. I also didn't ask him to be the one who found me when I drove off the road. But as much as I hate admitting it, he was there and the situation could have been much worse. And if it had been worse he would have been someone good to be there to help me."

Betty looked apologetic. "I know, honey. I can't argue that he's not a good man—my goodness, look what he does for a livin'. But he just isn't the right one for you. You know I worry about you."

"Betty, I have this under control." She glanced at the clock and knew if she was going to break the contracting news she needed to do it soon. "Actually, I need to tell you something before appointments start rolling in."

"Why is it I suddenly get the idea I ain't gonna like what you've got to say?"

Susan cleared her throat. "I don't think you are. But it couldn't be helped or, believe me, I would have done something different."

Betty's green eyes narrowed.

Susan gulped—*she never gulped!* "I hired him to take over the construction on the clinic."

Betty whacked the appointment book. "Well, if that just don't beat all. What were you thinking?"

"Well, I needed someone and he was available." Susan's temper flared. What else did Betty expect her to do?

"That may be so. But you better be on guard is all I've got to say. I've said my piece." She clamped her mouth shut for five seconds. "And further more, if you think I'm gonna *smile* and make nice when I know what he's up to—well," she harrumphed. "Then you better just tell Mr. Cole Turner he don't need to be comin' around here, 'cause I'll put a finger in his chest and back him up to that there door so fast he'll think a herd of bulls done ran slap over him!"

What did she think Cole was up to anyway? The man was simply helping her out of a hard situation… *and now you're taking up for the man?* "Betty, really, you are overreacting." She was relieved to see a truck drive up. "It looks like the day is about to begin."

Betty grinned as she picked up her pencil and plopped into her chair behind the reception desk. "And ain't that just lucky for you. I'll shut up now."

"Oh, but I'm certain it'll only be for a few minutes." Susan laughed and headed toward her office, still confused about what exactly Betty thought Cole was up to.

Behind her Betty's grumble was loud and clear. "You got that right."

"So is Wyatt coming to town or what?" Cole asked his brother as he buttered biscuits. He'd squeezed in some time with Seth and his new sister-in-law before heading over to get things rolling at his new job—the job he was still a little startled to have.

"Your guess is as good as mine," Seth said as he set a plate of sausage and bacon on the table while Melody finished dishing up the scrambled eggs at the stove. "Didn't he tell you it would be Wednesday or Thursday?"

"Yeah, but I'll believe it when I see it."

"Oh, I hope he does," Melody said. "Seth, did you know he was supposed to be coming home?"

Seth nodded at her and Cole caught the glimmer of love in his brother's eyes as they connected with his new wife's. Cole really was happy for them. His heart still tugged every time he looked at them, but it was a good tug. Wyatt had been wrong when he'd thought he wasn't happy for them.

Bittersweet at what he was missing, yes, but overjoyed that God had put them together. God and *Wyatt*. It was still strange every time he thought of his big brother setting them up.

Seth started refilling their coffee mugs. "You know how Wyatt likes to run the show. He sounded to me like he had a motive for wanting you back in town, Cole. Any ideas?"

Cole's head jerked up at the question. He wasn't going to tell them that Wyatt was holding his unresolved issues of losing Lori and *their* happy-ever-after over his head. "I think he wanted me home so I'd get to know my new sister-in-law better. I sort of skipped out on y'all early after the wedding…not that the two of you were noticing anything but each other."

"I have to agree with you," Seth said, setting the coffee carafe back on the burner. "I barely noticed you'd left. Sorry, brother."

"Seth, that's horrible!" Melody looked up sheepishly as Seth dropped a kiss on her cheek. "But," she squeaked, "it is true. I was so happy to be Mrs. Seth Turner that all I could think about was Seth. We really are glad you came home, though."

Cole liked Melody. She was sweet and kind and perfect for Seth. "I am, too," he said, and meant it. That wasn't so a week ago. He thought about that as he carried the biscuits to the table. What had changed?

Seth said the blessing a few moments later and Cole felt a peace in the room as the prayer ended and they tucked in. He'd been working so hard and running, as his brothers knew he was, from the past but Cole was happy for Seth and Melody. It was a precious thing— the joy he saw in their eyes.

"So," Seth said after food was dished up and they'd started to munch on bacon and eggs, "I'm still surprised you took on Susan's remodel. But it's a good thing."

"I know she'll appreciate it," Melody said. "She's about run ragged. We've all been so happy that she decided to do this especially after her falling asleep at the wheel."

"Stubborn woman," he grunted before taking a chunk out of a biscuit.

"She is," Seth said. "But good as gold and driven. She told me once that she was the success she was because her daddy raised her up to stand on her own two feet. She hasn't said much but his death hit her hard."

Cole let that sink in. She'd lost someone she loved. "She's a tough one, that's for sure. I can see where a dad raised her. What about her mom?" Okay, so he was curious.

"Susan doesn't talk about her. But once she mentioned that she didn't remember her."

Melody sighed. "I'm hoping she finds a good man. Someone who'll love her like she deserves and fill the empty holes I believe she fills with her work... I used to do that," she said, reaching out for Seth's hand. "And then I met you."

Cole took a swig of coffee and tried to ignore the way those words made him feel.

It seemed he and Susan had more than a few things in common.

Chapter Eight

The sun was high in the April afternoon sky as Cole climbed from his truck and headed inside the clinic. From the cattle pens around the back of the building he could hear the low bawl of a few cattle and from inside the clinic, the hectic bark of dogs.

He opened the door—he'd expected from what she'd told him that it would be busy…he hadn't expected chaos!

"Get that dog back—" a pint-size woman yelled from behind the counter as she waved a magazine at a huge shaggy beast of a dog. The owner of the animal was straining to hold the leash while another woman was trying to coax a hissing cat down from the shelf behind the angry woman.

The dog barked like the echoing of a cannon as Cole closed the door behind him. Cole had made some bad choices in life, but in that instant, walking into the fray had to be at the top of the list. The terrified cat sprang toward him claws out and hit Cole square in the chest— it did *not* feel good.

"Hold him!" *all* the women screamed—as if he

needed to hold on to a cat using him as a scratching post. Thankfully, one second the yellow tabby was hooked into his chest and the next it flew to the floor and under a magazine table.

The overexcited woofer spun. Magazines exploded everywhere as the dog hit the small brown table like a linebacker.

Cole hadn't moved, too stunned by what he'd walked into to move. This was *crazy,* he thought, lunging for the leash in an attempt to save the cat.

But before he could help the cornered tabby it took charge, reared up and with a terrifying hiss, slapped the bully across the nose.

Three wide-eyed women flattened against their chair backs clutching their trembling pooches as a new battle threatened.

Cole stormed across the room, snagged the leash and yanked the dog back just as the fed-up cat launched toward it—

Cole's timing couldn't have been worse.

He stepped straight into the line of attack as the cat overshot the dog! Cole had turned back into a human scratching post when Susan rushed out of nowhere and threw a sheet over the cat.

Startled, the terrified cat let go of his arm and Cole watched in shock as Susan disappeared into another room with the secured animal.

The room went silent.

Everyone—including the dog at his side—seemed to be holding their breaths.

"I don't know who you are," the pint-sized woman

said, breaking the silence. "But, oh, boy, am I glad to see you."

"Not sure I'm glad to be here," he growled about the time Susan came striding back into the room—*without* the cat.

"Betty, please take Sampson into exam room two. You," she barked the command to Cole. "Come with me, you're bleeding."

He had never been happier to be bossed around in all of his life.

He gladly turned over the leash to Betty then followed Susan into the exam room.

Oh, yeah, he was bleeding all right. He left a trail as he went.

"What *was* that?" he asked, as she pushed him to sit on the edge of the small animal exam table.

"I'm not exactly sure. Sampson is just a big puppy and normally a doll. But I'd just given him his shots and he was a little shaken up, I gue—" She stopped speaking and was staring at Cole's arm in horror. "I'm so sorry you got caught up in it."

"It's okay." He didn't want to make her feel any worse. She shook her head and reached for his shredded shirtsleeve. A quick and gentle roll exposed a not-so-pretty sight.

"I'm not even going to ask if that hurts—I know exactly how it feels." She leaned closer, her fingers trailing along his arm as she cataloged his injuries. "It doesn't look like you'll need stitches." She looked up and met his gaze.

"I'm sure you've been attacked many times in this line of business," he said, feeling no pain, only her gentle touch.

She batted her Mediterranean blues at him and for a moment he was lost in them.

She suddenly backed up, spun away and began washing her hands at the sink as if realizing she'd forgotten to sanitize before touching him. "It's a job risk," she said briskly. "I seem to keep involving you in all my job risks."

"True. Maybe we should stop meeting this way."

She gave a tiny smile, more grimace than anything. "I agree. No more mishaps from this day forward. Mine or yours."

He grinned at her as she began cleaning the punctures.

"Do you often have to deal with that sort of craziness?"

She shook her head. "Betty usually foresees disaster before it happens. She orchestrates the waiting room and exam perfectly. But today..." She frowned. "Her timing was off."

Maybe not, Cole thought, watching her work. He would have missed the feel of her touch otherwise as she gently put antiseptic on the wounds. As crazy as it sounded, the sting of alcohol had never been more welcome. Her blond hair was in its usual ponytail, falling over her shoulder as she worked. She lifted serious eyes to his.

"This may get infected."

"I work disasters, Doc. It'll be fine. I've been attacked by scared animals before."

"Really?" Her eyes widened. "I hadn't thought of that."

He shrugged. "You name it, I've most likely tangled with it."

She started to wrap a bandage around the worst wound. "Did you get some sleep last night?" he asked.

She stepped away from him. "Yes, I did. That's two nights in a row. It was wonderful. I may not be so lucky tonight."

"Let's hope the emergency night calls hold off until I get your clinic done. Speaking of which. I stopped by to tell you that I've picked up enough Sheetrock and supplies to get started tonight. By the time I get back to Mule Hollow this afternoon the demolition should be complete."

"You're kidding?"

"Hey, don't look so startled. I told you I knew what I was doing."

"Yes, I know. I guess I wasn't expecting you to jump in the very next morning."

"Why not?"

"Where did you find the help so quickly?"

He liked surprising her. The thought hit him that he liked seeing the light it brought to her eyes. And the touch of a flush it put in her cheeks. "You *see,*" he drawled, "that's where it comes in handy to have hired hands already working at the ranch. Cowboys are some of the best jacks-of-all-trades you can find."

She crossed her arms and leaned her hip against the counter. "Yes, they are. But still I didn't expect anyone to have the time."

"Seth helped out on that end by making the time for them. He's managing for a few days." He didn't need to tell her that it was a tough time to be loaning out help. Susan knew the business. "The whole town wants their favorite doctor safe."

He half expected her to bridle at the mere insinuation

that she might not be safe. She didn't, though—must have been because he was injured.

"I'm ready to be there, too. You look like that shocks you."

"I'm just startled that you didn't jump on me for suggesting that you couldn't handle the drive and the work."

She smiled, her lips turning up just enough that she looked apologetic. "Speaking of work. I hate this happened to you, but I need to get to my appointments before they pile up so far back we have all kinds of cat and dog fights in the waiting room. Are you sure you're okay?"

"I'm good as new, Doc." He hopped from the exam table and rolled his tattered sleeve down. "It's out *there* that worries me." He yanked his head toward the door and grinned. "Who knows what waits on the other side of that door."

"Oh, I promise I'll get you out of here without any more damage to your body. You just stick with me," she teased, moving to go out ahead of him.

"I'm feeling good about my chances with you in the lead. Hey, I almost forgot. I came by to ask about some wall placements." She leaned against the door and listened as he quickly explained a couple of minor changes to what they'd talked about the day before. Hearing she liked his idea, he felt satisfaction knowing she appreciated an improvement and recognized it as such.

She made the move to open the door. He touched her arm, drawing her attention. "When do you think you'll get to come out?"

"Um." Her brows crinkled. "It will be tonight after work if I can catch up—which I will, if the rest of the day goes without mishap."

"Then, I'll be there. If for some reason I miss you, you know, like if Seth needs me at the ranch or something like that, then call this number and I'll meet you there." He tugged his billfold from his back pocket and withdrew a business card. "Hopefully, we will both have uneventful afternoons."

She opened the door and he walked out into the reception room, which was in perfect order. The pint-size woman hurried from around the counter.

"Thanks again for saving the day. Dad-blame horse of a dog had a bee in its bonnet after Susan stuck that needle in him. I'm Betty, by the way."

Cole took the hand she offered him and shook. "Glad to meet you, Betty. I'm Cole Turner." No sooner was his name out of his mouth than Betty's mouth clamped tight and her eyes beaded.

She shot Susan a weird little look that he was certain had some kind of hidden message in it.

He lifted a brow and hitched a half grin. "Is something wrong?"

"Oh, *yeah,* Buster Brown. You planning to hit the road again after you get that building done?"

"Betty!"

Cole not only heard the warning in Susan's tone, but saw it in her eyes. What was going on here? It was clear that Betty was none too pleased with him. "Most likely. Is something wrong here?"

"No. Everything is just fine." Susan glared at her receptionist.

"It is not," Betty huffed.

Cole chuckled. Tiny Betty was like a miniature hen protecting her chick. What was up with her? Did she think he was here to play around—

"Someone needs to put all the cards out on the table. He needs to know I won't tolerate him—"

"Betty, please. Clients," Susan said under her breath as she took Betty by the shoulders and hustled her toward one of the exam rooms. "I need you to go and check on Tabby and make sure that he's calmed down after that scare he had."

"He is—but—"

"Go, Betty. I mean it." Susan opened the door and practically pushed Betty through the opening. Before she disappeared, Betty got in another glare at him that said this conversation would be continued.

Susan swung around and leaned against the closed door. "Sorry. Betty tends to get riled up easy."

"You don't say? What was she—"

Susan blushed…a full rose-pink. Not the pink cheeks like he'd seen before but an all-out hairline-to-neckline color change. And then he got it. "Ohhhh, she thinks—"

"I really have to get back to work." Susan glanced self-consciously about the packed waiting room and the women who'd all seemed to lean forward in their seats. Cole laughed, knowing that Susan was trying to stomp out a fire that was already well out of control.

She was definitely the talk of the town—or towns, since this was Ranger and there was no doubt in his mind that the same speculation was happening in Mule Hollow.

He grinned at her and she did not take it well. Oh, no, she snapped a hand to his good arm, yanked open the front door and shoved him outside.

"I'll see you tonight," she hissed, then pulled the door closed in his face.

Cole couldn't help laughing. Small-town life…he

chuckled halfway home thinking about the look of horror on Susan's face. There was one thing for certain and that was Susan wasn't lovin' life in a small town right now.

Chapter Nine

"Wow!" Susan exclaimed when she walked through the front door around seven that evening.

Cole pulled the trigger of the nail gun, shooting the last nail into place on the wall he'd just studded in. "It looks different, doesn't it?" He studied her, having wondered how she would act when she arrived. She had composed herself, it seemed, since there was no pink in sight. He missed it instantly.

"Are you kidding me? This is unbelievable. You're practically ready to install Sheetrock." She was clearly amazed. "How fast do you work?"

He glanced at the progress, unimpressed. "It's not that big a deal. Do you know how easy it is to tear stuff out when two men have sledgehammers and Sawzalls? By the time I got back to town the fellas had things cleared out and the place swept. All I had to do was start cutting and nailing. Piece of cake."

"To *you* maybe. I wouldn't have known the first place to start."

"And I'm quite sure that your animal clients would rather you know how to set a bone rather than how to set concrete or use a reciprocating saw. Sampson would have eatin' all of us if I'd been the one who gave him a shot." He held up the nail gun, pretending it was a needle.

Susan laughed. "You're right. Please don't remind me. How are your wounds?"

He shrugged. "I'll live." He started to ask how Betty was but decided she wouldn't find the subject funny. He'd been thinking about that blush that had overcome her after what Betty had insinuated. An antimatchmaker... Smart woman that Betty.

Still, he'd been thinking about Susan off and on all afternoon. That blush showed the softer side of the doctor. He wondered if she showed that side of herself to anyone—freely. Today it had been forced.

"You want to help?" he asked, deciding to steer away from what he knew she was embarrassed about. After all, she'd slammed the door on him. He hid his grin. "I mean, you don't need to. I have it under control. But anytime you want to learn a little about the construction business you just let me know. I'm your man." He was teasing her, but she bristled.

"I don't think that'll be necessary," she said primly. "I have plenty on my plate." No way was she helping him.

"Susan, relax. I was just teasing. I wasn't really expecting you to learn construction."

"Right. I knew that. I— Well, it's been a frantic day and I'm still a little keyed up," she said with an embarrassed laugh. "I actually do know how to use a hammer. My dad made sure of that."

"Well, that's a good thing," he mused, enjoying watching her. The fact that they were alone in a big room that suddenly seemed to shrink about them had his attention.

She looked away and it hit him that they'd been staring at each other for a lengthy moment. He plopped his boot to the concrete—*back to work*. "Let me show you what will be happening tomorrow." He grabbed the plans and rolled them out on the plywood board set across two sawhorses. "You can change anything you don't like now, but if you want the job finished quickly, I'd hold off on changing things as I'm working."

She moved to stand beside him and studied the pages. He couldn't help taking a deep breath—she'd obviously showered before she'd driven to town and she smelled of soap; it was as appealing as the clean crisp air of a new spring morning. Nothing floral or too sweet for Susan; this scent fit her. He forced his attention to the plans, wishing she'd smelled of dogs, horses and antiseptic... only problem was he didn't think even that would have taken away from the way she had his attention.

"These are the walls we talked about and the changes we discussed this morning." Whipping the pencil from behind his ear, he pointed to the prints he'd drawn. "On these four walls I added a few more plugs for you. No one can ever have enough."

"You're right about that." She leaned forward and studied the page. Tucking her loose hair behind her ear exposed her profile more clearly. Again, there was nothing about Susan Worth that resembled old Doc Crampton—the crotchety old man who had been the veterinarian in this area for as long as Cole could remember. When he'd been a kid, Cole had thought Doc Crampton was a hundred years old. But Doc had only just retired a few years ago.... Nope, Susan didn't look like the vets he was used to seeing. And he liked it—matter of fact, if he lived in Mule Hollow he'd be tempted to manufacture emergencies just so she would be at the ranch as much as possible.

"It looks just like what I explained to you," she said. Turning her head to face him, she caught him staring. "I like it."

He liked her. The knowledge hit him like a hundred-mile-an-hour wind gust. As if feeling the same blast, Susan inhaled sharply, gave him a tart nod and stepped away.

There was chemistry here.

Wide-open attraction…and he was enjoying it. He grinned at the idea. Not Susan, though. Oh, no, the good doctor's eyes narrowed, making him want to grin bigger. He didn't.

"I think you have everything under control," she said. "I'll leave you to it, then, so you can get home at a decent hour." She glanced at her watch as if to underscore her words.

"That sounds good," Cole said. Dropping his pencil on the plans, he removed his tool belt, still holding her gaze as she backed toward the door. "This is a pretty good time to call it a night."

"Oh. Okay," she snapped, turned and strode quickly out the door.

Ran was a better word for how fast she exited. He followed her, pausing to set the lock and pull the door shut behind him. "I thought I'd head to Sam's for a bite to eat. Want to join me?"

She stopped with her hand resting on her car door handle. "I don't think that would be a good idea."

"And why is that?" he asked. He'd expected her to

turn him down but hadn't expected it to be so disappointing. "You have to eat. I have to eat," he pressed—crazy as it was, he did it anyway.

Crazier still was her hesitation. "This is true…but I just think you and me together, dining in public, isn't a good combination. This—" she waved her hand toward the clinic "—this is a business association. Nothing more."

He held his expression blank when he'd felt like hiking a brow at her tone. He got her message loud and clear. A message he found a little insulting, truth be told. "Sorry I stepped over that line. You have a nice evening, boss."

He stalked to his truck. Sure it was a business relationship. It wasn't as if *he* was the one trying to do all this matchmaking. He wasn't even interested that way. Sure there was chemistry there—big-time. But so what? He was doing this job and hitting the road. She and Betty didn't need to be all up in arms thinking he believed in any of the town's nonsense.

He climbed into his truck. Susan hadn't moved. She was glaring at him from the same spot she'd been standing in as he walked away. Oh, she was hot at him for walking away—he'd given her what she wanted and now she looked insulted. He tipped his cap to her, then turned the key and revved the engine like a sixteen-year-old.

What a horrible day! Make that a horrible week. She watched Cole's truck disappear down the road and wondered—as she'd been wondering ever since she hired him—about her sanity.

Betty had been right on with her concern. Susan

wasn't sure how her receptionist had zeroed in on Susan's attraction to Cole and the flaws inherent in that but she had...even before Susan had taken a bite of a doughnut that morning.

Not that Susan needed to be told she'd be alone with an aching heart if she let herself act on her feelings.

Feelings. They were something that needed to be controlled. Her daddy had taught her to work, achieve her goals and not let feelings get in the way of those goals. Especially feelings for men. She figured out as she'd gotten older that part of that stemmed from the fact that he wanted to spare her the pain of losing someone she loved...but she'd learned after his death that that pain couldn't be avoided. Still, she'd hardly dated all the way through college. She'd worked so hard to make her daddy proud. He hadn't been there to push her, but his memory had and continued to give her the spur she needed.

She blinked against the emotion that welled up and threatened suddenly to overflow. She sniffed and brushed a tear off her cheek. She didn't cry much. What good did it do? Certainly none to cry over Cole Turner.

She swiped her fingers across her cheek, catching a lone tear as she stared at her new clinic. She should be happy. This was a great day. A turning point in her life. She'd been alone since her dad's death. But this was going to change that. She just needed to stop thinking about Cole.

And she *was* thinking about him. Ever since hiring him she'd fretted that she'd made a major mistake. Today had confirmed that on all counts. There was a chemistry between them that she couldn't deny when she'd tended the wounds Tabby had inflicted on him.

Especially every time she touched his arm. Feelings. It was only feelings. Taking the advice of her dad—as always—she knew she couldn't let her emotions lead her where Cole was concerned. She was looking for a forever cowboy. A cowboy who'd be there for her and help her in her business. Someone who would think she was worth loving and sticking around for…a man who would not only be there for her but also for their children.

Nope. Susan was moving to Mule Hollow to find a cowboy she could love…not one who loved the road.

Cole walked out onto the porch of the stagecoach house. The night air was cool and heavy with the scent of honeysuckle and he inhaled, hoping it would calm his restless spirit. Churning thoughts had finally driven him from bed and out into the night.

He'd dressed in jeans and boots and decided to take advantage of the moonlit night, see if it helped him.

He'd stopped having sleepless nights over Lori some time ago. Six years was a long time. He missed her and regretted every day of the life they'd not had the chance to have, but he'd stopped waking up over it during the second year. It had just happened, as if his subconscious had accepted that some things couldn't be changed.

God did make some dreams come true. Some people's.

In his job he got to help rebuild lost dreams.

It was a satisfying endeavor.

He'd come to enjoy it and it helped ease his discontentment. Tonight, he'd awakened with Susan on his mind and he had stirred that discontent inside of him tenfold.

He didn't really know her. All he knew about her was that she was a hard worker, stubborn and well respected. She was also beautiful, but he'd been around many, many women since Lori and none of them had cracked the wall he'd built around himself.

"You're not looking for Susan to crack it, either," he reminded himself.

He would be heading back to the coast as soon as he finished this job for her. And when he finished doing his work there he'd move on to the next town that had fallen victim to a natural disaster.

He'd only taken this job of Susan's because she needed him—why he took all of his jobs, really. He had the ability to fix someone's problems where his hands and backbone were concerned. It was something he was driven to do. It was something he wouldn't give up.

He'd always liked to travel. He'd dreamed of seeing the world through a cowboy's eyes…it had been his dream. But dreams changed. His had changed when he'd met Lori.

Her sweet face hovered in the back of his memory like the delicate flower of a woman she'd been. Pressing it aside, he concentrated on the sound of his boot steps as they clicked along the stone sidewalk. It led to the aged stone wall at the back of the stagecoach house. Needing the distraction, he let his mind wander. The stone wall had probably been built at the same time the house itself was built. The fireplace running up the side of the house was built from the same stone, so it was a good indicator. He liked that the low-slung wall with its iron gate was built in the early 1800s, too. He loved the family history of this place, the lasting power it represented, too. The hinges creaked as he opened the gate, the noise almost lost in the sound of the rushing river. The moonlight sparkled off the twenty-six stone steps that led down to the rocky river edge. It was a great place to think. He'd come here often growing up.

Mostly he'd come here to dream of seeing the world—of leaving.

Tonight he came because a tall blonde wouldn't get off his mind. Susan had drifted into his dreams and thoughts of her wouldn't be denied.

He tucked his hands in his pockets and wished his agitated musings could be tucked away as easily. Not so.

Susan had dreams. She'd worked hard for them and from what he could tell she didn't know when to say no. She didn't have a balance in her life. For her own good, she needed balance.

He could help there. God had brought him home at the right time to help her. When he finished her clinic, living there would help her be safer, hopefully more rested. Then again, if she was moving to town to find a husband, that'd mean she was going to date. And dating might take up more time than the driving she'd done between Mule Hollow and Ranger.

Unwanted, the idea of her dating sat in his gut like a sour lump of milk. He shifted his weight from one boot to the other and frowned. The doc might be planning to date, but she was keeping *their* relationship on a business level. He raked both hands through his hair as he stared up at the sky.

Bone-deep loneliness settled into him. He'd coped with the loneliness over the years by focusing his energies on his work. Things had been fine. Thoughts of Lori had driven away any desire to look for female companionship. He was young—his buddies hadn't been able to understand how he "stayed out of the game" as they'd called it. But it had been easier than they could ever know.

Ask her out again. There they were again: the words that had driven him from his bed. They rumbled through his thoughts and his lonely heart ached.

Chapter Ten

"So what do you think about this color?" Lacy asked on Saturday morning as she stepped back from the wall she'd just painted green. Holding her paintbrush in one hand she propped it on her jutting hip while she waved her other pink-tipped hand toward the wall. "It looks like green apples to me. Not that I don't *love* me some green apples, but this is a small room. As weird as it is for me to admit it, all this loudness might run you crazy."

She was right—but Susan was so shocked to hear that *Lacy* was actually thinking the bright color was too much. Lacy never backed down from color—why, her hair salon was pinker than her fingernails! The woman had talked a bunch of down-home cowboys into painting Mule Hollow every color God had ever created. But now, standing here in the tiny living room of what was about to become Susan's home, the irrepressible blonde bombshell was questioning the brightness of a relatively mild color. It was a bit confusing—kind of like Susan's life in general right now…with work, moving and Cole. Thoughts of the man had complicated her life all week— but she wasn't dwelling on that today.

"Are you sure you feel all right?" she asked, focusing on what was going on right now.

"Yeah," Molly Jacobs gasped through the open window of the porch. She was confined to outdoors painting because she was pregnant. Mule Hollow was having a run on pregnant women. Several were expecting and many were thinking about it. Before long the population was going to explode. That would make the matchmakers happy, since it would mean their original idea to bring women to town to marry the lonesome cowboys was an all-star success.

Molly was the local syndicated newspaper reporter who'd been here from almost the moment Lacy and her friend Sheri had driven into town in Lacy's 1958 pink Cadillac convertible. The matchmakers had the original dream and Lacy had come to town, bringing spunk and momentum to the plan.

But Molly had taken the plan to the next level when she'd joined in on the campaign. She'd come to town to do an article for her Houston newspaper about the wacky little town. She'd ended up staying on and creating a weekly column that people across the nation had begun to follow. The exposure still brought women to the tiny growing town.

The story fascinated Susan even after three years and all she could hope was that one of these days one of the cowboys would be hers.

Cole Turner's face appeared in her mind's eye like a thorn digging in. It had been a week since she'd told him she didn't want to have anything but a working relationship between them. He'd been overly careful at every meeting since to keep it just that.

So much so that it was beginning to irritate her.

Why exactly was that?

And why was she so scared to have dinner with him? She knew the facts—that he was leaving. So why not enjoy dinner and let it go at that? She was an adult, after all.

Because that was just the way it needed to be. The safe way.

Pulling her head out of the clouds, Susan focused on the candy-apple-green swiped across her living-room wall.

"Seriously," she said. "Why is this tone wrong for me? I might like bright colors, too. Or are you saying I'm too boring?"

Lacy rolled her baby blues at the teasing comment. "You know I like to be unpredictable," Lacy said. "But, Susan, face it, you're more reserved than me—this green paint *might* just make you crazy."

From the porch, Molly's hoot of laughter broke Lacy off and covered up Susan's own chuckle. "We all know a *lot, lot, lot* more reserved would be the accurate wording."

Molly stuck her head back in the window. "But then everyone is a lot more reserved than Lacy! Hey, heads up, the cavalry is arriving."

Molly had barely gotten the words out before the sound of numerous vehicles could be heard heading up the drive. Susan shot Lacy a startled look. "What's going on?"

Lacy grinned. "Surely you didn't think we were going to do all the work, just the three and a half of us? I got here early to butter you up. Molly's been slacking off on the painting to take notes for her column, as always!"

Molly wagged her tiny pocket notebook through the window.

"I should have known," Susan groaned as Lacy took her by the arm and led her toward the door. Unexpected tears welled in her eyes at the sight of the smiling folks hopping from their trucks and cars.

Mule Hollow might have started out with only the matchmakers, who were striding her way, but it now had a wonderful group of gals calling it home. And they were here to help and welcome her. Susan suddenly felt overwhelmingly blessed. God was good. Losing her father had been so hard but this felt so right...like she was at last making a home.

Haley Bell Sutton, the local real estate agent who'd sold Susan this place, came up the steps, her curly blond hair bouncing. She handed Susan a frilly bag. "Happy housewarming." She engulfed Susan in a hug. "I'm here to paint, but you know what a klutz I am, so you might want to keep me outside with the babies or something."

"You are not a klutz. Thank you so much for coming."

Before she could say more, Rose Cantrell came sweeping up the steps. "We're so happy you've finally decided to join us as an actual resident." She hugged her and held up another bright package. "I'll start a stack over here by Molly so you won't have to try to juggle them all."

A truck bounced to a stop and Tacy Jones hopped out. "Whoo-hoo—thought I was gonna be late!" She jogged up the steps with a red package tied with a red bandana. She was a cowgirl through and through, even down to her gift wrap. "Are we glad to have you here! Birdy and her new pack of pups send you their love."

Susan chuckled as Tacy hugged her. Birdy was Tacy's excellent blue heeler and she'd recently had some beautiful, healthy puppies that buyers were anxiously waiting to take home with them. "Speaking of Birdy and her crew, I'll be out first of next week to give them their last checkup before they go to their new homes."

"Roger that," Tacy said as Esther Mae stepped up. She, Norma Sue and Adela had been unloading refreshments from their truck with the help of Lacy and Molly.

"I'm getting me a new dog, Susan," she punctuated her announcement with a bear hug. "Thought I'd better get you ready. Me and my Hank are heading over to pick her up tomorrow."

"Great. I'll be glad to see her—"

"Tell her what kind," Norma Sue broke in, shaking her wiry halo of gray curls. "It's the dumbest thing I ever heard of."

"Now, Norma," Adela called from where she was slicing a cake. "Don't start." Her bright blue eyes sparkled with teasing.

Esther Mae's grin widened. "A Dorky!"

"A what?" The question rippled about the group that was growing by the carload.

"A Dorky," Norma Sue said, loud and clear. "One good thing about it, the name fits Esther," Norma Sue chuckled the last words.

"A Dorky," Susan said. "I've seen the little dogs and they're cute as can be—dorky-looking but cute."

"What are they?" Haley asked.

Esther Mae patted the edge of her hairdo with pride.

"A cross between a dachshund and a Yorkshire terrier. You know, a Yorkie. They call the little darlings Dorkies. You should see my baby." She cooed the last sentence. "I'll get her tomorrow. She's just a teacup of fur right now. Some of them are straight-haired but my Toot is curls, curls and more curls."

"What made you decide to get a puppy?" Susan asked.

"Well, with all these new babies being born I just thought a cute little puppy to play with would be fun for them. You know me, it's all about the brownie points and I want these babies to love their grandma Esther best."

"Ha! We'll see about that," Norma Sue huffed.

Adela came over and slipped an arm around Susan's waist. "Let's get this housework started and get Susan ready to move in. Norma Sue and Esther Mae can fight over their grandma status any time," she said.

As always, when Miss Adela spoke, everyone listened. She was the tiny, soft-spoken one but she was the leader when all was said and done. She always, always led by example and Susan wished she could be half the woman Adela was. She was a strong woman of faith. As were most of the women she knew who lived in Mule Hollow. They all just lived their faith in different ways. Lacy was an all-out in-your-face believer compared to Adela's quiet, steady faith—both were joyful. The idea hit Susan out of the blue. Her faith was more plodding. Did she have joy in her faith?

Why was she asking herself this? Her life was great. What she didn't like about it, she was changing. In the midst of the time she was supposed to be happiest, she was suddenly questioning things about herself that she'd never ever thought about before.

But now the group of women had reached critical mass and Susan was swept into a welcoming party she hadn't anticipated.

The gifts and food were wonderful. However, the sweetest thing of all was that everyone came dressed to work.

"Thank y'all for coming," she said. "My daddy always said that a true friend was the one who showed up to do the work." That got a big laugh, but looking around the porch full of smiling women, she felt extremely happy.

Despite her questions, her future seemed awfully bright. As she stood there, the sound of a saw slicing through wood drifted from the clinic building... Cole.

She was suddenly overcome with the insane notion to walk over there and ask him if he wanted to go out to dinner sometime.

Maybe Lacy was right. Maybe the apple-green paint was making her crazy after all.

Cole stretched the measuring tape out on the two-by-four then glanced up at the sound of another car headed toward Susan's house.

Something was going on—it looked like a meeting of the entire town of women. He was marking his measurement when a truck pulled up outside and stopped.

A few minutes later Seth stepped through the doorway.

"It's about time you showed up," he said, finishing his mark.

"Don't you be giving free labor a hard time," Seth

grunted. "I had to tend to my own business before I came down here to offer my services."

"Yeah, yeah, stop with the sob story," Cole said, heading over to start framing another wall in. He and his brothers loved to give each other a hard time. He and Wyatt especially enjoyed needling Seth, since he'd always tended to be the serious one. Of course, Cole had been a whole lot more serious since falling in love with Lori and watching her die. Watching someone fight that hard to survive changed the way a person viewed life.

Then again, it also made a person grateful for family, and his brothers had stood by him even in the darkest moments. Even when they hadn't known how dark his days had gotten. He'd sent his horse home and bought his Harley the same day they'd laid Lori to rest in the tiny cemetery outside her hometown in Colorado. He'd hit the road unsure of where he was going or what he was doing. All he'd known was he had to go. His brothers had been worried, but they'd stood back and let him do his thing while making sure he knew they were there for him when he needed them. It had been his cousin Chance who had set him on the course of working the disaster areas. Chance was a rodeo preacher and he'd been helping rebuild some of the thousands of miles of fences that had been wiped out by Hurricane Rita. He'd encouraged Cole during a brief phone call to come help with the devastation. He'd started with Rita, and when Ike had hit the coast two years ago, he'd continued to do what he'd been doing. It was odd how disaster had been a blessing to him when he'd needed something to pour his grief into. God had put Chance where he needed to be.

He could see it now.

"Any idea what's going on up at the house?" he asked.

Seth grabbed a board and handed it to him. "They're having a housewarming and paint party. Melody's over there."

"I must have missed her as she drove by."

"So how are things going between you and Susan?"

"Nowhere for things to be going."

They worked in silence for a few minutes, then Seth stopped fitting a board into place. "Cole, what's going on inside your head these days? Aren't you getting the least little bit ready to settle down?"

Cole shot a nail into the board then leaned back on his haunches to stare up at his brother. "Honestly, I think about it every now and again. Lately it's been there."

Seth's lip twitched upward on one side. "I was hoping you might. Seriously, Cole. I'm starting to need some more help on this end, not to put pressure on you or Wyatt. I've been happy to run this ranch, but since we bought the other ranch, it's taking up more time than I'm wanting to give. I'm married now."

Cole stood. "Why haven't you said anything about this before?"

"I've talked with Wyatt about it."

"But not me."

Seth lifted a shoulder. "I'm talking to you now."

Cole knew Seth like a book. His brother wouldn't say anything unless he meant it. "So what exactly are you saying?"

"I'm saying it's time for you to come home. It's time for you to put your past behind you."

Cole was caught off guard. "What if I don't want to?"

Seth locked eyes with him. "It's time."

There was more in those two words than business. This was about more than ranching and Cole knew it. "You'd force me to come home?"

Seth laughed a harsh laugh. "You know me better than that. All I have to do is hire a manager from yours and Wyatt's profits and that'd solve the problem right there…which was Wyatt's second suggestion."

"But I was his first suggestion?"

"Bingo. I didn't think you were ready, but I went along with him getting you back here. Now I believe it is time. Wyatt is right."

"Wait…you went along with it?" That got Cole's attention. "Do you know how he got me back here?"

"Some crazy story about me and Melody thinking you were upset about us getting married and being happy."

"I should have known," Cole said, feeling like a fool. His big brother was always pulling stunts like this. "I didn't believe a word of it when he first started in on his tall tale. But you know how good he is at spinning tales." Wyatt was true-blue Turner. He'd inherited their great-great-great-great-grandpa Oakley's knack for spinning a tall tale. Oakley had been known to make people believe anything he said. Wyatt had the knack.

"I honestly couldn't believe you fell for it. Wyatt must have pulled out all the stops to make you believe that I would ever think you weren't happy for me."

Cole frowned. "Not as much as you think, Seth. I didn't want you to be unhappy but I'll confess it messed with my head. I left early because it just opened up old wounds. I was in a bad spot for a little while."

"Wyatt is as good at picking up on unspoken things

as he is spinning tales," Seth mused. "I'm sorry you went through that and I hate that we deceived you, but honestly I agree now—it's time you came home. I need you. Forgive me. How's it going? Being here I mean?"

He knew how restless Cole got. "Strangely."

"In a good way?"

Cole set his nail gun down and scratched his jaw as he thought about how to put into words what was happening in his head. "I'm not sure. And I'm also not sure about pitching in here full-time. I hate to tell you, but as it stands you better start looking for a ranch foreman."

Chapter Eleven

The sun had gone down by the time the women of Mule Hollow packed up and called it a day. Susan still couldn't believe that every room in the small house had been painted. Her kitchen had also been scrubbed and the cabinets lined so that she was ready to unpack her things the minute she brought boxes over...of course she had yet to pack those boxes and everyone had volunteered to help with that, too.

Feeling restless, she glanced toward the clinic and saw Cole's truck was still parked outside. Taking a deep breath, she walked over. It had been an odd Saturday. For starters, she'd not scheduled any appointments so she could work on her house. Then, she'd arranged for the new vet buying her clinic in Ranger to start taking emergency calls over the next three weeks and she'd just be available for consultation during the change-over time. She'd been pleased when the vet had agreed and startled that she'd come up with the idea.

But it was the right move. Her clients there were going to have to get used to her being gone and she was going to have to let them go. She was at peace with it, though. Today she'd never thought twice about it—except to acknowledge a hopeful sense of things to come.

Cole had the large rolling bay door open leading into what had been the oil supply storage area. The door would now act as easy access for large animals and access to the holding pens that would be brought in and set up over the next couple of weeks. "Hello," she called as she entered.

"Hello, down there." Cole's head popped up over the edge of a rafter.

She laughed nervously, looking up at him.

What was she doing? "What are you doing up there?"

"Running electrical wire to the new plugs. Want to come up?"

"Sure." Susan walked to the ladder propped against an exposed steel beam. When she reached the plywood Cole met her.

"It's secured, so it's safe," he said, taking her elbow.

She stepped onto the board. "Thanks."

"Don't want anything happening to the boss." He let go of her arm instantly and went back to the coil of electrical wire he'd begun rolling across the ceiling.

"So it's looking good," she said, trying to ignore the boss comment—after all, she'd been the one to get it started.

"Thanks. It's coming along. I'll have the new paneling up on all the walls next week, and then I'll build the counters and that front area will be good to go. It'll take me the last week to get this area finished out—"

"Do you want to go to dinner?" She forced the words out before she could back out of it.

He cocked his head to the side to look up at her from

his kneeling position. "Well, Doc, I'm not too sure my boss would let me off for something like that."

"Would you *stop* with the boss stuff and answer my question." She was crazy. Slap crazy!

"Since you put it that way, I guess I'd better say yes or my boss might fire me. When?"

"How about tomorrow after church?"

He stood up. "You sure about this?"

"I asked you, didn't I?"

He laughed. "Well, yeah, you did. I'll be there."

"Good." Susan's knees were knocking and her stomach was lurching side to side so drastically she felt seasick. She'd just asked Cole on a date… "I better go," she blurted, not because she wanted to but because it was the only thing that her frazzled brain thought to say.

"How'd you manage to get off for your little shindig today?"

The question had her hesitating. He went back to work rolling out the wire. She relaxed a touch—maybe he'd just interpreted her invitation as just dinner.

"I made a deal with the new owner. He's taking over weekend emergencies in that area up until the sale date. So I took today off."

He paused and stared at her, clearly astounded. "That's good, Doc. Real good. How'd it feel having some freedom?"

His praise washed over her like warm water and in that instant her knees stopped knocking and her stomach calmed down. She smiled—she couldn't have hidden it if she tried. "It felt great. Of course, I'm on call here in Mule Hollow."

"And amazed you didn't get any calls?"

She leaned against a steel support pole that ran from

the slab below to the roof. "I am, actually. I had a couple of calls since I last saw you but other than that it's been quiet."

He'd reached a connection box. "Not my fault if that's what you're thinking."

She laughed. It had been days since she thought about how mad he'd been at Seth for getting her out to save that baby calf. "Oh, I'm glad to know you're not wasting your hard-earned cash to pay my clients not to call me."

"Don't think it didn't cross my mind the other night. You were so tired you needed someone to step in and change something."

Someone else might have thought that was a sweet thought. She didn't. "Cole, I didn't need anyone to step in and change my life. I'm quite capable of doing that myself. When *I* deemed it necessary." Here they went… right back to square one.

Her pager went off just as Cole was about to say something she was certain she wasn't going to like. This right here was the reason asking him to dinner was a ridiculous thing to do. They'd argue most of the night away.

The smug man just thought he was right about everything. It would be nice to be so perfect!

"I have to take this."

"Duty calls."

Even that irritated her. "Catch you later," she snapped and headed toward the ladder.

"Holler if you need any help," he called as she started down.

"Yeah, um, thanks." Yeah, right—like that was going to happen. Not, was more like it. Nope, she shouldn't have asked him out. He just simply took too much for granted. Her accepting help from him obviously gave him the impression that he had a right to voice his disagreement with her life. It was weird. And not something she was going to tolerate.

Cole hung his head, exasperated at himself. Why couldn't he keep his big mouth shut? He crossed to the ladder—fully intent on catching up with Susan. They'd been having a decent conversation and it had taken his mind off the things he'd been dwelling on ever since Seth dropped his bombshell that morning.

She'd thrown up the do-not-trespass sign the instant he'd said something about her lack of responsibility where her safety and well-being were concerned. Knowing her as he was beginning to think he did, she'd taken what he said as a complete slap in the face about her entire life.

The woman was hard to talk to. Skimming down the ladder, he followed her voice toward the waiting area. They'd had a phone line installed in the office on Tuesday for just such a thing as this. She was just hanging up when he walked through the door.

"Something wrong?"

"Yes. Lilly and Cort Wells—a local horse trainer—are out of town and one of their mares looks like she may be going into labor early. The young guy who is feeding for them called it in. I'm going out to make sure everything is okay."

She'd been walking toward the door while talking and Cole followed her. "You want some help?"

No way, the look she shot him over her shoulder said. "No. I'm fine."

"I might be able to help." He followed her into the night air.

She didn't give him another glance, but kept right on walking across the drive, heading toward her truck at a quick clip. He felt at loose ends as he watched her go. None of his business, though—what had he expected after what he'd said?

He'd just pulled down the large rolling door and locked up the building when she drove past. She didn't give him even a glance.

He stalked to his truck, watching her pull out of the parking lot. He should let it go. She didn't want or need his help.

As he drove onto the road, he could see her taillights in the distance. When she turned onto the main road into Mule Hollow, she went left. Cole turned right and headed the opposite direction.

He would do as she said. Mind his business and grab a chicken-fried steak at Sam's diner. Susan would be fine. She was just checking on a horse. She could do that in her sleep and there was no need to worry that she would get into any trouble out there by herself. She knew what she was doing.

Still, accidents happened.

Chapter Twelve

"Hey, Samantha, what's up?" Susan called to the mischievous donkey. Samantha ruled the roost out here at Cort and Lilly's place. They let the little donkey roam at will and had just tried to Samantha-proof the place as much as possible. "You're behaving, I hope."

Samantha batted her big brown eyes and grinned, curling her lips back, exposing a wide row of teeth. Her sidekick, Lucky, a hairy little beast with scraggly hair and whiskers, came barreling around the corner at the sound of her arrival.

Toenails scrambling for traction, he went crazy barking an enthusiastic greeting.

"How are my two favorite patients?" she asked, scratching first Samantha between the eyes, then Lucky before she headed inside to look for the mare.

Behind her she could hear Samantha's hooves prancing on the concrete as the donkey followed her. Lucky raced ahead of them barking, as if announcing her arrival to the entire barn of horses. Susan half expected all the horses to be running around free since Samantha had a habit of opening their stalls and letting them loose so she could eat their feed. Lilly had told her that she'd gotten better about that little problem since Cort had installed harder-to-open latches.

"How's our mommy-to-be?" Susan spoke soothingly as she unlatched the last stall's gate where Sweet Pea was pacing restlessly. The horse nickered and threw her head from side to side looking very unhappy. Moving inside, Susan approached her cautiously. Despite her name, Sweet Pea was pretty high-strung and Susan knew to take care.

Jake had made a good call. She was definitely in distress. She gently rubbed the mare's soft nose then ran a hand along her belly. "Not feeling so great, are you, girl? Hang in there, it's going to be okay."

Sweet Pea nudged her hard with her nose and grunted, as if to say "easy for you to say." "Believe me, I've brought plenty of colts into the world. I promise you'll be fine," she said as she examined her. When she finished she was glad to see that everything looked fine and the birth should go smoothly. Still, Susan knew to expect the unexpected.

She'd removed her rubber gloves and was tossing them through the stall gate into the trash bin Samantha was sitting beside. The donkey was on her haunches watching what was going on. Just as if she were sitting at the movies. Susan rubbed her nose before turning back when Lucky started barking—and just like that the unexpected happened....

Sweet Pea jumped, swung her hips around and slammed into Susan. Knocked off balance, Susan went down—just as Sweet Pea began to buck like a rodeo bronc.

* * *

Cole couldn't help it. He didn't like the idea of Susan being out there by herself. *Forget about it.*

Right. She didn't want him out there. Against his better judgment, he parked in front of Sam's and got out. On Saturday nights, the little town had metamorphosed into a happening place. The new theater that had opened up on the outskirts of town was partly to blame for the phenomenon. People drove into town to attend the live show and stayed around to dine at Sam's. Even during the day, the town had come alive with tourists…tourists—the very notion that his hometown now had tourists was just so weird to him. He was having to adjust to the idea. Thankfully nothing had really changed the atmosphere of Mule Hollow.

Sure, the town's clapboard buildings were now painted every color of the rainbow, but the base of the town, the good people—the roots of the place—were still the same. It was as if the town had simply spruced up a bit and become what it had dreamed of becoming. And it was drawing people to it.

When he entered the old diner, the hum of people talking and laughing almost drowned out Faith Hill singing "Mississippi Girl" on the jukebox in the corner.

There was a cute college-age gal taking an order from a large group in the far corner and through the swinging café doors leading into the kitchen he could see someone working the grill. Sam grinned at him from behind the counter.

"How goes, Cole? Coffee?"

Cole nodded. "Got you some help, I see," he said, sliding onto a stool. As long as he could remember Sam had worked the diner alone. It was a sure sign the town had grown.

"Yup. Since I'm married to Adela, I enjoy a little time off."

Cole should have guessed it. The conversation he'd had with Seth that morning shifted from the back burner of his mind to the front burner at full boil. Seth wanted more time off, too.

He wanted Cole home. Wanted him to pitch in and take responsibility beside him for the legacy they were trying hard to preserve with the ranch. Cole understood where he was coming from but it had come from left field.

"How's it goin' out thar at Susan's?" Sam said, grinning.

"It's coming along. I'm on schedule."

"That ain't what I meant and you know it. How y'all gettin' along?"

"How do you think?"

Sam chuckled. "That good, huh?"

There was a cowboy in his early twenties sitting at the counter and he tuned in to the conversation. "I just called Susan about thirty minutes ago about one of the mares out at the Wells place."

"Cole. Jake. Jake. Cole," Sam said, introducing them. "Jake here has been looking after the place."

"Nice ta meet you," Cole said, shaking hands. "She was in the office when you called."

"So did she head out there?"

"Almost before hanging up." He still wasn't happy about her being out there alone.

"That gal works too much by herself," Sam said, frowning at Cole. "Why'd you let her go out thar alone?"

"Now Sam, hold on. I offered and she shut me down."

Jake looked worried. "That mare's pretty skittish and in trouble. I'm thinkin' that foal is gonna need some help being born."

"I'll go," Cole said. "Sam, how about two of those barbecue plates to go?"

Sam's wrinkled face crinkled upward. "Sounds like a plan ta me. I'll even toss in a couple of peach cobblers."

What am I doing? "Wait. Scratch that," Cole said, thinking about how adamant Susan was. The woman was right—she was an adult who'd been on countless late-night calls. He was here only to get her building up and running. Not overtake her life.

"Scratch it?" Sam asked in disbelief.

"That's what I said. Susan'll be fine. She'll be hotter than a poker stick if I go out there. Y'all told me that from the very beginning."

"Yeah, but—" Sam scratched his head. "You sure?"

No, he wasn't sure. But what was he supposed to do? Ignore her wishes and force himself into her life whether she wanted him to or not?

Susan rolled, trying to escape Sweet Pea's hooves. She winced when one grazed her hip. Pain shot through her and she covered her head with her hands as she rolled toward the stall gate. Totally agitated out of her mind, Sweet Pea came down again. This time the blow grazed Susan's shoulder—thankfully it wasn't a full impact. Still, pain ricocheted through Susan. She cried out.

Trapped and feeling fear for the first time, Susan braced herself for the worst. Suddenly Samantha let out a loud hee-haw, the stall gate flew open and Lucky and Samantha came charging to her rescue.

* * *

Something was wrong.

The incessant barking of a dog had Cole barreling from his truck the minute he pulled up beside Susan's truck. Tearing into the barn, he came face-to-face with the most unexpected thing he could have imagined: Samantha the donkey dragging Susan from a horse stall.

Samantha, more roll-poly than he remembered her from years ago, had a tight grip on Susan's collar and was backing out of the stall. The dog had planted its feet between Susan and the pregnant mare and was holding the frantic horse back with its yapping.

It was a circus. Racing forward, he pushed the donkey away, grabbed Susan under the arms and hauled her clear of the stall.

She was awake. Her startled eyes looked up into his as he halted in the center of the barn. She winced as he dropped to his knees and leaned her against him. "What happened? Are you hurt?"

"I got knocked over and caught under Sweet Pea's hooves. Samantha and Lucky charged to my rescue."

He touched her shoulder and the ripped shirtsleeve. "You're hurt. Where? Is this the only place?"

"It's nothing."

"Where?" he demanded.

"Just a bruised hip, shoulder and ego. That's the worst."

His temper flared. "This was just the kind of thing I was worried about happening to you." His hands tightened about her arms and he had the overwhelming urge to slide one around her and hug her tightly. "You know how fortunate you just were, don't you?" He heard the clipped edge in his voice as the strain of losing it warred within him. She could have been killed.

"Are you okay?" Cole said. His hands shook as he looked down at her. Emotions he'd locked away threatened to cave him in but he held on as Susan nodded. Their faces were close and his lips moved to her temple in a kiss before he caught himself. She stiffened in his arms and sanity flooded his mind... He swallowed and yanked back. "Good." She hadn't moved, but blinked, studying him. What was he thinking? He shot to his feet.

"Let's see if you can stand. Careful," he said, trying hard to get his focus back on being angry with her and not on the fact that he'd just kissed her temple. Barely stopping himself from giving her a real kiss.

He could have lost her.

The idea slammed into him so hard his knees went weak. She sucked in a painful breath as she leaned on his arm and rose to her feet. Immediately, she took a couple of steps away from him. He didn't move. *She's not yours to lose,* he reminded himself.

Not that way, anyway. She was not Lori.

"I'm fine," Susan said. "Nothing broken. I'll probably limp for a few days, and this arm is going to let me know it's there every time I move it, but I'm good."

Cole blinked hard. "What if you'd gotten *trampled?* What if you'd lain out here all night with no one around?" What if he hadn't listened to Sam and he'd gone on home.... His stomach twisted and he felt like throwing up. She was staring at him, stunned.

"You have no business making large-animal calls by yourself," he said, yanking the stall gate closed. Needing something, anything, to do other than to look at her.

"Don't start with me, Cole."

"Why, because you don't want to hear the truth?" He told himself to back off. Told himself this was none of his business, but this was twice he'd been there—it wasn't a coincidence. He had to get through to her. He had to make her take better care of herself. "Why are you so stubborn?"

"Because I am. Because I need to be. It's my business and my practice. I know how to handle large animals. I'm not incompetent."

They were standing toe-to-toe, both breathing hard from emotion—anger on her part. Fear and…desperation on his part. He needed to make her understand that she was precious and had a great life ahead of her. He yanked his thoughts to a stop.

What was he doing? He raked his hands through his hair, his fingers trembled against his scalp and he quickly tucked them into his pockets to hide the emotion they exposed.

He had so much he wanted to say, but it wasn't his place so he tried hard to hold back. "Is the mare okay?" he asked instead, masking the anger and worry raging inside of him.

"Yes, she's just anxious." Her fingers went to her temple and she rubbed.

Cole wondered if she realized she was touching the place he'd kissed. He realized it. His fingers curled and he dug them deeper into his pockets.

"She didn't mean to harm me. Lucky just started barking while she was hurting and it simply got too crazy for a minute."

It *was* crazy out here. "So what's the plan?"

"The plan?"

"Yeah, are you going home or what?" He wasn't surprised when her brows dipped ominously.

"I'll be staying here, watching her. I may need to help her along from the look of things." She walked to the stall, studying the mare.

Her limp wasn't bad, but it could have been. And that was what mattered. He had a choice here. He could explode and get nowhere with her. Or…he strode toward the end of the stable.

"That's what I thought," he said. "Good thing I brought dinner."

"Dinner?"

"Yeah," he tossed over his shoulder. "Someone has to make you take care of yourself."

Her growl of frustration followed him to the end of the barn.

"I don't need you taking care of me, Cole Turner. Just because for some unknown reason I've had accidents when you were around does not mean I need you."

He halted at the doorway. "That may be so, but it's clear you need someone," he shot back.

Stubborn woman made him nuts—yeah, nuts, that was exactly what he was.

She got to him more than any woman ever had…and it wasn't a good thing.

Chapter Thirteen

Calm down. Calm down. Calm down.

Samantha nudged her arm as Susan tried to get a rein on her temper. Big, cold lips nibbled at her arm, as if to console her.

"Don't worry, girl. I'm fine. It's him who might not live through the next few minutes," she said. Understanding seemed to flow from the donkey's big brown eyes. Samantha was known for her almost human qualities. She had a wonderful sense for when someone was in need. Susan wasn't the first person for whom she'd saved the day. "Thank you for helping me, you little darling."

Lucky had followed Cole outside and now Samantha spun and pranced like a show pony on tiptoes. Her hooves tapped down the long concrete alley between the stalls like a plump ballerina.

Susan followed, glad she hadn't gotten kicked in the head and wasn't seeing two dancing donkeys.

Cole was right. She'd been stupid.

But the very idea of his being right fired her irritation all the more. She'd been totally irresponsible coming out here alone. With practically no cell-phone reception to speak of in this part of the country, she might very well have been kicked in the head or gotten a broken leg or something and been stuck out here all night. Hurt and alone.

Or dead.

She grimaced and took a step toward the outside where Cole had disappeared around the edge after telling her she needed someone. Needed someone—as if she didn't know that already! Didn't he understand she was looking? Of course he was talking about an assistant… She was going to look for one of those, too.

Movement didn't hurt as much as she feared when she marched forward. Her pride had sustained the worst damage.

It hadn't escaped her notice that God had been watching over her. It was a blessing that Sweet Pea hadn't stepped on her worse than she had.

Glancing down at her shirt, she was glad to see that it hadn't been ripped too terribly by Sweet Pea's clawing hooves. There was hay everywhere, though, and she dusted it off as she walked, her shoulder tightening up with each movement.

"What are you doing here, anyway?" she asked, disregarding the way her heart skipped at the sight of him beside his truck. She had a lot to ignore as instantly the feel of his arms around her came pushing into her thoughts. The feel of his lips against her skin—her breath caught at the memory. She'd been too stunned earlier to think about it, but now there it was. He'd had his arms around her and…and *nothing*.

She shoved the thought away. "Why are you here?" she demanded more adamantly.

He lifted a couple of boxes from the seat of his truck and grinned.

His grin caught her off guard and might very well have caused her insides to melt like warmed butter *if* she'd let it. But oh, no—she fought that sensation off with a vengeance!

"What's that?" she asked, recognizing Sam's to-go boxes even as she asked the question. Food. Food was good.

"Jake was at Sam's when I got there and he said, from the looks of the mare, he felt like you had an all-night affair—little did I know I was going to find you being hauled out of harm's way by Samantha."

His expression darkened and she knew he was fighting off saying more. Instead he held up the boxes. "Anyway, here's your supper."

She wanted to tell him so badly to take his supper and hit the road, but her stomach roared like a hungry lion.

He cocked a brow. "Don't even try telling me you aren't hungry. Not with your stomach cutting up like that." He walked past her to the mesquite bench swing next to the entrance of the barn. "Sam said you drink your tea unsweetened. Hope that's right," he said as he passed her again.

"Um…sure," she managed through clenched teeth as a new issue hit her. "So everyone knows you brought me dinner?"

"Oh, yeah. Sam insisted." He brought two paper glasses from the truck and sat down in the swing. Placing the glasses on the ground in front of him, he patted the seat beside him. "Come on. I don't bite."

So he said! Susan eased into the swing and took the

box of food he offered her. Might as well eat and hopefully then he would leave. The aroma of barbecue brisket caused her stomach to let out another roar, this time so loud Lucky's ears lifted as he plopped at her feet and waited for handouts. "This smells wonderful," she admitted grudgingly.

"Yep. No matter where I go I always miss Sam's cooking." Cole opened his box, closed his eyes and inhaled. "That is Texas gold right there. *That's* what I'm talking about."

Susan almost choked watching him. His dark lashes rested against tanned skin and his lips were turned up at the corners… Gracious, she couldn't stop staring! "Yes, I know what you mean." She sighed. His eyes popped open and she dropped her gaze to her box—snapping the lid open so fast she almost threw the food off her lap. Lucky barked and wiggled, thinking he'd very nearly hit the mother lode.

Needing something to do other than think of how handsome the ornery, oh-so-bossy cowboy beside her was, Susan grabbed a roll and chomped on it. She could only hope Cole didn't notice that unlike Lucky, she wasn't thinking about barbecue.

Maybe she had been kicked in the head after all!

"Why are you so stubborn?"

His irritating question shouldn't have surprised her. It did. "If a man conducted his business as I do, there would be nothing said about him being stubborn. He would just be taking care of business. You, Mr. Turner, are just—"

"Yeah, I am." He held her gaze unapologetically. "Sexist. Is that what you were about to say? Because if you were and it is—I know you—then so be it. If me thinking you don't take good enough care of yourself puts me in that category then I'm in and proud of it."

Unexpectedly his words sent a longing so strong through her that it took her breath. She chomped into her roll and chewed as if dogs were chasing her. *Do not let your guard down. Don't do it!*

He was bossy and irritating, but he was trying to look out for her. Trying to protect her…and it felt oddly nice.

Not since her dad had she had anyone want to protect her.

A lump formed in her throat. *Whoa, stop right there. You are moving to Mule Hollow hoping to find someone who can put up with your way of life. Someone who can love you despite it…not someone who thinks your life is all wrong.*

They ate in silence for a few minutes. She wasn't sure where to go or what to say, so she just ate. Her head was full of thoughts. She placed a piece of meat in her palm and held it down for Lucky, then rubbed his head after he snapped it up. "You love your job, don't you?" she asked, because it was the easy question. The safest question. It wasn't the one asking why he didn't stick around in town or settle down. That was what she really wanted to know…why hadn't Cole Turner settled down? *Maybe because he's so ornery!* Well, that was the truth, but she knew God made partners for even the orneriest of them.

He reached for his drink; in the glow of the big light on top of the barn she watched him shake the ice around. "I'm not sure if I'd call it love."

That struck her as odd. "But you live on the road. You go from place to place—I just assumed you loved it."

"I help people. I like that. Don't get me wrong. But…"

But what? She toyed with her food then closed the lid and placed the box on the seat between them. "But?" she finally asked, intrigued when he remained silent. She watched his Adam's apple bob.

"You love your job?"

She nodded. "It's pretty evident."

"Yeah. Anyone who dedicates almost every waking hour to something and totally ignores her safety has to love something."

"So we're back to that." Disappointment shrouded her as new anger flared. "I need to check on Sweet Pea," she said, pushing out of the swing, glad her hip didn't protest too much. "Thanks for the dinner."

"That hip hurting a lot?" he asked, following her out of the swing.

"No. I've been kicked and stomped on before. It's—"

"Part of the job," he said, disgust dripping from the words as he finished her sentence for her.

"Yes. It is," she snapped, stalking into the stable, trying not to limp too noticeably. What did the man expect from her? A person couldn't be a vet and not expect to get dirty or kicked a few times…or tired. She shot him a glare when he fell into step beside her.

"Look—" he started.

"No, *you* look." She turned on him. "I don't need you strutting around here judging me. This is what I do. This is who I am. If you can't accept that, then I really don't need you hanging around. I didn't ask you to come here. And as for lunch tomorrow—forget about it. The offer is retracted. And if you're thinking about hanging around tonight, don't. This isn't my first foal and it won't be my last." Her knees were shaking as she stormed away. Her daddy had told her she'd have to sacrifice things to get what she wanted out of life and she was willing to do it. If she didn't get rid of him now, she might regret it. For the first time in her life, she was scared she might be tempted to give up more than she wanted. All this fear he had for her was stifling. *Wasn't it?*

Cole was not good for her. Not good at all.

"Go home," she insisted. "And I mean it. Get out of here."

Cole raked his hands through his hair and watched Susan disappear inside Sweet Pea's stall. He'd really overstepped his boundaries this time. What was it about Susan that had him tied up in knots with concern? Sure she'd had a couple of accidents when he'd been around, but things happen. She couldn't live in a glass cage—

What was he thinking? He walked to the stall, boots dragging as he tried to figure out what he should do.

What he needed to say. When he reached the stall he saw that Sweet Pea was down and the birth had started. Only a few minutes earlier the mare was struggling, and now in the blink of an eye the foal was coming. Susan was down beside her helping and he started inside to help her, but she shot him a glare, jerked her head in the direction of the barn exit and had him stopping in his tracks. Clearly she was serious about wanting him to leave.

So be it. He spun and strode to his truck. Susan didn't want him hanging around and she had things under control. He, on the other hand, didn't have anything under control. Nothing at all.

"Wyatt, are you coming to town or not?" Cole paced the floor of the stagecoach house. When he'd first arrived home, he'd stared at his Harley for twenty minutes before talking himself out of hitting the road back to Galveston. Instead he'd decided it was time to call his big brother—after all, it was Wyatt's fault he was in this mess.

"Sorry, brother, but I'm not making the trip. This case—"

"Don't even go there," Cole growled. "Seth already told me about the plan to get me here and then keep me here."

"I'm not denying that," Wyatt said. "I thought it would be good for you. It's time for you to come home, Cole. You used to love that place out there. Until Lori. I really was coming home to talk to you face-to-face about this, but I'm tied up with an unexpected turn in this case. I'm about to board a plane to New York right now. But listen to me, Cole. It's time to let Lori go. It's time to stay home where you're needed."

"I'm needed—"

"At home. That's where you're needed now, and where you should stay long enough to come to terms with whatever's hounding you."

"I'm not hounded." Cole leaned against the counter and stared at the hundred-year-old cabinets in front of him. His roots ran deep here in this cabin and on this land. But his heart— "I need to leave, Wyatt."

Wyatt didn't say anything for a long moment and the clock on the mantel ticked off the seconds. Every second weighed on Cole. He needed the road. He needed… what? This wasn't the same as the other times—this was different.

"How's the remodel coming along?" Wyatt said at last, breaking into Cole's troubled thoughts.

"I'm getting there."

"If you're thinking about leaving, remember you signed up for that job. Running away isn't going to help that pretty vet get into her place. It'd be real sorry of you to leave her high and dry."

"What are you, my mother?" Cole ground out.

Wyatt chuckled. "No, bro, I'm your big brother and don't you forget it. You are my responsibility and I keep tabs. So how's the good doctor?"

"She's an ill-tempered, stubborn woman who is probably ruing the day she hired me. I know I'm not too happy about signing on. Whoever that contractor was that skipped out on her, he must have gotten a tip-off that working for her wasn't going to be a walk in the park."

That got a big hoot on the other end of the line. "So y'all are getting along that well."

"Well? We barely tolerate each other, but—" Cole broke off, shifted his weight from boot to boot, and frustration clawed at him. "Wyatt, I can't stay," he blurted out at last.

"Why? Because you're attracted to someone?"

"Ha—like a moth to a flame!" He was doomed if he stuck around. It was a no-win situation.

"That's better than living half a life."

"You have no idea." Cole's temper was rising. As kids growing up, Wyatt had always been the leader. He took his position as eldest seriously and Cole knew it had taken willpower on his part not to step in and try to fix Cole's problems beforehand. He'd obviously realized that what ailed his baby brother was beyond even him. Cole hoped he kept thinking that way.

"Cole, I've stayed out of your business for six years. But I'm done. Talk to me."

"You can't fix everything."

"Maybe not but that doesn't mean I'm going to give up. You know me—when have I ever given up on anything that I thought was important?"

"Never." It was true and Cole knew it. Cole suddenly had an uneasy feeling. "Wyatt, what have you been doing?"

"Whatever I needed to do. Do you remember I was at Seth's wedding, too?"

That was weird. "Well, duh."

"Duh is right. I was standing beside you most of the night, remember?"

"Yeah, what does that have to do with anything?"

"You were only there in body most of the night. And then Susan walked in. For the first time in a long time, I saw life in your eyes when you and the Doc locked gazes. I sure thought it was interesting."

"You would," Cole drawled, but couldn't help smiling. The Turner men came from a long line of men who enjoyed "campfire stories." Wyatt could hold his own up against the best of the best and often did in the courtroom.

Problem was, this wasn't the courtroom. This was his life and Cole wasn't exactly certain what to make of Wyatt's little fairy tale.

"You need to ask her out. The two of you need to talk."

"No."

"Ask her out, Cole. Not to work at the clinic or to work cows. Ask her out to a nice place. It'll remind you about what it's like to sit down in a nice restaurant with a lady and enjoy a good meal."

Cole had just eaten with Susan and there wasn't anything about the experience that could be called pleasant. "If we went out to a restaurant, it would probably end in a public fireworks display, compliments of the temperamental doc. No, thank you."

"Don't leave, Cole." Wyatt's words resonated across the phone lines. All teasing was gone. "The Cole I grew up with was fearless and tenacious and had a heart that was ten times bigger than mine.... Stick around and finish what you signed up to do for Susan. You can't run when someone else needs you. You've never done it before and I know you won't do it now."

Cole looked at the floor and shook his head, hating that his brother knew him so stinkin' well.

Chapter Fourteen

The Mule Hollow Church of Faith was a quaint, white-washed church built back when the older folks of town had been kids. It had always given Cole a sense of homecoming when he entered the front doors. He could still remember as a boy being hustled into the fourth pew on the left by his mother as she lined her family up to worship the Lord. His cowlick would have been slicked down at least four times before he'd picked up a hymnal. By the time the preacher got up to give the message Wyatt would have already told a couple of jokes under his breath to make Cole and Seth giggle… and their dad would have already shot them "the look" that said sit up and get right.

Memories here were good ones.

When he'd left for college, the town had been the color of dried-out cardboard, windblown and struggling. The church had held about a hundred and fifty people in boom times, but wasn't even half-full now. Most of the kids his age weren't planning on coming home after college. Not unless they were like Seth, who'd never wanted to be anything but the man who kept their heritage alive for the next generation. People like Seth, Clint Matlock, Norma Sue, Esther Mae and Adela and their husbands had been the ones who kept the dying town alive for people like him to come home to…eventually.

"Can you believe the crowd?" Applegate said, meeting Seth in the doorway and handing him a bulletin. "It's done grown since the last time you were here," he boomed, obviously without his hearing aid, since half the church would have been able to hear him if it hadn't been for Adela on the piano banging out "Give Me That Old Time Religion."

"Yes, sir, it has," Cole said, running a hand over the cowlick that seemed determined to relive old memories.

Seth stepped up beside him and grinned. "Mom had fits with that cowlick of yours."

"Yeah, I've tamed it pretty good but walking in here always brings back memories."

"You boys better hurry or your pew is gonna get taken."

"We're waitin' on Melody," Seth said. "She had nursery duty during Sunday school—"

"I'm here," Melody called, coming up the steps in a rush. Her cheeks were a pretty shade of pink and her dark hair seemed to accent them.

Cole watched Seth kiss her on the cheek and give her a hug as she placed a hand on his brother's heart and whispered something in his ear.

"No kidding?" Seth said, looking amazed by what she'd said.

"It's the truth. She just told me," Melody assured him.

"Told you what?" Applegate bellowed, not in the least bit embarrassed for having butted in.

"You'll see. It's not for me to tell."

"But ya told Seth." Applegate's thin face fell in a cascade around the frown.

"That's because he's my husband and we're one and the same."

Cole thought Seth was going to burst he looked so happy as he took Melody's arm. "That's one of the beauties of marriage. We better take that seat."

He looked around the room for Susan, but didn't find her as he followed them down the aisle to an empty pew—not pew four but five—his brother was shaking things up, it seemed.

He shook hands with Stanley, who was sitting in pew number six with Pollyanna and Nate Talbert, and he shook Nate's, too. He was turning back around when he saw Susan enter the back door. She wore a red dress and when she smiled at Applegate, he wished it had been sent to him—a wish he didn't want to have. The notion was like a kick in the gut, so real that for a minute he lost his breath. He spun toward the front and stared at the choir. Made up of mostly cowboys and the matchmaking posse he found himself staring straight at Esther Mae. Her red hair was topped with a white hat with pink daisies that matched the hot-pink dress she wore. But it was her sparkling green eyes and her possum grin that had his attention. Beside her, Norma Sue, in her blue-striped dress, was smiling so big her plump cheeks almost touched her eyes. He frowned, realizing the cowboys standing behind them had their eyes glued on Susan as she found a seat.

Cole's eyes narrowed on the cowboy at the end.

"You thinkin' of taking him outside?" Seth asked

through the side of his mouth. "Or you just giving Norma Sue and Esther Mae something to talk about?"

"Huh." Cole stiffened and saw the two singing ladies grinning at him. Okay so he was losing it—what had gotten into him?

"Yeah." Seth chuckled. "I'd tone that down a notch if I were you."

Cole scrambled to grab a songbook. Was he jealous? The question rolled around in his head the whole time. To be jealous you had to have feelings for someone. Did he?

Pastor Allen took the podium. God seemed to smile through him as his gaze swept the gathering. Seth hadn't been to the church since he'd taken over, but he could feel good vibes from the older man. "We have an exciting announcement this morning. Ashby and Dan went to the hospital last night and delivered a healthy baby girl!"

A wave of clapping ensued. "God has been good and is building the church and the town population. This is exciting. As you know, Lacy and Clint Matlock want a baby and have been trying for over a year now to do their part to build the congregation. Lacy, why don't you tell them?"

Everyone had already turned toward the couple. Lacy was beaming as she hopped to her feet in the middle aisle. "God is just so awesome. We're finally having a baby, everyone!" she exclaimed and threw her arms around Clint and kissed him.

At the news, Esther Mae squealed like a schoolgirl and Norma Sue did, too. They scrambled over their husbands, practically knocking them down to reach Lacy and swallow her up in hugs. Adela left her pew beside

Sam and followed them. She had the most satisfied expression on her genteel face as she took Lacy's face in her hands and kissed her cheek.

Melody leaned around Seth. "This is wonderful news! She wanted to surprise the ladies here in the sanctuary because she felt like God had brought them all together and it was important to share the blessing here to give Him honor."

Minutes later, after everything had calmed down, the pastor gave a great sermon on giving God the praise and the glory even when times are rough or life isn't turning out as you expected. He used Lacy and Clint as an example, in that they'd been praying for a baby for some time, but they'd had to wait until God made the way. The pastor emphasized that the couple had walked the walk of Proverbs 3:5, "Trust in the Lord with all your heart and lean not unto your own understanding." That even when it looked like they might not have a baby, they'd worked hard to trust God in the situation. Even when it wasn't easy.

Cole swallowed hard as the words rolled around in his mind. He'd trusted the Lord and hadn't had a happy ending… Oh, he'd gone on with his life, but there was no way he'd ever understand why sweet, spirited Lori had suffered and died so young.

"Come on Cole, stay for lunch and volleyball," Norma Sue said after services, blocking the path to his truck.

"Sorry, Norma Sue, I'm not hungry and I haven't played volleyball in years," Cole hedged, angling toward his truck.

"You might as well say yes," Seth said. "Norma's not going to let you go. Don't you remember she gets every cowboy who ventures through that door out on that sandpit? Give it up, bro."

"And besides," Norma Sue snorted, "I remember you used to play a mean game of it, so pretending you don't know how won't cut it with this ole gal."

That made him grin despite the disquiet churning inside of him. "I didn't say I couldn't play. I said I haven't played in years."

"It's just like riding a bicycle."

Seth grinned, enjoying watching Cole lose the discussion.

"Besides," she added, "we have to celebrate Lacy and Clint's news and if you leave that'd be mighty rude of you."

It would be a distraction from the memories, too. "I'll stay," he drawled. "But, be warned, I'm not going down easy. I remember that you might be short, but you set well and serve fierce."

Over the top of Norma Sue's head he saw Susan out in the parking lot getting into her truck. "Hey, I'll catch y'all inside if you don't mind." He sidestepped toward the parking lot. He needed to talk to Susan. Norma Sue and Seth both glanced her direction.

"We don't mind at all. And fair's fair," Norma Sue said. "You go grab that gal and bring her back here."

"You do that." Seth chuckled. "And don't take no for an answer."

Cole dipped his head to them, spun on his heel and jogged the distance to Susan's truck. She'd already started the engine and he slapped the side to get her attention. "Hey, hold up," he called, rounding the fender. "Where do you think you're going?" Skidding to a halt in the white rock, he smiled at her and placed a hand on her open window.

She lifted her hand to shield her eyes against the sun that was high and bright behind him. "I have too much to do at home to stay and play."

He didn't miss the curt tone—and understood his behavior at the stable elicited it. "Nope. If I have to stay then you have to stay," he coaxed, feeling lighter just looking at her, knowing he wanted to bring a smile to her face. Norma Sue had had a great idea; a play day would be good for Susan…and him. Might even help him forget some of the heavy things on his mind.

"Ohh, no. I certainly don't."

"Okay, I get that hanging with me is the last thing you'd want to do. But c'mon, it's Sunday. You're supposed to rest on Sunday, remember?" He went to open her door but she grabbed the windowsill and held it in place. "It'll be fun and you know it. Besides, Norma Sue told me not to let you go anywhere." He tugged the door open as her eyes turned to cute, feisty slits. He smiled—couldn't help it. Man, he felt good suddenly.

Her shoulders sagged slightly. "Cole. I really don't feel like it."

"Look, if this is about last night, you were right, I stepped over into your business. I still think you put yourself at risk, but it's not my place. This is your life. Stay. It'll be good for you and I'll leave if it'll make you feel better."

She expelled a heavy sigh of frustration. "Don't be ridiculous. Your leaving isn't necessary. I'll stay." She snapped the ignition off.

He pulled the door open wide and held out his hand to her. "Let me help you, ma'am," he drawled.

"I can make it on my own," she said and slid from the seat. "And *believe* me, a few minutes into this game, you'll be needing *my* help."

Susan watched the ball descend toward Cole on the other side of the net. Taking a step, she gauged her defensive move to his. He stepped then jumped into the air—she left the ground a split second later, arms up. Just as he hit the ball, she hit it right back at him—he missed the shot and looked shocked as the ball landed at his feet like a cannonball.

"The girl can play," Cole said, grinning.

"Ya don't need ta take his head off," Applegate yelled from the sidelines as laughter and loud whistles erupted.

Susan ignored it all, intent only in keeping Cole Turner from making any points off her.

She hadn't actually wanted to hang around if he was going to be here. He'd made her so mad out at the barn the night before that she hadn't been able to sleep. But dad-gum the man sure was cute grinning back at her through the net.

As the game started up again, the voice in the back of her mind chattered like it had all night long—*he was simply concerned for her.*

It was nice to have someone concerned for her—or at least she'd *thought* it would be nice. She'd never thought about how a husband's overprotectiveness could hinder her work. Not that Cole was remotely being considered for the job—still, it had her disturbed more than a little bit.

"Susan," Esther Mae exclaimed from the left of her. "Your ball! Your ball!"

Susan jerked back to attention and spotted the ball just as it whizzed past her head. "Sorry," she grumbled.

"Where's yor head?" Stanley called.

"It ain't on her side of the net," App grunted.

Susan cut her eyes at him. "I just lost my train of thought for a minute—"

"We saw that," Esther Mae said. "Cole must be up there winking at you just like I told him to do."

"What?" Susan asked, glaring at Cole. He was grinning like a schoolboy.

"She suggested it, but I'm innocent. I told her a wink from me would only make you madder at me and then you'd really whip us for sure."

She arched a brow in agreement. "You got that right."

His smoky-blue eyes brightened and he chuckled. Delight wrapped around her heart—unexpected and aggravating. She did not want this, but it was as if God was playing an April Fool's joke on her and she was falling for it hook, line and sinker.

"Game ball!" Norma Sue bellowed, holding up the ball that would win the game for Susan's team if Cole's team didn't hit Norma's serve.

Though she was a short, robust woman wearing boots, rolled-up jeans and a headband that had her kinky gray curls rivaling the look of Richard Simmons, the woman was deadly on a volleyball court. Cole hadn't expected the game to be this big a battle.

Across the net, Susan hunkered down into position and gave him the look—the one he'd come to realize in the past hour meant she was about to try to eat his lunch.

"Cole, better watch out," Stanley called from the

sidelines. "I'd be plumb embarrassed if she got two in a row past you."

"Yep, yep," Lacy yelled from over by the food. "You better dig deep, Cole Turner."

Seth chuckled behind him and Esther Mae harrumphed beside him. "You can do this, Cole. If it comes my way this time, I'll get out of your way. I don't want you knocking me over again."

Him knock *her* over—Cole cut his gaze to her in surprise and when he came back to Susan, her eyes were twinkling—that was good at least. She'd seemed to have difficulty gaining focus at the first of the game, but then she'd come out swinging and he'd been hard-pressed to defend his position at the net. She was excellent at spiking the ball and had several times nearly taken his head off when she'd leaped into the air and slammed the ball. He kept getting distracted watching her fluid grace.

Of course only now did he learn she'd put herself through vet school on a volleyball scholarship—a nice bit of info he'd somehow missed.

Norma Sue tossed the ball then slammed it, sending it skimming straight at him—he was well aware that it was a deliberate hit that would have him and Susan fighting at the net. He and Susan rose as one to block the other's shot at the same time. The next minute he felt wind by his ear as she drove the ball back past him straight into the ground.

He grinned as he landed. "Well done, Doc."

She laughed. "Not so bad yourself, cowboy."

"I think that means the loser buys the winner a soda," he said as everyone swarmed about them in a flurry of congratulations and consolations.

She hesitated. "I guess it would be kind of sorry on my part as the winner if I turned down an offer like that."

"You're right. After beating the socks off me, it would look pretty bad to tell me no. In fact, I think it should be lunch." He was thinking of the date she'd canceled—the one they were supposed to be having now.

"So are you saying *yes?*" Cole asked, thinking he'd misunderstood, since she'd agreed so easily.

"Well, it's the sportsmanlike thing to do," she said as she headed toward the group gathered around the tables.

Cole was quick on his feet. Moving as if he was dodging an angry bull, he shot out in front of her and blocked her path. "Oh, no, you don't. I just worked entirely too hard for this lunch date and I'm not looking to entertain a crowd anymore today."

She studied him with slight mistrust in her eyes. "So what exactly do you have in mind?"

Chapter Fifteen

Susan held on to Cole's waist and couldn't help but enjoy the feel of the sun on her face and the wind in her hair as they rode through the beautiful hillside. Riding with Cole on his motorcycle was the last place she'd expected to be...or wanted to be. Wasn't it?

She blinked against the wind and tightened her hold around his waist as they rounded a curve. Playing volleyball reminded her that she was moving to Mule Hollow to try to begin a new life. To try to *have* a life. Following volleyball with a motorcycle ride was a good way to start... Cole just might be right.

There had been much teasing and a flurry of excitement as Adela and Lacy threw together a sack lunch for them and hustled them on their way. It had been embarrassing.

As they headed toward his black-and-chrome Harley he'd smiled at her and made her smile when he told her that he'd enjoyed watching her have a good time, even if it was at his expense.

The man had a way about him—when he wasn't being a domineering oaf—that seriously drew her to him…dangerous thing to admit but it was true. He was so different from his brother Seth. Susan had thought at one point maybe she and Seth would have made a great couple. Seth was so settled and sure of his spot in life that they'd gotten along great from the moment she'd first begun working in this area and they'd become friends. He'd been in what she'd thought was a serious relationship and then when he'd broken that off, she was dating someone—of course that didn't work out. But when they both were single and she'd thought now was the time, he'd fallen for Melody. She'd been happy for him, but sad for herself. She'd not been able to help thinking that she might have missed out on the best man she'd ever known.

The man she could have trusted would never leave… but the first time she saw him and Melody, she knew they were meant for each other. There was a beautiful spark between them. That "thing," that unspoken connection, that everyone around a man and a woman in love can see. She couldn't help but be thrilled for them.

At their wedding when Cole had walked in, she'd thought instantly, "Now, there is a man."

He was nothing like his brother, oh, no. One look at Cole and she'd felt as though she was stepping out on a tightrope. With Seth she felt an easy feeling of comfort. Not anywhere near the tightening of her stomach, accelerated heartbeat and the we're-going-over-the-edge-of-the-cliff feeling she got when Cole was near…

That impression had solidified and done nothing but gather speed since he'd come home. Being around him was always like a roller-coaster ride. But it was all surface stuff.

So now here she was with the sun on her face and

the wind in her hair as she took this step to get to know him better. She was terrified…her daddy had always told her fear was her best friend if it helped propel her forward. Susan had no idea if forward was good in this situation but forward she was determined to go.

She had to find out if this spark she felt when she was around him was what she feared it might be…

Energy filled Cole as he jogged down the old stone steps to where she stood on the large flat rock that jutted out into the water. The river swerved around the rock and rapids gurgled and swirled as the rock ledge on both sides of the area narrowed. Susan shielded her eyes and looked at him.

"I never knew this was back here," she said, amazed. "Can you imagine what a welcome respite this must have been for those stagecoach passengers a hundred and fifty years ago when those stages rumbled to a stop at the house?"

He looked about thoughtfully, taking in the beauty and the timelessness of the place. "I've thought of it often. Actually as a kid I'd come here to this spot for respite myself. It's special."

"I can see you here," she said, her eyes sharpening with interest. "I bet you dreamed of all sorts of things."

He tucked his hands in his pockets—the logical way of keeping them from reaching out to her. Which was suddenly exactly what he wanted to do, right here at his special spot. He'd never brought anyone here before. But he'd made the decision to share it with her the instant she'd agreed to have lunch with him.

He held up the plastic grocery bag Adela had handed to him before they'd left. "Are you ready to eat?"

"I can't believe they threw that together in the few moments we were telling them we were going for a ride."

"Adela and Lacy are quick-handed women, is all I can say." He led the way along the wide rock to where another ledge made a good place for them to sit. "As a kid, I pretended this was my thinking couch."

She sat down with a space between them for the sack of food. Scooting back so her feet dangled, she leaned against the wall. "It reminds me of one. All we need are a few pillows to soften it up a bit."

He nodded as he extracted two bottles of water, some turkey sandwiches and a large, half-full bag of chips from the sack.

"This looks good," he said, his mind racing for an opening.

Susan nodded. "Can I ask you something?"

"Shoot away." His interest spiked instantly by the hesitancy he heard in her voice.

"When you were sitting here, did you dream of settling down?"

There was his opening…as if God was telling him to open up like he'd wanted to do.

He laid a sandwich on the napkin Susan had just removed from the sack and placed in front of him. He steadied his thoughts. "I didn't. I dreamed of being a rodeo star and seeing the world. I brought my rope here and I practiced to the sound of the water rushing by."

"That's kind of what I'd put together about you," she said before taking a bite of her sandwich. She looked away, studying the water as it flowed past.

"But things change."

"How so?"

"First, I never figured I was needed around here.

I love this place, the land, the fact that it has been in our family all these years. I love coming home to it—"

"But you hardly *come* home. I mean, at least since I've bought the clinic and been doing work around here, you haven't been home much."

He grinned. "Been keeping up with me even before you knew me. Impressive."

"Yeah, you wish." She laughed. "That *Seth* has mentioned you a time or two is the *only* reason I even knew you existed."

"There's no need to be embarrassed. I'm sure my gals, Norma Sue and Esther Mae, have mentioned me to nearly all the single gals just like yourself. They're always looking out for a suitable match for their favorite prodigal son."

She shook her head. "Hate to burst your bubble, but they never once mentioned you to me."

He let out an exaggerated sigh. "And here I thought they were on pins and needles waiting for me to come home to roost."

"Don't feel too bad. They've been busy with all the cowboys *already* living here."

"This is true. Still, I'm wounded."

"So—it wouldn't really matter. Right?"

"Actually, at the time I left it, it wouldn't have. The rodeo team at college was my ticket to see more of the world. I never meant to leave home forever. But my third year at school I met—" He had to pause as emotions slammed into him at the thought of meeting Lori.

Susan's gaze went still and she studied him with open curiosity. "Who?"

"A very special girl. Her name was Lori and she'd been on the team the year before I signed on." After all this time it was just like yesterday. "She was an excellent barrel racer and sister to one of the ropers. And, well, she'd had to drop off the team due to a rare form of cancer. The team admired her and dedicated most of their rides to her so even though I'd not met her, she was there in spirit every time we went out."

Susan placed her sandwich on her napkin and listened, unmoving. He studied her thoughtfully, her healthy glow and vitality so in contrast to Lori's sallow coloring when they'd met… "She came to the arena one day. She'd lived longer than the doctors expected her to and had beaten the odds, as some would say. She gave all the glory to God for every second she was alive. And she believed God had kept her alive for a reason— she was convinced of that and had been trying hard to figure out what it was that day when she walked into the arena." Cole took a shaky breath, remembering that moment as if it was thirty minutes ago.

"She changed my life in ways I never thought possible. She was frail—so frail I thought she might need to sit down to catch her breath as she walked up the wheelchair ramp to the bleachers."

"What happened? Did she make it?"

"Yes. She made it into the stands and sat on the bottom bleacher and watched the practice. I roped my calf, but when I went off my horse to tie his hooves she let out a whoop and I slid in the dirt and went down. I was laid out flat on my back in the dirt and heard her soft chuckle. For the first time in my life, I didn't care that I'd missed." He smiled. "All I could think about was going over and meeting the girl I'd heard so much about." He glanced at Susan and widened his smile…

thinking about how hearing that rich laugh coming from such a fragile woman had affected him.

"She must have been a great gal?"

He shook himself out of his nostalgia. "That's all I could think, too. I mean when someone makes an impression like she had on so many, it gets a person's attention."

"So what did you do?"

"I picked myself up, dusted myself off, walked over and…and, I gave her my heart." He swallowed hard and caught the surprise in Susan's face. "Yeah, hard to believe, isn't it?"

"You fell in lov—" Her voice caught, which caught him off guard. "You fell in love?" she asked, her voice hushed.

"Like a rock." He leaned elbows on knees and hung his head. "When I looked up through those arena bars into her eyes—so shadowed and hollow, but…extraordinarily full of life—I knew I would never be the same." He wasn't exactly sure why he felt so compelled to open up to Susan about Lori but it felt good to talk to someone. Why her? Maybe it was so that she would stop and take less risk with herself. Not take her life or the quality of that life for granted.

"Was she recovering? In remission?"

"No." He gave a slow head shake as he held Susan's startled gaze. Sure she was probably unable to believe he had the capacity for something like that—he hadn't known it himself. Feeling compassion for someone in that situation was one thing, falling in love in a heartbeat—some would say was crazy. And they had said it plenty. Pushing forward, he continued—details were hard. "We had three months. People called me crazy.

Who would pursue someone who was dying? If I could, I wouldn't wish it on anyone. But I wouldn't change it for me. Lori was the best thing that ever happened to me."

Susan's pain-filled eyes bored into him but she didn't say anything.

"She taught me what was important. Look, I've never told anyone all of this. I don't exactly know why I brought you here to tell you this, but I did. Life is precious. You should enjoy it and take care of yourself. There is more to life than your career. Don't take it all for granted."

Susan's heart hammered with Cole's words. The man had fallen in love with a terminally ill woman—it was heartbreaking. "What did you do?"

He rubbed his knee, as he seemed to go back in time thinking. "I'd hurt my knee and was struggling competitively in my rodeo events. My dream was dying and it had been killing me. But after meeting Lori, it wasn't important anymore. I started seeing things in black-and-white in terms of importance. Which makes it even more difficult to handle what happened after she died…

"I shut down and for a while nothing was important to me, nothing at all. Thinking about those weeks now, I'm ashamed because I feel like I let her down. She'd wanted me to let her go easily. She'd been prepared to die. But even knowing this, there was no way—" His words died abruptly and he turned his head away from her.

Susan's heart broke for him. She wanted to comfort him, touch his shoulder, something, but she couldn't move.

"I couldn't understand how someone so wonderful

had to go through so much," he said, his words harder, his eyes flat when he turned back to her. "I still don't. It's a part of life I don't get." He shook his head in distaste. "I didn't mean to get into that, that isn't why I started telling you this. I was just trying to let you know that you need to take care of yourself. Do more of this type of thing. Play volleyball, laugh. Hire an assistant who will be with you when you go out on call. You shouldn't be so stubborn about it."

So that was what all of this was about—he slipped that assistant in there so smoothly. What exactly had she hoped it was about?

More.

The man had just given her a look inside his heart and even said he didn't do that with many people. No one in town, other than Seth maybe, knew this side of him. She would have heard something about it…she remembered Norma Sue saying she thought something had happened to him, but she didn't know what. Now, Susan knew and she'd felt touched, even honored, that he would confide something so personal to her. He'd just described giving his heart to Lori in an unbelievable instant. He'd still stepped over that line and given his heart to her, knowing that he would suffer such a void after her death. But obviously he hadn't confided in her because he felt connected to her…

Oh, no, hardly. She blinked and stared away from him. Had she really thought his telling her meant more than it did? And why, oh, why did she care? She knew he was merely trying to use the experience to get her to slow down and hire an assistant.

"You want to know why I'm so stubborn?" she asked, more disappointed than angry at his continual soapbox stand on her life. "I understand the void you feel. Not exactly in the same way but, still, losing people you love is hard. Even with God's comfort. My mother died giving birth to me. She was forty-five. They'd wanted a child so badly, but had given up years earlier and so when my mom found out she'd conceived me she was ecstatic. She was cautioned to give me up because of some complications, but she refused. She basically gave her life to bring me into this world." The very idea of it had truly overwhelmed her growing up. Her mother hadn't had to die for her. But she'd loved her. "I always think of Jesus when I think of my mother's sacrifice. Jesus died on the cross for us because He loved us so much, and my mother died in labor because she loved me so much. Even though she'd never seen me. It's overwhelming sometimes when I think about it."

Cole took her hand. The contact was so unexpected it took her breath.

"I'm so sorry for your loss," he said, his smoky-blue eyes darkening like gray skies before a rain.

Susan felt his sincerity and as she looked into his eyes she felt comforted. "Thank you." His hand tightened about hers and his thumb soothingly caressed her skin. "My daddy and I were everything to each other. He was fifteen years older than my mom, though, and he felt like I needed to be able to stand on my own two feet in case something happened to him. He died just after I graduated high school and was getting ready to enter college. Though he'd prepared me, I still had lessons to learn." Had she ever. Thinking about how hard those years were reminded her not to feel bad about her stubbornness. She'd been alone and grieving when she'd entered college. She'd also felt all of her father's expectations while feeling lost at the same time. "I'm stubborn and determined and driven for a reason, Cole. Yes, I'm moving to town to try to have a life. But I can't change who I am." And that was what he would have her do—she pulled her hand from his. "I am the child my father raised. Knowing your story helps me see why that bothers you. But I will make my father proud in my short lifetime." She stood up, too troubled to stay seated. "I think we should go back now."

She'd confided too much and knew it had simply been the result of a long two days…a long two weeks. That was it.

He would be through with the clinic by the end of the next week if he hurried it up, and then he'd move on. He'd be gone. Back to the altruistic life he'd chosen after losing the love of his life.

All she had to do was not think about that. Not think about how she would love to be the one to take away the pain she'd glimpsed in his eyes as he'd talked of Lori.

Chapter Sixteen

"So how's it goin?" Sam asked on Tuesday morning when Cole walked into the diner with Seth. From their seat at the front window, Applegate and Stanley tuned in. They called out a "howdy" and leaned a bit closer to make sure their hearing aids picked up all bits of conversation.

"Don't ask," Seth said. "Cole might bite your heads off."

Cole shot him a grumpy glare as he took a stool. He'd avoided the diner on Monday because he knew he'd get the fifth degree from the old fellas. He'd already gotten it from Norma Sue, Esther Mae and Adela. The three ladies had visited the clinic first thing Monday morning. They hadn't even tried to hide their real reason for dropping by and had immediately begun drilling him about Sunday afternoon.

He'd told them little. What was there to tell? That he'd opened up to Susan and had completely come across the wrong way. She'd empathized with him over Lori but hadn't gotten why he'd told her...he wasn't sure he completely understood why he'd told her.

The last thing he'd expected was for her to reveal what she had. He'd had no clue what she'd been through and he seriously doubted that anyone in town knew that she'd lost everyone so close to her…early in her life. No wonder she was so independent.

"I'm almost done with the clinic, if that's what you mean," Cole offered.

Applegate spat a sunflower seed into the spittoon. "I heard Susan was out most of the night last night," he boomed. "She was back and forth between here, thar and yonder with one emergency after the other. You seen her?"

"Nope. She hasn't come by."

"That ain't good," Stanley yelled across the room.

Sam set cups in front of Cole and Seth. "Nope, sure ain't."

"She's busy. It's her job," Cole snapped, watching as Sam filled his with coffee. "Thanks," he grunted. He took a cautious swallow. Black and caustic, the coffee burned all the way down his throat and settled in his stomach like acid on acid. He took another swallow.

"Shor she's busy but…" Sam drawled. "It still ain't good that she's burning both ends of the candle. The little gal is dancin' with disaster if ya ask me."

Cole couldn't agree more. He wasn't the only one in town who thought she put herself in dangerous situations. Or was stubborn. Or needed someone to watch over her. She might be a certified veterinarian, but she was a woman alone at all hours of the night and no matter how she explained herself to him he could not and did not think it was safe for her.

Chauvinistic—maybe by some people's terms—but to him it was just plain and simple fact that any woman he cared about was going to have to understand that he'd have her safekeeping in mind at all times. Who, at night, would know if she didn't return home after being called out on emergency? Who would know until she didn't show up for work that she had run into trouble? Had a wreck? He yanked his thoughts away from her and her business. Or at least he tried. The woman was starting to obsess him. She seemed close to Betty but still she lived all the way in Ranger.

"Earth to Cole," Sam said, topping off Cole's coffee. "Did she say when her new equipment is gonna arrive? From what I gather, she did real good in the sale of her other place. Got all new stuff comin' for the new clinic."

"I don't know about all that, but whatever it is it's supposed to arrive Saturday. I'm working to get everything ready for it."

Applegate stood up and ambled over to the counter. He was moving slow—limping, too.

"Is something wrong, App?" Cole asked, noticing the way the older man was moving.

Stanley spit several sunflower seeds into the spittoon. "We been helping Norma Sue bottle-feed some ornery baby calves." Stanley chuckled. "One of 'um got the better of ole App yesterday."

App grunted. "I'm still sore. The calf decided it was a goat and tried to mow me down."

"That's the truth," Stanley agreed. "If Norma Sue hadn't grabbed it when she did, ole App might'a got the boot right out of town."

"Now thar's an idea," Sam said, rubbing down the counter.

Cole chuckled listening to them. They always gave each other a hard time. But since they'd all been friends for sixty years or more, it didn't look as if they were gonna split up or anything.

"So when you movin' back here, Cole?" App asked, ambushing Cole with the sudden change of subject.

"I've told him I need him," Seth said.

Cole shot him a hard look. "I'm enjoying what I do."

"Humph," Sam snorted. "From what I hear you ain't even got a home ta call yor own out thar. Livin' in a hotel room ain't no life fer a man. Especially when he's got responsibilities back home and good reason fer being there. Yor brother is a newlywed—you should thank about him and also yorself."

"That's right. Just like I jest did by beatin' the socks off this old sourpuss," Stanley said, jumping several of App's checkers. "Remember roots are good. Especially fer raising kids."

"That's what I'm telling him," Seth said.

Cole drank his coffee in silence and let them carry on with their ambush.

A few minutes later after avoiding answering their questions and making his escape, Cole and Seth left the diner. Cole couldn't help thinking that roots were good. Having people around who cared about you and knew you so well they could say anything—might drive some folks crazy but knowing those folks cared about you was a nice feeling. That was what Mule Hollow was made of.

"Some things never change," he said as he climbed into Seth's truck.

"Nope. It's a good feeling, isn't it?" Seth's eyes were serious beneath his Stetson.

Cole gave a short half laugh. "You're trying real hard to make me reconnect, aren't you, brother?"

"You know I am. I want you here, Cole. Plain and simple. It's more than just about me needing you at the ranch. It's where you belong. You always said you were coming home to raise a family. So come home. Settle down. Find a good woman and have that family. Lori would have wanted that for you and you know it."

Cole didn't want to get into this and yet…it was unavoidable.

"And what about Susan?" Seth prodded. "If I'm right, there's something there, isn't there?"

"Drive, Seth."

Seth slapped the steering wheel. "I was right. I knew it," he said. Cranking up the truck, he backed out. "What are you scared of?"

"Nothing."

"That's a lie and you know it. Come on, Cole. Talk to me."

"I have obligations—"

"You and I both know you don't have anything going that you can't get out of. And, besides, even if you did, it's easy enough to plan to come home as soon as those are up."

It was true. He'd freed himself up before coming here but there was plenty of work that still needed doing. "You know as well as I do that I can walk away from life as I know it at any minute. But that doesn't mean I want to."

Seth shot him an irritated look. "Why, because coming home would mean you'd be tied to responsibilities that aren't so easy to get out of? You'll never find peace unless you make a stand, Cole. You have to stop running."

It would mean, also, that he'd be in town—around

Susan…as of Sunday he wasn't sure if that was a good thing or a bad thing. "Out on the road I'm able to be happy most of the time…. I'm managing. I'm helping people." And any disgruntled feelings that would besiege him from time to time could easily be pushed aside and ignored while he worked at solving other people's problems. "It's a good way of life for me. Here. Honestly, Seth, I don't know how it would be. I don't know if I can handle it."

And Susan. Well, Susan complicated the situation tenfold.

Seth pulled the truck to the side of the road. "Cole, you can handle anything. With God's help, you can conquer this fear or sadness or whatever it is. You are not alone. I know without you telling me that you blame God for taking Lori. And I know you felt powerless watching it happen. But, Cole, you have to know you deserve to move forward and have a life, too. One built around roots and family and not driven by anger and sadness and emptiness. You're my baby brother and I saw you when we lost Mom and Dad. When you hurt you bottle it up. You hold it in—you smile and joke but it's there. Truth is truth, Cole. And the truth is, it's time to stop."

It was seven in the evening when Susan turned into her new driveway. Cole called to say he needed her help with something, but he hadn't told her what it was. She'd been out nearly all night and was dragging, but her energy level surged upward dramatically on seeing him standing in the doorway.

She'd thought about him almost constantly ever since Sunday. But she'd stayed away. She wanted to be the woman who took away the pain she'd glimpsed in his eyes. It was a dangerous thing to be thinking.

He wore his tool belt today—a reminder that, yes, he worked for her. His lean jaw was scraggly with stubble as if he'd been working as many hours as she had. His wavy brown hair curled from beneath the ball cap and his eyes seemed to light up as she approached. She couldn't help thinking that the smartest thing she could do was get back in her truck and race in the opposite direction.

But she was no chicken. Or at least she'd never been before. "Hi," she said and smiled, feeling self-conscious about all she'd revealed to him about her past. She was still amazed that she'd done that.

"I'm glad you could make it out, finally. I hear you've been busy the past four days."

She couldn't tell if he realized she'd been avoiding him or if he really thought it had all been about being busy…she went with busy. "Very. So what's up?" she asked, keeping her focus.

He moved aside and let her pass into the building. The caustic scent of stain and varnish hit her. It wasn't strong enough to cause her eyes to tear up or to run them out of the building but it was there making itself known.

"You look— I, well, I had an idea that I wanted to run by you."

She almost smiled at the way he'd changed course on telling her she looked tired. Because it was more than obvious that was exactly what was buzzing around in his mind. The fact that he'd decided against saying it was good, so she pretended not to notice as she followed him to the reception desk.

The place looked fantastic. The cedar walls looked beautiful and the cabinetry he'd done in pine, opting to clear-coat it so the wood would show and match the light weave of blond running through the red of the cedar. He'd done her counters in the same wood and they looked very rustic.

"I still have to finish out the bathrooms and some cabinets in the dispensary and surgery. The front area is done, except for adding a clear coat to the front of the reception desk and the counter. I waited to do that because I had this idea about putting a few brands on them first. What do you think?"

Susan's interest peaked. "That sounds interesting. Like take a bunch of different people's brands and burn them into the wood?"

"Exactly!" He beamed at her. "I figured you'd get the idea pretty quick. What do you think?"

"I *love* the idea. I really do." She met his smile with one of her own and time just sort of sat there between them. *Focus, girl, focus.*

"Good," he said. "I had a feeling you would. Follow me," he drawled, crooking his finger and then heading toward the doors leading into the back area. "I took the liberty to round up a few irons and thought since it's your building you should have the honor of doing the first brand."

Oh, boy—wasn't that thoughtful? A warm sense of pleasure filled Susan and she hushed the small voice yelling "focus" in her head. He had several branding irons heating in a gas warmer and she pulled a few out and recognized the brands. "I really love this idea." It seemed to be the only phrase she could string together at the moment.

"I'm assuming you've handled irons before?"

"Actually, no."

"Really?"

"Yeah, don't do branding. Some vets do, some don't."

"Not a problem. I'll show you how it's done."

"I really— That sounds great," she said, catching herself before she repeated herself again.

He grinned. "Then we had better get busy. Are you driving back to Ranger tonight?"

She heard the "you don't need to" tagged onto the end even though he didn't say the words. "No. I'm staying here, at the house."

"That'll help us get this done, although this shouldn't take more than a couple of hours. Hopefully you won't have any emergency calls and you can get some rest."

The man had tried, but hadn't made it five minutes. But instead of it irritating her as much as before, she felt that same sense of pleasure flowing through her. He seemed genuinely to care about her overworking— if she relaxed a bit, she'd admit that it was a nice feeling. *Wasn't it?*

"What brand do you want to start with?" he asked.

"Is the Triple T in there?" she asked, knowing that was the Turner Ranch's brand.

"Right here." He pulled it from the batch and handed it to her.

"Then that's it, in honor of you thinking of this and also for getting me out of a bind."

"I really love that idea," he said, his eyes twinkling as he mimicked the way she'd said the words.

She liked the teasing side of him. "Where is Cole and what have you done with him?" she asked.

He reached for a brand, his smile fading. "It's all me.

I can have a lot of fun when I'm not stepping over into someone else's business." The side of his lip hitched upward again. "But when a lady isn't watching out for herself it's kinda hard for me to keep my mouth shut."

She thought of Lori and wondered if he was, too. "I think…that's an irritating, but commendable quality—"

His eyebrows shot upward in surprise. "Susan? Is that you?"

She gave a short laugh at his startled words. "That doesn't *mean* I like being bossed around," she warned him, giving him a look, "but I know you mean well."

"I do, Susan."

She heard the sincerity in his words and she believed him…. Her heart caught realizing how much she wanted to believe his actions for her were motivated by more than just concern.

She took a breath and looked at the brand in her hand. It was time to change the direction of the conversation or take the chance of exposing her emotions.

"Are you okay?" he asked.

"Y-yes. I think this brand has grown cold." She struggled to sound normal. It was a hard thing to do when she felt as if she were losing control of her heart.

Chapter Seventeen

Cole stared at Susan and felt off-kilter. He'd come up with this idea about the brands the day before, after he and Seth had had their little talk. He'd been in such a foul mood that the last thing he wanted to do was spend time with Susan. Nope, he'd planned to avoid her at all cost, until he finished the job and hit the road. Which would be next week—unless he could get done early.

But this idea was too good to pass up. When it hit him he'd known he was going to have to put off clear-coating everything and call Susan to come out to get her opinion and her help.

Looking at her now, he was almost overcome with the desire to pull her into his arms. He stepped back. He was leaving. Nothing good could come from testing the waters between them. He wasn't looking for that. He was interested in keeping her safe. And in getting her into her building.

They'd had to put the Triple T brand back into the heater to fire it up again.

"So how do you do this?" Susan asked again as they

waited, sounding as if she was searching for something to fill the awkward silence between them.

Cole went with it, needing the distraction. "When you press the iron to the wood, you have to keep it steady. Give it even pressure and it'll do the work. It's easy. You ready?"

She nodded.

"Then let's do this." He pulled the brand from the heater and handed it to her. Their fingers brushed, drawing their gazes together. He let go instantly. Heading back inside, he held the door for her to pass. "I'm glad you came," he said, unable to not tell her the truth.

She paused, her eyes serious. "Me, too. I should have come out more. I—I didn't mean to abandon you during this project but I— Well…" She swallowed hard and he could tell she didn't know how to move forward.

Welcome to the party.

"Anyway, I'm glad I came." She hurried through the door and once inside she studied the front of the four-foot wall of the reception desk as if her life depended on getting this right.

Susan was just as mixed-up about what was going on between them as he was. At least that was what he thought. She was probably even more intent than him to keep this business—like she'd said from day one. She'd been right about that. But denying his feelings was getting harder and harder to do. And that was not something he'd anticipated.

Finally, Susan positioned the Triple T's brand almost perfectly in the center and pressed. The muscles of her arms tightened as she leaned into it.

"You're doing good," Cole said, enjoying watching her. Susan liked to get things right. It was obvious in the way she applied herself to anything she did. He liked that, despite worrying about her. He'd come to realize there was much about Susan that he liked, which was exactly where all of this other emotion was coming from.

"Thanks." She studied the brand, now burned black into the blond wood in a nice contrast. "It's just a tad off on one side, don't you think?" Leaning her head slightly to the right she contemplated her work.

"You aren't going to lose sleep over that, are you?" His teasing got him a glare...but unlike other times, this glare instantly faded to a smile.

"I'm not *that* much of a perfectionist."

He grinned. "That's a relief," he said, teasing yet totally truthful. "Come on. What do you say we get this show on the road?"

"I say let's do it!"

They got new irons, and Susan walked back into the front area. She stared at the desk for a long moment and wondered if she was going to line it up perfectly with his brand. He hoped she would do what he'd envisioned and start branding the wood in random order...some slanted, some sideways, some straight.

"Here goes nothing," she mumbled, then pressed the brand at an angle.

Yes! He laughed then took his brand and pressed it beside hers.

"Now, that looks good. Once again, great idea, Cole Turner."

"Glad to be of service, Doc. It's working out better than I thought it would."

It was true, he realized. It had been a long few days and he'd missed her...

The idea flowed through him as if trying to settle in where it wasn't welcomed.

He *had* missed her. Very much…

And no matter how much he was trying to deny it— or put off that he was merely feeling things out of concern or in friendship—he couldn't. Question was, what did it mean? What did he want it to mean?

Susan was trying hard to act normal and not let Cole see the conflicting emotions she was fighting. She'd been doing that a lot lately. Focusing on the branding helped, but when he suddenly grew quiet she raised her gaze to his, just as his brows crinkled and his eyes dimmed.

She couldn't move as he took a step toward her. The ringing of the phone broke the silence, but not the tension of the moment. When the phone rang in the evening it was usually the dispatch office with an emergency call. Reaching for it, she couldn't help thinking she had an emergency going on already…one she was not at all prepared to deal with.

Turning her back to Cole, she listened as the dispatcher relayed the message. She could feel Cole's eyes staring at her the entire time.

"What's happened?" he asked the moment she hung up the phone.

"Mrs. A. is at the emergency room in Ranger with a broken hip. She's demanding to see me." Her heart was pounding as she headed for the door.

"Hold on, let me cut off the furnace," Cole said, racing out the door into the back area again.

She didn't slow down. She was already behind the wheel of her truck when he came jogging outside.

"Wait up," he demanded, slamming the clinic door behind him.

"Cole," she protested through the open window, snapping her seat belt into place. "I don't have time! I have to go. She won't let them operate until I get there." She knew he was thinking of coming with her. She didn't need the distraction, and she started to back out.

"Don't you dare back up," he warned, jogging to the truck even as it moved away from him.

"Cole—" She pressed the brake as he yanked open the passenger door and slid into the seat next to her.

"Now drive," he growled.

She glared at him. She didn't have time to argue with him. And she didn't appreciate him just—

"Would you stop looking at me like that and just drive? I'm not going to mess anything up, if that's what you're worried about."

Easy for him to say, she thought as she hit the gas, shooting the truck back like a bullet. Stomping the brake hard, she pulled the gear into Drive, pointed the front end toward Ranger and floored it.

Beside her Cole flew forward then was yanked backward against the seat.

"You might want to put that seat belt on," she snapped.

"Ya don't say," he drawled, but reached for his seat belt.

She glanced his way and he cranked a brow up and casually stretched an arm across the back of the seat. He looked entirely too settled. Entirely too comfortable—

"Maybe you need to look at the road," he advised, ever so calmly, nodding toward the road ahead.

She planted her eyes forward immediately and had to swerve to keep from running off the shoulder!

She half expected him to say something smart, but instead he just asked, "Did they give you any details about Mrs. A.?"

"No. It was my evening answering service and they didn't have much info. Just that she needs surgery but she insists on talking to me."

"I hope she'll be okay. Any clue what she wants you there for?"

"Not sure, unless it has to do with Catherine Elizabeth. I don't know why else she'd request me."

"Do you want me to drive?"

"Cole, stop!" She scowled at him. "Don't start that. I'm telling you right this minute that I'll pull this truck over and kick you straight out of here if you go mothering me."

"Mothering you?" He held up his hands.

"Yes," she warned, feeling more like herself.

"Okay, okay. I'm behaving. But the offer is there."

Susan grunted and kept her mind on the road. She was worried about Mrs. Abernathy. She didn't need to have the aggravation of Cole Turner riding shotgun beside her, butting into her business—making her think about how he'd looked only moments ago when she'd thought he wanted to kiss her. *No!*

She just plain and simple didn't need him. He was all wrong for her...had been since he drove into town, and nothing had changed.

Except it feels nice to have him, doesn't it?

She bit her lip as the notion tangled her up inside. This was not the time for this. Not the time at all. And yet he was here...but he wouldn't stay. She had to protect herself from that. She had to. *Didn't she?*

He reached over and turned on the radio. The sun

had gone down and the night air whirled about them as it whipped through the open windows. The unromantic scent of stain and clear coat had seeped into their clothing and now the scent swirled about them—maybe all those fumes were the reason for her weird thoughts.

She suddenly was wishing there was more time for them. More time for him to be around…and more time for her to get him to see things her way. If the man could understand her viewpoint they might be able to act on this crazy attraction…or at the very least become friends. Because despite his irritating stand against her way of working, she still couldn't get over that fact that the man's heart was big enough to fall in love with a dying woman. And then big enough to devote his life so far to helping others… But no matter how much they didn't get along, there was just too much about the man for her to admire. Even if he was stubborn and totally ignored what she wanted.

It suddenly hit her—had he been this way with Lori? How had she felt about him falling in love with her? Had it given her something to regret leaving behind? Had it made her dying harder?

Chapter Eighteen

"Oh, you brought your man with you!" Mrs. Abernathy said the minute Susan and Cole walked into her room.

Susan didn't take the time to point out that he wasn't her man—he just wouldn't listen to her. She was too concerned for Mrs. A. to think about Cole. She looked so frail in the big hospital bed. Especially with the IV in her arm and the monitors beeping all around her. She also looked like she was feeling no pain. They must have given her something to make her comfortable. The nurse had told them before she showed them in that they were ready to take her to surgery the minute she spoke to Susan. The nurse and the orderly followed them into the room and began getting ready to roll.

"Mrs. A., you poor thing. What can I do?" Susan asked as Cole moved to her bedside and took her hand in his.

"We're here to do whatever you need us to do," he said, smiling sweetly when Mrs. A. looked up at him with slightly glazed eyes. Tears formed as she nodded to him.

"My Catherine Elizabeth is out there alone. I need you to find her. And, Susan, I need you to fix her up for me and then keep her while I'm recovering from this dad-blamed weak hip. I tried to tell them when they picked me up that my baby was lost in the woods somewhere. But there were only two of them and they said they had to get me in the ambulance. No one would go search for her."

Distress filled the old woman's eyes and Susan's heart broke. Gently Susan took her hand with the IV hookup and gave it a gentle squeeze. "You don't worry about anything. We'll go find Catherine Elizabeth."

"Yes, we will. You can count on that."

Susan felt reassured by Cole's words. She knew the old dog's problems and worried that it might already be too late to help her. "What happened to Catherine and where should we look?"

"I was at the Stony Creek Cemetery where my Herman is buried. Catherine Elizabeth was with me. We were putting flowers on Herman's grave. I looked up and saw Catherine Elizabeth running across the country road—can you imagine my baby running? She was chasing a rabbit and looking like she was a big puppy. I started to go after her but fell and that's when I broke my hip. A car was passing by and the man helped *me,* but he wouldn't leave me and go find my Catherine Elizabeth. No one would. She's out there alone and you know she's sick."

There were tears in her eyes and her blood pressure and heartbeat had increased. The nurse stepped in. "I'm sorry, but we need to get her to surgery. We've waited as long as we can. The doctor is waiting."

Susan nodded and met Cole's stormy blue eyes.

"We're on our way," he said, looking back at Mrs. A. "I promise you I'll find Catherine Elizabeth."

Susan's heart kicked up. Cole Turner was not a man to give his word and back down. She suddenly wondered how many people over the past six years since Lori's death he'd made promises to. Promises to rebuild their homes, their businesses. Their dreams.

Mrs. Abernathy had leaned forward in her agitation, but now looking at him she relaxed. Part of that was due to the meds the nurse had slipped into the IV drip, but still, Susan could tell she had total confidence that Cole was going to do as he said.

"Thank you, Cole," she said, her words slurring. "I'll pray for her and for you to find her. Susan, will you watch over her?"

"I will watch over her until you are able to move back home and reunite with her."

"Good. Good."

The nurse nodded to the orderly and they slipped her onto the gurney.

"We'll see you when you come out," Susan said, letting go of Mrs. A.'s hand at the door.

"Don't you worry about anything," Cole called.

"Oh, I'm not now. God sent you and He's taking care of everything."

"Cole, wait up. What is wrong?"

Susan was fast on his heels but he didn't slow down until he reached her truck. "I'll drive," he said, stopping at the driver's side and holding out his hand.

"No. You're too upset."

"I'm not upset. I have a dog to find and no time for this. Now, give me the keys."

Susan studied him hard, as if trying to look inside his head, then she dropped the keys into his hand. "They're all yours. Now let's find Catherine Elizabeth."

Cole didn't talk as he drove.

"What's the matter, Cole?" Susan asked after they'd left the town behind and were speeding toward the country graveyard.

"How bad is this for Catherine Elizabeth?"

When Susan didn't answer he glanced her way. "Susan?"

"She isn't used to being outside. She could just be scared and hiding. But she could also be in trouble. I'm not sure if Mrs. A. would do well if something happened to Catherine Elizabeth. She loves that sweet dog. They are family."

Cole gripped the wheel. He wanted to believe God would take care of the old dog. Especially since it was the most loved thing in Mrs. A.'s life. But he wasn't getting his hopes up for divine intervention. He would, however, do everything within his power to bring Catherine Elizabeth home to Mrs. A. There was no way he was going to face her with anything but good news. Being in the hospital had reminded him all the more of how it felt to lose your loved one.... Mrs. A. already knew that feeling, because she'd lost her husband. He couldn't let her go through that again.

He didn't ever want to go through it again himself.

"Cole." Susan laid her hand on his back three hours into their search. "Are you okay?"

He shrugged off her hand and moved away from her. "I'm looking for a dog that could very likely be dead."

"She could still be alive."

He shook his head in disgust. "Don't patronize me, Susan. I'm not one of your little ole lady clients you need to cheer up. We both know the odds are against her. You said it yourself earlier. If she was able to come to us she'd have already been here. She knows and loves you. The fact that we haven't even heard a whimper is not good, and you know it."

"That's true—I did say that earlier. And…" She rubbed the back of her neck and scanned the area as if believing Catherine Elizabeth was suddenly going to appear and prove him wrong. "And I was thinking the same thing as you only a very few moments ago. But, Cole, I don't think this is all about a dog. Is it?"

He frowned. "We're wasting time."

Susan stepped up close. He went totally still when she suddenly placed her hands on his face. "I believe God is going to come through here tonight," she said with full conviction that it would be so.

Cole stared into her beautiful eyes. If only he could believe that. "God lets people down every day." He took the best of the best—how then did she think He'd care for a dog? He'd taken Lori despite all the prayers. Despite all the trust.

"Do you believe that God is going to come through here tonight?" she asked.

He looked away.

"Look at me, Cole Turner," she said, forcing his face back so she was staring into his eyes. They were a mere breath apart as she leaned in and stared hard into his dead-feeling eyes.

"God said to have confidence in Him," she said sternly. "Remember 1 John 5:14 says, 'This is the confidence we have in approaching God, that if we ask anything according to His will, He hears us.'"

Cole broke away from her. "Don't talk to me about confidence. I learned the hard way that God takes what He wants and it doesn't matter what kind of confidence I have in Him."

"Yes, it does."

"No, it doesn't. I prayed for Lori and I had confidence that He was going to work a miracle and heal her. I trusted Him then, so don't start with all of this. He gets to do as He sees best. But He can't expect me to put my heart on a platter and believe He's going to answer my most heartfelt pleas. I can't play that game anymore."

He couldn't. "I rely on the abilities He's given me to accomplish answering prayers. He might not choose to answer them, but if I'm in the picture I'm going to do everything in my power to do it."

"And you've given up on saving Catherine Elizabeth."

"Yeah, I have. It's late. She's old, sick and more than likely she's out here curled up somewhere dead." Susan wiped a tear from her eyes and knelt in front of him. "What are you doing?"

"I'm going to pray, Cole. You're right. God has the right to do what He wants. But He is going to do what is best…for everyone. Not just for you and your selfish wants. But for everyone. He knows the future. He knows what is coming in the lives of all those around. You don't know what He saved Lori from in the future. You don't know how many people she touched as they watched her live—from what I've learned from you— was an extraordinarily close walk with Him during the days of her illness. How many lives did she touch? How many lives did her unerring faith change for the better? She felt like every day she was alive was a gift. You told me that. I had that with my dad. He knew every day we had together was precious and a beautiful gift. And he prepared me for life after his death. He prepared me for every way possible and I've been hard-nosed and determined to be the woman he prepared me to be. But you know what, Cole? I forgot something until this very moment. He prepared me most importantly for his passing by giving me a strong faith. He knew when he died that I was going to be okay. I'd forgotten that he told me to be strong and stand up for what I wanted but that without God on my side none of my accomplishments mattered. I believe God sent you Lori as a gift. He knew He was taking her home for reasons we will never know or understand. But He gave you those precious, beautiful three months together. I think Lori recognized them for what they were and she tried to prepare you."

"So what are you praying for?" His question was a bare whisper.

"I'm praying that God is going to show you a miracle tonight." She held up her hand to him. "Come pray with me. Please."

"Susan," he said. He couldn't believe she was doing this. "This is useless."

"Please, Cole. Come down here. Please."

This was the last thing he'd expected from Susan. He couldn't move. What she'd said about Lori weighed heavily on him. Lori had touched every life she came in touch with. She had been a gift. He'd felt privileged for every second he'd had with her. She'd felt the same way. But this was about believing in God answering his prayers. And He hadn't answered the one that meant the most to him.

Susan took his hand and continued to look up at him. "God tells us to ask and believe, Cole. To ask and believe and then trust that He is going to do what is best. I'm going to pray Catherine Elizabeth is okay and that we are going to find her. And I believe with all my heart that if it is His will, that sweet dog is going to come walking out of the shadows, and her return will show you that He worked all things out for good where Lori's life was concerned."

Cole couldn't move. He stood still with Susan's hand grasping his so tightly it hurt. She smiled gently up at him then bowed her head and prayed.

Cole stared at the top of Susan's bowed head. His heart was thundering in his chest and he closed his eyes. She believed. She really believed. He prayed for her sake that God would answer her prayer. But he didn't hold any high hopes that it was really going to happen.

He opened his eyes when she finished to find her smiling at him. He pulled her up and hugged her. She melted against him and wrapped her arms around him. He felt her comfort and strength flowing through him. He kissed the top of her head. "Thank you for that. But—"

"No buts, Cole. No doubts. God is going to provide. I feel it."

He glanced around and saw nothing in the darkness. There was no sound other than the crickets and the tree frogs. There was no sign of Catherine Elizabeth and no sounds to say she was near. "Come on, Susan. It's time to go back to the hospital and check on Mrs. A. She's going to need us."

Susan rested her head against his shoulder and her heart pounded against his. *Please, God, show this man that You had a plan for his life. That You let a beautiful soul into his life not to leave him sad and discouraged but to give him hope and to make him into the man You wanted him to become.*

She looked into his eyes then glanced around. There was nothing. She wanted to be disappointed but she'd prayed for God's will to be done. She didn't understand what that plan was but she had to trust that He was working it out for Cole's benefit. And God was not her puppet on a string.

"I'm ready. God's will be done."

"You tried," Cole said as he kept his arm around her shoulders and walked her out of the woods. "What is Mrs. Abernathy going to do?"

Susan sighed as he tugged her closer to comfort her. It felt good to be comforted by him, but… "I don't want to believe that Catherine Elizabeth is dead. But if she is, Mrs. A. will be fine. She was strong, so strong when her Herman died. She is a woman of faith and I don't believe you've realized that about her."

"I'm glad to know that," he said.

They stepped over a log and headed the last few steps to the edge of the woods. Susan tried not to cry, but her heart was heavy for Cole. She wasn't sure why she was so compelled to prove this to him. But again, God's will be done.

She blinked and wiped tears from her eyes as they stepped out of the woods. Cole stopped and went still. She looked up, and there wagging her old gray-tipped tail was a grinning Catherine Elizabeth.

Chapter Nineteen

Cole pressed the last brand into the counter and waited as the hot iron burned its way into the wood. From her pallet in the corner Catherine Elizabeth watched.

"So what do you think, ole girl?" he asked. Pulling the brand away, he moved to stand beside the dog. He scratched her ears as he studied the front of the pine reception counter. "It has a certain charm about it, don't you think?"

Catherine Elizabeth barked and turned her head so she could nuzzle his hand with her cold nose. He still couldn't believe she'd been sitting there right in front of them the night before.

Susan had been convinced that God had answered her prayer to prove to him that He cared for Cole. That He'd had a plan for Lori's life and for his. Susan was convinced of all kinds of things the old dog's miraculous survival was supposed to prove to Cole. Truth was, Cole didn't know what to think. When Mrs. A. had awakened from her successful surgery he'd been overjoyed to tell her that her old companion was alive and well.

"That must have been some rabbit hunt you went on last night," he said, bending down to look into her chocolate-colored eyes. He'd volunteered to keep her at the house with him and then bring her along to work.

"All that worry and you were taking a nap," he said, giving her one last rubdown before heading out back to turn off the branding heater.

He couldn't stop thinking about Susan dropping to her knees like she'd done. He'd fallen to his knees like that and begged God to save Lori.

He'd bargained and pleaded with God to spare her. To heal her. His prayers had gone unanswered. He was glad for Mrs. A. that Susan's had been answered.

Cole pushed the memories out of his head and went to finish installing the fixtures in the bathrooms. It was the last of the work here…once he finished the cabinet doors in there and put the top coat on them and the reception desk he'd be done.

And he could hit the road.

He needed to do that as soon as possible. He knew if he stayed around much longer, he'd have to admit that he'd fallen in love with Susan.

And he couldn't admit that.

Couldn't let his heart open up that much. Couldn't chance setting himself up for the heartache of losing the one he loved ever again. He'd been afraid Mrs. A. was going to have to face that last night over Catherine Elizabeth. She'd already lost her beloved Herman and no matter what Susan said about her being a woman of faith, he'd seen the terror in her eyes when she'd feared for her dog. He'd known that fear as he'd walked out of that hospital. He'd remembered it as if it was yesterday and, faith or no faith, Cole couldn't willingly open himself up to that ever again.

It smelled as though Cole had just clear-coated the reception area. Susan walked into the clinic later that day and smiled as she looked at the room. She loved the cool mix of rustic functionality—the branded desk was one of the highlights.

"Cole. Catherine Elizabeth," she called as she pushed open the door to the back. The place still smelled of clear coat even with fresh air billowing in from the open bay doors.

"Cole," she called again, looking up to see if he was in the ceiling working like he'd been that one night.

"Hey, Doc," he called, peeking around the door of what would be the women's restroom. Catherine Elizabeth came ambling out to greet her. Susan dropped to her knees and gave her a hug. She looked good, as plump as a plum, but good. Cole had been sweet to keep her with him so that she wouldn't be so lonesome while Mrs. A. was recovering. It was amazing how much peace it had given Mrs. A. knowing she was going to be with Cole. To her, even just the outward appearance of him was reassuring. He was a walking, talking hero. Mrs. A. told her this morning that God had sent him to take care of her Catherine Elizabeth. She'd also said that he needed healing and time.

Susan had been startled when the older woman had taken her hand and told her that. Her perception had amazed Susan…or perhaps Susan was wearing her feelings on her sleeve now, and if she wasn't careful everyone might be able to see that she'd fallen in love with Cole Turner. Obstinate, hardheaded man that he was…

It was crazy. The last thing that should have happened. But obviously love was not logical.

"I just finished hanging the last door in here. Come have a look. See what you think."

She stood but her feet seemed rooted to the cement floor as she looked at him. His hair was tousled and his clean-shaven jaw made her want to place her hand against it.

Move, she told her feet and was happy when they obeyed. *Act natural,* she told herself. Hard to do when she wanted to run over and throw her arms around the man.

Crazy. That was precisely what she was. She needed to prescribe "reality" medication for herself. Only problem was she was pretty certain they didn't make anything for humans or animals that would cure what she had.

"Wow," she said, staring at the finished room. "This is so cool."

"Are you sure you like it? Because if you don't, I can rip the tin off the walls and install Sheetrock in a day."

She couldn't stop smiling. The walls halfway down were lined with corrugated tin. The bottom half of the room was cedar with a chair rail dividing it from the tin on top. She'd liked the creativeness of the room before, but with the cabinet doors installed, the finished product was fantastic. "Are you insane? Clients are going to love everything about the clinic. I don't want you to change anything."

"Then we're done here."

He studied her with serious eyes that caused Susan's heart to stumble. He was so close and yet she felt closed off from him suddenly—as if he'd pulled a barrier between them.

"How was Mrs. A.?" he asked.

"She's great. The doctor says with her strong constitution and determination she should make a full recovery. I told him it would take more than a broken hip to get her spirits down. I also assured her that for as long as she needed me to, I'd take care of Catherine Elizabeth."

"Good." He tucked his fingers in his pockets and nodded.

"She loved that you were watching over her this morning," she said, feeling an urgency to break past the barrier but not sure how. "She told me— Well, she told me you were sent from God to watch over her sweet dog." She'd said that several times.

Cole's expression tensed. "I'm glad to help out, but you were the one who had the faith last night."

Susan wondered, especially looking at him, if anything she'd done had gotten through to him. She was afraid it hadn't. Afraid actually that she may have done more damage than good with her actions. She was still amazed at how God had worked everything out in His own way…she was well aware that He might have chosen not to answer her prayer in the way that He did.

"The, ah, the equipment should be here before noon," Cole said, leading the way toward the front. Taking them to different territory both physically and conversationally.

She pulled her thoughts back and followed him. "Sure. Then all it will take is a little setup and some organization and I'll be up and running."

"Sounds like a plan."

He was being too pleasant, she thought as he held the door open for her. "Thank you."

"You're welcome. App and Stanley came out early

this morning and helped finish up. They put outlet covers on and cleaned windows."

"You mean they didn't play checkers this morning?" She couldn't believe it.

"Nope, said they wanted to do something for you."

She blinked at the sudden welling of tears. "They are so sweet. Even with those scowls they wear half the time."

"Marshmallows," he said, and his expression seemed less distant. Less removed.

"You noticed, too?" she asked as her heart quickened when he laughed.

"The two grumps and Sam grumble and gripe like crows bickering over cornstalks, but they've got each other's backs when it comes down to it."

Susan ran her hand over the counter and traced the Triple T brand—she'd branded it into the counter several times and liked the way it looked. Liked that it stood for the Turner men—for Cole.

Beside it was an *OT* with the *T* turned sideways. "This one is your ranch's original brand, isn't it?" she asked. She knew it was, but needed something to talk about. Something to keep the wall from going back up between them.

He stepped beside her, his arm brushing hers as he placed his hand on the counter beside hers. "Yes. It stands for Oakley Turner, my great-great-great-great-granddad."

Susan's nerves jangled as an electric current of connection flowed from his shoulder to hers. "Do you play poker as well as he evidently did?"

"Nope. Not a gambler. Or a horse trader like he was. The man could sell a man a horse and throw in a saddle to sweeten the deal. The buyer wouldn't even realize he was buying a saddle he already owned until he'd already paid the money and Oakley was hotfootin' it down the road."

Susan laughed. She'd heard many stories about the Turner man with the questionable morals who'd founded the ranch from a poker win. Seth had no respect for the man, yet loved the land. She traced the brand and her hand touched Cole's as she traced the *O*. "How," she began, sounding like a frog, "how do you feel about your granddad?"

He shrugged and let his finger fall into the trail behind hers. She swallowed and her stomach tilted.

"I'm with Seth on the subject. Oakley was pretty sorry when it came to life skills. He could lie and swindle with the best of them and probably gambled away his family's food money on more than one occasion. No one can figure out how a woman like my great-great-great-great-grandma Jane could have fallen in love with a man like that."

Her hand had stopped tracing the brand and Cole's hadn't. He drew his finger right to the tip of hers then stopped with their fingers touching. It was excruciating for Susan. "A person can't control who they fall in love with," she said softly. "Maybe Jane had no control. She fell for the local bad boy whether she wanted to or not." Just like she had—not that Cole was a bad boy.

The truth settled over her once more like a noose around her heart. She was in love with Cole Turner and it couldn't be denied. He'd loved and lost and she seriously doubted that with the way he'd described his journey to love anything else would ever stand up to it in comparison.

She pulled her hand back and put some distance between them. Her knees were weak as she forced her legs to propel her across the room to a safer distance. Safer—but not safe.

He hated her way of life and didn't understand her actions—and yet illogically that didn't seem to matter. Love and logic didn't play from the same deck.

He would be leaving…and he would take her heart with him and never know it. Of that she would make certain.

She blinked hard as she pretended to study the trim work surrounding the window. "So, you're done?"

"Yes."

How could a simple flat answer be so devastating? "I'll write you the last check and you'll be free," she managed and was startled by the steadiness of her voice. She shouldn't have been. She was her daddy's girl, pulling from the reserves of strength he'd empowered her with so well. "When will you leave town? I'm sure you're needed and missed. Wherever it is you're going."

She was moving to Mule Hollow to get a life and that life was about to ride off into the sunset. She pushed the thought from her mind.

"I'll be leaving in the morning," he said quietly. "I returned a couple of calls this morning to set up a few appraisals in a tiny town near the Louisiana boarder. It still has lots of displaced families living out of temporary trailers."

"I see." It was all she could manage as she closed her eyes, praying for God's strength. Her own wasn't going to be enough to get her through watching Cole leave. It was ridiculous.

Cole would leave and she *would* get on with her life.

It wasn't as if she'd really known him long enough to fall *madly* in love with him. Not the kind of love where she couldn't live without him…that kind of love— Well, that kind of love took time.

Drawing her shoulders back, she told herself she was really feeling infatuation. That was it exactly. "Well, then," she said, "I'll write you that check, that way you won't have to wait around any longer. I'll take Catherine Elizabeth and you'll be free. More people than me need you now— I mean—" she coughed with embarrassment "—other people need you. Now that you've finished here."

Chapter Twenty

"So he's leaving," Norma Sue said, sliding into the booth beside Adela and looking across the table at Susan.

Susan nodded. She'd decided to stop by Sam's and have lunch sitting down in a booth. It had pleased Sam no end that she'd come. But then Esther Mae and Adela had joined her. And now Norma Sue. At this point, Susan wasn't sure what she'd been thinking when she'd come. She should be at her clinic waiting for the afternoon delivery of her office equipment but after Cole walked out, check in hand, goodbyes said, she hadn't wanted to be alone. If she stayed alone she would have fallen to pieces.

And Susan Worth did not fall to pieces.

Beside her Esther Mae's expression fell. "That's what Susan just said." She scanned the group. "What are we going to do? We can't just let him ride that motorcycle off into the sunset."

"I agree," Adela said, clasping her fine-boned hands together. "I think we need something to buy us some time."

"I agree," Norma Sue said, thumping her fingers on the table.

Susan looked from one to the other, her mind whirling. "Y'all, he's leaving. There isn't anything any of us can do. He's a grown man who has other places he'd rather be."

Esther Mae harrumphed. "Crazy man, what is he thinking?"

"I just don't know," Norma Sue grumbled. "We need to figure a way to keep him here for a little longer—at least until he comes to his senses."

"But what do we do?" Esther Mae asked. "Could you tinker with his motorcycle, Norma Sue?"

"What!" Susan exclaimed. "Certainly not."

"Hold on to your bloomers, Susan. *If* I could tinker with his motorcycle I might be tempted to do just that. But I don't know a thing about them contraptions. And why in the world wouldn't you want me to keep that man here?"

"Yeah," Esther Mae quipped. "Look at you, honey. You're all flustered and agitated."

"That's right, dear," Adela said. Her eyes twinkled mischievously—very un-Adela-like. "You are *very* agitated and I believe *very* much in love."

She couldn't deny the truth, so Susan clamped her mouth shut. This was all very strange.

"Come on, admit that my Adela is right," Sam said, walking up with a coffeepot in one hand and mugs and cups clutched in formation in his other hand. He placed the cup in front of Adela. "Here you go, girls," he said then leaned closer. "So what's the plan?"

"No plan," Susan said. "Really, y'all. A woman has

to have her pride. I refuse to have Cole Turner stick around because someone tricked him into doing it."

"Oh, you do have a point," Esther Mae gushed. "But, then again, what if he doesn't know how you feel? What if you let him go without telling him that you love him?"

"I never said I loved him—"

"*Oh,* you said it all right. Just not out loud," Norma Sue drawled. "Now what are you going to do about it?"

"Yeah," Esther Mae said. "You're someone who works hard for what she wants. This wonderful career of yours proves it. So don't sit there and say you're just going to let the love of your life sneak on out of town because you don't want to rock the boat."

Susan started to remind them that she hadn't even said she loved him and certainly hadn't called him the love of her life—but what was the use? They had her number.

So what are you going to do?

She stood up. "I love y'all dearly, ladies and Sam. But I don't have a clue what to do. I really don't." She started for the door.

"Well, don't just run off. Let's come up with a plan," Norma Sue said.

"No, I have a delivery that needs to be met. And I need to think. But," she added, managing a smile, "thank you all for caring."

Norma Sue watched Susan leave and then she looked about the table. "We can't just sit here and let this happen."

"I'm tellin' y'all he loves Susan," Sam said. "I kin feel it. But if it ain't love yet, it's on the fast track ta bein' that way. I thank they jest need more time. If he hauls off and runs away because of whatever it is that happened to him after college then we might not ever get him back here again."

Norma Sue hunched her shoulders, and stared at the jukebox that sat across the room.

"But, Sam, Norma doesn't know anything about a motorcycle. She can't fiddle with it," Esther Mae said with a long sigh. "So how else are we supposed to keep him around?"

Sam frowned. "That thar is the problem. Maybe you gals can jest go over thar and remove a few parts."

"Yeah, you mean steal them," Norma Sue huffed. "I can just see Sheriff Brady or Deputy Zane coming to haul me into jail."

"Okay, back up and time out," Adela said gently. "We can't break the law. We have to figure something else out."

"Yor right, sweetheart," Sam said. "I wouldn't want them ta have ta arrest you—now Esther Mae and Norma he kin have."

"Not funny," Adela said. Reaching across Norma Sue, she patted his arm. "No one is doing anything to put Brady or Zane into a compromising position. We might not be able to fix this situation. If Susan isn't going to speak up then God will have to step in."

"That's right," Norma Sue said, lifting her cup. "Let's just pray something happens between now and in the morning that changes Cole's mind."

Esther Mae gasped. "I can't just sit here and twiddle my thumbs. There has to be something we can do."

"Patience, Esther Mae," Adela said, patting her friend's hand. "We have to learn to trust God just as much as everyone trusts Him."

Esther Mae frowned. "I just can't sit here. Sure, the Bible says for us to have patience and wait on the Lord. But it also says in the book of James, 'You have faith, I have deeds. Show me your faith without deeds, and I will show you my faith by what I do.' Well," she harrumphed, "I think it's time for a deed. *Or two!*"

"So you're leaving," Seth said, clearly not happy.

Cole had saddled a horse and ridden out to where he was checking calves. It felt good to be on a horse. His thoughts were troubled as he'd ridden but even so he'd enjoyed being out riding across the land he loved.

"I told you I was leaving the other day," he said, shifting in the saddle and glancing out toward the ravine where he, Cole and Wyatt had spent many a day exploring. "You'll have to hire someone else." He met his brother Seth's penetrating gaze.

Seth's jaw tightened and Cole knew he was trying not to let his anger overtake his words. Seth was like that, calm in a storm. Steady as rock.

"You miss this." He nodded, letting his gaze flicker about the land before tagging him again. "You can't run for the rest of your life, Cole. I feel like I'm a broken record, but how else am I going to get through to you? All the good works in all the world won't bring Lori back to you. Won't change the past."

"I'm not in denial. God gave me the ability to help people and that's what I'm doing."

"That's all noble of you and you've changed lots of lives doing what you do but I need you here and at the other ranch. I need you to help me. You need to put some structure in your life here on the ranch. And what about Susan?"

"What about her?"

"You don't have any feelings for her?"

Cole swallowed; he wanted to deny the question but he couldn't. He couldn't tell Seth a lie. "I care for her. But she needs more than a man who, as you put it, is quote 'living in denial' unquote. She needs more than I can give."

"More than you can give or more than you're willing to give? There's a big difference, little brother."

Cole didn't like the way that sounded.

"Look, Cole, I had issues of my own to deal with when I met Melody so don't think I'm judging you about this. I just know that I've been blessed because I resolved those issues and took hold of the love God was offering me. I just want you to have the happiness I know He has in store for you, too. And my gut tells me Susan is the one to make you happy. Don't leave. At least not yet."

"Sorry, Seth. I'm leaving after church tomorrow. After I say goodbye to everyone."

Early Sunday morning, Cole walked out of the stagecoach house and stared at his motorcycle. For six years it had represented escape to him. When things started caving in around him, he'd tied up his loose ends quickly and hit the road.

But he'd hardly slept all night as his thoughts and his heart fought. He wasn't so sure if hitting the road was what he needed now.

Maybe Seth was right. Maybe if he didn't make a stand at some point, he'd never come to peace with the things he didn't want to face. Was it all about denial? Was the entire past six years of helping others simply denial on his part?

The thought pained him.

He'd believed he was helping others out of a good heart when it may have simply been a coward's way of not facing issues—point-blank and real… He'd not faced the pain and resentment he felt eating him up inside over Lori. God should have spared her like He'd spared Catherine Elizabeth…and all those whom Cole had witnessed survive disaster and illness. God should have spared Lori.

He set his saddlebag on the porch and sank down on the steps. He knew Seth was trying to make him step up into his responsibility…and this ranch was his responsibility as much as it was Seth's. But could he stay? Did he want to stay?

It was eight o'clock. He'd planned to be on the road by six so he'd get an early start—or was it to avoid saying goodbye to anyone? He'd told Seth he was going to church, but he'd decided it would be better not to. He'd already said goodbye to Susan the day before at the clinic.

And he'd driven away from her with rocks in his stomach.

Susan. He was leaving her behind. His heart ached thinking about that.

He hadn't told any of that to Seth when he'd ridden out to give him the news that he was leaving.

It would have only made Seth more determined to keep him here. Cole grabbed his bag. It was time to go.

Time to stop thinking and ride.

Susan hadn't slept a wink. She'd paced back and forth all night and the fact was, she couldn't let Cole go. She'd not had the power to keep her mom or her dad with her—but she had the power to at least try to keep Cole in her life. No, she *couldn't* let him go.

Not without telling him that she loved him.

Not without at least trying to get him to stay.

The ladies were right. She'd fought for everything she'd ever achieved. Her daddy had taught her to set a goal and go after it. That meant keeping the love of her life in her life, too!

Storming off the porch, Susan had her truck door open and one foot on the floorboard when Catherine Elizabeth lumbered down the steps.

"Stay, girl. I can't take you with me," Susan called and hopped inside. A pitiful howl filled the air. "Not now," she groaned. She'd waited so late that she was afraid Cole had already ridden out of town. She didn't expect him to hang around for church. He'd realize that if he went everyone would be on his case to get him to stay. So she figured he'd probably rode off toward the sunrise. But there might be a chance that he hadn't.

She didn't have time to waste. But Catherine Elizabeth looked so sad, and lonely... Jumping out, Susan jogged over to the driver's side and opened the door. "Come on, girl. Let's go get 'my man,' as Mrs. A. calls him." And as she wanted him to be.

Catherine Elizabeth ambled over and waited as Susan bent to lift her. It was like trying to lift a cow all by herself. "Okay, I can do this," she gasped, adjusting her hold and giving it another try. Nothing happened.

Susan had to get the dog into the truck. Time was of the essence. She was a vet. She lifted animals onto exam tables all the time. She should be able to lift Catherine Elizabeth, too. Wrapping one arm beneath the overweight dog and the other around her back legs,

Susan took a deep breath and *heaved*... "Don't want to hurt your feelings," she grunted as she managed to lift her, "but we're putting you on a diet while Mrs. A. is recouping."

"A smart woman once told me to lift with my knees. Maybe it'll work for you."

The slow drawl behind her had Susan almost dropping poor Catherine Elizabeth on her well-rounded bottom. Thankfully Cole stepped from behind Susan and rescued the sweet dog before injury happened.

"Where did you come from?" Susan's heart was thundering in her chest as she looked at him. All tall and broad-shouldered, he looked so rock-solid—in a much better way than Catherine Elizabeth—as he hugged the old dog. "Wait a minute." She glanced around. She hadn't heard a truck or motorcycle drive up and, examining her surroundings, she saw neither. "How did you get here?"

"Seems I ran out of gas," Cole said, gently placing the plump pooch on the ground and giving her a gentle pat before he straightened.

"Where?"

"About five miles from your turnoff."

"But…" Susan's brows dipped—*surely, the ladies did not do this*. A vivid image of the ladies on a covert mission flashed to the front of her mind. "How?"

He studied her with light eyes. "I was too intent on leaving town that I forgot to fill up."

"Thank goodness." Norma Sue and Esther Mae hadn't snuck out to his house and drained his gas tank.

He grinned. "Really. And why exactly are you so happy that I forgot to fill up with gas?"

"No, I meant—" She stumbled to a halt, about to

deny that she hadn't meant that when in fact she'd meant it very much. It didn't matter that he had just confirmed he'd been in so much of a hurry to leave town—to leave her—that he'd forgotten to put gas in his tank. It didn't matter. The only thing that mattered was that he was here.

"I meant thank-goodness-you-didn't-get-out-of-town-before-I-could-tell-you-that-I-love-you," she blurted out at the speed of light. "I realized I couldn't let you leave town without telling you. I was on my way to try to stop you when you walked up. I know you don't like my lifestyle. I know you loved Lori. And I know you love what you do. It's impossible and crazy for me to even think—" She halted, as a big grin spread across Cole's face.

"Thank goodness." His eyes seemed to caress her face as he smiled at her.

"What?"

He took a step closer and placed his hands on her shoulders. "Thank goodness you love me," he said. "Because I love you, too, and I would have hated walking that entire five miles just to have you tell me it was for nothing."

"Are you sure?"

Cole laughed and tugged her into his arms. "Yes, I'm sure I love you. I've never been more sure of anything in all of my life. I was leaving and made it as far as the crossroads and I couldn't do it. I knew that this time I didn't want to leave. I was running just like Seth said. I was angry at God for not answering my prayers and too stubborn to see what a beautiful gift He'd given me in knowing Lori and loving her. You helped me see that. But I realized when I got to the crossroads that God was giving me another gift…you. I certainly don't deserve a second chance at happiness, especially since dummy me was trying to run away from you. I prayed all the way here that you would tell me you loved me, too."

"Oh, Cole," Susan whispered. "You prayed for me."

Cole took her face in his hands, so tenderly she wanted to cry—and she did as a tear slipped down her cheek. He kissed it away, his lips warm and gentle brushed across her cheek, and caused her breath to catch in her chest.

"I prayed all the way here, believing that God had a plan when He'd brought us together. *Believing* just as you'd showed me when you prayed for Catherine Elizabeth. I knew I didn't deserve it and I was willing to accept it if you told me you didn't care for me. But I believed with all my heart that you would love me, too."

"Oh, Cole. I love you so much."

"Even if I'm hardheaded when it comes to you taking care of yourself?"

Susan cherished the feel of his arms wrapped about her. It was a feeling she knew she would never grow tired of. "I decided I love having someone to watch over me. Someone who loves me enough to want what is best for me—"

"Then in that case I'm your man. But I'm also going to want to support you in what you do. I'm proud of what you do, Susan. Don't ever think I'm not. I just want you safe and I want to help you in any way I can if you'll have me," he murmured, his lips only a breath from hers.

Susan smiled against his lips and wrapped her hands around his neck. "I'll take you for the rest of our lives," she said, and then as his lips claimed hers she sighed with happiness. In Cole's sweet embrace, with his heart beating next to hers, Susan knew God had answered her prayers and given her the blessing of a lifetime. He'd given her her very own forever cowboy. And He was giving her a future with a man who would challenge her, as she would him. One she knew would never be boring…and as she kissed him back with a love deep and true, Susan knew she wouldn't have wanted it any other way.

Epilogue

"So when's the wedding date?" Wyatt asked, his piercing dark eyes locked on to Cole. His big brother had *finally* arrived in town a week after Susan had agreed to marry Cole.

Today was the grand opening of the Mule Hollow Veterinary Clinic and the entire town was here. It was like a small-time festival with all the door prizes and refreshments and fun going on. He'd been slapped on the back so much he thought he might need to be the first in line for the beautiful veterinarian's tender loving care…not a bad idea.

"We're looking at the dates and we're pretty sure next month we're having a wedding. You're going to make it, I hope."

"Wouldn't miss it for the world. You're happy, aren't you, little brother?"

Cole smiled. He couldn't help it. "I'm happier than I've ever been. Thanks for insisting I come home when you did. God really seems to have had everything worked out with the way Susan and I met that first night. And then when the contractor up and quit like he did— Why are you grinning like that?" Cole asked, recognizing the mischievous glint in Wyatt's eyes. Growing up, he'd seen that look often.

"Tank told me he had a great time on his fishing trip—"

"Whoa, wait a minute! *Tank*. Is that the same Tank you used to play poker with?"

Wyatt hiked a jet-black brow. "Way back before I saw the light—in my wayward days, I made a bundle off that man. Seems only right that I give him a trip of a lifetime to make everything up to him."

Cole couldn't believe what he was hearing…then again, yes, he could. This was Wyatt, after all. "It was you all along! I should have known."

"I told you I'd do whatever it took to get you home," he said, clapping him on the shoulder. "When I saw you and Susan at Seth's wedding, my mind started working. I figured you two were made for each other…and I couldn't pass up the opportunity to bring you together."

Cole laughed. He met Susan's gaze across the room. They'd come a long way and were looking forward to the life before them. He'd thanked God every day for her. "How could I be mad when I have Susan standing over there looking at me with all that love?" And it was true. "Now, if you'll excuse me, I believe I'm going to go hug my beautiful fiancée—but watch out, big brother. What's best for two Turner men is better for all three—so you're next in line."

"Hold on there, Cole. Wait just a minute!"

Cole chuckled and left his brother sputtering behind him. God was going to have to step in and be the matchmaker for Wyatt because Cole had other things on his mind… Susan was going to be his priority. And besides,

Cole knew it was going to take one very special woman to put up with Wyatt, and only God could be the matchmaker where that one was concerned.

Boy, would it be fun to sit back and watch.

* * * * *

Dear Reader,

Hello—I'm so glad you decided to spend some time with me and the gang in Mule Hollow! I always try to make it a great place for you to kick up your heels and escape for a few hours.

Her Forever Cowboy is the first of three books about the Turner men. I introduced them in *Lone Star Cinderella*, which was about Seth Turner. I love the background story in that book and felt compelled to continue the story line of Cole, Wyatt and Chance, the cowboys whose roots go six generations deep in the Mule Hollow ranch they own. We've named the three books Men of Mule Hollow, and I hope you'll be on the lookout for them.

In *Her Forever Cowboy,* Cole and Susan are both hurting and struggling to heal—both are ready to move forward. As always, I love showing that God's timing is always the best timing. I pray that, whatever you may be going through, you'll trust God to take care of you and to comfort you. He loves you and has a wonderful plan for you!

Until next time, live, laugh, love and seek God with all your heart!

Debra Clopton

YULETIDE COWBOY

When I am afraid, I will trust in you. In God, whose word I praise, in God I trust; I will not be afraid. What can mortal man do to me?
—*Psalms* 56:3–4

This book is dedicated to my home church:
Cowboy Church of Leon County.
Thank you all so much for your huge hearts!
You are changing lives…mine included!

A special thank-you and dedication
to our pastor, Tuffy Lofton—you are
a cowboy preacher with a true heart for God.

Chapter One

Chance Turner stepped from his truck as country singer Craig Morgan crooned "Small Town USA" on the radio. He was home in Mule Hollow, Texas, which definitely fit the song's positive image of small-town life in the USA. A smile tugging at his lips, he reached into the truck bed for the large box his sister-in-law had instructed him to deliver to the church.

Colorful strings of Christmas lights overflowed from the box. Melody was late for work, she'd said, and didn't have time to deliver the lights to the church secretary. That had been her pretense anyway, but Chance had no illusions about why she'd asked him to run the errand for her. It was the church.

She wanted him to be as near the church as possible. She had hopes that being here would fix "his problem"…if only it were that easy. He could have told her that seeing the church, being on the premises, wouldn't help him. Instead he'd done as Melody asked—it was easier that way. The last thing he wanted to do was talk about his problem.

And he didn't want to think about it either.

Pushing the dark thoughts aside he focused on delivering the lights. He'd get this done, then he'd head back to the ranch, back to the solitude he'd come home to find. Just him and his horse, and the land that had been in his family for six generations. He wasn't the first Turner to contemplate the state of his life riding in the sanctuary of the vast Turner family ranch. Sanctuary—not exactly something he deserved. Not when he couldn't see past the guilt eating at him.

Still, right now he needed what the solitude of the ranch offered him.

He wanted to ride across the pasture, just him and his horse…but, before he could saddle up, he had lights to deliver.

Hefting the box into his arms he strode toward the quaint white church he'd attended off and on for the better part of his youth. His boots crunched on the white rock and his spurs jangled as he headed down the sidewalk toward the office. The squeals of kids' laughter, shrill with excitement, rode the chilly November wind. Chance had just reached the door when, like bulls out of the chute, two small boys pounded around the edge of the building. Trailing behind them was a monster of a dog.

He tried to sidestep the first kid but he was already on a collision course, and the rest was a blur. One-two-three he was hit by the first kid, fighting for balance as the second kid tangled up with them, and the horse of a dog launched himself at the box of lights in Chance's arms. That was the kicker.

Boots up, head back, Chance sailed straight to the ground, landing like a hundred-and-eighty-pound sack of bad luck!

* * *

"Oh, my goodness," Lynn Perry gasped when she opened the door of the church office to find her twins and a long-legged cowboy sprawled on the grass. Rushing forward she grabbed Gavin by his belt and hauled him off Chance, setting him to the side where he stood giggling as she reached for Jack. The poor cowboy was on his own with Tiny, though. The big dog was all over him like butter on toast.

"Tiny, get off of him." Lynn grabbed the dog by his collar and tugged. Nothing happened. "Move, Tiny, you big bag of rocks. Come…*on*." The beautiful, slate-gray Catahoula had a pale buff face outlined in rich chestnut. The giant blinked his silver-blue eyes at her, clueless as to what he was doing wrong. After all, he was simply having a great time sitting on top of the new cowboy play-toy.

Looking less than pleased, Chance scowled as he pushed the dog off him.

"Are you all right?" Lynn asked, holding Tiny back when he flopped his tongue out and made a last-ditch effort to swipe the cowboy's face. "I'm so sorry," she said. The last thing she'd expected to find when she'd heard her kids squealing was Chance Turner, rodeo preacher, beneath the pileup of her twin boys and their dog. Poor man was covered in Christmas lights, too.

In the two years that she'd lived in Mule Hollow the handsome preacher had come home only recently to perform his cousin's wedding. But here he sat sprawled on the sidewalk, his serious green eyes looking through the curtain of Christmas lights hanging from his cowboy hat. Thankfully, those gorgeous eyes were crinkling around the edges as his lips turned up in a smile.

"We had a bit of a wreck," he drawled, instantly sending butterflies into flight in her chest.

Startled, she ignored the response. "A wreck?"

"Yeah, Momma," Gavin offered, grinning like an opossum. "We done run him down. Tiny didn't mean to do it."

Jack looked intently up at her. "It was an accident."

She had to smile and Chance did, too. His lips hitched to one side in that signature Turner grin he shared with his three cousins, a bit crooked with a hint of mischief. Her pulse skittered crazily when his eyes met hers in shared humor.

"Well." She swallowed hard, pushing Tiny out of the way and the frog in her throat, too. "I'm certainly glad it was intentional."

He wore a tan insulated jacket, cowboy-cut at the hips. Tall and lean with dark good looks and a strong jawline, he looked especially cute as he tugged the lights off him. At her words he cocked a dark brow.

"I mean, it *wasn't* intentional," she protested.

He chuckled as he rose to his feet in a smooth motion. "I know. I just got in their way when they came around the corner." He shook his head and lights slid to his shoulders—the boys giggled.

Mortified, she went into action and reached for the lights. "Here, let me help." She began untangling the strings of lights, without much success. "I still don't understand. How a big man like you ended up on the ground? I mean, they're little—" Her mouth was saying things her brain was trying to stop.

"Yup, I do tend to be clumsy. My momma used to say the Lord gave me two left feet when He passed them out."

"Oh, dear, I didn't mean to say that." If the man had a clumsy bone in his body her name was Reba McEntire!

He chuckled and the sound made her feel all warm and happy, like drinking hot cocoa—where in the world had her brain gone?

Gavin stepped up. "We just come around the corner, Momma, and *boom,* there he was." He used exuberant hand gestures to help explain the situation.

"We didn't mean to knock him down." Jack shook his dark head, his big blue eyes looking suddenly worried. "You all right, mister? Tiny's sorry."

Tiny was waltzing about them happily.

"I'm fine. But you two sure pack a punch. Are y'all football players? Or maybe your dog is." That won him a round of giggles.

A crimson tide of humiliation crept warmly up her cheeks when Chance's gaze locked with hers.

"I'm so sorry. I can't believe they knocked you off your feet. As big as you are—I mean. Well, you are a man." Most definitely a man, no doubt about that.

His eyes crimped around the edges and it seemed almost as though he could read her thoughts. Her crazy-unable-to-understand-them-herself thoughts! No mistake about it, despite not wanting to be, she was attracted to Chance Turner. Heart-thumpingly, breathlessly attracted. Okay, so she wasn't dead.

"Last time I looked in the mirror I was a man. But you've got two dynamos here. They took me out like pros with the help of their linebacker there."

Tiny sat on his haunches and cocked his big head as if he knew they were speaking about him.

She scanned the cowboy for damage. Though he was a bit rumpled there were no tears in his long-sleeved shirt, no rips in his jeans. "Are you hurt?" she asked anyway.

"My pride is stomped on, but I don't have any broken bones."

Lynn laughed with a mixture of relief and nervousness. "I guess for a former bull rider like you that is a little hard to swallow."

"You're a *bull rider?*" both boys gushed in unison. They loved bull riders. Something she wasn't thrilled about in the least. To Lynn, riding a bull was right up there with swimming in a shark tank.

"I was a bull rider," he said to the boys, then cocked his head slightly toward her. "Have we met?"

Lynn realized her mistake. "No, not exactly. I'm Lynn Perry. I saw you at Wyatt and Amanda's wedding but we weren't introduced. I heard though that you used to be a bull rider before you became a preacher. They need all the prayers they can get," she added, and realized she'd probably stepped on his toes a bit as he stiffened before taking the hand she held out to him.

She was instantly hit by the strength in his large hand as he wrapped it around hers. Warm pinpoints of awareness prickled across her skin at the touch of his calloused palm. In his eyes she saw a spark of recognition—as if he felt the same sensation—she pulled her hand from his as her pulse kicked up a notch.

"It's nice to meet you, Lynn. I'm Chance, but you already know that." If he was startled by her reaction, he hid it well, tugging a strand of lights from his shoulder as if he didn't notice anything out of the ordinary. "I guess these lights are for the church? Melody, my sister-in-law, said I was to bring them here and give them to the secretary. Is that you?"

"That's me." Had Melody meant them for her? They hadn't discussed lights. "I didn't know we were expecting them though."

"Are they *ours?*" Gavin's eyes widened as he looked up at Chance in awe.

"We need some lights, for our house," Jack piped up, beaming at the assortment. "We don't got none do we, Momma?"

Any other time she would have corrected his English but not now. It had been a hard month getting moved from the shelter to the house she was renting. Settling in and making it a home had cost more than she'd planned, and with Christmas right around the corner money was tighter than ever. She'd been saving every penny she could over the last two years while they lived at No Place Like Home, the women's shelter from abuse. Most of her savings had gone toward rent, deposit and getting all the utilities turned on. Christmas lights hadn't been in the budget and yet the boys talked about them all the time. Trying not to dwell on what she couldn't give the boys, she focused on what she had accomplished and quickly moved past the tug of feeling sorry for herself. She refused to give in to those types of feelings when they snuck up on her. Instead she smiled at the boys.

"Let's pick them up. We'll put them inside the office until I talk to Melody and find out what they're for."

Gavin and Jack whispered to each other, then stared up at Chance.

"You're a preacher?" Jack asked.

Chance hesitated before answering, which seemed odd to Lynn.

"I'm taking a break, but yes, I'm a rodeo preacher."

Chance knelt and began rolling up one of the strands of lights into a ball.

Lynn did the same and each boy grabbed a strand of his own, imitating exactly the way Chance was coiling his.

"You boys are doing a great job." Chance flipped the overturned box upright and laid his coiled lights inside. The boys followed suit. They were all grins and eyes full of awe…she understood it. Despite her misgivings, she was attracted to this handsome cowboy. She dropped her lights into the box and gave herself a talking-to—she had no interest in men. Not yet. She'd come a long way since she'd escaped with her sons to the shelter over two years ago, but she hadn't come far enough along to think about bringing a man into the mix. She was building a life with her boys and that was all she cared about doing.

That was what she needed.

Gavin dropped another messy coil into the box, then put his hands on his hips and looked Chance straight in the eyes. "If you're a preacher we need one."

Jack nodded. "In the worstest of ways."

Lynn smiled at his word choice. Jack had heard Applegate Thornton, one of the more colorful older men, saying that at church on Sunday.

"Yeah, the worst," Gavin repeated. "Are you going to fill the puppet?"

Chance laughed in a rich baritone. "No, I'm not preaching right now. I'm taking some time off." The box was full and he picked it up. "Where would you like me to put this?"

She was startled by his answer. "In here." She led the way into the office and he followed her inside as the boys trailed in behind him. She couldn't remember them being so taken by a man before.

He set the box on the table and looked around the office. It was a cozy room with a dark oak desk that gleamed from the polish she applied to it every week. The double bookshelves were full of reference books for a new pastor, who would call this his office when he showed up.

She wondered what Chance thought about the room. He didn't quite fit here. He was too rugged, too masculine—not that a pastor couldn't be both those things. It was simply that *rodeo pastor* fit Chance Turner. "Thank you for bringing the Christmas lights to town," she said, not sure what else to say.

He swept his hat from his head, revealing jet-black hair with a hint of wave. "You're welcome." His gaze was strong and steady as it took her in, causing her pulse to drum faster—despite her will. There was a charge in the room between them that left her breathless. He broke the moment by letting his gaze drift about the office again.

Gathering her wits she took a deep, shaky breath. "It's a bit sad to me." She felt disconcerted by him but tried to seem unaffected. "It just seems wrong for this office not to belong to someone. Ever since Pastor Allen retired we've had a problem finding a pastor who feels called to fill our pulpit."

"That's what I've heard. The right man will come, though," he said, then added, "in God's time."

"Why cain't a rodeo preacher preach here?" Gavin asked, moving to stand right beside Chance so he could look straight up at him.

"They can if they aren't preaching a rodeo," Chance explained.

"Are you preaching a rodeo this week?" Jack asked. For nearly five he and his brother were pretty smart.

She didn't miss the troubled look that shadowed Chance's blue eyes. He shifted uncomfortably as if biding time while he searched for answers. Odd.

She decided to help him out. "Hey, guys, why don't y'all go back outside and play. I'll be out in just a minute. And don't run over any more visitors."

"Okay, Momma," Jack said solemnly. "You want ta come swing with us?" The question was his way of making up to Chance for knocking him down. A child's innocence.

Chance looked surprised and a little pleased. "I'll come watch you before I leave. First I need to talk to your mom."

Jack nodded. "You promise?"

"I promise."

Gavin stopped at the door, holding it open for his twin. "We'll be waitin'. Remember you promised."

Chance smiled at her as they stampeded off but their singsong voices told her how much a promise meant to them.

"You've got good boys," he said the minute the door closed.

"I think so. Rambunctious, but then that's just boys. So, I know you said you weren't preaching right now. But are you doing weddings? I know you did Wyatt and Amanda's. And my friend is really needing a preacher right now."

He shook his head almost too quickly. "No. I'm not doing any pastoral duties right now."

"I guess I didn't think about a pastor taking a vacation," Lynn murmured, not exactly sure how to handle the information. "From what I've heard you're a dedicated man of the Lord. It's just one wedding and it would mean so much to her."

"I'm sorry but I'm taking time off."

He didn't say the words unkindly, but still the man acted as if she'd just asked him to stand in front of an oncoming train. "Maybe if you met Stacy and Emmett. They are—"

"I'm sorry, I really am, but I'm taking time off right now," he said and his tone firmly shut the door on that discussion.

Baffled, she was at a loss for words. The man wasn't thirty yet and he'd been a rodeo pastor for about four years—at least that was what she'd heard someone say down at the diner. And he'd seemed so content when she'd watched him at Wyatt's wedding. Maybe he just needed a rest. Pastors took time off, didn't they? She didn't know what else to say so she just waved a hand toward the lights. "Then, I guess that's a wrap. Thanks for bringing this by. I'll give Melody a call and find out who they're for." She picked up her purse and strode to the door. The man had a right to do what he wanted, but his refusal, without even hearing Stacy's story, irritated her. Really fried her bacon, and that didn't happen often. After all, this was sweet Stacy she was talking about.

"Look, I'm sorry."

She couldn't help hiking a brow at him. "I'm sure you are. Don't let it bother you. I'm sorry my boys accosted you."

"They didn't mean to. I should have been watching out. It was a hard shot to my pride, that's for certain."

He held the door for her and she walked past him, more than a little aware of him as she went.

"I can lock up. You go ahead."

He pulled his hat from his head and met her gaze full on. "Is it all right for me to go watch the boys swing for a minute like I promised?"

"Sure." Some of her irritation at him eased as she watched him saunter off in the direction of the boys' shouts of laughter. Chance Turner might not want to pastor right now, but he'd promised her boys he'd watch them swing and he was doing just that.

Such a promise was worth more than most people could even fathom to a pair of boys who'd never had that from their dad.

Lynn didn't want to think about that though. She took a deep breath, walked to the side of the building and watched the looks on their little faces as Chance strode their way. When their eyes lit up she had to fight the lump in her throat and a sudden flood of tears from a past that she had no intention of revisiting.

When the women's shelter in L.A. had burned she'd been thrilled that it had relocated to the sleepy ranching town of Mule Hollow, Texas. Here the cowboys and small-town folks had rallied around them and made a safe haven like nothing she'd ever dreamed of. Her little boys had been too young to remember the life they'd been living before she'd gotten them out. Here in Mule Hollow they had role model after role model of what real men were supposed to be like. Here her sons had the chance to grow up with loving, loyal, honest men and women surrounding them.

What they didn't have was a father. And they wouldn't. Lynn had already come to understand that falling in love wasn't an option she was willing to explore. The safest way to give her boys a good life was to keep it uncomplicated. Besides, she didn't have what it took to cross that line and start looking for love. To love meant to trust and trust wasn't in her anymore. Not trusting with her heart anyway.

But… Chance Turner was intriguing still.

Lynn's heart fluttered as her boys squealed in delight when he said something to them. The flutter just proved that she was still a woman who could appreciate a good-looking, nice man when she saw him. And Chance Turner was a nice man. He'd be nicer if he hadn't refused to perform Stacy's wedding.

Intriguing or not, he was just one more friendly cowboy that her boys could look up to. He was no different than Sheriff Brady Cannon or Deputy Zane Cantrell. Or Dan Dawson or any of the wonderful, Christian men of the community who'd stepped up to be father figures for the kids at the women's shelter.

He spread his legs shoulder-width apart and locked his arms across his chest, watching Gavin and Jack. *Why was he not preaching?* The question niggled at the back of her mind. None of her business though, right?

Right!

"Okay, boys, it's time to hit the road," she called. No use making Chance watch them swing for too long and no reason for her to stand here contemplating issues that had nothing to do with her…except she wished he would consider marrying Stacy and Emmett. *It's none of your business, Lynn.*

"But, Momma—"

"No buts, young man," she said to Gavin. "It's time to head home." She suddenly wanted to grab the boys

and hurry away before she opened her mouth and butted
in where she shouldn't. The man had a right to preach
or not preach. Besides, this was a traditional small-
town church. Chance was a rodeo preacher. He moved
along with the rodeo circuit, preaching and mentoring
the cowboys who couldn't make it to church because of
the rodeo's schedule. It was an honorable calling. She
liked the idea of what he did…still, while he was here,
couldn't he do one wedding?

What could that hurt?

*Give it up, Lynn, the man made it clear he was tak-
ing time off.* Mouth shut, she headed toward her car.
She had to bite her tongue again as Chance reached his
truck and tipped his hat at her after telling her boys to
have a great day.

"Momma, we like him," Jack said the minute he
climbed into the seat and buckled his seat belt.

"Yeah," Gavin added, meeting her gaze in the rearview. "Maybe he can teach me how to bull ride."

"There won't be any bull riding for you, mister."

"Aw, Momma. I ain't gonna git myself kilt or anything. Chance ain't dead and neither is Bob or Trace."

Bob Jacobs had been a bull fighter and Trace Craw-
ford had ridden bulls, too. Both men had survived and
many other cowboys around town had, too. Still the
thought of her little boys growing up to be bull riders
didn't sit well with her. "You concentrate on being a little boy and leave the bull riding to the men."

"Aw, Momma, you ain't got to worry. Don'tcha know
I'm gonna be the best there ever was."

The hair at the back of her neck prickled but she decided the best thing for now was to let it go. The less

said on this subject the better. At least she prayed that was so.

"Well, sugar baby, I think you're the best there ever was already."

"What about me, Momma?" Jack asked.

She turned in her seat. "You know I'm talking about you, too. God must have thought I was pretty special to have blessed me with the two best boys in all of the world."

Chapter Two

"So how are you? Did you get settled into the stage-coach house all right?" Wyatt asked.

Chance hadn't wasted any time getting back to the ranch after his meeting with Lynn Perry and her twins. He'd just climbed into the saddle when Wyatt rode into the yard.

"I'm fine. And yes, I'm settled. How are you? You're looking good. And I'm happy to see you in the saddle again."

Wyatt had insisted on saddling a horse and riding with him. Wyatt sitting in the saddle was a good thing to see, since less than six months ago after his plane crash he'd been relegated to a wheelchair.

Wyatt's lip hitched as he urged his horse forward. "I have the best physical therapist in the world."

Wyatt's wife was his PT. They'd met when she'd come to help him recover. Chance had performed their wedding just a few months earlier and had never expected to be here now. "You don't look like you're doing all right," Wyatt said, shooting Chance one of his penetrating looks. "So don't tell me you're fine. Look,

Chance, I know you feel responsible somehow for that bull rider's death but you know as well as I do that it's a profession full of risks."

Perspiration beaded beneath the brim of his hat and his fingers clenched the reins too tightly. Willing himself to relax, Chance studied the flat pasture and welcomed the cold wind on his cheeks and the sting in his eyes. It gave him a barrier to the bitter chill that ran through him each time he thought of Randy. How could he sweat bullets and feel cold to the bone at the same time? *Guilt, that's how.* Gut-wrenching, soul-shredding guilt could make him sick as a dog it tore him up so bad.

"Talk to me, Chance."

"I let him die. Nothing you can say will convince me that I didn't do what I should have done." *I'm just not ready,* had been Randy's last words to Chance before he'd climbed over the rail and settled onto the bull's back. For the last five years Chance had held services every Sunday morning before a rodeo and then he'd stood on the platform with any cowboy who asked. Randy had wanted him there until a few weeks before his death. He'd stopped attending services and avoided him for weeks prior to his last ride. Instead of seeking Randy out, Chance had let other things distract him from going to Randy and showing his concern. Chance knew he was hanging with a rough crowd. He'd known Randy was in danger and yet he hadn't gone the extra mile to try and help him.

"Randy didn't give his life to the Lord. Never accepted the gift of salvation that Jesus offers every person." Wyatt listened intently. "It haunts me." Chance lowered his head for a minute with the weight of the guilt. "I didn't step up when he needed me the most."

"But you were there on his last ride."

He jerked his head up. "Yeah, I was. But he still wasn't ready to commit. I don't know why he asked me that night. It's like he knew in his gut that his time was running out but he couldn't do it. I don't know, Wyatt. I have been over it and over it a thousand times in my mind and I can't figure out what I did wrong. I presented him with every verse and concept about salvation that I could come up with. And I always come up empty…and he always comes up dead. I can't shake knowing that I should have done more. At least stopped him from getting on that bull when I knew he might be doing drugs. It—"

"You can't hold yourself accountable for that."

But he did, and the assortment of prescription drugs that had been found in Randy's gear only made it worse. "I should have stepped in. Rumor had it that it he'd gotten hooked on painkillers after his shoulder injury. His eyes were glazed when I looked at him the moment before the gate opened. And I didn't say anything."

Saying the words was hard for him. Chance knew that logically Randy's death wasn't his fault but that didn't change the way he felt.

"What could you have said? The ride was already in motion. You have to let it go, Chance. I'm telling you it's not your fault." Wyatt's expression was etched with determination. That was Wyatt, always wanting to charge in and save the day. But not this time.

Chance gave a short shake of his head and stared into the distant horizon. He'd messed up. There was no way to wash Randy's blood from his hands. "By omission I let that kid die both physically and spiritually. How am I supposed to live with that?"

"That isn't true," Wyatt snapped, his eyes flashing. "It isn't. You aren't a superhero. The kid was on drugs and he was avoiding you. I get that you hold yourself up to a higher standard, but come on, Chance, let it go."

"I can't, Wyatt. And until I can come to terms with it, there's no way I can stand up in front of a bunch of cowboys or a congregation feeling the way I do. Knowing what I've done."

"Lynn, you need to bid on a bachelor tomorrow night."

Lynn looked up from the centerpiece she was arranging for one of the many tables set up in rows in the community center. Several ladies were scattered about decorating the room for tomorrow night's fundraiser for the women's shelter.

"I'm helping with the benefit, Norma Sue, but I'm not taking part. I've already told you that."

Norma Sue Jenkins hooked her thumb around the strap of her ample overalls, tilted her kinky gray head to the side and grunted, "Hogwash."

"Now, Norma, none of that," Adela Ledbetter-Green admonished in a gentle voice that always made Lynn think of the sugar and spice and everything nice that little girls were made of. God's goodness and grace just radiated from her with a sincerity that made everyone around her feel happier just by being there. It was that loving, sweet spirit that could be misleading to some at times. Because within the elegant, almost fragile-looking form of Adela beat the strong heart of a woman of wisdom, unafraid to speak her mind and give advice and direction whenever she felt the need. Obviously she felt the need, and for that Lynn was grateful.

"Thank you," Lynn said, more than glad to have her support.

Adela smiled and studied her with vibrant peacock-blue eyes. "Well, dear, I didn't say I didn't agree with Norma Sue. I do. I simply think she should be more tempered in her encouragement."

And here Lynn had been thinking all these good thoughts about her!

"Honey, don't look at me so surprised. We just love you to death and want you to be happy."

"I am happy. I just don't want to be pushed." Not even by these ladies she loved so much. And she knew how they could push when they got it in their heads that a woman needed to be matched up and married off. "There will be plenty of women here for y'all to mix and match without me."

"But what about your boys?" Esther Mae Wilcox, their third partner in crime, huffed as she scooted from the table on the other side of Norma Sue. She wore a red velour warm-up suit that clashed totally with her bright, reddish-orange hair. "Don't you think it's time to at least go on *one* date?" At her impatient tone she glanced Adela's way. "Yes, I know I'm pushing when we said we were going to go at this nice and easy. But Adela, I just can't." She hit Lynn with her green eyes. "You were the strongest woman who climbed off that bus two years ago. You have jumped into life here in town with ease and have given your moral support and encouragement to all the other women who have passed through the doors of No Place Like Home. You are always working to help others move forward with their lives and yet you don't."

Lynn couldn't deny any of this. It was true. She'd attended every class at the shelter on overcoming being a battered wife. Every class on coping. Every class under any name, anything that would help her be the woman she needed to be for her boys. She could tell others how to do it and she could help her friends when they needed her. Outwardly she seemed to have her act together and so everyone assumed she did. "Esther Mae, I just moved my boys into their very own home. That's moving forward. I'm happy. I'm content and I'm not bidding on a bachelor."

"Did I hear you say you weren't bidding?" Lacy Brown Matlock asked, coming up behind Lynn. The hugely pregnant hair stylist pulled out a chair beside Lynn and eased down into it. "I'm telling y'all that the doc says this little gal of mine is coming no sooner than two weeks out, but mark my word it'll be sooner rather than later. This baby has a mind of her own and is trying to kick her way out right now!"

Relieved to have someone else join in the conversation, Lynn chuckled. "She's independent like her momma." And they didn't come any more independent than Lacy. She'd moved to Mule Hollow after reading the matchmakers' ad in the newspaper. Just like that, the spunky blonde had followed her heart, determined that if women answered the ad for wives they would not only need their hair and nails done to catch their men, but also they just might need the Lord. Lynn had arrived at the shelter, spirit verging on broken, and gained much inspiration from Lacy. She also knew that Lacy was as much a cupid as the other three ladies.

"*Independent* is the truth," Norma Sue echoed. "I have a feeling Lacy's baby girl is going to hit the ground running."

Esther Mae grinned. "None of us will be able to keep up with the live wire she's destined to be."

"Lacy will," Adela added, reaching across to pat Lacy's arm. "You do look tired though."

She did. Lynn could see fatigue in the high-octane blue of Lacy's eyes. She was glad for the distraction from the subject of Chance, but she wished Lacy didn't look so weary. "Are you sleeping?"

Lacy waved a cherry-pink-tipped hand. "Sleep, what's that? I gave that up weeks ago." She laughed good-naturedly. "Clint says the baby is taking after me with its impetuous nature. We never know when she's going to settle down and when she's not. If I knew, then maybe I'd get some sleep. But when I lay down— at night or even for a little nap—she starts kicking."

"How's Clint holding up?" Lynn liked Clint. The hard-working cattleman sometimes looked at a loss for the things his wife came up with, but there was always a glowing admiration and love in his eyes…even though she'd seen a time or two when he was exasperated. Lacy tended to do that to people though. She got so caught up in what she envisioned for couples that she often acted before thinking things through. Despite that, he loved her…or actually, from what Lynn observed, he loved her because of it. Lynn wouldn't know what that was like. In her marriage she'd learned, slowly, not to voice her opinion, much less make an impulsive move. It had happened over time, practically sneaking up on her. The mental abuse started long before the beatings had occurred.

"Lynn, so you aren't going to bid?"

Lacy's words pelted through the fog of memory like

buckshot. "No. I'm not." She braced herself for Lacy to jump on the bandwagon.

"Too bad. I've been praying God would lead the right man to town for you and your boys." Lacy rubbed her extended belly and took a long breath.

"Lacy, you look really tired," Lynn said, concerned.

"Why don't you call it a night?" Norma Sue called out. "You're standing on your feet too much."

Lacy gave a smile—not her normally exuberant one but a smile nonetheless. "You've been talking to Sheri! I sit down when I need to—"

"Ha!" Sheri exclaimed from her perch on a ladder across the room. She cocked her spiky brown head to the side and looked down from where she'd been tacking up red-and-blue bandanna decorations. "You lie, Lacy Matlock! You don't sit down nearly as much as you should. If it were up to me I'd hog-tie you to a couch and make you stay there till our baby comes."

Lacy laughed. "Okay, okay, I get it. I've promised Clint that I'm going to start taking it easy so y'all relax and let me talk to Lynn." Lacy's eyes twinkled like they usually did when she was inspired. "You should bid on Chance. If not for yourself then for him. The man could use some distraction, I think. And you and your sweet boys might just be what the doc upstairs has in mind for him."

Inwardly Lynn groaned as all eyes returned to her. Lacy, the sneak, was trying to turn the tables on her. "I'm not bidding on Chance or anyone else…"

Chance pulled into a parking space in front of Sam's Diner and got out of the truck. There was no way he could come home and not drop by for breakfast at

Sam's. His cousins' trucks were lined up along the plank sidewalk and he knew he was running late. Hurrying, he pushed open the diner's heavy swinging door to find Lynn Perry standing on the other side. She was carrying a stack of carryout boxes and coffee in a paper cup. When she saw him she stopped in her tracks.

For a little while the day before, he'd rolled over their meeting in his head, and for the life of him he couldn't stop thinking about her. There was something about her that had edged under his collar and wouldn't let go. She was pretty, with her dark hair and shimmering midnight eyes, but he'd sensed a tough girl underneath her soft image. A tough girl determined to make it for herself and her boys. He liked that.

But she had a keep-your-distance wall erected around her and it was firmly in place right now, even though she was smiling at him.

He tipped his hat and gave her his best smile. "How are you this morning?"

"Great. How are you? I hope you didn't have any lingering aches and pains from yesterday. The boys really didn't mean to lay you out like that."

"I'm fine. Don't worry about me. I've been thrown from horses and bulls that make being taken out by two pint-sized four-year-olds a piece of cake."

She flinched prettily. "It still had to hurt, but I'm glad to see you aren't limping."

"Like I said before, only my pride was hurt."

"Yes, well, that's good—I mean it's good that's all that was hurt."

She sidestepped him to go out the door. "Here, let me," he said, pressing his back to the swinging door and opening it. She edged past him and he got the sweet scent of chocolate as she passed. He couldn't help but lean her way—just his luck, she turned and caught him.

"You, ahhh—" *What?* "You smell good. Is that chocolate?" *Slick, Turner. Way to stick a boot in your mouth.*

She colored rose-pink and he could tell he'd flustered her. He'd flustered himself! He could flirt with the best of them but it had been a while since he'd done it. He was about as rusty as a bucket of wet nails.

"I've been mixing chocolate bars since seven."

"Sweet. I mean, sweet job."

He figured she was probably ready to toss her coffee on him but she chuckled instead and walked off without another word. She probably thought he was a lost cause. Come to think of it, maybe he was. He watched her cross the street and push open the door to the candy store.

"You jest gonna stand thar and stare all day or ya gonna come in and have a bite to eat?"

He should have known Applegate Thornton would be sitting at his usual seat by the window. The old coot's booming voice probably could be heard across the street at the candy store. But at least it had Chance moving back inside and not standing halfway out on the sidewalk.

Ignoring the laughter from the table in the center of the room where his cousins were sitting, he strode to the window table to see App and his buddy Stanley Orr. "It's good to see you two are still holding down the fort. How's it going?"

Applegate grinned. "We ain't doin' nearly as good as you, son. Lynn was lookin' mighty sweet at you. Stanley, you ever seen Lynn lookin' at anybody like that?"

Stanley was slightly balding, plump and about

the easiest-going man Chance had ever been around. "Nope, can't say I have. You got a ticket to the steak dinner tomorrow night?"

"Yes, he has a ticket," Cole called from the table where he, Wyatt and Seth were watching Chance like hawks.

"I didn't buy a ticket."

"The ranch bought it for you," Seth said.

He took the fourth cane-backed chair at the table and sank into it. "I don't remember saying I wanted to attend a steak dinner."

"It's for a good cause," Seth said, taking a drink of his coffee, just as Sam, the owner of the diner, came striding toward their table with coffeepot in hand.

Small and wiry, with a quick step, Sam gave a hearty smile. "It's good ta see ya, son!" He set a coffee mug in front of Chance then shook his hand fiercely. "I was sure sorry ta hear about that bull rider. A cry'n shame is what that was." Shaking his head he poured coffee into the mug.

Chance wrapped his hands around the warm cup and felt the stab of deep regret. "Yeah, it was." All eyes were on him right now. He didn't want to discuss this.

"All you could be was there fer them if they needed you."

Chance met Sam's wise, gray eyes. How could he say that he hadn't been there for Randy? That in his heart of hearts he felt—

"Yor taken his death pretty hard, ain't ya?"

"Yes, he is," Cole answered for him.

Chance met his gaze across the table. His cousin had been running hard from his past for years after his fiancée's death. He was settled and happy now, thanks to a beautiful country vet named Susan. Cole was more content than he'd ever been and he and Susan were planning on starting a family soon. He'd been through a lot and found solace in helping disaster victims rebuild their homes during the time that he lost his way. Chance stared into the black coffee and wondered if that was what he'd done…lost his way. Ever since that horrible night he just couldn't think of himself as a pastor. It ate at him.

"That's what makes you good at what you do, Chance," Cole continued. "You care. You can't be a pastor, a shepherd to your sheep, and not care."

He felt as far away from being a shepherd as he could possibly get. Talk about a gulf…

"So don't keep beating yourself up with things that were out of your control," Seth, the control freak of the Turners, added. Chance looked at him in disbelief. Seth grinned. "Yeah, you heard right. That coming from me. I've been learning to let God handle things more. Not that it's been a bed of roses. Old habits are hard to break. But I'm working on it."

Chance had been handing out advice right and left, thinking he was making sense. Funny how it all seemed out of focus to him right now. "Can we talk about something else?" He didn't want to be rude but he felt like he was swinging zeros.

Sam squeezed his shoulder. "You were reckless but you always was one to take the world on yor shoulders. You got a big heart, Chance, even after all you went through. I gotta git back ta work, but you listen ta these boys and pull yourself out of this spot yor in. My eggs and bacon'll help ya. That all right by y'all?"

Everyone gave hearty agreement and Sam strode off

on his bowlegs. Chance knew Sam had been referring to Chance's childhood…he'd long ago come to terms with the fact that his dad had had better things to do than raise his son. Chance had been hard to deal with at an early age and his mother hadn't known what to do with him. He'd spent many summers here in Mule Hollow with his cousins. Their dad had loved him and treated him like his own, worked him hard and given him as much direction and love as he gave his own sons. But in his early teens Chance had rebelled against his dad's lack of interest and he'd hit the road…it had been a hard time. Too heavy for him to think about right now.

"Look, Chance, take it from my experience." Seth glanced around the table at his brothers. "God is in control even when we don't understand or don't agree. You've given us all that advice at some point in time."

"Yeah, I was pretty liberal handing it out, wasn't I?" He grunted, his mood taking a downhill turn and picking up speed.

Wyatt frowned. "You hand out great advice. I owe you and there's no two ways about it. God sent you to me with the advice I needed to hear just when I needed to hear it. I was about as low as a man can get and you helped me see what I needed to do to help Amanda. You just have to heed your own good advice and give this over to the Lord. We've all been where you're at, and it's not a fun place to be."

Applegate and Stanley had been pretending like they were engrossed in their morning checkers game—why they were even pretending was a mystery to Chance. For two men who couldn't hear they heard everything. It was a miracle beyond understanding, which made Chance smile—some much-needed relief from the downturn of this conversation. App spat a sunflower seed into the brass spittoon at his feet and Stanley did the same. Both hit the opening in the conversation dead-on.

"Sounds ta me like that steak dinner is jest the place you need ta be. Don't you thank so, Stanley?"

"Yup. Ain't nothin' like a good steak and the company of pretty women ta pull a man out of the dumps."

"A woman is the last thing I need to be thinking about."

"It ain't us that caused Lynn ta blush," App grunted. "You got a free ticket and a woebegone attitude that needs sprucing up. Put on some starched jeans and a crisp shirt, slap on a little smell-good and join the festivities."

Sam came out of the kitchen loaded down with plates. Chance had never been so glad to see a plate of eggs in all his life. Maybe putting food in their stomachs would get them off him.

"And speaking of other thangs," App drawled, his lean face cascading into a dour look. "We need a preacher. No two ways about it. I been thankin' that thar is the reason the good Lord brought you home." App had made it clear at Wyatt's wedding that he thought Chance should come home to Mule Hollow and become the pastor of the church. Chance had told him then that he didn't feel called to preach in a local church. That should have ended the discussion, but App wasn't known for letting go of things and it looked like he hadn't let this go either. "So what do ya say?"

Chance looked at the steaming breakfast plate and took a long, slow breath. So much for thinking the food was going to get him off the hot seat.

Chapter Three

The morning after Chance had flustered her by telling her she smelled sweet, Lynn *dreamed* about him! Oh yeah, but thankfully she was awakened from dreaming about the hunky, dark-haired bachelor by her horse of a dog, Tiny. Her unlikely hero bounded onto her bed and pounced on her with all four of his huge paws! The power of the attack knocked the wind *and* the dream right out of her.

"Thank you," she gasped, trying to get her breath back as she stared into Tiny's pale face. His excited are-you-ready-to-play eyes danced as he gaped at her. She relaxed, relieved to be awake...it wasn't unusual for her to have nightmares. Though they had slowly become less frequent and they were always about her ex-husband... Dreaming about Chance Turner was disturbing on an entirely different level. Thank goodness for Tiny.

"What are you doing in the house?" she asked, making certain not to scold. The boys sometimes tried to sneak the giant animal into the house, or when they went outside they forgot to close the door and Tiny would sneak into the house by himself. On those occasions there was never any telling what he was going to get into. And if you scolded him he tended to leave puddles—and that wasn't a good thing.

The sound of erratic hammering filled the air outside her window. She glanced at the bedside clock—seven o'clock. Tiny danced on top of her, tail wagging, breath huffing, eyes twinkling, he barked excitedly and looked toward the window.

"Okay, okay. I get it." Gently pushing the oversize pup off her, she padded to the window and pulled aside the curtain.

Before going to help decorate for the auction—and getting attacked by her friends—she had worked a full day at the candy store. Her boys had spent the day at Amanda Turner's place. Amanda couldn't have children of her own and since marrying Chance's cousin, Wyatt, she often enjoyed having Gavin and Jack over to play when Lynn needed a babysitter. She and Wyatt were in the process of trying to adopt, and there was no doubt in anyone's mind that any baby would be blessed to have her and Wyatt as parents.

Just after Lynn had told everyone that she was not bidding on a bachelor, Amanda and her two sisters-in-law, Susan and Melody, had arrived with the kids.

Melody had asked about the lights and the boys had immediately told everyone about how they'd caused Chance to fall and dump the lights all over himself. Everyone got a good laugh and she'd seen the spark of excitement burn brighter in the three matchmaking buddies' mischievous eyes. That was all it had taken for them to be off and running with stories about Chance when he was growing up—Chance Turner had been a handful. Of course, her boys had jumped right into the fray, giggling at stories of the things Chance and his cousins had gotten into.

She had also been informed by Melody that the Christmas lights he'd brought up to the church were for her, and that they were to be used to decorate her new house. Lynn had been touched by the gift and told Melody so. All their questions about Chance and what she thought of him had taken her by surprise and left her suspicious. Mule Hollow was known for its matchmaking, after all.

She and the boys had been late getting home and they'd all been tired. The last thing she expected to see when she looked out the window this morning was Gavin and Jack outside attacking the large oak tree in the backyard with hammers.

"What are they doing?" she asked, looking down at Tiny.

The dog placed his paws on the windowsill and whined as he studied them. His tail wagged impatiently, signaling that he wanted to be out there with his boys. "Come on, let's go." That was all it took. The dog shot out of her bedroom like a flash. Lynn grabbed her housecoat off the bed as she passed. It was chilly in the house and she stopped to turn the thermostat up a notch or two. She put on her leather slides beside the back door, which was cracked open but not enough for the dog to escape. Lynn guessed that he'd snuck inside when the boys left it ajar and then the draft must have sucked it shut, trapping him.

Tiny wiggled with anticipation and the instant she pulled the door open he shot outside and was gone. Lynn agreed with him—life was never dull with Gavin and Jack around. She trailed him.

Jack had both hands wrapped around the middle of

a hammer that was as long as his arm. Gavin held a twelve-inch piece of old barn wood against the tree. Both of them looked up at her as she approached. Tiny stuck his nose into the mix and Gavin pushed it away.

"What are you two little mischief makers doing?"

"Workin', Mom," Jack answered, slamming the head of the hammer at the nail protruding at an angle from the piece of wood. He missed.

"We're gonna build a tree house." Gavin nodded toward the old shed at the back of the yard. "There's a whole bunch of wood in there we can use." His high-pitched voice was shrill with excitement.

Jack again whacked the nail, which bent over and smashed against the wood. She cringed—better the wood than his finger. His shoulders slumped and his face fell as he let the hammer drop to his side. He looked so dejected it was all Lynn could do not to scoop him up and hug him tight.

Gavin scrunched his brows together looking at him. "That's okay, Jack. I didn't do no better."

Her little men, her heart tugged. "Building a tree house sounds like a great plan, guys. But let's put the hammer up for now. It's time to get ready for church. When we get home I'll come out here and we'll take a look at what's in the shed and see what we can do." Like she could actually build something! Who was she kidding?

"But you're a girl, Momma."

Oh, the challenge of it. "Yes, Jack, I am. But girls can build tree houses, too." She was sure some girls could. Whether or not *she* could was yet to be seen.

"You sure?" Gavin asked, looking as skeptical as she felt.

"Yes, Gavin, I am. Now come inside and let's get dressed for church."

"Momma, I bet Chance can build a tree house."

Not again. Her boys had been around Chance for only a short time and for some reason they were fascinated by everything about the man. "Gavin, I've already told you he's Mr. Turner to both of you. And he probably is very good at building things," she admitted as she opened the door for them. "Wipe your boots off." They made extravagant swipes of their boots on the rug and then hurried off to their rooms. Tiny tried to follow but Lynn grabbed him. "Oh, no you don't, buster." She pulled him outside, patted his head and then firmly closed the door.

She walked to the sink and stared out the window at the tree with the board attached and the hammers leaning against it. Chance probably could build a tree house her boys would be proud of. The man looked like he could do anything. There was just something about him that gave off that vibe. She felt it, and that had to be what her boys were sensing even though they were too young to realize it.

"Mom! Jack won't give me my shirt," Gavin yelled from the back room.

"It's my shirt," Jack yelled back.

She closed her eyes and shook her head. Her boys got along for the most part, but brothers would be brothers… Pushing thoughts of Chance from her mind she went to see what was going on. She was so happy to have the small house of her own that even the sounds of her boys fussing made the place seem homey. It was wonderful to know that she was providing a roof over her sons' heads in this peaceful ranching community.

The other women who had arrived with her in the van from L.A. were also moving on with their lives, slowly but surely, just like Esther Mae had said. Lynn had helped many of them in some way. Rose, the only mother with a teenage son, had been the first to move out of the shelter and had married not too long after that. Nive was still at the shelter, and so was Stacy, who was about to get married. All of them had come a long way since arriving here in Mule Hollow. And there were others after them who came, too. Some had used the facility as a temporary stopping point before finding a permanent shelter elsewhere, but for the original four Mule Hollow was now home. It was a great place to raise boys. The country life suited them and it suited Lynn, too.

"It's mine—"

"No. It's mine—"

She found them having a tug-of-war over a blue shirt. "Guys, what's going on here?"

"It's my shirt," Jack said.

Gavin shook his head. "It's mine."

Lynn looked at the shirt. "You both have this same exact shirt… Let's take a look at them." Getting dressed for church was not always an easy process. Raising boys was challenging, but she wouldn't give it up for anything. Sometimes, though, she worried about the future and not having a man in their lives to help guide the boys. Should she start looking for a man to fill the blank spot their dad had left? The thought hit her at times like this. When things like the tree house cropped up. It made her feel guilty that she wasn't ready.

The ladies pressuring her about the bachelor auction didn't help either. They didn't understand—how could

they know how she felt when she'd never told them?
All her life she'd lived in turmoil where men were concerned—until now.

No one knew exactly how bad her life had been prior
to escaping to the shelter. She wanted it to stay that way,
too. Hiding her emotions had worn her down, but for
the first time in years she was living life contentedly.

With no man in the picture there was no danger. No
broken trust, no risk of being hurt…it was easier. Safer.

Both physically and emotionally. It had taken the
love and fear for her sons to drive her from the cycle
of abuse. Knowing that if not for them she might still
be there undermined her self-respect and scared her.

No. It was better this way. Better feeling strong and
content that her boys were her life. They were safe and
happy as they were. And no matter how guilty she might
feel because they didn't have a father in their lives, she
wasn't ready to change that, not even for them.

Church had started when Chance slid into the
back pew. He felt awkward arriving late but he hadn't
planned on coming at all. At the last minute the Lord,
or habit, had him heading to the church. Normally his
church was a dusty or waterlogged arena prior to a competition's start.

Miss Adela had been playing the piano for the Mule
Hollow Church of Faith all of Chance's life. She had
just finished playing the welcoming hymn "When We
All Get to Heaven" as he slipped into the pew beside
Applegate.

"This back pew's not the place fer you, Chance Turner," App leaned in and whispered loudly.

So much for thinking he'd gotten his point across yesterday. "Good morning to you, too, App."

Applegate hiked a bushy brow. "What's good about it? We're at church and the only preacher we've got is sittin' in the back row with me."

Several people turned at his words. Since App was hard of hearing and talked loud enough to be heard in the choir loft it was a wonder the entire congregation didn't turn and look at him. Well, okay, so most of them did. Chance had known this would happen but here he was anyway. It was like the Lord wasn't going to let him go even when He knew Chance was struggling. "App, sir," he whispered, "now isn't the time for me to be up there."

App crossed his arms and grunted just as Brady Cannon stepped up to the podium. The sheriff taught the singles' Sunday school class, and he and his wife, Dottie, had turned his ranch into a shelter for abused women. Chance respected them both very much. Dottie ran a candy store on Main Street where she taught the women how to run their own business. Being self-sufficient was a goal of the shelter along with helping the families overcome their abusive pasts.

Wyatt had told him that Lynn, the woman he'd met yesterday, had recently moved from the shelter into her own place with her two sons. He wondered about Lynn. He'd hated to hear she'd had a hard time in her life. How a man could hurt a woman was beyond him...but how he could vow before God to love and cherish her and then strike and abuse her was even more incomprehensible.

"As most of you know I'm a sheriff, not a preacher," Brady began to speak. "I'm just the best you've got this morning. Or at least that's what the elders tell me. I'm pretty certain there's some of you out there who could do a much better job than me of preaching this morning. I hope whoever you are that you'll step up and fill the need."

App shot Chance a sharp look, and he felt eyes on him from everywhere else, too. Looking to the right he saw two small heads, one dark and one blond, turned his way. Gavin and Jack were barely able to see him over the back of the pew but they were watching him. Their mother sat beside them with her gaze focused straight ahead on Brady. When the boys saw Chance looking, the blonde raised his hand and waved. The dark-headed one followed suit. Lynn caught their movement out of the corner of her eye and automatically turned. Her midnight eyes locked with Chance's and unexpectedly his mouth went dry and his pulse tripped all over itself, pounding erratically.

Something in that look hadn't been there before. Something in the way her eyes blazed into his hadn't seared into him like that yesterday. The moment lasted less than a second before she let her gaze drop to her boys, tapping them each on the head and telling them, with the swirl of her finger, to turn around. Less than a second but he was hung up…

App elbowed him. "Like I said yesterday, she don't look at jest anybody like that. If you was in the pulpit you wouldn't have ta be lookin' at the back of her pretty head right now."

The woman in front of him almost choked on her laughter as she tried to hide that she'd heard what App had said. Why hide it? Everyone would have heard him, but they were all listening intently to Brady. Chance knew there was no way they hadn't heard App, but they were doing a good job not disturbing the service any more than it already had been.

"App, cut it out," he growled.

Thankfully, App decided he'd said enough. He crossed his arms and stared straight ahead for the remainder of Brady's lesson.

The sheriff did a good job over the next twenty minutes. His words were about being a good steward of the talents God had given each church member, something Chance had thought he was doing until Randy's death.

Though Chance listened, his heart was closed off to any emotional response. It had been that way ever since Randy had fallen beneath the hooves of that bull and Chance had realized he probably wasn't coming out alive. App could push all he wanted but Chance wasn't up to being in that pulpit right now. And honestly, he wasn't sure when or if he'd be ready. He felt as if a heavy horse blanket had been thrown around his heart, smothering out all the light.

Everyone kept saying he needed time. That was why he'd come home. Time could heal most everything.

Chance hoped it was true.

He'd given many a cowboy a similar sermon at different times of trial in their lives. Now he was seeing how much easier it was to spout the words when you were giving advice to someone else. It was different when you were the one in the midst of the storm.

He let his gaze slide toward Lynn once more. Something was bothering her, too. He saw it in her eyes just now, and it cut him to the core.

Chapter Four

"Hey, mister. Mr. Chance, hold up."

"Yeah, hold up!"

Chance had cut out the second the prayer was over. He wanted to keep right on walking but no way could he ignore the small voices hailing him. He'd made straight for the parking lot and was almost to the edge of the grass, almost to the white rock and fifteen feet from his truck... He'd almost made it.

App's grumbling during the sermon had convinced Chance that if he hung around he'd never hear the end of it. But no way could he ignore Gavin and Jack.

Feeling roped and tied he turned on his heel to find both boys charging after him. Lynn followed at a slow, reluctant pace. And he groaned at the sight of the Mule Hollow posse behind her! Norma Sue Jenkins and Esther Mae Wilcox were two of the older ladies who kept Mule Hollow running smoothly. They, along with their buddy Adela, had saved the tiny town with their matchmaking antics.

They'd come up with the idea a couple of years earlier to advertise for wives for all the lonesome cowboys who lived and worked the ranching area. Despite the disbelief of everyone around them, lo and behold, women read the ads and had begun to come to town. Since then the ladies were always coming up with special events that would draw women to the town. Like dinner theater with the cowboys singing and serving, or festivals where the cowboys and ladies would meet up. So far it had worked well. He appreciated the three women, but they were also among the ones who were adamant about him coming home to preach.

Watching their approach he prepared himself for a lecture.

"Boys," Lynn called, coming to a halt behind the two little dudes.

He couldn't help but wonder what was bothering her so…why she looked pensive and almost frightened. Was she scared of him?

"Mr. Turner was leaving. You don't need to bother him."

"We ain't, Momma." Gavin batted big eyes at her and then at him. "We was just wonderin' if you know how to make a tree house?"

"Yeah," Jack drew the word out dismally as he wagged his dark head back and forth. "We got a *mess* at our house. A pure mess."

"Boys!" Lynn exclaimed, turning red as a poinsettia, her big dark eyes widening like she'd just been prodded with an electric cattle prod.

Esther Mae and Norma Sue came to a halt, catching the end of Jack's declaration. Chance had a feeling Lynn was just as reluctant in their presence as he was. Matchmakers. Scary stuff for people who wanted nothing to do with the subject.

"Y'all are building a tree house—how fun!" Esther Mae exclaimed. Her red hair almost matched the color on Lynn's cheeks as they flamed up even brighter.

"We—well, the boys—started one this morning."

"That's a wonderful idea," Norma Sue boomed. "You boys probably do need a man to help you get that tree house up and working."

Chance didn't miss the flash of alarm in Lynn's eyes when Norma Sue spoke. He understood. He didn't know what to say. He didn't want to build a tree house. He wanted to be alone right now. To go back out to the stagecoach house where he was staying to contemplate the state of his life. Alone. And he could see that was what she wanted, too.

But Jack and Gavin were looking up at him with adoring eyes! *Adoring*—what exactly had he done to deserve the look in those eyes?

He met Lynn's now fiery gaze and his mouth went dry for the second time that day. She was struggling to hold her temper. It was obvious she didn't want his help. He told himself this had to do with her background. This was wariness or maybe distrust that he was feeling from her. He didn't like what he saw in the depths of her eyes and his own hackles went up at the idea she'd been mistreated. How bad had her abuse been? The question dug in like spurs.

"I could help if you need me." What else could he say? The boys yelled jubilantly and began jumping around with happiness.

Lynn pressed her shoulders back and shook her head. "Thank you," she said, stiffly, "but we don't need help building our tree house."

"I don't mind." *Chance, what are you saying?*

"He don't mind, Momma."

"Gavin, you're showing very bad manners. Again, thank you but we're fine," she said firmly. "Come on, boys, we need to go."

"But, Momma—"

"Jack, we need to go home. Remember we have Christmas lights to put up, too."

Both boys looked reluctantly at him but obediently headed off to the car. Lynn didn't meet his gaze as she said goodbye to Norma Sue and Esther Mae. He thought she was just going to walk off but then she paused. "I'm sorry. Thanks for the offer though," she said, then strode away.

What had she been through?

Chance's cousins walked up. "What was that all about?" Wyatt asked.

"That was Lynn being stubborn," Norma Sue offered. "Gavin and Jack were trying to get Chance to help them build a tree house, but Lynn is Miss Independent and having none of that."

Esther Mae harrumphed. "She needs to get over that."

Wyatt got a thoughtful gleam in his eye. *"Really."*

Cole grinned. He was the youngest brother, about Chance's age and his former partner in crime. "Did you tell them you were a master tree house builder?"

"I think we can both swing a hammer better than we could back then." Chance chuckled. He and Cole had tried to build a tree house when they were about eight years old. "We were stubborn back then though. We refused help from everyone."

"Until Dad stepped in," Wyatt added. "Y'all had the

biggest mess. Dad finally had to insist on making it safe for y'all to use."

"Thank goodness." Seth gave a laugh that was more of a grunt. "Oh, by the way, I forgot to tell you Melody said thanks for taking those lights up to the church for her."

Esther Mae beamed. "Lynn told us about that last night when we were decorating for the fundraiser. What a cute way to meet," she gushed. "Are you coming to the fundraiser tonight?"

Chance had already told Wyatt and all the guys the day before that he was going to pass. Wyatt hadn't liked it and had told him that being around people would be good for him, but he understood. Now, looking at Esther Mae and Norma Sue, Chance wasn't sure what to say. They had worked hard on this fundraiser, evidently, and it was for a good cause. His conscience pricked at him. He was startled that they hadn't yet mentioned his preaching. He was relieved by the reprieve. "I'm not sure—"

"Sure you are." Norma Sue looked serious. "Chance, we just heard what a hard time you're having dealing with the loss of this young man. The best thing is for you to get involved with your family...and we are your family. I expect to see you there." She shot Wyatt a firm look. "See to it."

Wyatt gave a slow grin. "Yes, ma'am. You heard the lady, Chance."

He was dug in deep for patience.

Esther Mae dipped her chin, causing the yellow daffodils on her hat to bend forward as if they, too, were watching Chance. "I'm expecting you there, too. So don't disappoint me. I know you'll enjoy it. And it will be good for you. Lynn will be there, too."

Great, just what he needed. Chance wondered what Lynn would think if she knew what was going on.

"And you'll enjoy the auction, too," Cole drawled.

"What auction? I haven't heard anything about that."

Seth hiked a shoulder. "Aw, it's just stuff for the ladies."

"But you'll still enjoy seeing them bid," Norma Sue added quickly, and Esther Mae grinned and nodded.

Everyone was acting strange. He knew they cared for him and maybe they were right. "I might be there," he offered.

Chance thought about Norma Sue's words all the way back to the stagecoach house. As he drove down the gravel road to the house that had been in the Turner family for almost two hundred years, he felt a small semblance of peace. His home was basically on the road, but when he needed time out this was where he came—always had been. All the memories he had from his years spent visiting and living at the ranch were the good times. Yes, he'd come home for much-needed solitude and time to think. But as he pulled up in front of the stagecoach house and got out of the truck he knew at six o'clock he'd be getting back in the truck and heading back to town.

This was a fundraiser…and the least he could do was go up there and buy a steak to help raise money for the women's shelter. There was no denying the good the shelter did. It was evident in Lynn and her boys. He'd spend some time alone tomorrow, but he knew he wouldn't feel good about himself if he didn't go up there and make a contribution to the shelter. Many benefits had been held to help Randy's family after his death. He'd only made it to one of them and he'd been asked to speak. He'd almost not made it through that… No, helping out the shelter here at home was the least he could do.

The women must really like whatever was up for bids. They were everywhere.

Chance walked through the door of the community center, which was just down the sidewalk past Pete's Feed and Seed. He'd had to park all the way at the opposite end past Sam's Diner just to find a parking space.

There were lots of couples sitting around and mingling in groups, but it was immediately obvious that the room was overrun by single women. He should have known that any gathering the town was organizing would bring even more women to Mule Hollow to meet single cowboys. His cousins had expanded their cattle operation, as had several other large ranches in the area, increasing the cowboy population even more. All in all, Mule Hollow had grown in the last year, and by the crowd it was apparent.

Glancing around, Chance had thought maybe he'd see a bunch of beauty-treatment baskets or jewelry or stuff that ladies liked, lining a table somewhere to be auctioned off. But he didn't see anything like that.

"Chance, over here," Wyatt called, waving him over to join the family. He wove his way through the tables, greeting people as he went.

"Boy, you weren't kidding when you said the women were going to bid. What's up for bids?" he asked, taking a seat beside Wyatt. There were two women at the table in front of him giving him the once-over... He felt like *he* was the one on the auction block.

Wyatt's wife, Amanda, gaped at him like he was crazy. "You don't know?"

"Know what?" He glanced around the table. Seth, Cole and Wyatt had on poker faces that would have made their great, great, great, great, great Grandpa Oakley proud. Oakley wasn't the most respectable Turner in the clan and immediately Chance was on alert. Melody, Amanda and Susan's expressions of disbelief sent an uneasy feeling coursing through his veins. "What have I missed?"

Amanda pushed her short dark hair behind her ear. "I can't believe no one told you?" She gave Wyatt a cute scowl. "Or that you didn't see the flyers on the fronts of the stores announcing that this is a dinner and bachelor auction."

Chance choked. "A what? What flyers? You said a *bachelor auction?*" He cut his gaze to Wyatt, then Cole and Seth, and he was pretty certain his scowl wasn't cute. He hadn't been in town all that much, but now that he thought about it he had seen a flash of yellow on the windows. Suddenly he remembered seeing Sam crumbling up something yellow when he was getting out of the truck for breakfast the day before. He'd also been grinning when he greeted Chance at the door. "What exactly are y'all up to?" he asked, knowing he'd been set up.

"It's harmless," Susan said, shooting Cole a disbelieving glance. "The women or anyone who wants to can bid on the bachelors who have agreed to be auctioned off. The high bidders have to fix dinner for the cowboy they win and then he gives them a few hours of work around their house."

Melody leaned around Seth and smiled sweetly. "You know, like help with putting up their *Christmas lights,*" she said, drawing out the obvious. "Or cleaning up their yard to get ready for the holidays."

Had that had been why she'd given all those lights to Lynn? Was Melody expecting Lynn to bid on a bachelor? As if summoned by his thoughts he spotted Lynn across the room dishing salad onto plates. He noticed the waiters then, about fifteen cowboys carrying plates to the tables.

"Are those the cowboys who agreed to be auctioned?" he asked Wyatt.

"Yup, that's them."

"You know cowboys," Cole drawled. "They'll sacrifice themselves for a good cause."

Yeah, right. *Big sacrifice.* Judging by the grins on their faces they weren't hurting too bad. Chance massaged the knot that had formed in his neck. It was no coincidence that everyone had conveniently omitted that this was a bachelor auction. Why?

Across the room he caught sight of Lynn. She was busy, in and out of the kitchen with several other women and men. Applegate and Stanley were manning the grill out back, so he'd been told. Every once in a while he saw them carry in pans of steaks. Lynn was putting food on plates. She looked as pretty as a summer day wearing a yellow sweater with her jeans. She caught him staring at her several times—he'd make an effort to stop staring but next thing he knew, he was right back at it. It was nothing short of rude, so why was he doing it?

Feeling eyes on him, he glanced around and caught

Brady watching him from the next table. The sheriff leaned toward Chance across the space between the tables so he could speak quietly to him.

"It was good to see you in church Sunday. You were far more qualified than me to be in that pulpit though."

"You did a great job."

Brady rested his elbow on his thigh. "Don't know about that, but seriously—I know your heart is at the arena with the cowboys, but we could really use you while you're in town. With Christmas coming and no preacher in sight… I mean, to be honest, we haven't gotten any replies to our request. I can only do so much because I'm not a preacher. I have faith that God's going to send the right man for the job, but I'm not sure when that will be."

Chance really admired Brady for what he was doing. If there was ever a born leader Brady was it. Not only was he a big man physically but he was a man of big integrity, too. He deserved an honest, open answer. Chance leaned closer so their conversation couldn't be overheard. "Look, Brady, I've got to sort out some personal issues right now before I could stand up there in front of the church. My heart has to be clear and since Randy died—"

"That's the bull rider that got killed a few weeks ago?"

"Yeah, that's him. I'd been witnessing to him for some time. He'd gotten mixed up in some bad stuff but all I needed was a little more time. I know he'd have accepted the Lord…with just a little more time. I don't know why God didn't allow that."

Brady hung his head then, met his gaze with regret in his eyes. "I guess preachers are human too, aren't you? We can look at a preacher and expect you never to have a crisis or any anger…but it happens."

Anger. It was true he was angry. And he was in a crisis of faith. Brady had him pegged. But then, he was a sheriff with skill in reading situations. "Yeah, it happens. I'm sorry. I'd like to help out, but even though I'm out of sorts right now I still have confidence that God's going to send the right man to Mule Hollow."

Brady nodded. "You're right. I'll just keep plugging away best I can. I'll also pray He'll help sort out things for you." He started to sit up straight and let Chance get back to his table but halted halfway and leaned back toward him, speaking quietly again for only Chance's ears. "Lynn over there is a great gal. She's sorting through her own issues at her own pace. Dottie and I are praying God sends the right man into her life when the time is right. She deserves it."

Chance wasn't sure if he was getting a warning but he nodded. "She seems like a good person."

"She is. All these women are, in the shelter. They've had it rough but they're fighters. Lynn's their advocate in many ways, pushing them to heal and move forward with their lives, but…" He paused as steaks were brought to his table. "I'm talking too much. It's time to eat, then I have an auction to get underway. You think about what I said. If you need to talk, come by my office."

"I'll do that." Chance glanced up and saw Lynn making her way toward him. She took the empty seat at Brady's table directly across from him, and as she sat down she caught Chance watching her. Again. She gave him a tentative smile, then began talking to a pretty blonde whose gaze was riveted on one of the cowboys—a nervous fella who was barely getting his job done for looking back at her.

"Who is that lady sitting beside Lynn?" he asked Wyatt.

"That's Stacy. She and Emmett are planning on getting married—*if* she ever decides on who is going to perform the ceremony. And if you haven't figured out who Emmett is, he's the cowboy who keeps bumping into tables because he can't function without looking at Stacy."

It was pretty obvious who Emmett was. The red-faced cowboy was going to dump a steak on somebody if he didn't watch out where he was going. Chance remembered Lynn asking if he performed weddings. "So, if they're getting married why is he one of the waiters? Didn't you say the waiters were the ones getting auctioned?"

"They needed more men and since he's a nice guy who is grateful the shelter brought Stacy into his life, he offered to fill in."

"I see," he said, but really he didn't. He sliced a piece of his steak. It was tender and, like all the steaks at a shindig like this, cooked medium to save on confusion and time. He watched the cowboys pass out the last plates, flirting with the ladies as they served. "From the looks of things the shelter might make a pretty penny." His gaze slid toward Lynn. She was watching him, though she looked away quickly and concentrated on her own meal the moment their eyes met.

"Hey, cousin, we want to auction you off." Cole cocked a brow.

"That's the plan," Wyatt agreed, and the rest of the table nodded enthusiastically.

"Oh, no, you don't." Chance got all hot under the collar looking at them—his ears were hot, he was so tense. "I told y'all not to go gettin' any ideas," he warned, glancing across at Lynn and seeing a pink stain on her cheeks. Though she wasn't looking at him, he got the feeling she'd heard everything.

Wyatt shot him one of his piercing looks and Chance could see the wheels in his lawyer's head chugging away. This wasn't good. When Wyatt got an idea about something there wasn't much to stop him. Even so, Chance tried. "Wyatt, don't even think about it." Could they not see that she didn't want any of this?

"I was just thinking about those little boys this morning wanting you to help them with their tree house. It would be nice to help them out."

Chance saw Lynn stiffen and her sharp gaze met his briefly before she looked away—no doubt about whether or not she'd heard that. "She didn't want my help," he said, his voice low to keep it from carrying. "She made that clear." He looked at Wyatt with real warning in his eyes. It was then that he noticed how quiet the table had grown, and his attention was drawn around to the bright, well-intentioned eyes of his family. Not one of them was paying his warning any attention.

His gaze slid back to Lynn. Randy hadn't wanted his help either, and Chance had failed him because he hadn't pursued helping him anyway. But this wasn't the same.

Not the same at all.

Chapter Five

❧

"Who'll give me one-fifty for Emmett? He's a hard worker, *and*..." Brady paused to grin at the roomful of people before zeroing in on Stacy, who blushed profusely when all eyes turned to her. "From what I hear he's a good cook, too. A bit on the shy side so you might have a hard time getting any talk out of him." A round of laughter erupted from across the room. Red-faced, Emmett stood beside Brady. When a lively round of bidding instantly ensued he looked even more embarrassed. Lynn's heart went out to the lanky, quiet cowboy. The poor guy was not the most handsome cowboy in the room—some might even say he was homely because he was so thin and red-faced. But within his skinny chest there was a loyal heart of gold. A humble man of honor, he'd given his heart to only one lucky woman in the room. He'd fallen in love with Stacy the day she stepped off the van that had brought Lynn and the others to No Place Like Home. God truly had worked in mysterious ways to get them here, and she was forever grateful.

Stacy had been through so much, having grown up

with an abusive father, then continuing the cycle by marrying an abusive man. The shelter had saved her and when they'd moved to Mule Hollow, Emmett had patiently, sweetly been there for her over the last two years as she healed emotionally. Both he and Stacy were quiet, and it had taken a year to get them to actually talk more than a few sentences to each other. It had been a touching thing to watch. Lynn knew she'd been a part of helping Stacy let go of some of the pain from her past and reach out for the bright future she could have with Emmett. Knowing this gave Lynn great satisfaction.

When the bidding finally eased up after going another hundred dollars higher, Emmett shifted and looked pained. The bidding had slowed now but he seemed ready to bolt. He'd known when he entered the auction that Stacy wouldn't have a lot of money to bid on him and he'd thought that was okay because he didn't figure there would be much bidding going on for him anyway. Still, he'd confided that he was worried about the situation. He hadn't counted on Norma Sue and Esther Mae jumping in to take care of him. They were intent on outbidding each other, but more focused on outbidding a young blonde who had apparently decided Emmett was the man to spend her money on.

As soon as Brady asked for more bids, Norma Sue shoved her hand in the air and glared at Esther Mae. "You might as well back off. Both of you."

Brady chuckled, acknowledged her bid and asked for more. "Who'll make it one-sixty?"

The young woman shot a perturbed look toward her competitors and then waved a bid.

Poor Emmett turned slightly green.

Stacy had shredded her paper napkin and was now

starting on Lynn's. "Why is she trying to get Emmett?" she whispered in alarm.

Lynn patted her arm. "It's all for a good cause. I wish you could bid but it'll be okay. Emmett only has eyes for you."

The younger woman was obviously looking for a date and knew a good thing when she saw it. The way she kept bidding, Lynn thought maybe she wasn't going to quit until she won him.

"Who'll give me one-seventy?"

"I will!" Esther Mae exclaimed, shaking her red head enthusiastically.

Emmett looked relieved.

The determined young woman was not happy and the minute Sheriff Brady rattled off the next amount she jumped to her feet. "I bid *two hundred!*"

"What?" Stacy gasped and ripped Lynn's napkin in half.

Chance and his family had been cheerfully rooting for the bidding, along with all the other people in the room. Lynn had been distracted by Chance and was finding it hard not to stare—the man had green eyes as vivid as cool creek water. She'd caught him watching her several times and each time butterflies had filled her chest. She found her gaze drawn back to him now, just as Brady called, "Two-twenty?" Chance tugged his ear!

She sat up straighter. Was that a bid? Had it not been for the fact that sharp-eyed Brady acknowledged it as such she might not have caught it. But he confirmed her suspicion by instantly accepting it and moving on to the next bid.

Esther Mae, Norma Sue and the determined blonde looked around to see who else had bid, but Chance gave no indication that it was him. If anyone else saw his inconspicuous bid they didn't give him away either.

He was good. As the next few minutes passed in heavy war Lynn was fascinated by him. When the bid hit two hundred and fifty the blonde finally huffed and gave up. Norma Sue and Esther Mae searched the room to see who was bidding against them.

"Who is it?" Stacy whispered for the fourth time.

Brady was having a great time with the secret and Lynn couldn't help being happy about it, too. "It'll be okay," she assured Stacy.

Norma Sue's gaze landed on Chance as he nodded his head. Brady, a good auctioneer, had been careful not to make direct eye contact with Chance since he'd picked up that it was an anonymous bid. Norma Sue hiked a brow then grinned, crossed her arms and settled back in her seat without giving a bid. Not so quick to catch it, Esther Mae started to open her mouth but Norma Sue elbowed her, gave a hard shake of her head then whispered something to her.

"Oh! Ohh." Exclaimed the excitable redhead and with a chuckle she settled down, her mouth zipped up tighter than a vacuum seal.

"Going once, twice…"

Chance scratched his chin and Lynn saw his finger subtly pointing in Stacy's direction.

"Sold to anonymous third party and gifted to Stacy."

"What?" Stacy gasped the same moment that Emmett did.

The room ignited in a roar of good cheer.

"You won him, Stacy!" Lynn exclaimed, hugging her friend as Sheriff Brady's gavel slammed down on the podium.

"But I didn't bid."

"That's okay, someone did it for you as a donation. Now you can fix Emmett a good meal and he can help you with decorating the shelter. It's perfect."

That was the end of the auction and Lynn was relieved. She'd been tense as the cowboys were auctioned off. She'd heard what Chance's cousins had been saying and she was afraid one of them would do something crazy. But they had behaved.

"Well, that concludes our bachelor auction and we've raised a good amount of donations for the shelter tonight. Thank you all and I hope you ladies make these cowboys work hard for their suppers. As an added tag to the evening, earlier in the day we had a donation made to No Place Like Home by Wyatt, Seth and Cole Turner on behalf of their cousin. You all know Chance."

There was chair scraping as everyone shifted to stare at Chance. Lynn's stomach went south with an uneasy feeling. Chance sat up straight in his chair. As if reading her mind, his gaze shot to her then straight to Wyatt and the rest of his family. They were all grinning at him.

Lynn's cheeks began to burn even before anything else was said....

Sheriff Brady kept on talking. "The donation stipulation is a bonus for the evening. It seems that Chance has agreed to be auctioned off to Lynn Perry and her boys for an entire day of work at their new home. Let's give him a hand and everyone else who participated in the evening."

Lynn was floored. "I don't need help," she said, looking at Chance and the table of people responsible for this. Chance had a resigned expression that embarrassed her even more. It was obvious that he'd not volunteered to help her and her boys. And if the man didn't want to help she certainly didn't want his help. She hadn't asked for any, that was certain. If there was one thing she hated it was feeling needy. Oh, she had been there—very much in need—but she didn't like it. And right now she was in a position where she was helping herself, standing on her own two feet. That was a feeling she *liked*.

She did not need Chance Turner's help, nor that of his wealthy cousins!

It was one thing to help Stacy but this… *This is for the good of the shelter,* said a little voice in the back of her head.

She ignored it and marched straight over to the group. "Thank you for the thought. But I don't need the help." She tried to keep her rising irritation out of her voice. "I hope you'll give the donation to the shelter anyway."

Wyatt gave her a crooked grin, one that all the Turner men had in varying degrees. "Lynn, he's just coming out to hang some lights."

A heavy tug of embarrassment hit her. "I know that. It's just that I don't need any help." Her gaze slid to Chance, who still didn't look any happier about the situation.

Amanda looked worriedly at her. "We just thought with this being the Christmas season and you and the boys being in your own place that some help would be nice."

"And we wanted to make sure Chance didn't get bored or become a hermit out there at the stagecoach house," Cole drawled. "If not for yourself, think of our poor cousin."

Chance shot Cole a long-suffering look. It was easy to tell he was used to being teased by his cousins. "Yeah, think of me," Chance said at last. "If you don't let them do this I'll never hear the end of it."

Not because he wanted to. "I don't think so." She refused to have a man working around her house who didn't want to be there. Especially when *she* didn't want him there in the first place. Despite her words everyone continued to watch her expectantly. Did they think this was all it took for her to be herded into their way of thinking? She had a mind of her own. "No thank you," she added more firmly for clarification. She had a right to make her own decision without feeling guilty about it! Before she acted like a total jerk, she turned and headed out the door with her back straight. She knew they were all probably thinking she was being rude but she couldn't help that. She and her boys could put up their own lights. They could.

She was within a few steps of escape when she heard her name.

"Lynn, wait." Norma Sue left Esther Mae talking to a relieved looking Emmett and a still baffled Stacy. "Did I hear you say you weren't going to accept Chance's help?"

People were milling around in groups and Lynn shuffled out of the way of a wave of folks talking excitedly among themselves. She glanced toward the door. "No, Norma Sue, I'm not."

"But you have to, honey. They paid that money and it isn't going to hurt anything. And you really deserve some help, what with all you have going on, working, taking care of those boys, and the upcoming children's pageant."

The pageant wasn't going to be much trouble. The kids were practicing the songs on Sunday mornings and Adela and Esther Mae were doing the costumes, so all she had to do was oversee a dress rehearsal. No trouble at all. "Norma Sue, it's embarrassing," she confided. Norma Sue, Esther Mae and Adela had been wonderful to volunteer at the shelter. They'd kept children when needed and offered moral support and shoulders to cry on. In doing so Lynn and all the other women at the shelter had come to love them like family. They also knew that Lynn had issues—issues she didn't like to dwell on. Or talk about. They knew this. So why were they pressuring her?

"Don't get any ideas about me and…*him.* Don't you dare do it. I told you the other day not to." She whispered *him* long and hard, giving the notorious matchmaker a warning eye as uncomfortable thoughts of being alone with a man pressed in on her. She'd not let her thoughts dwell on old fears that hid deep inside her. She held her emotions in a tight coil.

This entire situation had matchmaking written all over it—just like she'd been afraid it would. Lynn hadn't realized until now that Wyatt Turner had hooked his brothers up with their wives before he himself fell in love and married Amanda. That being the case, it hit her instantly that he would want to see his cousin married off, too.

Surely not with me.

Surely yes, and she knew they were thinking it could work. Chance's stay in town would be his perfect opportunity. They had no idea how wrong they were. None… The room suddenly felt far too closed in… She swayed slightly and fought to stay calm as her past swept like a dark, clawing shadow choking her—like Drew had done so many times. She couldn't breathe. Couldn't think.

Esther Mae was heading their way like an excited bumblebee in her yellow-and-black velour jogging suit, followed by Adela. They were so happy with their good intentions. So totally misguided. Lynn pressed a hand to her stomach and demanded her body and her emotions not betray her but it was a losing battle. Suddenly, the room seemed to implode about her.

Breathe. Her pulse rate skyrocketed and her stomach plummeted. It was that weird, unkind feeling that had taken over in the midst of trying to escape the violence of her life. She'd thought that once she escaped her husband's fist she'd be okay. But that hadn't been the case. Her panic attacks had eased up over the last couple of years but this was a bad one.

She made it out the door in seconds, rushing off the plank sidewalk and around the side of the building, where she managed to fight off the need to throw up. Drew's twisted, violent face filled her mind's eye and she gagged. Her stomach rolled.

"Dear God, help me," she gasped, and stumbled toward her car. She had to get home. No one could see her like this. No one.

Almost before the words were out of her mouth she felt some semblance of control returning. Not completely, but a portion.

She headed down the street and felt relief as she reached her car.

Christmas was coming. This was the time to be happy and to count her blessings. She inhaled the cold, fresh air and willed her pulse to slow. It didn't. The last thing she needed to do was let this pull her down further. She thought of the good in her life. She had a great life going for her now.

Some women needed and wanted men in their lives. The only two men she *wanted* or *needed* in her life were her twins. They were the loves of her life and she was satisfied with that.

She did not need Chance Turner's family or anyone else, *including* Chance, interfering with the life she was envisioning for her and her boys.

And that included how she chose to decorate her house for Christmas!

"Lynn, wait."

No. She spun, startled by Chance's voice. "I need to go pick my boys up," she said, praying for strength in her words.

"Look, about what happened in there—"

Miraculously she calmed. "I won't be railroaded, Chance. And that's exactly how it felt in there. I'm the first to know the auction was for a great cause, but I would have bid on a man if I'd wanted one. And I didn't, don't and won't be forced, no matter how good the intention."

"And I'd have put myself in the running if I'd wanted a woman." He stopped a few steps from her. "Believe me, the last thing I want is to railroad you. I just came out here to say I'm sorry if we offended you. I know that is the last thing my family wanted to do. They thought they were doing you a favor—"

"They were trying to match us up."

He had the decency not to deny it. "You're right. I think that was apparent. But still, there was no offense intended. I can tell you're upset. Are you okay? Is there something I can do?"

She shook her head, tears suddenly threatening. "I—I'm not offended. Not really. Look, I have my own plans and I'm hoping everyone can understand that and honor my wishes."

"Yeah, sure they can. I'll relay that to my family." He stepped toward her, concern written in his expression. "You aren't okay."

"I'm fine." She pulled open her car door. "Don't worry about me. You have your own plan you came to town to work on, I'm sure." Why she added that she wasn't certain, but he got an odd look on his face. His jaw tightened and he glanced down the street for a long moment. Pain? Was that what she'd just seen?

When he looked back at her his eyes were troubled, confirming that she had just seen a flash of hurt. "I do have my reasons for being back here. Anyway, you be careful picking up your kids. The deer are getting hungry this time of year and probably thick along the roadways."

Her heart tightened for him as he headed down the street in the direction opposite from the community center. Apparently he'd had enough, too.

She got inside her car and sat in the silence, giving herself time to calm down before driving. This wasn't a new thing to her. She'd been upset far too many times in her life and knew driving while her world was spinning was risky.

She was still thinking about that troubled look in Chance's eyes when she finally headed to pick up the boys. Instead of worrying and dwelling on what had happened to her, she couldn't stop wondering what had brought Chance home.

She'd heard there had been a tragedy and a cowboy

had been killed by the bull he'd been trying to ride. But that didn't explain why Chance had come home. He was a rodeo preacher—tragedy happened. And he was a man of faith. So what had put that pain in his expression…in his heart?

It was none of her business.

And she wanted it to remain that way. She did not want to get into Chance Turner's business and she didn't want him in hers.

Period.

With a capital *P*.

Chapter Six

Chance just couldn't let it go. Sitting in the truck at the end of Lynn's drive he stared at the house in the early morning sunlight.

It had a steep gable roof and a porch on the front with a matching roofline. It was one of those roofs that Christmas lights looked great on, but a man could break his neck hanging them on the high pitch. The thought of Lynn attaching those lights herself bothered him as he pressed the gas and drove down the gravel driveway. Not to mention the fact that he couldn't stop thinking about how upset she'd been last night. He'd noticed that even upset as she was she'd shown concern for him in the end.

Pulling to a halt in front of the house, he stepped from the truck and hesitated before striding to the porch. He'd come for a reason, not an excuse. *Not* because he hadn't been able to get her off his mind.

The boards creaked as he stepped on them and one— no, several—he noticed at closer inspection were in need of replacement. He knocked on the door and waited. When there was no answer after a couple of minutes he knocked again. Lynn's car was parked at the edge of the house in the metal carport so she had to be home.

It was likely that she'd peeked out the window, had seen him and decided not to open the door.

He hoped not though. On the other hand, he couldn't blame her if she did exactly that after everything that had transpired last night.

In the short time he'd been home the weather had gone from the forties to today's seventy degrees. It was a beautiful balmy December day in Texas—they were having a snowstorm up north and Texas was having a breezy summer day in the middle of the winter. It was one of those perks of living in the Lone Star State. He rapped his knuckles on the door one last time before heading back to his truck, more disappointed than he wanted to admit.

Laughter coming from behind the house called for a detour.

Careful to watch for running twins, he strode around the corner and spotted Lynn and both boys hard at work on what appeared to be the beginnings of a tree house. But the only indication it was a tree house was the fact that a tree was involved.

Their backs were to him, huddled together studying their handiwork. Lynn said something and the boys laughed.

A ball of unease settled in his gut. What was he doing?

The Catahoula was sprawled on its back off to the side enjoying the sunlight. He must have caught Chance's scent on the wind because he suddenly sprang to his feet, belted out a war cry and charged his way.

Uh-uh. Not happening again. Chance braced himself, stared at the dog and commanded, "No."

Instantly Tiny dropped to his haunches and stared at him like a tiny puppy being scolded. His wide head cocked and his eyes pleaded an explanation but he sat still.

"Chance!" Gavin exclaimed first. Without waiting the boy raced toward him and grabbed him around the knees. "I told Momma you'd come help us."

"Hi, Gavin. What kind of help do you need?" The zealous greeting took Chance by surprise.

Jack was right on his brother's heels. "With the tree house," he exclaimed, latching on to his other leg. Despite the frown on Lynn's face there was no way Chance couldn't smile.

"So you're building that tree house. Sounds like fun!"

Without hesitation they each grabbed a hand, tugging him forward, chattering all the way. Tiny pounded about them in a circle barking excitedly. Chance had trouble following what they were saying: They were building a tree house, they found wood in the old barn, Gavin wanted to climb the ladder but his momma wouldn't let him, Jack couldn't hit a nail for nothin'! Chance laughed at that one.

It was amazing how much information poured out of them in the twenty feet between the house and the tree.

"Good morning," he said to Lynn. "It looks like you could use a little help." She might not want it but it was glaringly apparent that Lynn needed help with this project. Once again he felt bad for her—caught in a situation she didn't want and all because of him. She'd been nailing a board to a tree limb—he assumed this was going to be the floor of the tree house. He eyed it, not wanting to be critical, but he was really glad, for safety reasons, that the thing was only about five feet off the ground. Lynn was standing on a lightweight fiberglass ladder that she'd leaned against the limb. He didn't want to tell her that her structure wasn't going to be very safe.

"Hi," she said, climbing from the ladder. Her hair was in a ponytail and she wore a soft blue sweater that made her skin radiant. "I'm just starting."

He also didn't want to tell her that it didn't matter if she'd been working all day it wasn't going to get any better. "I was just passing by and thought I'd drop by. You know, see how you were this morning." He'd gone in for coffee at Sam's and been put through more of the same from Sam, App and Stanley. He couldn't explain in front of the twins that he needed to talk to her, so he left it at that. "This is going to be the floor, I'm thinking." He tried to sound light.

She didn't find that amusing. "We're learning."

"We got a mess." Jack crossed his little arms and studied the situation seriously. He looked like a miniature man contemplating his next move.

"Sure do," Gavin agreed. "Momma done nailed that board on there nine *hundred* times!"

Jack crunched his eyebrows looking up at Chance. "We're havin' a learn'n' experience, all right."

"Hey, it's not that bad." Lynn chuckled, and then sighed. "But close. Apparently I have no talent with a hammer and on top of that I have no clue what I'm doing. But we're getting there. We are definitely having a learning experience."

Chance felt for her. His own unease lessened a bit. "Can I talk to you for a minute?" He didn't want to talk about the money from the auction in front of the boys.

"Sure. Boys, why don't you go get a carton of juice. You deserve a break."

Both boys yelped excitedly and started toward the house only to halt.

"Are you gonna help us?" Gavin asked.

Chance felt a tug on his heartstrings. What did he say to that? He couldn't overstep their mother. "We'll see."

That got him two frowns. Lynn intervened. "Go on now and get your juice. You can add a cookie, too."

The offer was too sweet to pass up, bringing big grins as they raced each other to the back door. Tiny trailed them, flopping on the step to wait when they disappeared inside.

It was quiet the moment the door slammed shut behind them. Feeling suddenly ill at ease, Chance snagged his hat from his head and held it in both hands. "I came to tell you that my cousins gave the donation to the shelter with no strings attached. I didn't want you to feel bad or worry that your decision caused them not to get the money."

Her shoulders relaxed and her pretty eyes softened. "Thank you. I didn't want them to lose out on such a generous donation because I didn't accept the offer."

It was easy to see that she was a nice lady, just guarded. And hurt, giving her every right to protect herself. He couldn't help being curious about her. "I know we talked about this last night but I just want you to understand that my family meant well. They really did. They just overstepped their boundaries. The Turners are known for being overzealous at times. Or maybe the word is *overbearing*."

Lynn's shoulder lifted slightly. "Overzealous can be a good thing. I'm just into planning my own life these days. I hope people can understand that. If I hurt any feelings I'm sorry, but that's just the way it has to be."

Her back stiffened. She was closing the door between them again.

"You need to do what works best for you, Lynn." He glanced again at the poor tree house. "I could help if you'd like me to."

"No," she said too quickly. "We'll figure it out."

That was easy enough. And for the best, he guessed. "I'll head out then. I just wanted to tell you not to worry. You have a right to turn their offer down."

She nodded. He wondered why she was so wary. Of course it was easy to figure out that she came from an abusive situation, since she'd lived in the shelter. But how bad had it been? He'd seen the panic in her last night. Lynn looked strong. Nothing about her hinted that she would have allowed someone to lift a hand to her… but apparently she had. He knew that all too often there was a misconception that abused women were weak. That wasn't always true. He also knew there were ways to abuse someone other than physically.

No matter how much she pushed away his conversation, he couldn't get the idea out of his head. When she'd fled the building last night it had bothered him a great deal. He'd followed her but she hadn't been happy about it and had seemed glad to see him leave. He had a feeling she would be happy to see him leave now also.

He hadn't come home to Mule Hollow to hang around anyone. He'd come home for the solitude the ranch offered him. "Well, I guess I'll be drifting on out of here then." He tipped his hat and turned to go. It took all his considerable willpower not to offer once more to help…but considering that she wasn't even going to thank him for coming by, he decided keeping his mouth shut was the right option.

He was almost around the corner of the house when she called his name. Her voice was soft and there was a hesitancy to it that touched a chord inside him.

"Chance," she called again when he didn't immediately halt and look back. When he turned she hadn't moved.

"Thanks for stopping by. And…" She raked a hand over her hair. In the morning sunlight it gleamed like the blue-black coat on a raven. "… And thanks for understanding."

He nodded, then got out of there. She had not asked for his help and hadn't looked as if she had any plans to do so. The lady had simply said thank you.

It should have been the easy out he was hoping for. He'd taken the easy out with Randy and the bull rider had come up dead. This wasn't the same and he knew it, but that didn't stop him from thinking about Lynn all the way back to the ranch. One thing was certain. He'd come here for peace and solitude. He'd come here to get away from God and everyone else.

Except God wasn't having any of it.

But then Chance already knew that it didn't matter whether a person was mad at God, or stumbling in the dark. God was always there waiting. Calling His own back to Him.

It was Chance who wasn't ready to let go. He felt as if he'd helped kill a man—some would say he was crazy for thinking such a thing. But that was how he felt. Randy might have gotten mixed up with the wrong crowd and avoided Chance in the last few weeks before his death, but Chance knew in his heart that despite the bad feeling he'd had about Randy, he'd not heeded God's nudge to seek Randy out. He had not gone the extra mile to help the young cowboy, who was clearly in a danger zone. It wasn't something Chance could forget or forgive. And no matter who said he wasn't responsible, in his heart of hearts he felt like God was holding him accountable. He felt like he'd failed Randy and God at the same time.

Emotionally and mentally Chance was not in a place to entertain thoughts of the single mother of two. But no matter what he did, Lynn continued to enter his head.

The heavy scent of rich, dark chocolate filled the candy shop. Lynn added sugar to the commercial-size pot and stirred. "No, I didn't accept the offer. Come on, don't you two give me a hard time."

Stacy bit her lip as Lynn and Nive Abbot squared off across the counter. Lynn didn't miss the way Stacy tensed at the very idea of her friends having words. Though she was wrong—Nive and Lynn weren't having words. They were simply having an excitable conversation.

"I'm not pushing in that way," Nive said, holding her plastic-gloved hands up in surrender. "I understand you aren't looking for a man but some help around the house from a man of God…that sounds like a plan to me. You know, I never thought about marrying a preacher but, hey, have you looked at that guy? Whoa! He has dreamy green eyes."

Lynn prayed for patience. "I'm not interested in his help, but I'm not dead. Who wouldn't notice his eyes?"

"They are nice," Stacy interjected, slicing the fudge in front of her.

Stacy already had cold feet about getting married. That was the only way Lynn could describe her reluctance to hire a preacher to come marry them. Yes, she was crazy in love with Emmett in her gentle, timid way, but she had spoken of recurring doubts that plagued her. The fact that Lynn was so against letting a man into her life wasn't helping matters. Lynn had noticed a change the instant she'd walked into the candy store that morning. She felt horrible that her decision was having a detrimental effect on the future of Stacy and Emmett. She hoped Nive would get the hint and clam up.

"I saw him watching you," Stacy added, pausing in her steady slicing. She smiled timidly. "A lot."

Her softly spoken words startled Lynn. "Watching me?" she asked. She'd noticed it herself but thought it was just because she couldn't seem to keep her eyes off him.

Stacy nodded her paper-cap-covered head and began slicing again. "He kept glancing your way over and over again. I think he looks sad."

"Me, too," Nive said. "I saw it in his yummy eyes. When he wasn't looking totally perplexed by his cousins teasing him. I heard something bad happened at one of the rodeos he was at. I think a bull rider was killed during his ride."

Lynn concentrated on stirring the chocolate mixture. Burning the bonbons wouldn't be good but her thoughts were not on her job. "I heard something similar—it was terrible. I meant to ask Norma Sue but too much other stuff was going on. I don't understand why cowboys want to get on the back of one of those killers. And my boys talk about becoming bull riders. I hate it."

She cringed at the thought of her babies growing up and climbing on one of those huge monsters.

"It's a wonder more of them aren't killed," Stacy said.

"I know they know the risk they're taking but I just can't stand it. It would have to be hard on someone like Chance who was working with them." A mental picture of Chance witnessing to the riders week after week popped into her mind. It was easy to see that he would be a caring and compassionate preacher. And yet he had said he wasn't preaching right now. Whatever had happened had affected him deeply. She'd glimpsed sadness when he'd followed her to her car. It was there, along with the kindness she'd seen in the depths of his lush green eyes.

Okay, so maybe thinking of his eyes as lush wasn't the best way to put the man out of her head. But they were. The color didn't make her think of hard green stones but tall grass swaying gently in the breeze. As a little girl she'd always begged her mother to pull over when she saw a field of high grass tossed in the wind. It had looked like the perfect, safe place to run to. A perfect place to find peace. Funny how she hadn't thought of that in a very long time.

The Lord makes me lie down in green pastures, He leads me beside quiet waters, He restores my soul. The passage from Psalms echoed through her like a gentle whisper that lifted her spirit. God had brought her a long way from that childhood innocence. He'd carried her through darkness and into the light. She wondered if Chance was struggling in the darkness right now?

Men of God struggled. It was foolish to think they never had pain…but that was none of her concern. He had family and friends here who she was quite certain were helping him with any problem he might be having. He didn't need her worrying over it.

"I wonder if Chance would marry me and Emmett?" Stacy asked.

It was the same thought that Lynn had had when she'd first met Chance outside the church.

"That would be a great idea," Nive said excitedly, pausing in the midst of wrapping the freshly sliced fudge in colorful cellophane. It would be decorated with ribbon in preparation for the gift shops they supplied all across several counties.

Lynn removed the pot from the heat but kept stirring. "Actually, I asked him about that and he said he wasn't preaching right now."

Stacy turned hopeful blue eyes to her and it was easy to see her disappointment. She had hoped to wait until a preacher took over the pulpit who would mean something in their lives through the years. She didn't want to have a stranger marry her. When she wasn't having moments of cold feet, this marriage meant the world to Stacy. "This is my new beginning. My fresh and beautiful union that I desperately want God to be a part of…" Her voice trembled and she went back to work. "I just don't understand. I want God involved in my wedding and that starts with the pastor who recites our vows. Why do I keep coming up against closed doors?"

Lynn couldn't stand the frustration in Stacy's voice. She closed her eyes and asked God to help her make this happen for Stacy. Opening her eyes she met Stacy's gaze and, despite her need to back away, Lynn knew what she had to do.

She was going to ask Chance Turner once more.

Chapter Seven

The sun had just peeked over the distant treetops when Chance saddled Ink and rode out of the barn. They'd ridden for a good hour, checking fence line, looking at the cattle and simply riding. Ink's ears had been back and he'd been jumpy at first, but now the black gelding had relaxed. Chance had, too, feeling the tension ease from him as he rode across the plains on the Turner ranch. Hauling from one rodeo to the next could wear on horse and man. Being at peace and roaming the wide-open space was good for both of them.

He'd awakened bound in his sheets and sweating bullets with Randy on his mind again. He couldn't stop thinking about that last ride. He had witnessed to Randy, told him that no one knows what the future holds, and he'd asked Randy once more to commit his life to the Lord. But it had been a no-go. Instead, Randy had wrapped his gloved hand with the bull rope, gripped it tightly and then grinned. "Not today," he'd said. "This is gonna be a good ride."

Chance saw his unfocused eyes in that instant and

got the uneasy feeling that tragedy was in the making. But the gate opened and it was too late.

How many times he'd replayed in his mind yanking Randy out of that box and stopping that ride.

Bull riders at the top of their game were athletes. They trained hard and respected their bodies and clear minds. You didn't ride against the toughest bulls—bulls with bigger reputations than the cowboys in many ways—without being prepared. Bull riders died all the time. It was a risk they accepted and they knew not being sharp upped their risk of death. But injuries caused problems. Ever since his shoulder injury two months earlier, Randy had come around more, asking questions. Chance had sensed a need in Randy to change his life. And yet he hadn't done it. Instead he'd continued hanging with a rough crowd to play with a lifestyle that Chance knew from his personal experience led only to dead ends and heartache. Why hadn't he done more for Randy? Why?

Chance was heading home, as unsatisfied as when he'd headed out, when he saw a car approaching the stagecoach house. He recognized Lynn Perry's aging auto as it drew closer. The vehicle had seen better days, but he figured Lynn was probably doing her best raising two boys on her own and putting a roof over their heads. There was much about Lynn to admire. He'd thought about that yesterday when he'd stopped to stare at the moon before calling it a night. She seemed very levelheaded and in forward motion. He liked that about her. She was cautious about giving the wrong impression to men. And with reason. She'd been hurt before and now he'd seen it in her eyes—she didn't plan on being hurt again. He also figured she was looking out for her kids. A person didn't take all the risks involved in fleeing an abusive husband only to jump right back into a relationship. Not when she'd been trying to protect her kids in the first place.

So why was she here? He urged his horse forward across the space separating them. By the time he made it into the yard she'd gotten out of her car. She shielded her eyes from the glare of morning sun and watched him ride in.

She was beautiful standing there, and his heart lifted looking at her, beating out a bongo rhythm despite everything he knew about her and everything he'd come here to escape.

She gave him a terse smile as he approached. Clearly she was disturbed about being here.

"Hi." He dismounted as he spoke. As soon as his boots hit the ground he tipped his hat and couldn't help smiling at her. He suddenly felt the weight on his shoulders ease up. "I'm a little surprised to see you way out here. But I have to say I'm glad to see you."

"I'm surprised to be here, too," she said, unsmiling.

"But obviously not happy about it." He couldn't help teasing her.

She tugged the collar of her jacket closer around her chin and continued to look ill at ease. He waited for her to continue. The edge of her dark hair lifted from her cheek in the chilly breeze and she sucked in a breath. Serious eyes watched him.

"Is something wrong?" he asked.

"No. I'm sorry. I'm just...not sure how to do this."

His lips lifted and he gave her his best smile. She wasn't the easily flustered type and yet she was now. The idea that she was flustered just being around him set his heart to pounding all over again. *In your dreams, Turner.* "I promise not to bite. Say what's on your mind."

She nodded and took a breath. "Gavin smashed his finger this morning when I was getting ready for work."

"Is he all right?"

"Yes, but…" She rubbed her temple and looked away momentarily. "But I feel horrible."

"Little boys like working on tree houses. There are hard lessons sometimes, but you have two very creative little boys who clearly want to learn. He'll be all right, that one."

He had no doubt about it. Her boys were determined little tykes. He'd thought his words would reassure her but they didn't. She shifted from one foot to the other and looked more distressed.

"He wasn't working on the tree house. He and Jack had moved that old ladder we found in the barn from the tree to the house. I don't know how they managed to get it standing against the house but they did."

This was going south quickly. "He didn't?"

"Gavin climbed the thing to the eaves and was trying to hang Christmas lights." Distress sounded loud and clear in her voice. "It's a wonder he hadn't fallen and hurt himself. He's only four—well, more five than four, but still. He could have been hurt because I'm so stubborn and want to do everything my way."

Chance stepped closer to her and had the urge to tug her into his arms and comfort her. Instead he smiled, hoping to ease her anxiety, though he was more concerned about the situation than she could know. "God took care of him, it seems. So don't beat yourself up over it."

"Easier said than done." Her lip curved slightly. "I seem to have made a mess of things. They wanted lights on our house for our first Christmas, but I got side-tracked trying to help them build a tree house—which is a disaster. By the time I figured out that I stink at carpentry it was too late to hang the lights. I haven't had time since to get them up. This is what happens when they decide they need to do things themselves."

She was upset. No two ways about it. She was a mother alone with a lot riding on her shoulders. Not only raising her two boys and providing for them but also overcoming whatever had sent her to the women's shelter. Chance wondered again what kind of heartache she'd gone through. And what kind of effects lingered from the past. "Come on, let's go sit down and let me get you a glass of tea." When she didn't move he took her arm. "Come on."

She took a deep breath and let him lead her to the porch. He opened the door and led her inside. The stage-coach house had a long, wide hall from front to back, its walls lined with old photos, some dating all the way back to the eighteen hundreds. He led the way into the living room, which was connected to the kitchen and separated by a large wooden table that had been here, as far as they knew, from the beginning. He liked the place. Its rustic stone fireplace and scuffed wooden floors were right up his alley. Their link to the past made it more special. "What can I do?" he asked as he pulled a chair out for her, then got a glass and filled it with ice from the automatic ice dispenser—there were a few modern conveniences that he enjoyed.

Relief and a mixture of embarrassment, if he was reading her expression correctly, washed over her. "I was wondering if that offer of your services was still open."

He pulled a pitcher of tea from the icebox as excitement hummed through him at the idea. He filled the glass and set it in front of her. "Yes, ma'am, it is." He sat down across from her. "And even if it had time limitations I'd be honored to help out you and your boys."

It was the truth. He and God might be having a difference of opinion right now, but that didn't matter when it came to down-home decency. This was the right thing to do. It was easy to see she was still struggling. Was it the idea that she needed help at all that was bothering her?

"Thank you so much," she said, taking a sip of her tea. "I'm sorry I lost it. I'm not usually so upset, but all the way out here I kept thinking about what a close call Gavin and Jack had. Gavin dropped his hammer and it almost hit Jack. My stomach keeps getting sick thinking about it."

He automatically covered her hand with his. "I'm sorry you had to go through that alone." Her hand was soft and he was tempted to keep holding it but drew his back. He sure liked the touch of her though.

"The boys will be ecstatic," she said, tucking her hands into her lap. "And despite all my efforts, your family, my friends and the matchmakers seem to be brewing up ideas about us with every passing moment. It worries me."

He hadn't mixed up any signals from Lynn, but his manly pride was getting a bit defensive that she'd easily dismissed the idea of being set up with the likes of him.

"As far as I'm concerned they can brew all they want. If I'm not interested in becoming involved in a relationship, I won't get involved. No matter who's doing the pushing." Was that a flicker of feminine prickle he saw in her eyes at the notion that he'd so blatantly refused involvement? If so she hid it well, because the next instant her lip crooked upward.

"Good. We're on the same page. What day will be best for you to come out?"

"I guess since you've got four-year-olds trying to scale your roof I'd better start as soon as possible. How's today?"

"Today—I'm sure you had something planned for today, penning cows or working them or something. Honestly, I'm not much of a cattle woman so I'm not really sure what all you do to them, but whatever you had planned I hate to take you away from it."

She was cute. He hadn't figured the slightly uptight lady for being cute, but she was. Sure, she was pretty, but a woman could be pretty and have no cuteness about her. "I had the big plans of just hanging out here by myself. I can do that tomorrow if you'll let me hang lights today." It hit him then that he was glad for the excuse not to be alone with his thoughts anymore today.

She smiled and he felt good… He hadn't felt good since before the day Randy leaned forward too far over B-par's back, and the hulking bull's powerful head had slammed into Randy's face full force. The move had dazed him and when he hit the ground B-par continued—

"If you're sure," he said, pushing the thoughts away and focusing on her.

"I'm sure." Something about the entire situation drew him. The last thing he'd expected to do when he came home was spend time with anyone, especially a pretty woman and two little boys. But it looked as if that was exactly what he was about to do. And as downhearted as he was feeling, the idea brightened his day more than he could say.

More than he deserved.

"I gots a smushed thumb under here." Gavin lifted his hand and showed off the bandaged thumb.

"I guess you learned about climbing all the way up there." Chance nodded toward the eave of the house where he was about to begin work hanging the boys' Christmas lights. Lynn had worked until two and then picked the kids up from the shelter. She'd explained that the women took turns at the shelter watching the children so that everyone could work in the candy store.

He could have come earlier but he'd felt it important to let the boys be a part of putting the lights on their home for the first time. When he'd chosen to do that, Lynn had looked pleased. Though she hadn't voiced the words, he got the feeling he'd earned points by wanting to include them. He wasn't looking for points or getting on her good side—that hadn't been his objective. He'd simply known the boys would have fun and he would enjoy their help. He also wanted to talk to them about the dangers of climbing a ladder.

"I wasn't scared. Jack told me he didn't wanna do it."

Jack shook his head back and forth in methodical rhythm, as if he were watching a tennis match. "My stomach hurts when I get too high. I told Gavin not to do it. But I held the ladder for him, like I seen Miss Dottie do for Sheriff Brady when he was workin' on the barn roof."

"Only when I dropped the hammer it done almost hit Jack on the head!"

Chance got a vivid picture of the little dude holding the ten-foot ladder and dodging the hammer.

"Momma said it was a *miracle* I didn't fall when I smashed my thumb."

"And another miracle the hammer didn't hit me in the head."

Chance's heart clutched at the thought…the same way he felt looking back on Randy's last ride. He hadn't done anything about Randy's situation but he could do something here.

The idea coursed through him like a wildfire. He tamped it down. These were just little boys wanting to be handy around the house. Randy had been hyped up on drugs, strapped to the back of one of the most ferocious bulls on the circuit. It had been a deadly combination…a train wreck in the making and he hadn't seen it coming. But maybe there was some redemption here helping Gavin and Jack.

Maybe he could make a small difference in these boys' lives by at least getting up the Christmas lights they'd been talking about since the day they'd first run him over.

The memory made him smile. "You boys are all right. You know that?"

They beamed at the praise just as Lynn came out the front door. She'd gone inside to change out of her slacks into jeans and an oversize, cream-colored sweater that hung below her hips. She'd pulled her hair into a ponytail once more and Chance missed the way it hung around her face. She also had changed from boots to canvas shoes that had seen better days. The outfit looked as if she had loved and worn it for years.

He sure missed her hair hanging down though, no matter how much he tried not to think about it.

"Did you come to help, too, Momma?" Jack asked.

"Sure did." She hugged him and gave him a kiss on the head, making him giggle. "Is that okay with you fellas?"

Gavin crunched his brows together skeptically. "Long as you don't use the hammer. You're worse with it than me."

"Hey!" Lynn laughed cheerily. "That's not a nice thing to say about your ol' momma." She engulfed him in a swooping hug and growled against his neck. He squealed and wiggled attempting to escape.

Jack hopped from foot to foot excitedly. "Get him, Momma! Get him."

Chance had climbed the first two rungs of the ladder but paused to watch them. They were good together. The three of them. Lynn had done a great job. She should be very proud of herself. Laughing and breathless from romping with Gavin she let him go and smiled at Chance. Her cheeks were soft pink and she had a happy glow about her as she held his gaze. His stomach tilted looking down at her and he felt peaceful.

"I wish I had some of those plastic gadgets you hang lights with. It would make things a lot easier, I think."

He held up the staple gun. "We'll do it the old-fashioned way."

"You ain't usin' a hammer?"

"Nope, Gavin, I'm afraid I'd hit my thumb if I tried to hang lights with a hammer."

"You don't want ta do that. It hurts."

"Yeah, I reckon it did." He climbed the ladder carrying a strand of lights and all three jumped to hang on to the ladder.

"We won't let you fall, Mr. Chance," Jack yelled at the top of his lungs.

"Thanks. I'm in good hands. I can see that."

"There are none better than my boys," Lynn called, her voice bright with affection.

Chance looked down to find her smiling up at him as she said the words. She looked so pretty and so happy at that moment that he almost missed a rung on the ladder.

Chapter Eight

"So, what do you think?" Chance asked as he hopped to the ground. He'd hung several strands of lights, and the old house was looking great.

He was standing close to Lynn and she could feel the warmth from his body through the down vest that he wore. She'd helped him for the last hour and he'd been great with her boys. And, okay, the man smelled wonderful.

"Momma, don't ya got yor ears on? What do you think?" Jack asked, tugging on her arm. It was what she always asked him and Gavin when they weren't listening to her.

Boy, where had she been? How embarrassing was that? "Ear one and ear two are both on and ready to do their jobs," she said lightly, careful not to look at Chance.

She hoped Chance hadn't noticed her embarrassing lapse. She stole a glance at him. He caught her and the wink he gave her said he'd noticed plenty.

"You were taking a nap," he drawled, a teasing smile

tugging at his lips as he grabbed the ladder and moved it down three feet.

A flutter erupted inside her chest at his words and she watched him. He moved with an athletic grace she'd been admiring all morning.

Leaning the ladder against the house, he placed a hand on his hip and grinned. "Seriously, I think a mother of active twin boys deserves to grab a power nap any time she can get it."

"Thanks, they are few and far between." Her mouth felt like she'd stuffed marshmallows in it when he gave her a crooked grin.

"Hey, remember I'm the hired help, so if you need to go grab a little shut-eye I'd be more than glad to watch these two cowpokes of yours."

"Oh, that is so tempting." True, she wasn't looking for a romance. Or a date even. But there was nothing keeping her from liking the guy. And the more she knew of him, the more she liked him.

"I'm serious," he said, looking at the boys, who were stretching out the strands of lights like he'd shown them, checking for burned-out bulbs. Jack plugged one end into an extension cord. "We've got this."

The thing was that, as a single working mom of two active boys, she literally dreamt of sleeping... "No. I'm good. I want to do this with the boys." *And you.* So she was human. She was a woman drawn to a man. But that was all. Nothing more.

He grinned and it was like a bolt of sunshine. "Sounds great to me."

What was a great guy like Chance Turner doing still single? The man had never been married and he was about twenty-eight, if she had her figures straight.

He was a year older than Cole and they'd had a small gathering for Cole's birthday three weeks ago. Not that being twenty-eight and never married was a bad thing. She assumed his lack of a wife had a lot to do with being on the road so much.

Not that it mattered to her one way or the other. He was simply a nice guy who was kind to her kids.

And you're having a great time with him.

"Hey, Chance, got one," Gavin yelled, waving at him to come to the end of the strand.

"It's blown, all right," Jack added.

"Duty calls." He tipped his hat, eyes twinkling. "Want me to show you how to change a bulb, too?"

"Sure, sounds great," she laughed, her heart feeling as light as the breeze blowing in across the yard.

She watched him show the boys how to replace a bulb with one of the extras in a little plastic bag that was still attached to the strand.

Her boys huddled with him, their little brown and blond heads bent next to his black one. When the light popped on like the rest of them they whooped and gave each other high fives. Guys.

"There ain't nothin' to that," Gavin gushed.

Chance grinned at him. "You're right. It's easy once you know how to do it."

"What if there's not any extras with the lights?" Jack asked, looking at the strand that lay next to them.

"You can get a little pack of them for less than a dollar, I think."

"Did you hear that, Momma? I got a dollar. I can help."

"I got a dollar, too, Jack," Gavin added, not wanting to be outdone.

"And that is one reason I love you two so much, because you are my little helpful men."

They beamed at the praise and Chance winked at her once more. There was nothing meant by the wink other than agreement with what she'd said, but that didn't stop her insides from feeling suddenly as if she'd been turned upside down. She stepped back, having somehow moved to stand a bit too close to him.

"I guess I'd better get dinner started. You're upholding your part of the deal so I'd better get mine together. Do you like King Ranch chicken?"

"Does a horse like sweet feed? It's my favorite."

A warm bloom of pleasure spread through her at the way he was smiling at her. Self-conscious, she glanced at her boys, who looked in shock at each other, then up at him.

"It's our favorite, too!" Gavin exclaimed for both of them, and Jack nodded, his big blue eyes locked on Chance in admiration.

Shaken by the attachment that her boys seemed to have formed so quickly, she had to force her voice to sound normal. "Then while you boys are finishing up I'll go start on that." She should have already started it, but she'd been unable to walk away from hanging the lights.

It was nice seeing her boys with a good man. The neighbors had helped with several projects at the shelter. Men like Dan Dawson, who'd lived in a shelter growing up, came by to play football and hang out. And others like Mule Hollow deputy Zane Cantrell spent time with the boys, especially after he'd married Rose, who'd lived in the shelter with them. And there were all the others like Clint Matlock, Pace Gentry and Cort Wells who helped the boys with their riding skills. The list went on and on. Mule Hollow was full of great cowboys and everyone she'd thought about was now happily married to friends of hers. The single guys came around too, and it never failed to bless her soul to see men willing to mentor kids who weren't lucky enough to have a man in their life. It was special.

So why, she asked herself with one last glance before heading inside, did it seem her boys had latched on to Chance Turner like they'd never before latched on to anyone?

Chance was having a hard time concentrating. He'd helped with the lights and had a blast with the boys. They were quick learners and interested in everything. While Lynn had cooked supper they'd taken him to the backyard tree house. Chance didn't want to think or say anything derogatory but there was no denying that they needed an intervention.

He'd crossed his arms and studied the poor thing. The boys flanked him and he bit back a laugh when he realized they were copying his own stance.

How easy it was to influence those around you. He'd made a lot of mistakes in his rebellious wild days, during the beginning of his riding career. It had taken one fateful night—a bar brawl had gone bad and a drunk had pulled a knife on him and a riding buddy. Thankfully, his buddy had lived after being stabbed and in the emergency room Chance had come to know the Lord. That E.R. doctor had intervened in more than a physical crisis. He'd also stepped in and brought Chance to his knees before the Lord. Ever since then, Chance had tried his best to be the man that God had intended for him to be. He'd wanted to be like Doc Stone…a man who stood in the gap and boldly told others about God.

He'd made plenty of mistakes along the way. But that hadn't stopped him from trying, striving to be a man of integrity, one the rough-and-tumble riders could see living his witness, day in and day out.

Looking at the boys standing beside him gave him a reprieve from the feeling of failure that had weighed on his shoulders since Randy's death. He knew it was temporary and undeserved, but he wasn't able to walk away from these two without offering to help them on the tree house, too. Even if the solitude he craved called to him back at the stagecoach house.

"It's a sad situation, ain't it," Gavin said, solemnly.

"Hopeless," Jack sighed heavily.

Even Tiny looked depressed about the scary way the boards tilted between the tree limbs.

"It's not hopeless." All three—dog included—looked at him with hope. There was no way he couldn't help. *No way.* "All it's going to take is a little know-how. Your momma has never built one of these before, but I'd give her an A for effort anyway."

"Yeah, she tried." Gavin let out a long sigh.

"You did um, ain't ya," Jack said, sounding more and more like Applegate.

"Yes, I have, Jack. But my first one was a disaster, too."

"Worse than ours?"

Chance laughed. "Yes, Jack. Worse than yours. But, see, my uncle had to come help me and my cousin Cole rebuild it. We couldn't do it on our own."

"Your uncle helped you. Not your dad?" Gavin was studying him, probing. The look in his eyes pulled at Chance's heartstrings.

"No, not my dad. It was my uncle." His dad had spent a good deal of time away from him.

"We don't got a dad to help us either," Gavin continued and Jack nodded.

Chance swallowed the lump that formed in his throat. He'd been too young at the time to realize that it wasn't normal for a kid to spend so much time away from his dad. And his mom. He'd had his cousins and his uncle and aunt to fill in the holes. He'd been lucky. It wasn't until he was a little older that he understood. "You don't have a dad, but God gave you a mom who loves you and tries very hard. That's the best thing ever."

"Yup," Jack sighed. "That's good, ain't it, Gavin?"

"Yup."

As if that was all that needed to be said on the subject, they went back to studying the dilapidated tree house.

"So what do ya say? Do you want me to help you?" He knew the minute the words were out of his mouth and the boys turned jubilant smiles up at him that he was in trouble.

Chapter Nine

"Well, that was some day and a great meal," Chance said. He and Lynn were standing on the front porch and he was getting ready to head home. They'd gotten most of the Christmas lights up and had a meal better than anything he'd eaten in a long time. Lynn Perry could cook.

"Thanks. I can make a few dishes pretty decently. But I'm pretty iffy on the rest."

He laughed and looked down at her. He was getting partial to looking into her deep blue eyes. He kept finding himself trying to figure out what she was thinking and feeling. When she looked at her boys it was clear as blue skies what she was thinking. But it was the rest of the time that had him hooked.

"I know you're being humble now. There is no way you can cook a dish that mouthwatering and not be able to cook anything else you wanted. That was awesome. Really, Lynn."

In the porch light, she looked pleased. His gaze dropped to her lips, full and expressive, their corners tight with uncertainty. Her lips. Chance pulled back, tugged his jacket closed and stuffed his hands into his pockets—for safety. He'd been thinking about pulling her into a hug and kissing her. That's what you did at the end of a date—but that was just it, this was not a date.

He wasn't here for a date.

But that was exactly what it had felt like sitting around her kitchen table with her two sons enjoying her excellent King Ranch chicken.

"Well, I guess as a mom, I'm just happy the boys like my cooking." She had pulled on a coat when she'd walked him outside. Now she tugged it close and took a deep breath.

He did the same as silence stretched between them. It was time to go but he was reluctant. He felt more at peace right now than he had in what seemed like ages. Part of that had come from her, and part from the boys. They'd touched a chord in him that he hadn't even known was there. He'd bent down and given them a hug before they'd gone to take their bath. And they'd asked him once more about the tree house, their excitement overflowing.

"So you're fine with me working on the tree house?"

"I don't want to impose. But the boys are so excited."

"You can say that again." He chuckled. "I don't have anything pressing right now. And I enjoyed today...and don't think I'm not getting something from it. It was good for me."

It had been very good for him.

In the porch light her blue eyes darkened. "Are you all right? I heard you came home because of something to do with that bull rider who was killed."

He shifted his weight from one boot to the other and hefted a shoulder. "Randy was his name."

"You were close?"

Chance rubbed the edge of a curling porch board with his boot and fought a tightness in his chest. "I'd been witnessing to him. I'd known him for a while though he was only twenty-five. I felt responsible for him."

"It must have been really hard on you."

"Yeah." He inhaled the chilling air, feeling cold to the bone. "Harder on Randy. He just needed a little more time."

She startled him by placing a hand on his arm. He could feel the warmth of it through his jacket. The simple act warmed his heart more than any words could have.

"You could only do what you could do. You can't make choices for other people."

His mood shifted suddenly and he gave a harsh laugh. "Boy, don't I know it."

She squeezed his arm and then tucked her hand back into her jacket. He felt colder instantly.

"I know what you're feeling about that," she said. "If it had been up to me I'd have made several decisions for others in my life. But it wasn't possible. For my children, yes, and I made the most important one for them when I took them to the shelter in L.A. I know that I only have them for a short season in life and then they'll be on their own. I'll be praying that I did everything and gave them everything I could to help them make the right choices. That's all you could do for your friend. For Randy."

He hadn't told anyone else how he felt about the drugs. Other than Wyatt. "I could have done more, intervened about the prescription drugs and the bad decisions he was making."

"Maybe, but maybe not."

He nodded. "Look, it's cold. You better get back inside. Thanks for the evening. And the company." He had to move. The guilt was on him once more like a heavy shroud.

"Chance, wait."

His heart thumped against his ribs when he turned to find her right beside him. "Please do come build the tree house," she said and then she took his breath completely away when she hugged him. As easily as the breeze, she slipped her arms around his waist and hugged him tightly. Her face rested against his heart as she held on to him. She was warm and soft and smelled so sweet. And she was holding him.

By the time he tugged his hands from his coat pockets she was stepping back.

"Come tomorrow if you can. I get off at two again," she said, smiling. She slipped inside the house.

Tiny, who'd been flopped across the bottom step, lumbered over to whine at the door.

Chance didn't move at all. Not for a full minute.

He just stood there staring at the door.

"You hugged him!"

"Well, Nive, you had to have been there. He just needed it."

"Hey, I didn't ask why. I'm all for it. When he gets there this afternoon, you going to hug him again?"

"No. I just did it on the spur of the moment. He looked so sad. He feels responsible for Randy's death. Even though you and I both know we can't be responsible for someone else's actions." They'd both learned that after years of letting abusive husbands make them think it was their fault they were getting beaten. It just didn't work that way. For anyone.

"So the kids really like him." Nive leaned over the glass counter and put her chin in her palm. Her amber-colored hair was pulled into a messy topknot and loose tendrils fell around her heart-shaped face.

"It's scary how they've attached to him."

"It's cool. Wonderful."

Lynn frowned. "Nive—"

"Don't look at me that way. Do you seriously not think you're going to remarry?"

Lynn laid her pencil down, finished with the list she was making. "In my heart of hearts I just can't see it happening. I mean, well, you know how it is. Those two precious boys are my responsibility. What if I made a mistake? What if I could trust a man again and he… and it turned out bad. I don't want to think about it."

"Are you sure you aren't just using them as an excuse?"

"Maybe." She was honest about it. "Because I sure can't read my mixed-up heart. The one thing I'm positive about in life are my boys." She loved them and they loved her and they were her life. And God loved them. She was certain about that also. So two things. Three—God had brought them here. It was good. So there were plenty of things she was sure of, but she wasn't sure that she could ever truly open up to a man and be a wife, emotionally, physically, mentally. She had baggage even she didn't like looking at.

If she did find a good man he would deserve more than she could give him.

"Well, I think it's great you're going to let him help you with that tree house. Gavin and Jack told me it was horrible."

"The little toots!"

Nive made a face. "Seriously, Lynn. You weren't going to let them walk around on those boards after you nailed them in? Jack said you nailed one in and it fell right off the tree and stuck in the ground. Those were his very words."

"All the more reason to be glad I decided to let Chance help."

"How's the Christmas shopping going? Did you get a tree yet?"

"Nive, I just got the lights up. Hopefully we'll get a tree this weekend, because next weekend is pageant practice. I've got to go. Wish me luck. I'm going to talk to Chance this afternoon about Stacy's wedding if the time seems right. I really think he'll do it. He's just hurting right now. But I feel like if I just explain everything he'll do it."

Nive didn't move from her position but lifted a hand and waved. "I'll say a prayer. I want that girl married so bad it's not funny. If ever there was a need for a happy ending it's for Stacy... I'd even give up dreaming about my own if Stacy-girl could have hers."

"That's really sweet of you, Nive. But don't worry. I feel like God has this under control."

"Hey, He might have more than you think under control where you and this cowboy preacher are concerned."

Lynn was opening the door when Lacy practically waddled in. Her blond, erratically wavy hair framed her adorable face and she looked a little puffy under the eyes.

"How are you?" Lynn asked, pulling the door closed to keep the cold out.

"Priscilla is kicking like an Olympic soccer player. She needs a container of peanut brittle. Now!"

Nive was already moving. "Tell her to hold her horses. I'm getting it."

"You have eaten your weight in peanut brittle," Lynn said.

"Yep, yep, yep, and I've enjoyed every ounce of it! I'm holding up my bargain and I'm off to kick my feet up at home, munch on peanut brittle and let Priscilla watch a little *Love Me Tender.* That Elvis movie's got some soothing music in it, so maybe the little whirlwind will settle down and stop kicking."

"You and Elvis." Lynn laughed. She had her Elvis-pink Caddy and loved his music. "Do you think if you stopped feeding her so much sugar it might help?"

"Hey, I'm monitoring my sugar intake. I'm not eating it in anything but candy."

"Lacy," Lynn gasped. "You're so bad."

"Hey, I'm a pregnant woman." She took the bag Nive held over the counter. "I can crave what I want. So back off, sister." She plopped her money on the counter, grabbed a tissue from a box and greedily reached inside the bag for a piece of golden brittle. She took an exaggerated bite.

"You are crazy." Lynn laughed.

"Blissfully. That's the way God wants me to feel. I mean, goodness gracious—look how He's blessed me. I certainly don't deserve any of it, so I'm surely going to enjoy it like I'm supposed to."

"You have got to have the most optimistic mind of anyone I've ever met."

Lacy's electric-blue eyes settled on Lynn, seriousness overtaking mirth. "Oh, Lynn, after the year it took for me to conceive I'm just so grateful."

"It's hard to believe it was that long."

Lacy started to bite down on another piece of brittle but paused. "I was beginning to think I couldn't get pregnant but it was just God's timing. The man upstairs was just telling me to hold on to my horses till He gave me the go-ahead. And He taught me a big lesson in compassion and patience while I waited."

That was pure Lacy, always trying to figure out what God was trying to teach her. Lynn wasn't always so good at that.

"Well, I hate to run out on great company but I've got to go. Enjoy your time at home this afternoon."

Lacy grinned. "Will do and you, too. I hear you've got some handsome help coming over. Y'all have fun!"

Lynn stopped with her hand on the doorknob. "And how did you know that?"

"Little birdies told me. Well, big birdies, actually. Chance told Cole when he saw him this morning that he was helping you this afternoon. Cole told Seth and Wyatt, and it went like wildfire as soon as App and Stanley got wind of it. And yes, the posse knows, too."

Lynn let out a groan. "Great. Just great. Now everyone will instantly jump to conclusions. I'm just letting the man help me build a tree house."

"Yep and I'm only eating one piece of this brittle. Relax. Enjoy and build a *great* tree house. Who knows where that will lead…. Lynn and Chance, sitting in a tree. First comes love and then comes—"

"I'm outta here." Lynn laughed despite herself and headed toward her car. She heard Lacy continue the song as the door closed behind her.

She glanced around and felt like she was sneaking out of town as she got into her car and drove down Main Street. The entire town knew Chance was coming out to her house again. And she knew exactly where it would lead. Straight to overblown hopes for love and romance, which wasn't happening. Yes, the man was gorgeous. Good to her boys and extremely useful around the house... Her ex-husband had been none of those things. So it really felt unfair to let her experience with her ex color her view of Chance. But she painted all men with that brush where she and her boys were concerned.

Where this was going? Nowhere. She'd just gotten carried away with her soft side, and Chance had looked so woebegone and sad last night that on a crazy impulse she'd hugged him. Hugged him for a pretty long time.

An extremely nice, long time. And now she knew... No hugging allowed. None. Zero. Never again.

Chapter Ten

"If you'll hold this then I'll attach it," Chance said several hours later.

Lynn was crouched beside him, shoulder to shoulder, on the now sturdy floor of the tree house. They were using a cordless drill to attach the walls to the floor with screws. Below them the boys and Tiny ran in circles playing cowboys with their popguns. They were thrilled with the tree house.

"I would hope you know I would never have gotten this done without you. My boys would have probably hurt themselves in what I could have built them."

Chance pushed the power button and the screw ate through the wood in less than ten seconds. He sat back on his knees and let the drill rest on his thigh. "You were trying. That says something. And the best way to learn is to be taught. I'm a good teacher, if you haven't noticed." He gave a cocky grin and it did crazy fluttery things to her insides.

This was a glimpse of Chance Turner, relaxed and not being so hard on himself. Until that moment she hadn't realized exactly how difficult Randy's death had been for him.

But now she knew his unguarded side and realized that Chance Turner could be dangerous. She tried to look unaffected and casual. "You're a little cocky for a preacher, aren't you?" She laughed.

"Hey, God never said a preacher was supposed to be a passive, no-personality kind of guy."

She was hyperaware of where her jean-clad knee was touching his. "I guess you have a point."

"You're right, I do. Look at Peter. There was nothing about him that was passive. Passionate, yes. Passive— no way. Strong men can be Christians."

"Hey, you sound a little defensive," she teased, enjoying herself more than she could fathom. It was a beautiful, crisp winter day, the sun was sparkling, her children were playing and she was having an entertaining, enlightening conversation with a devastatingly handsome cowboy. It was lovely.

He crunched his straight black eyebrows. "Oh, believe me, there are some out there who think a preacher has to have a milkweed handshake and his chin to his chest. But God tells me and all His other kids to be bold. Courageous. Men of courage. Patient and kind, yes. But there is a balance." He paused. "I guess that could sound arrogant. Believe me, I'm not. The Lord has forgiven me a lot. I'm no better than the lowest sinner out there. None of us are. But I try to be the man God would want me to be." He took a deep breath and turned his head to the side, staring out at the cattle in the distance.

"You aren't preaching right now. Why is that?" she asked. "You are clearly called to it."

He was passionate. It was obvious now. But he was

deeply caring and compassionate to have been so affected by one from his congregation. She guessed that was what Randy had been. Having church in an arena didn't change that.

Chance pulled himself back from wherever his thoughts had gone and reached for another board. "I don't have it in me. I just feel like my well is empty." He stood the board up and she grabbed it and held it like she'd done the other one. Their fingers brushed as hers replaced his, and the butterflies that had been dancing on and off all morning exploded into motion.

She tried to concentrate on what was being discussed and the importance of it and not this attraction she was feeling toward him. "When you talk just now you don't sound empty. You sound like a man with a lot to say and to offer. But I know what you mean. Not from a preacher's standpoint, but I know what you mean about feeling empty. I never thought about it exactly that way, but that's kind of how I feel about the thought of remarrying." Why was she going there? It had just come out. "I know everyone sees me and my boys and they think it would be so lovely for me to find a good man—a cowboy—and remarry and live happily ever after." She gave him an embarrassed smile. His eyes were serious and caring as he listened. "I've thought about it. But unlike Stacy, who is trying to get married, or Rose, who married Zane, I just don't think I have in me what it takes to be a wife again. I feel like I can be a good mother."

"You are a good mother. A great mother."

Her heart jumped at his soft words of reassurance. "Thank you. But as far as a wife, I feel like my well is dry, too." She was totally embarrassed. Waving her hand, she huffed, "Ignore all of that. It isn't anything at all like what you are feeling. I shouldn't have even tried to make a comparison. It probably makes no sense at all."

He set the drill down and grabbed her fluttering hand. "No. Stop. You make perfect sense. I don't know what all you went through, but you're a strong woman. I can tell that. You've come out on top here with your boys. No one can judge or even try to know someone else's heart. But God does know, and with time He'll heal even that dry well. One day you may be able to love again. Your time to heal is your own. No one else's."

He was rubbing his thumb across the back of her hand and his words comforted her…as did his touch. Lifting her chin, she looked into his eyes and felt an overwhelming sense of…assurance. He was good at what God had called him to do.

"Thank you," she said. "I was feeling some pressure from several sides."

"They mean well." He winked and gently laid her hand on her knee, patting the back of it once before picking up his drill again. It was almost as if he regretted letting her hand go.

She concentrated on placing the next board of the tree house in place. Her thoughts guiltily went to Stacy. She'd yet to ask him again to perform Stacy's wedding. Knowing what he was going through now, she was conflicted.

"So about you?" she said. She hadn't meant to sidetrack talking about him. "You were ministering to me just now. You do it naturally."

"Some things come naturally. That doesn't mean I'm not stuck on the sandbar in the middle of river. I'm sorry about your friend's wedding. I've been thinking about that ever since you asked me, but that's her special day and I just don't feel like I'm where I need to be to be involved in it."

Looking at him no one would guess Chance Turner would ever get stranded. "I wish you were. She—" Lynn stopped. This was about him right now. "And this has to do with Randy's death."

The pain instantly dulled his green eyes to a pale hue and his handsome features went slack with the weight of the burden he carried. Lynn's heart cracked seeing it. She leaned the board against the attached one and gave him her full attention. "Is it that you didn't realize he was on drugs?"

He took a deep breath, and let it out slowly through tense lips. "Funny how I can counsel and give advice and can't get it in my own head and mind."

A sharp stab of empathy sliced through Lynn. She got it. She understood exactly what he was saying. "I guess it's the eighteen-inch rule. Many people miss Heaven because of the eighteen inches between their brain and their heart. The two don't always connect." She started to say, *Believe me, I know,* but held back. She couldn't keep bringing the conversation to herself.

This was about Chance.

"I'm just taking time off, trying to find my way. Giving God time to pull me off the sandbar. Helping you and the boys is a good thing." He lifted the drill and pulled the trigger. Twice. "So put me to work," he said over the whirring roar.

"Okay, anything I can do."

"Momma, can we come up there yet?" Gavin skidded to a halt at the base of the ladder.

Jack was right behind him. "We ain't gonna fall."

He grabbed hold of the ladder and jumped on the bottom rung.

"What do you think, boss lady?" Chance's eyes twinkled. "Do you feel safe enough to let them come up and maybe start helping build this thing?"

She looked around at the two sides that were finished. "If they stay on that side I won't worry so much that they'll try to jump from the floor to the ground."

"Nice way to not say they might fall."

She laughed. "Knowing those two, they would jump intentionally just to see if they could do it."

"Come on up, but careful," Chance called. Jack scooted up the ladder like a squirrel up a tree.

Chance took him by the arms and helped him onto the deck of the tree house. "Dude, I thought you said you were scared of climbing a ladder?"

Jack's face blew up with a radiant smile. "I'm not scared of *this*. I'm scared of *that*." He waved toward the house and the tall eaves. "That's e-*nor*-mous.

"It ain't enormous. Clint Matlock's barn, that's enormous," Gavin declared, hot on the heels of his brother. Chance reached for him also. "And I'm not scared of any of it." Gavin beamed, then looked at Lynn. "But I'm not gonna scare you again, Momma. Just like Chance told me."

He was scaring her all right, just by his big talk! "What did Chance tell you?" she asked, her curiosity spiked.

"That boys can be daredevils but calcu-lated. They got to be prepared and trained up for dangerous stuff so's it balances the scale. But sometimes they just gotta think about their mommas."

She laughed nervously. "Well, thank you for thinking of me. If you become a daredevil I'm going to grow old before my time."

"And she's too pretty to grow old before her time. Don't you boys agree?"

Chance had just called her pretty. The compliment was just to tease with her boys and yet there was no denying the way it washed over her. It had been a very long time since a man had told her she was pretty.

She didn't look at him. Instead she looked at her grinning boys.

Gavin spoke first. "We ain't gonna do that to you, Momma. Are we, Jack?"

Jack shook his head. He turned serious. "You think my momma is pretty?"

Chance hiked a straight black brow charmingly and showed his even more charming half grin. "I think you've got a beautiful mom inside and out."

Gavin and Jack stared at her with the excitement of two children who'd just won the Toys "R" Us lottery.

She laughed, self-conscious about the moment. "You don't really know me," she said, teasing but serious.

He looked shocked. "So you're telling me you aren't nice?"

"Oh, she's nice," Gavin said. "Except when we don't do what she says!"

"Oh, yeah." Jack giggled when she shot them a teasing scowl. "She makes us sit in time-out forever!"

She knew he was playing, getting into the spirit of things. She poked him in the rib and he jumped away squealing. Chance caught him around the waist and poked him, too, as Jack wrapped his arms around Chance's neck. "Your momma is just teaching you right from wrong because she loves you."

"We know," Gavin said, launching himself toward Chance, wanting to be included in the hug. Lynn's heart caught—partly because they were up so high and partly because of how hungry her boys were for male affection.

Laughing, Chance caught him and pulled him close, keeping him safe.

Lynn took in the sweet picture. It sent an ache of longing through her like nothing she'd experienced.... Her boys were on the safe side of the tree house with Chance in between them and the edge. Looking at them, it was easy to see what they were missing. Her boys were missing the man in their life who was supposed to love them and protect them from the hard, dangerous things in life.

Her boys were missing that because she thought she was enough for them.

But was she?

Meeting Chance's eyes, she smiled back at him and tried to enjoy the moment and not make more of this than she should.

She and her boys were doing great. And if she looked at it from Chance's point of view, this was good for him, too. This moment was a way to relieve some of the strain he was feeling from Randy's death. That's what this was. A great moment for her boys and for Chance.

She didn't need to complicate it with all this other stuff suddenly rolling around in her head. Like the realization that Chance Turner was a man she could trust. He was a man she could trust with all the shattered pieces hidden inside her heart.

A shattered piece of glass wasn't fixable. There were too many pieces crushed to dust particles that were irreparable. It was the same with her heart. Some women at the shelter with worse stories than hers were moving on. Stacy was one of them. But as hard as she'd tried to encourage others to take the step, she'd realized that her heart was too shattered. She couldn't and wouldn't put herself through believing in someone again.

But seeing her boys with Chance told her that they were going to suffer in the long run because she couldn't let go of her past.

Chance was wrong. She wasn't pretty on the inside or she'd be able to forgive and forget and move on.

Her ex had been manipulative and mind controlling. And though she'd finally gotten out, it was a struggle. She'd come to realize deep in her heart that he still controlled her, even though she hadn't seen or talked to him in over three years. It made her feel weak.

She didn't like knowing this about herself, but as much as she tried she couldn't get past it. Some people could trust again. She couldn't. And it seemed nothing or no one could change that.

Chapter Eleven

Lynn pulled herself out of the dumps by the next morning and headed over to the shelter. Dottie had called and asked her to talk to a new resident, Sandra, who she thought Lynn could help. Though Lynn was able to help others, she often felt like a hypocrite because she still had her own hang-ups. But she never refused to share her experience or to listen to a new resident pour out her heartache. Lynn never omitted that she still had struggles—a hang-up where trust was concerned.

When it came to trust, each person had to work that out on her own timetable. It was much like grief. One person's time to grieve the loss of a loved one was not charted on the same schedule as someone else.

She did know and recognize that God had brought her through and she had a great life! She *did*.

Sandra was a nervous wreck. She was a small woman with a kind face that wore the bright purple marks of a fresh beating and a swollen eye full of blood. In her eyes, behind everything, Lynn saw the struggle. She'd seen this over and over again and every time it made her sick to her stomach. But unlike the way she'd almost lost it at the bachelor auction, here she always was able to hold on to her emotions. When she was talking to women like Sandra it was all about helping free them.

Dottie, tall and willowy with a slight limp left over from a near fatal meeting with a hurricane, had hugged Lynn the minute she arrived, and had introduced her to Sandra. Dottie was a Godsend for the shelter. They stood in an awkward moment as the boys raced each other to the large swing set the men of Mule Hollow had built them. A little girl sat on a swing hugging her doll.

"This is Margaret," Dottie said. "She's seven and loves babies."

"Hi, Margaret, it's good to meet you," Lynn said. She never asked a child how she was doing when she'd just arrived. Poor children were disoriented, afraid, usually confused and scared. But putting that into words right off the bat to a total stranger was hard. Lynn knew from her own boys' experience that it was best to let them acclimate slowly. Margaret didn't say anything, just hugged her doll closer and looked at her mother. Lynn's heart went out to the child, just for having to look into her mother's bruised and swollen face.

Overwhelmed with compassion and the desire to help, Lynn smiled at Sandra. "Let's go talk. If you want to?"

Sandra nodded.

"I'll watch the children." Dottie patted her five-month-old's padded bottom. "You take all the time you need. Margaret can help me babysit. How does that sound?" Dottie held her hand out to Margaret. The little girl glanced at her mother. Sandra nodded and Margaret reached out and took Dottie's hand.

Lynn led the way to the parlor that they used for

group sessions and one-on-one meetings. Brady's parents had dreamed of having a huge family and had built this giant ranch home in anticipation. But God hadn't had it in His plan and they'd only been blessed late in life with Brady. Brady had turned the house into No Place Like Home. And this parlor, which had been used little in the years before the shelter, had become a room where much heartache was shared and much healing begun. Brady loved to say that his parents had had a dream for the house, but God had had a bigger dream.

As she led Sandra into the pretty pale blue room, Lynn prayed that she could be God's facilitator of the beginning of Sandra's healing process.

To her surprise she didn't have to coax anything out of Sandra. She was ready to speak. Ready to try and find answers. Like Lynn had been when she'd finally left her husband, Sandra was seeking a way to stop the cycle. She was just trying to get her mind around how to do it. She opened up and everything flooded out.... She was so upset that trust wasn't an issue. She just needed someone. And she was worried that her abuse was her fault.

"No, Sandra, it's not your fault. You can't think about how long you stayed. You're out now," Lynn said, not too long into the conversation. "From this point on you have to look forward. God led me out of my abusive marriage, but I did the same thing as you. I let myself stay in that situation far longer than I should have. I was mixed up and I'd heard so many lies, and so many situations had been twisted, and over time I was turned inside out and unable to see clearly. Distance helps us see more clearly. Each passing day helps.... There may be emotional scars that take far longer to heal than those marks on your face. But life can be better for you and Margaret. I promise."

Sandra wrung her hands together in her lap. "But my mother despises that I've done this. She says that God hates divorce and that I'll reap the consequences of my actions for the rest of my life."

Good, well-meaning—and not so well-meaning— Christian folks could be so judgmental, so clueless sometimes. "You were living in a dangerous situation for you and your child. Yes, God wants marriages to last, but I don't believe God wants us to stay in a situation like that. I have to answer for leaving my marriage one day and, Sandra, I am proud to say that I kept my boys safe. You and I both have no one to be accountable to for our action except God."

Sandra contemplated that before nodding. "I understand."

"No one understands like those of us who have been down this road. For me, leaving was hard to do. Despite the pain and the fear I lived with and as unhealthy as my situation was, it was still hard to make myself leave." Drew had hit her during his drunken, emotional rages, and his infidelities, followed by contrite apologies, were always the same. And always painful.

She finally realized they were merely his way of manipulating her into doing exactly what he wanted her to do—abusive in so many ways.

"But maybe I could have done something different," Sandra said. "Margaret loves her daddy."

"It's not your fault, no matter what, when a man hits you."

Drew had always managed to make it Lynn's fault. Toward the end he'd grown more and more physically abusive, as if the more he hit her the easier it was. And she'd allowed it, believing the lie that somehow it was her fault. "We do things we shouldn't because we love our spouses—so we put up with things and believe the one we love when he says it's our fault. Sandra, God gave you Margaret to love and protect. You have taken the first step toward doing just that."

Lynn totally understood where Sandra was coming from. She'd started out as a strong person but somehow she'd lost her way. At some point her mind told her this was the way she was supposed to live. And the way it had happened…she'd lost herself and her path because of the worst part—how much she'd loved Drew and trusted him.

She was so ashamed to admit to herself or anyone that she'd loved a man who could do that to her. If it hadn't been for her boys she would have stayed there. It was humiliating to realize that about herself. With distance she'd understood that any love she'd ever had for Drew had been wiped out by the bad things he'd done. And that gave her freedom. But the issue remained that she'd misjudged him and loved him in the first place. How, how, she asked herself, had she ever loved a man like that? Was her judgment that bad?

She and Sandra talked for over an hour and Sandra seemed to feel better and stronger about what she'd done when they finished. A long road lay ahead, but at least Sandra was on the path to freedom and healing.

Lynn hoped she'd helped Sandra. But she was thinking about herself as she drove away. She would never allow herself to become embroiled in a bad marriage again. She feared it more than anything in life. It would not happen. God had helped her over the last few years to know what a great life she had now. And to believe that she and her boys would and could be okay. It was just that lately niggling doubts and worries had started in on her. Why now, when everything was going so well?

Chance's tires crushed the gravel of Lynn's drive as he pulled to a stop. It had rained but he'd noticed Lynn didn't have a Christmas tree. So what did he do? He asked her if he could take her and the boys to cut one. He'd come over two straight days and worked on the tree house and it was now finished. He could have disappeared and gone out to the stagecoach house for the solitude he needed, but the boys really wanted a tree.

He'd picked up some wood to repair Lynn's front porch. Lifting the lumber from the truck, he carried it around the back of the house to the barn. Tiny sloshed around in the mud, dashing all around Chance, and before he made it to the back door it flew open and the boys raced out. They wore rubber boots and coats that could repel the wet, cold weather. He felt good seeing them.

"Hey, buckaroos!"

"Merry Christmas, Chance," Gavin yelled, jumping in a puddle.

"No, Gavin," Jack exclaimed. "Momma said don't get wet. We're goin' ta get a tree. Now."

"Gavin," Lynn said, coming to a halt on the back step. "Your brother is right. What did I tell you?"

Chance hid a laugh as Gavin reluctantly stepped out of the puddle and looked up at his mother.

"Don't get wet," Gavin said. "I'll be too cold to go get a tree."

The kid was funny. "Then load up," Chance said. "Let's get us a tree."

The boys whooped and raced off around the corner, sloshing through shallow puddles as they went.

"Hi." Lynn sighed. "All I can do is try."

Chance instinctively gave her a one-armed hug as he met her twinkling eyes. "It's all good."

"Yes it is." She looked up at him. "Are you ready for this?"

His heart felt as if it were being pumped up like a balloon. Goodness, she took his breath away. "I was born ready."

But looking at her, holding her close and wanting to hold her closer, he knew he wasn't ready at all.

Chapter Twelve

Lynn walked beside Chance as they followed the boys through the woods on the Turner ranch. Her thoughts were distracted. When Chance had put one arm around her and looked into her eyes her world had begun to spin. She'd been thinking about him before he got there. Ever since he'd played with her boys in that tree house, she'd been thinking about it—how her boys were on the safe side, with Chance in between them and the edge. It had been so easy to see what they were missing. So easy to see what they could have if she were able to fall in love with a good man. Because she knew in that moment in that unfinished tree house, with two sides built and two sides open, that her boys missed having a man in their life to love and protect them.

Walking beside Chance, looking for a Christmas tree, underlined the fact in bold black.

Her boys were missing that because she thought she was enough for them.

But was she? No.

She'd looked into Chance's eyes and wanted him to embrace her like a man in love would do. She'd wanted him to kiss her…wanted to feel cherished and protected. She'd looked into Chance's eyes and wanted her life to be different. Wanted all the horrible past to have never happened. If it had never happened then there was hope for her—but she wouldn't have her boys. She closed her eyes and sighed, feeling the strength of Chance's embrace. Her past had happened and nothing could make it not so. Her boys were the proof that God could make good from any bad situation. She wouldn't choose a clear past over her sons.

And she and her boys were doing great. That was what she told herself when she'd stepped out of Chance's embrace. It was what she told herself as she'd pretended his touch hadn't affected her.

But it had.

"What about this one?" Gavin yelled. He was standing beside a gigantic cedar tree.

"I think that's a little too big," Chance called. He was walking beside her as Jack and Gavin bounded from one tree to the next.

"You sure are quiet," he said.

"Sorry."

"Is it something I did?"

"No. It's just stuff."

"Can I help?"

No, he couldn't, because the stuff she was dealing with was knowing Chance Turner was a trustworthy man. He was a man she could trust with all the shattered pieces hidden inside her heart. And yet she couldn't do it. She thought of Sandra and all she'd told her…. She prayed that, like so many of the others, Sandra could become totally free from her past.

Lynn hated admitting that she wasn't free from her

own past. Hated admitting that she was more fragile than she wanted to be. But it was true. She wasn't just cracked, she was broken on an emotional level.

"What is bothering you?"

She sighed and was glad for the cold air on her hot cheeks. "My ex was a manipulative man. And though I finally got out, it's been, and still is a struggle. I'm dealing with issues this morning."

His expression was understanding. And yet she knew he couldn't understand.

"I hope you know you can trust me," Chance said, as if he'd been reading her mind.

She stopped walking and studied a cedar. It was too small but it gave her something to concentrate on. "I have a hard time trusting men."

"I know. But I still hope you'll realize you can trust me."

"My boys are crazy about you. I guess you've figured that out."

His lips twisted in that pulse-igniting grin of his. "I don't know what I did to garner that honor but I like it."

"Kids are good judges of character."

"How about you?"

"Sometimes," she said, wishing she could say yes, but it wouldn't be true. "I misjudged Drew in the worst possible way and, though I no longer bear the physical signs of that mistake, psychologically I still have issues."

"Do you want to talk about it?"

She pulled her knitted scarf closer around her neck and shook her head. The kids were squealing in the woods ahead and that was where she wanted to be…not here, where she suddenly wanted more than anything to feel Chance's arms tightly around her. To feel the beat of his heart against her ear. How could she want that so deeply and still be scared to death of him?

She hated this. "You know what—enough." She inhaled and smiled like she meant it. "We came to find a tree and have a good time and that is what I want to be doing." She headed toward the laughter ringing through the trees. She was going to have fun and not think about all the dirt from her past. "Today is a great day," she said, her confidence building.

"Yes, it is. You're a brave woman, Lynn. A strong woman. I'm the first to tell you that I'm having issues of my own, which you are well aware of, so I completely understand what you're saying."

"I know. It's crazy, isn't it. I know God has gotten me to this point and it's fantastic, considering where I was. Why then can't I get past this moment?"

"Hey, look around at this beautiful place and listen to your children laughing." He took her hand. "This is a good moment." He paused, looking up at the treetops while the sound of her children's laughter echoed on the chilly air, and then he smiled at her. "Let's just think about this moment right now."

He was right. It sounded like a good plan.

Planting a smile on her face and in her heart on Saturday morning, Lynn headed to the church. She had to drop by the feed store and pick up some dog food first, and they ran into App and Stanley buying their weekly bag of sunflower seeds. While she paid for the dog food the two older men and her boys went outside. She watched through the window as they stood on the sidewalk and practiced their sunflower spitting. Boys would be boys no matter what ages.

As soon as she herded Gavin and Jack into the car they began copying the way App and Stanley talked. It never failed after being around them. Thankfully, it *usually* lasted only a few days before they went back to their normal vernacular.

"I ate me some *sunflours,* Momma," Jack drawled.

"Yup," Gavin said. "Them thar thangs is the best ta spit."

She bit her tongue and concentrated on getting to the church. It was less than three weeks till Christmas and practice was starting on the children's Christmas pageant. Like everything else around here, it had been started as a way to get women to come to Mule Hollow. Not just as a matchmaking endeavor but also as a witness with the story of Jesus' birth. Lacy had been in charge and she was always excited about spreading the good news and witnessing to everyone about God's ability to save and redeem. But this year she was due to deliver close to Christmas and had been unable to take charge. It just seemed that one thing after the other had kept folks from stepping up. The Barn Theater, started by Ross and Sugar Ray Denton, was having a Christmas-themed program involving several resident cowboys and cowgirls and so it really didn't seem necessary to have a community pageant. Lynn and several ladies had decided that the children needed a program and so Lynn had volunteered to head that up.

The last person she expected to see when she pulled into the church parking lot was Chance.

"Look, it's Chance!" the boys squealed in unison. They were crazy about the man. Crazy about him.

He was leaning against his pickup with his boots crossed at the ankles, his hat hunkered down low over his eyes against the sparkling winter sunlight. Involuntarily her stomach dropped and she smiled like a schoolgirl, which she certainly was not!

He nudged his hat back and grinned, coming to place his hand on her open door. "I guess I got the time wrong. I showed up thirty minutes ago."

"What are you doing here?"

"We invited him," Gavin boasted, jumping out of the backseat. He tilted his head all the way back and grinned up at Chance. "We didn't thank you was actually going to come though."

Jack jumped from the car. "We shor nuff didn't," he said, in his App-and-Stanley slang. Okay, so she might have to talk to the boys about copying everything the two older men said.

"Didn't you two tell me your mom needed help?"

Their eyes grew wide as saucers. Gavin spoke first. "You're not s'posed to tell her that."

"Why did you tell him that in the first place?"

Jack looked shocked. "But you said you did."

"I didn't mean—" She got out of the car, where she really felt hemmed-in looking up at Chance from her seat. "Do you really want to help?

He glanced toward the white church. "I do."

The man confused her. He didn't want to preach right now, he was struggling spiritually and yet he was volunteering to help with the children's ministry…. It suddenly hit her that maybe this wasn't about her, but was about Chance. Maybe God was using all this for him. Once more she bit her lip and she prayed she'd stop thinking about her own situation and focus on his.

Maybe God was going to use this to help Chance refill his well. It wasn't hard to see what a wonderful man he was. Though he was hurting inside, he was still reaching out to help her and now the children.

"Sure. That's great. Follow me to the sanctuary. Boys, do not, and I repeat, do not barrel around the corners of this church and slam into anyone. You may go play on the swing set until everyone starts to arrive but slow down around corners." The ground had dried up since the morning's rain but it was still moist in places. Although thankfully here at the church there hadn't been anything more than a drizzle. Mud and kids and a church were not a good combination.

"We'll try, Momma," Gavin said with a heavy sigh, as if trying to control his speed was the largest weight he could possibly bear. Jack had already raced off toward the back of the church.

"*Jack Robert Perry,* did you hear me?" she called in her sternest voice. The little tyke put the brakes on instantly and turned to look at her innocently. Right.

"I wasn't gonna run when I was coming back."

"Don't run going either."

"Okay, Momma. But little boys are supposed to run, don't you know that?"

She cleared her throat trying to hold back a grin. "Yes, I do know that, but they are also supposed to mind their mommas."

"Yes, ma'am," Jack said as Gavin reached him. They headed off together at a snail's pace, overemphasizing their dragging feet.

Chance chuckled watching them disappear around the corner. "You sound pretty mean there."

"Ha! I sound like a mother."

"That you do. You have a good poker face, too."

She gave him a look of shock. "You noticed that? And here I thought I was fooling everyone."

"Yeah, right. They turn you to mush, and me and anyone watching for two seconds can see it."

She pulled two bags of refreshments from the backseat. "I didn't think I was that transparent."

Chance reached for the bags. "Here, let me take that. And I'm just teasing you."

"You had better watch your step since we are about to be bombarded with ten kids—none over the age of eight—for this dress rehearsal."

"Sounds like fun." He fell into step with her, then waited at the front door as she inserted the key and opened the big oak door. "I'll be sure and look around all corners. So, what's the program?"

"It's the Christmas story from the shepherd's point of view. We wanted to have it be from the donkey's point of view and use Samantha—you know, Cort and Lilly Wells's cute donkey."

"Oh, yeah, I've heard about that donkey's shenanigans."

"The kids love that little donkey but we decided bringing Samantha into the sanctuary was not a good idea."

He cocked a brow. "Nope, not a good idea."

They laughed as she flipped on the light switch and then led the way down to the front of the quaint church.

The sun was filtering in through the stained glass, glinted off the dark wooden pews and made patchworks along the planked floor. "I love this sanctuary," she said, feeling the warmth of the place and the serenity. "There is just a sense of peace that overcomes me when I walk inside. As much as I love Samantha, her clomping down the aisle wouldn't be appropriate."

"I agree. On all counts. I can still remember my first time to come here to worship. I accepted Jesus as my savior right here in this very spot." He'd come to stand in front of the pulpit and was staring thoughtfully at it.

"Then this is a special place on a personal level to you. I think that's great. I want my boys to experience that when the Lord leads them to make a commitment. It's just so wonderful to have roots in the Lord."

And it was. "It means so much to me that my boys have roots. All the women at the shelter feel the same way." She paused and then couldn't stop herself from continuing. "That's what Stacy wants for her wedding. She is such a sweetheart, Chance. She's been through so much in her life and she has been so horribly mistreated by every man in her life…and yet she has a quiet spirit of survival. And she has found a dedicated, loving Christian man she is brave enough to marry—despite all the abuse she's lived through with her dad and former husband. You called me brave. *That* is a brave woman."

"Sounds like it."

"She would never believe that, but she is. And this wedding means so much to her. Finding a preacher to perform the ceremony who is connected to them is very important to her."

"What about Brady?"

"He and Dottie have been lifesavers to her and she could easily have him do the wedding. But she wants a man of God performing the ceremony. She wants to stand here, where we are in this church sanctuary, and say her vows before God and all of her new Mule Hollow family."

Chance looked thoughtful and she wondered what he was thinking. She wanted to come right out and ask him again to do the wedding but something inside her held her back. He was waging his own spiritual battle inside his heart and soul and he didn't need pressure from her. God would lead him as he was ready.

Chapter Thirteen

❧

"No, Wes, you carry it this way. Hold it up."

Chance stood to the side of the little troupe of children lined up at the front of the church. He was totally engaged in watching Gavin show the smaller boy, Wes McKennon, how to hold his staff in his pudgy hand. The dark-haired little boy was trying very hard to do what he was supposed to do.

"Gavin, you're doing a great job helping Wes." Chance bent on one knee, deciding he could help the tot hold the staff the correct way. "And you're doing a good job holding this staff, Wes." Chance knew the boy could hold the staff upside down or sideways and the audience was going to think he was fantastic no matter what he did. As for Gavin, rattling off instructions—the kid was born to be an organizer and leader. The boy was full of instructions for everyone and the other kids were listening when he spoke.

And not just kids. Chance still couldn't believe he himself was here. Gavin also had the gift of persuasion where adults were concerned—or at least where Chance was. Gavin had asked him to help with the program and

Chance had come. And he was enjoying himself. He'd also had fun cutting down the Christmas tree and helping the boys with the lights and the tree house.

"Okay, boys and girls, let's stand up straight and sing so the people on the back pew will hear you. You are doing a great job."

Jack was standing beside a toddler who was sucking his thumb and taking everything in with gigantic eyes. This was Stacy's baby. She was with the other mothers decorating the annex for lunch after the sermon and the program. The Mule Hollow Church of Faith was a busy church. He watched Lynn working with the kids. She'd said she wanted roots for her boys. As a cowboy preacher he hadn't really set any roots down for himself. He stayed on the road much of the time. When he wasn't at a rodeo he was at an auction barn or a roping or any manner of other places where he was called or invited. But that was where his heart was. That was where God had put him.

One lost soul. Randy. Why hadn't he been able to lead Randy to the Lord? Why hadn't he seen that Randy had a problem…. If he considered Randy his flock then why hadn't he recognized that he was in trouble? That torment had a grip on him that he couldn't ease. Why hadn't God given him the time to help Randy physically and spiritually?

"Mr. Turner, could I speak to you?"

The soft voice drew him from the fog of his internal debate and he turned around. Stacy was sitting on the pew behind him looking pensive.

"Sure," he said, wanting instantly to ease her discomfort.

"Outside?"

He nodded, glanced at the group of kids and Lynn as she led them in a song, then got up and followed Stacy. Lynn had told her that Stacy had a hard time trusting men. That she'd come a long way, thanks to some very special men in Mule Hollow who'd been kind and set good, godly examples for her of how real men should behave. On the porch she faced him. Her pale blond hair was pulled back in a clasp, totally exposing her fine, dainty features. She was beautiful in an almost angelic sense—the perfect choice for a Christmas angel. Sky-blue eyes, kind with a wariness that still could not be hidden, despite the kindness she'd been shown here in Mule Hollow. Just looking at her and knowing some of her story, he wanted only the best for her.

"What can I do for you?" he asked, trying to put her at ease, pretty certain he knew what she wanted.

"Lynn, I'm sure, asked you to perform my and Emmett's wedding ceremony. I know you aren't preaching right now, if I understand that correctly, but I was just hoping that I could ask you to please consider it once more." Tears welled in her eyes but she blinked and they disappeared in an instant. He got the feeling she didn't usually speak a whole lot. "I—I've decided I want to get married next Saturday." She glanced at the ground then, almost as if forcing herself, she met his gaze again. "I've been dragging my feet, coming up with all kinds of excuses for why now isn't the time to marry Emmett—there isn't a preacher I want, I'm afraid, I could be hurt again." She breathed in hard. "But I know it's wrong. I love Emmett and he loves me…."
She softly cleared her throat. Probably for courage to push onward—it was clear in her eyes how hard this was

for her. "So, I had to ask you personally if you might marry us next Saturday."

Chance's heart cracked, remembering everything Lynn had told him about Stacy. God help him, there was no way he could tell her no. What kind of man would he be to do that? Meeting her sincere gaze with one of assurance he said, "I would be honored."

"Chance, are you out here?"

Chance was repairing a broken slat on one of the old stalls in the stagecoach house's barn. He straightened and called, "I'm here," stepping out where Lynn could see him.

"You left without a word," she said as she saw him and strode toward him. "And then Stacy told me that you'd agreed to marry them next week and I couldn't believe it. I'm so excited! But, are you all right with that?"

He had been asking himself the same question for the last hour. "I guess I have to be. After she pushed herself to get the courage up to ask me to do it, how could I say no? Who could say no to someone as gentle and kind-looking as Stacy?"

"Oh, so you're saying I'm not sweet enough? That's why you so easily told me no?" Lynn crossed her arms and gave him an assessing look.

"No… I mean…" He stumbled over his words, realizing how that had sounded to her. "I'm sorry. That's not what I meant."

"Relax, I'm just teasing. I know what you mean."

She was laughing but he shook his head. "No. You're just as sweet, Lynn. I just didn't get it until you'd told me her story and then I met her."

A pale tinge of pink touched her cheeks and her eyes softened. "No. I'm not—"

"Yes, you are." He touched her arm then, realizing Lynn's background might mean she wasn't used to compliments.

She studied his hand on her arm then raised her gaze to his. "It seems that God isn't playing fair with you."

He scowled. "You probably think I'm not worth much, pulling back like I have."

"No. I think you are a man grief-stricken for a lost soul. Maybe a little angry at God about it, and that has wiped you out inside. I've been thinking about that dry well you were talking about, and I think God's real busy trying to fill it up for you."

His scowl dug in deeper and he went back to the stall. Grabbing another nail, he bent to retrieve his hammer and sank the nail into the hardwood with two strikes.

"Impressive," Lynn said, leaning against the top plank and looking down at him. She'd been happy about Stacy, but deep inside it was costing him. His soul did ache. It was easy to tell. "Nothing like a hammer and nails to vent with," she said, feeling led to see if he needed to talk. It didn't go unnoticed that he wasn't using his cordless drill and wood screws.

"You are enjoying this."

"No. I'm sorry. I really think taking your frustrations out with hard work is very constructive. You get to vent, think about it, pray about it, accomplish something constructive at the same time. Believe you me, I can do some heavy-duty housecleaning when I'm mad as a hornet. I buzz around, hotter than fire, and my house sparkles like Mr. Clean himself has been to visit. I just recognized the tendency."

He stood up and hooked the hammer on the wooden slat. "So you probably thought me running out on you like that was pretty pathetic."

"So, you did run out on me. I looked around and you weren't there. It wasn't until Stacy came and told me the news that I thought—well, I wondered if you were okay."

He nodded. "I'm okay. God's working with me."

She really liked that about him. He was angry at God for not giving him the opportunity to lead Randy to the Lord. Angry at God for taking Randy before he had time to get straightened out. And yet he was waiting and letting God work on him.

"Thanks for coming to check on me."

His quiet words washed over her like the touch of a whispery breeze. "You're welcome." He smiled and she felt almost faint, her heart was pounding so fast. "I'm just so pleased you agreed to do this for Stacy and Emmett." She needed to get to a subject that wasn't attached to her emotions. Maybe that was what was wrong with her suddenly. She looked around the interior of the barn, trying not to think about how his gaze had seemed to touch something deep in the dark corner of her heart.... "This place is really old, isn't it? Am I wrong, or would this have been the same barn they used all those years ago to stable the stagecoach horses?"

"It is. We try to keep it in as good condition as possible. For over a hundred and fifty years old it still looks pretty good, don't you think?" The stable was a low-slung building but the ceiling was steep in the center and high enough to house the stagecoaches if needed. Then the roofline sloped low on both sides where the horse stables were. It wasn't used much anymore but

Chance liked it. He enjoyed the relics left from days gone by, like the old horseshoes that were nailed along the top stable board running the length of the barn.

"Are these horseshoes from back then?"

"Yes," he said, pleased. "I wonder where those shoes have been?"

"It is a really neat thing, this history your family has here. Melody talks about it all the time."

Melody had met Seth because she was researching Sam Bass, the famous Texas outlaw. As a history teacher she was intrigued by the ranch and its past, and Wyatt had hired her to research their whole family. She'd done a great job and in the process married Seth.

"I love the stability of your family."

He placed his boot against the stall rung and leaned his back against the stall. "Oh, we have our share of dysfunction. No family doesn't."

"Yes, I know. But you have to remember all that I've seen. I really cannot express to you what this means to Stacy for you to marry them. It is like a blessing from God. And being able to take her children and grandchildren to the church one day and show them where it all started—that means so much to someone like Stacy. I know I sound like a broken record. But it is true. I pray that God will give you peace about it."

"Where are your kids?"

"They went with Lilly Wells to play with Joshua. They just love going out there as much as they love going over to Susan's."

"So you have the evening free?" What was he doing?

"Well, I hadn't really thought about it but, yes, I guess I do. I—"

"Would you like to ride into Ranger and have dinner with me?"

"Like a date?"

Her startled question flew back at him almost before he could register that he'd actually asked her out. Sure, he asked ladies out but not when he knew they weren't interested. But he enjoyed her company and he needed to eat.

"Um, if you want to call it that. I just need to eat." It was a lame attempt to make it no big deal. She was looking at him with shining eyes, almost black in the filtered light of the barn. And it hit him looking at her that he really wanted her to say yes.

She stepped away from him and shook her head. "No. Thank you though. But I, I don't d— I mean, I ought to go home and catch up on my washing. And tomorrow is the play and, well, I just came out here to thank you for consenting to do Stacy's ceremony—"

"Okay, halt." He gave the time-out sign with his hands and pushed away from the fence. "You are choosing washing over dinner?"

She shook her head. "I told you I don't date."

He knew it so why did it suddenly irritate him? "This is to celebrate me doing the ceremony. How about that?"

"That's not really fair, you know."

He held up his hands. "Hey, no strings attached and besides, you yourself said that God wasn't really playing fair with me and you're right. So I'd say if He can do it then I can do it."

"That's pretty arrogant, if you ask me."

"Yup." What was he doing? *Enjoying her company, that's what.* "So what will it be?"

Chapter Fourteen

What was she doing? Sure, she'd not technically agreed to make it a date. She needed to run by one of the large superstores that were open late and pick up some gold pipe-cleaners to make the angel a halo. She'd decided just last week not to put a halo on the angel, but an angel needs a halo and that was that.

In the process she did need to eat. A quick call to Lilly confirmed that she could keep the boys later than they'd planned originally. The fact that Lilly sounded too excited when she'd learned that Chance was giving Lynn a ride to the store in Ranger was to be expected. After all, everyone else would believe from appearance that it was in fact a date. When it wasn't.

Lynn stared into her closet of clothes. She'd stopped thinking about dressing up a long time ago—not that she was considering it now. But really, if there was a dressy occasion, she had nothing appropriate.

She bit her lip and tugged a red sweater from a hanger. And a pair of black pants…she'd gotten both pieces of clothing three years ago when she'd arrived at the shelter. There was a large room there with all kinds of donated clothes. She took a deep breath to still the queasy feeling attacking her, and changed with no second-guessing. She would just have to do.

She was applying a touch of mascara when she heard the rumble of Chance's truck. He was early! Her nerves kicked up in panic and she jabbed herself in the eye with the mascara wand when she heard his truck door slam. Wet mascara smeared below her eyes in a sudden blinking fit and she stared at herself in the mirror. Grabbing a tissue, she scrubbed at her eyes.

She was in a mess. Rushing to the window she peeked through the curtain and saw him as he strode toward the front door. The man had dressed up. He was starched and ironed and spiffed up from one end of his shined-up boots to the top of his cream-colored Stetson!

And he looked good.

"Who are you trying to kid, the man looks great," she growled as she struggled to get the black mascara off. The doorbell chimed brightly and she felt like she was going to be sick! This was a date.

She didn't date.

It had been almost eight years since she'd gone on her last date, and look how that had turned out.

"Calm down. Deep breaths," she told herself. "Your last date wasn't so hot but you got Gavin and Jack out of the deal." Some semblance of calm came over her. At least she wasn't going to throw up and her knees weren't about to give out on her. "You aren't marrying the man. You are going to the superstore and to dinner. Period."

The fact that he looked gorgeous was merely a benefit of the evening.

Still, there was no denying as she went to answer the door that something about Chance Turner told her she needed to be careful. It might have been the fact that the sick feeling in her stomach had somehow turned to anticipation.... Tugging the door open she tried to appear calm. Cool. Collected.

What a joke.

All it took was that totally mischievous, slow smile and his gaze sweeping down her and back up to let her understand exactly how ridiculous it was—she was not collected, cool or calm. More like nervous, insecure, scared.

"Might I say you are looking lovely tonight," he drawled, tilting his head slightly, his eyes teasing.

And that was all it took. She laughed, so taken by surprise. "You may say it," she said, smiling like a fool. "I have to say I've never had that line used on me before."

"But it's not a line."

She pulled the door closed, feeling relaxed somewhat by his teasing. She couldn't tell him that he'd come up with the perfect way of putting a woman at ease.

Chance had almost panicked, he was so nervous about this date. *It's not a date,* he reminded himself. He'd repeated the phrase the entire time he was getting ready.

She agreed, too. Lynn had made every effort to convince him it was not a date.

He wasn't so sure now. It felt like a date as he'd walked up to her door. His nerves were rattled as he'd pressed the doorbell. Those nerves hadn't gone away when she'd come to the door, and they hadn't calmed down as they drove toward Ranger.

He was taking Lynn Perry to dinner. He was extremely thankful for gold pipe-cleaners and angel halos. "You're great with the kids," he said, after they'd exhausted all other small talk and driven a couple of miles in silence. "They seem ready for tomorrow."

"Thank you. But I didn't do all the work. They've been practicing those songs and the Bible verses in Sunday school for weeks now. Adela and Esther Mae made the costumes while Norma Sue gave them moral support."

He laughed, concentrating on keeping his eyes on the road. "I gather Norma Sue isn't a seamstress."

"You know, she can fix a host of things—tractors, toasters, the projector if it messed up—but put a needle in her hands and she becomes all thumbs."

"So why weren't any of them there today?"

"I think they were matchmaking. They realized you were going to be there," she said, with a shrug. "What can I say?"

"You know, now that I think about it, I saw Norma Sue's truck pass by while I was waiting on you." He went back to watching the road.

"The sneak."

He laughed. "Wouldn't they have a field day if they knew I was taking you to pick up supplies?"

When Chance came home for some solitude to deal with Randy's death, he hadn't anticipated being set up by the matchmakers…not that they'd been set up. Lynn being in his truck had nothing to do with anyone else but them.

Marriage and settling down wasn't something he really thought about. He'd assumed that one day he probably would, but he'd loved his life, loved his calling. He'd been happy.

"So what would you like to eat?" he asked, refocusing his thoughts. "Steak, Mexican, Italian?"

"Oh, I'm fine with anything."

"Hey, it's the lady's choice tonight. What would you like?" He winked. "I know you have to have an opinion."

She was silent and when he looked her way she was frowning.

"Lynn, it's not hard. I'd just like to take you somewhere you'd like to eat."

"Sorry. I, well, I'd really like Italian, if that's okay?"

That sounded really odd to him. "Sure, if the lady likes Italian then the lady gets Italian."

She smiled then, a sweet, somewhat sad smile that had him wondering what he'd said to cause that look.

Lynn's heart was doing odd things and all because Chance had genuinely wanted to take her somewhere she wanted to eat. It was nice. Touching, actually, and it made her momentarily sad to remember how her ex-husband had chosen everything. Chance acted like he knew Ranger well, drove straight to a building with an aged-looking sign and whipped into the parking lot.

"I haven't been here in a long time but if my memory serves me well—which is debatable—they have great food." He hopped from the truck and by the time she had her seat belt off he was opening her door!

"What's wrong?" he asked as he held out his hand.

She was staring, she knew, and making all kinds of a fool out of herself, but this was too much. She'd seen several of the cowboys around town open a truck door for their girlfriends and wives and it always sent a shiver of envy through her. She'd never had that…until tonight. Chance Turner was not only generous in spirit and with his time, his smiles and his talents, he was also a gentleman. "Nothing's wrong," she said, taking the hand he offered her. "I'm just not used to the cowboy way."

She'd spoken as she stepped down from the truck and instead of him stepping back as she'd expected, he planted his feet and stayed put so she practically bumped into him. The man was going to cause her to pass out if he kept surprising her with this kind of behavior. Her pulse rate rocketed out of control as she looked up at him.

He was looking down at her with a quizzical expression. "I think you have been misled. This is the cowboy way but it's also a man's way. And you deserve it."

Breathe, Lynn. Just breathe.

Her head was spinning with the crazy commotion rioting inside of her. Her pulse was out of control, her head dizzy, her stomach sick—the odd combination shouldn't feel so beautifully wonderful but it did. If her boys complained of the same symptoms she'd have said they had the flu but this was not the flu. This was thrilling.

Chance tilted his head and she knew he was about to kiss her. And she hadn't wanted anything as much, ever.

Almost involuntarily her chin lifted and her eyes closed in anticipation…even as somewhere in the back of her mind she was reminding herself that she didn't trust any man with her heart. She didn't.

Tugging her toward him, Chance wrapped his arms around her. But instead of kissing her he placed his lips against her ear. "I'm so glad God kept you safe and brought you here. You deserve all the good things in life. I hope you truly realize that. You never deserved not to be treated like the lady you are."

Sucking in a sharp breath, Lynn breathed in the masculine, earthy scent of Chance's cologne. Unexpected tears welled in her eyes at the sweetness of his words.

All she could do was nod against his neck for fear the dam would open and she would cry. And how horrible would that be, to burst into tears!

He stepped back and gave her a cocky grin and a wink, which pulled an even more unexpected laugh of relief from her.

"Are you ready to eat?" Chance drawled, holding out his arm for her.

"That sounds lovely." Butterflies going nuts, emotions running crazy inside of her, Lynn slipped her hand into the crook of Chance's arm. He immediately covered her hand with his and escorted her into the restaurant. She had never felt so special in all her life.

She knew he was simply being kind but still he was going out of his way to make her feel good about the evening…and she did.

He pulled her chair out for her and helped her take off her coat. He waited while she ordered first, making certain she ordered exactly what she wanted, her favorite, Chicken Alfredo. And this restaurant made the best she'd ever eaten. Of course, with all the attention Chance was paying her it could have been scorched and five days old and she'd have thought it was the best ever.

Chance Turner seemed like the best man ever. He seemed almost too good to be true. Was he as special as he seemed? Children were good judges of character and Gavin and Jack had adored him from the first… but was it real?

She'd tried and tried not to feel drawn to Chance, but tonight she couldn't deny that she was.

The knowledge scared her to death.

Chapter Fifteen

Lynn was frazzled by the time she made it to the church the next morning. As the secretary she was supposed to open the church office for the visiting preacher. She hadn't slept well and the boys were bouncing off the wall the second their eyes opened. Of course they'd been over-the-moon excited since Chance had brought her to pick them up the night before.

Chance—she shouldn't have been surprised when he'd insisted on taking her to pick them up. Telling her he didn't mind and he would rather know that she and the boys were home safe and sound when he went home. Since there was room in his double-cab truck, she agreed. It was another gentlemanly trait that she wasn't used to.... How had she made such bad choices in her life?

Looking back, if she'd been reading a novel and a character she cared about was heading toward making the bad choices she'd made, as a reader she would have thrown the book across the room in frustration. But, she'd not had the good sense to see what she was doing. She'd been too close to the fire and the smoke had blinded her. Or at least that was the kindest way she could describe her choices…. Life was about choices and she'd chosen badly.

She had had the best evening of her life and then the past had surged up and driven it all away with doubts about herself. How had she chosen to marry her ex-husband? It was humiliating to think love could have blinded her to Drew's character.

Her mood didn't get any better when she walked into the church office and played the message on the answering machine….

Chance drove into the church parking lot earlier than he'd planned. He'd had a restless night after dropping Lynn and her boys off. That he couldn't get Lynn off his mind was an understatement.

Lynn Perry amazed him. And she also confused him. He'd have sworn she'd expected him to be a jerk last night. She wasn't used to the cowboy way, as she'd put it when he'd walked around to open her door for her. What was she used to? His temper had flared in that instant and it had been all he could do not to voice his opinion about her ex-husband in a very ungodly way. Instead, God had held him true to his calling and he'd reacted with positive words for her. She did deserve all the good things in life and he was glad God had brought her through that bad time safely.

Kissing her temple hadn't been in the plan. Holding her had happened out of concern and encouragement… but not wanting to let her go had had nothing to do with either. That had strictly been the man in him.

It was that man in him that was heading toward the church at eight-thirty when Sunday school didn't start until nine-thirty. Lynn would probably be there early because of the program. She might need more help.

"Chance, Chance!" The twins yelled, running toward him the instant they saw him pull into the parking lot. They'd been sitting on the front steps of the church looking slightly miserable…probably had been instructed not to get dirty, which for them was a real trial.

"What's wrong, fellas?"

"We ain't got no preacher for today," Gavin burst out.

Jack nodded vigorously. "He done canceled and left the church high and dry."

Despite the situation, a smile tugged at Chance's lips at the boy's word choice. App's truck was in the parking lot and he was pretty sure Jack was repeating something he'd heard.

Gavin took his arm. "You got to help us, Chance."

"Yes, sirree," Jack quipped, planting his hands on Chance's hip and pushing him forward. "You gotta help us."

This was not what he'd been expecting as he'd driven to the church, but then nothing since he'd arrived in Mule Hollow had gone as he'd expected.

"We brung him to ya, Momma," Gavin said excitedly, ten feet before they reached Lynn, who'd come out of the church office to talk to App.

Lynn had her arms crossed and looked a little stressed out. Applegate's bushy brows were crinkled like crawling caterpillars above thoughtful eyes. "Our stand-in fer the day left us high and dry," he grumbled. "Jest called in and said he wasn't comin'."

"App, now, he said he was ill," Lynn said firmly, giving Chance a look that said her patience was ebbing.

"I didn't miss a day of work in fifty years. You set

yor mind to it and you feel better after ya fulfill yor commitments."

"In *fifty* years!" Jack exclaimed. "What's fifty years?"

"It's a bunch, son." App scowled deeper as he hit Chance with a glare. "So I guess it's up ta you, son."

All eyes turned to him. The one thing he was thankful for was that they were the only ones at the church. He didn't expect that to be the case for too much longer though. "App, not so fast. What about Brady?"

Lynn's mouth fell open. "Seriously. You seriously just said that?"

"He did a great job—"

"There was a wreck at the county line that he is dealing with this morning," she said, curtly. "May I speak with you in the office?" She didn't wait for his answer, just took his arm and pulled him along with her. Gavin and Jack fell into step with them. She looked around him. "You boys go play."

"But you said we was in trouble if we got dirt on us," Jack groaned.

"Yeah, that's what you said," Gavin assured her.

Chance would have laughed at the entire situation had it not been hemming him into a corner.

"Boys. Go play, have a good time but please try to stay clean. Can you do that?"

They looked at each other then at their momma. It was clear they weren't really sure if they could do it or not.

"Sure we can," Gavin said, giving his best shot to being positive. Jack didn't look near as sure. "Tell her, Jack."

"What if we get a teensy-bitty little dirt on us?" he asked with a face that made Chance almost bust with laughter.

"Fine. Go play," Lynn said and he knew he was in trouble if she was so zeroed in on talking to him that she'd give them the go-ahead to get dirty before the program.

Still holding on to his arm she marched him to the office and kicked the door shut with her heel. Startled, he half expected her to tell him to sit, as if he was in the principal's office. As soon as the door slammed shut she let go of him and looked up at him like a puppy that had lost its favorite toy. "You have to preach today."

"No. I don't."

The puppy disappeared in a blink. "Chance Turner. What are you doing? You were thanking God for what He did for me and my boys last night but today you still won't go back to preaching. I don't understand."

She was right and he knew it. He hung his head and studied his boots before looking back at her. "You're right. I don't know what I was thinking."

Her expression softened. "Chance, you lost someone you cared about as a person but, more importantly, as a soul you desperately wanted to see in Heaven one day. It affected you. It hurt. Even as the man of God that you are, it affected you. There is nothing wrong with that. It is actually a wonderful thing. I love it—I mean—well, yeah, I love that about you."

He swallowed hard and his heart was thrumming in his chest at her words. It was true he cared deeply but he'd never before felt like he'd failed on such a personal level. "I can't shake the feeling that I didn't do enough. I needed one more moment with him."

"But who can gauge how many moments a person gets to hear about the Lord before their time is up? No one can. That's not your call. I don't know how to help you. But I have faith that God is in control and He knows your heart, Chance. He knows you wanted more opportunities to be a witness and that you regret not making more. But it's not all about you. It's about Randy. You couldn't make Randy's choices for him or any of your cowboys. You can only present them with God's enduring love for them—you know this."

"I know it. But it's like I'm lost in the yaupon thicket."

Lynn chuckled. "I'm so sorry, but I don't believe I've ever heard it put that way before. But you know that God can get you out of anything. Remember that God is light. If you walk with Him, He will lead you."

"And I thought I was the preacher." Looking at her his spirits lifted. He knew it all, had given advice, scrip-ture and counsel to many, and yet he needed these words and comfort from Lynn. "Thank you."

"So do you think you could bring a few words to the congregation as a prelude to the program? It doesn't need to be a full sermon even. Just whatever God leads you to say. What's it going to be?"

She was so proud of Chance. She sat with the kids on the front row as he stepped to the pulpit. She'd come to realize how much he cared for the bull riders though, and he seemed out of place to her. He was a rodeo preacher, she saw that so clearly now.

He was better suited to his ministry. Or maybe it was simply that she knew his heart through his concern for Randy. But either way she knew the men he led in wor-ship each week were blessed to have a man so heavy with concern for them. She hadn't seen him in action but she knew in her heart of hearts that he was as much a man of faith as any she'd ever been around.

"Good mornin'," he said, his Texas drawl reverberating across the room. "I've been straining against getting in this pulpit since I came home, but God pretty much laid the pathway clean this morning and roped me into it."

Laughter crackled across the sanctuary. Lynn smiled and caught Gavin and Jack completely enthralled watching him. Their little faces were upturned and their eyes bright and unblinking as they grinned at him. "Have you ever heard the saying, don't sweat the petty stuff, and don't pet the sweaty stuff?" He hiked a brow as the laughter rolled, then he sobered. "I told y'all I was a cowboy preacher. But seriously, what I've been dealing with since coming home isn't petty or sweaty, but it's been heavy on my heart. A very wise woman told me that God's got things under control for those who believe in Him." He winked at her from the pulpit and her stomach dropped to her toes.

She listened as he gave a short sermon on 1 John 5-7, *God is light and in Him is no darkness at all.* It was a good reminder that God sent His Son to walk beside all of his children as the light of their path. She loved the way he delivered the message and knew there were many, herself included, who needed the reminder. He had a plainspoken way with words, of cutting to the heart of the matter and she knew that was exactly the kind of preaching cowboys would respond to. There were no flowery embellishments with Chance. He was a straight shooter for the Lord. She understood that was exactly why he wouldn't preach until he felt his own heart was right, or at least on the path to right.

"I'm going to get out of the way now and let these kids get up here and bless y'all with their Christmas pageant. But I want to encourage you that if you haven't saddled up with Christ—if you haven't accepted this very special gift—that you'll do it today, you won't regret it. And if you're like I've been, caught up in the yaupon thicket, tangled up in your problems, then I pray that God will be your light and open your eyes and He will lead you to clear pastures."

The man was a preacher. Not conventional, but he'd touched her heart.

She leaned forward and motioned for the children to take their places as Chance headed toward them. Gavin started to go to his spot then came back to her. "Momma," he whispered loudly. "Why is God gonna put us in a clean pasture?"

Chapter Sixteen

"Those little darlings did so wonderful yesterday!" Esther Mae said as she burst into the candy store with Norma Sue and Adela on her trail. The sleigh bells on the door jingled merrily.

"It was even cuter when Joshua—or should I say the baby sheep—wandered up on the stage and started waving at his momma and daddy and then told them his costume was itching him."

Adela's eyes twinkled. "I thought my Sam was going to fall out of his seat when Joshua started to try and take it off and Gavin and Jack—sweet darlings—tried to talk him out of it. They were really taking on the responsibility of being the older boys of that group."

Lynn could have been embarrassed that the play had ended up being more humorous entertainment than anything but she wasn't. That was part of the joy of getting small children involved in a program. You never knew what was going to happen. She'd loved it. "I hated to have to go up on stage and stop them but Joshua wanted that costume off and I was afraid my two boys were going to wrestle him to try and keep it on him."

She'd tried to get their attention and get them all back into the lineup but they weren't listening. She'd finally looked at Chance, who was about to burst with held-in laughter—not helping her at all. She'd given him a teasing scowl, then walked up the two steps to where the boys were trying to manhandle three-year-old Joshua into keeping on the sheep costume. It was a towel they'd sewn pillow filler on so that it looked fluffy like a sheep. Fuzz was flying everywhere!

"I still haven't figured out what part of that outfit was causing him to itch. The towel was all that touched his neck."

Stacy had been placing a tray of chocolate-covered nuts in the glass display case. She straightened, looking fresh. "I'm just glad Bryce didn't try and strip down to his training pants and join them."

"Lynn stepped in just before everything hit the fan." Norma Sue chuckled. "Anyway, we came by for a couple of things. First, we've got a lot to do this week if we are going to have a wedding Saturday. I'm so glad Chance agreed to do this. I think our boy is coming around. He did wonderful yesterday."

"He sure did," Esther Mae gushed. "Hank laughed all the way home. He said he wasn't going to sweat the petty stuff anymore or pet the sweaty stuff. Out of all that was said, *that* is what my Hank got the most out of."

"He said he would preach next Sunday, too." Adela was watching Lynn, who wondered if she was picking up on her reluctance to talk about this. Adela was extremely perceptive. And Lynn had a major problem. As of yesterday she didn't believe that Chance would ever belong in a traditional church setting. Although Mule Hollow was packed to the gills with cowboys and the entire town pretty much lived the cowboy way, it was still hard to think about him sitting in that office day in, day out.

A wide grin cracked across Norma Sue's face as she stared at Lynn. "We've decided to have a Christmas Ball the week before Christmas. So that means we've got a wedding to get ready for, a Christmas Ball and then Christmas. What do y'all think about that?"

"Norma Sue, that sounds like fun," Nive said, coming out of the back. "Doesn't it, Lynn?"

Nive had been giving her a hard time all morning. "It sounds busy."

"Well, sure it is. But we need to do everything we can to encourage Chance while he's here and keep him from staying out there on the property. Him agreeing to do our Stacy's wedding is a good sign. That boy has a heart as big as Texas and he needs to share that with a family. Don't you agree?"

Lynn agreed to come out and help decorate for the wedding and she reluctantly agreed to attend the Christmas Ball, which had matchmaking written all over it! But she kept her mouth shut when it came to agreeing that Chance needed to be the new preacher at the Mule Hollow Church of Faith, or that he needed to share his big ol' heart with a family...namely her family. Maybe he was supposed to have a family but she—well, she might be tempted, but in the end she knew nothing would come of throwing the two of them together.

She wasn't interested in a husband. She guessed she was still tangled up in the yaupon thicket with her eyes tightly shut, because she wasn't seeing any light leading her to a clear pasture. Where being ready for a husband was concerned she wasn't seeing clear pastures anywhere!

No matter how wonderful Chance Turner was.

"I'm tellin' ya it ain't country music," App grunted. He slapped a red checker one spot forward and glanced at Chance and Wyatt as they walked into the diner. "Mornin'," App and Stanley said in unison.

Chance and Wyatt echoed their greetings and took stools at the counter. Growing up, Chance and his cousins used to have races to see who could spin the cowhide-covered stools the fastest. Today he folded his hands on the counter and glanced toward the checker game.

Stanley grinned and made a double-jump move. "Yor right about it," he continued as if his conversation hadn't been paused momentarily to greet the morning stragglers. "No complaints from me. I bet Alan Jackson and George Strait—and I know good and doggone well George Jones—are all wonderin' what's happenin' ta country."

"*Rap* country," App grumbled, so caught up in the discussion that losing two checker pieces didn't even bother him. "Whoever heard of such a thing? It was on every station when I drove into town this mornin'. Three different songs. How many of 'em are out thar?"

Stanley shook his balding head. "It ain't right. Before ya know it they'll be tradin' in thar belts and wearin' thar britches down around thar ankles."

"So how do y'all really feel about it?" Chance teased. He was feeling better about life in general today. God had helped him start finding his way. And he'd done it through a class act with dark hair and elusive eyes.

"We like yor preachin' a lot more than we like that garbage."

Wyatt cleared his throat. "Well, that's not saying a whole lot by the sound of it. I might be insulted if I was you, cousin."

Chance chuckled. "I'm a rodeo preacher, don't apologize."

The conversation ensued about cowboy preaching and traditional preaching and the differences. He wasn't at all surprised that questions about him and Lynn were interspersed throughout the conversation. He'd not been able to get her off his mind.

He and Wyatt were heading to Pete's Feed and Seed when he saw her leaving the candy store.

"I'll catch up to you in a few," he told Wyatt, drawing a knowing grin. He ignored it and strode across the street toward her. "Hey, Lynn," he called, and as she looked his way he thought he saw a flash of excitement. The idea of her being excited to see him pleased him more than he could explain.

"How are you this morning?" she asked, digging inside her purse.

"I'm good. Hey, I was wondering if you'd like to go to dinner again. I thought we could take the boys out. You know, reward them for a good job yesterday."

She stopped digging. "That's funny, Chance."

"Hey, they were only trying to help out and you have to remember they were shepherds watching out for their flock. They just went and tried to gather up their stray."

She laughed, making him smile at the bubbly sound of it.

"I keep thinking about that. It was just so cute. But it really was not the program I had envisioned."

"But you know what," he offered, realizing as he spoke that he'd moved mere inches from her. "God was smiling, I'm sure. Little children please Him just like they please us."

"I know." She pulled her keys from her bag. "I need to go pick them up now."

"Hey," he said, not wanting to let her go. "So how about that dinner and a movie?"

She looked like she was going to say no, then she hesitated—and his heart started pounding unevenly with hope. He wanted to spend time with Lynn. He wanted to see that shadow of wariness, of uncertainty, disappear from her eyes. He wanted her to trust him… but was that all?

"The boys, too?"

"Yeah." He grinned, feeling great. "Let's load 'em up and go find an early movie, then grab some pizza."

"You're sure?"

He wanted to run his fingertips across her jaw in a gentle caress. "Absolutely."

She smiled sweetly and her eyes lit up like candles on a birthday cake. "You are so good to my boys. That means so much to me."

His throat had seized up on him at that look. It dug in deep and snuggled into nooks and crannies of his heart. He grinned—it was all he could do for a couple of seconds. He'd almost tried to tell her that she meant so much to him….

"Three."

"Three?"

"I'll pick you up at three. Unless that's too early," he said, as shaken as if he'd just been dragged from beneath the hooves of the biggest, baddest bull of all time.

"That sounds great." She opened her car door. "If you're sure."

Oh, he wasn't sure about anything in that moment except that he had just stepped over a line into a world he had never been in before. "I love your boys, sure I'm sure. It'll be fun."

She was having enough trouble keeping her head out of the yaupon thicket without accepting another date with him! But he'd offered to take her boys. How could she refuse that? And there was absolutely no denying that his offer thrilled her. *He loved her boys.* Those words had melted her.

It was scary. And for a gal who thought she'd gotten her act together, who thought she was seeing life in clear terms—she wasn't. And if God was out there trying to light the way to a clear path she wasn't seeing the light!

Her heart was getting involved in a big way. And with her heart and her emotions involved…she was trying to fight against making any emotional decision where a man was concerned, ever again.

But, a few hours later, it was hard to think straight when the man was buying popcorn for her boys!

Gavin and Jack were jumping up and down with excitement over the animated movie they were about to see. The fact that they were seeing it with their hero skyrocketed the experience to the moon and back.

"Here you go," Chance said, turning to hand her a tub of popcorn. "If you'll carry this, I'll carry the drinks."

She barely heard him over the blood rushing through her veins at lightning speed. "Got it," she squeaked, when his fingers brushed hers in the handoff. Her stomach was in knots—a combination of thrill and disaster mixed together.

"You boys ready for this?" he asked, handing each one a small drink and leading the way toward the theater.

"I am," Gavin said, carrying his drink very carefully. Lynn knew he was trying to impress Chance by not spilling anything.

"Me, too." Jack practically sang he was so excited. "I want to see that dog fly!"

Chance chuckled. "I think he does a good job of it, from what I heard."

They reached the designated theater along the long hallway and Chance held the door as they entered. As she passed by he leaned close. "Are you having fun?" he asked. His warm breath sent tingles down her neck and racing along her spine.

She turned, startled, and found herself so close that they were practically kissing. "Yes," she said breathlessly. She was embarrassed. His eyes were twinkling.

"Me, too."

His gaze dropped to her lips and for a mere second she thought—

"Y'all comin' or ya just gonna stand there?" Gavin called from the front of the theater.

Thankfully a wall hid them from the people in the seats. She bolted and strode to her boys with Chance right behind her.

It was a great movie. Then again she only came to that conclusion from the boys' delighted reactions to it. They oohed and ahhed all through it. She'd had the storm of the century battling away inside her and the sinking feeling that her boat was about to capsize!

Chapter Seventeen

On Saturday before the wedding Chance was in the church office when Emmett poked his head in the door.

"Chance, got a minute?"

"Sure, I'm at your beck and call today. What's up?"

The cowboy pulled the door shut behind him and stood there with his black hat in his hands. They were both wearing black western-cut jackets and white shirts. Chance kept running his finger around the stiff neck of his shirt, straining against the pull of the western tie. As they looked at each other they grinned, realizing they were both doing the same thing.

"I'm not much for ties and top buttons," Emmett said, taking his hat between both hands.

"Me either. On the rodeo circuit a tie isn't required as preaching attire."

Emmett nodded, as his thoughts went serious. "I need you to pray with me."

On the circuit Chance was used to the tough cowboy who was hard to get to know and even harder to bring to the Lord. He was also used to the cowboy who'd given his life to the Lord and showed up rain or sleet to worship in the arena on Sunday morning before his ride that afternoon. When something was on their hearts it was written across them like the red letters of his Bible. Emmett had something on his heart… Chance had no doubt it was a timid, pale blonde with eyes only for him.

"I'm ready. What's on your mind?"

"I need prayers that I can be the man that Stacy needs. The one who can show her all God's love for her through my love for her."

Chance nodded, understanding full well his concern for his bride-to-be. "That is God's command to all husbands. I've been watching you and I've heard stories about how you've been there for the last two years, demonstrating your love to Stacy in quiet, faithful action. I'm going to pray for you, Emmett, but clearly, God intended your paths to cross and your lives to intertwine. Keep your eyes on God, your priorities in order—God first, your wife second, your children third and everything else after that."

Chance and Emmett knelt beside the desk there in the church office. He placed his hand on Emmett's shoulder, much like he'd done to many a cowboy before, watching him ease over the bars and sink onto the back of his bull. He wasn't standing at the gate but he realized as he prayed that he was in a sense doing that with Emmett and Stacy. This was why she was so intent on the pastor being someone she felt connected to. When they were through with the prayer he gave Emmett a hard handshake and a hug. "You ready?"

Emmett took a deep breath and met Chance with steady, sure eyes. "God said in Genesis that it wasn't good for man to be alone, so he created woman. I've waited my whole life for Stacy. I'm ready."

"I'm proud for you and proud to know you." Chance held out his hand and shook Emmett's. This was a man who walked humbly with God. Chance liked him. "If you're ready, and obviously you are, there's only one thing to say—*Let's ride.*"

"I now pronounce you husband and wife. Emmett, you may kiss your bride."

Lynn dabbed at her tear-stained face as the shy cowboy smiled, then took Stacy in his arms.

Stacy had wanted the three women who came on the bus together from L.A. to No Place Like Home to stand up beside her, Lynn, Nive, Rose. And also Dottie, who'd taught them and inspired them through her ministry at the shelter with Brady. Brady walked down the aisle and it was a touching scene as he handed her over to Emmett. Lynn's heart had ached watching them. Stacy, with so much reason not to trust again, had found love. She'd pushed through all her ugly to love and trust Emmett.

If only she could do that, Lynn would be able to give her sons everything they deserved....

Chance's eyes met hers as Emmett and Stacy kissed and she felt the warmth of his gaze all the way to her toes.

This was a man whose heart was big and bold and concerned with the things of the Lord. A man whose heart had broken because he felt he'd failed God and Randy. This was a man who loved God. A man who enjoyed spending time with her boys and whom her boys clearly loved. They talked about him nonstop, even more since the movie and pizza night. What a man he was.

Yes, Lynn. This is the man you can trust.

The words jumped out at her…as did the knowledge that Chance was a man she could love.

Chance didn't get to talk to Lynn at the reception. She seemed to always be where he wasn't. And she always seemed to be busy. Since Stacy had opted to have her reception at the small fellowship hall at the church rather than the community center, he felt pretty confident that Lynn was avoiding him. The place was only about as big as a doctor's waiting room. Lynn was keeping out of his way, no doubt about it.

After the birdseed was thrown and the happy groom tucked his wife safely into the seat belt of his truck, Chance stood on the sidewalk and talked with different people who came by to visit. Several women asked if he would consider doing their weddings when the time came. It had been a hard question to answer but he told them to call him.

"You might have started something," Cole said, coming up to stand beside him. They were on the church lawn and dusk was settling in. Through the window he could see Lynn and the other ladies cleaning up. Children were running around playing inside and also on the playground. He couldn't see them since they were out front, but he could hear the familiar whooping and hollering of Gavin and Jack. Those two boys were full of life.

It was a great evening. Though he was troubled by thoughts of Lynn, Chance felt a sense of peace and contentment. "Lots of gals have marriage on their minds."

Cole chuckled. "That's why they come here. Can you believe how alive this place has gotten?"

"It's always been a great place but it is nice seeing babies and families again." He remembered how it had been coming home to the weathered town. Mostly working cowboys and the town itself just a tired-looking bunch of buildings slowly going downhill.

"Uh-oh, here comes trouble." Cole grinned as Applegate, Stanley and Sam came striding up looking like stair steps. Sam, the shortest of the bunch, held out his hand.

"That was great," the wiry man said, shaking in his normal iron grip. "Ya did a fine thang, marrin' those two off."

"Yup," App boomed, clamping down on Chance's hand as soon as Sam let go.

Chance shook Stanley's hand, then crossed his arms over his chest. "I'm glad I did it. They're a special couple."

"That's the pure truth." Stanley eyed his buddies. "We've come on official business, Chance."

Cole tucked his fingers in his pockets, giving him an are-you-ready-for-this look. In the back of Chance's mind he'd known this was coming. He'd known the moment he'd stepped into that pulpit a week ago. He just hadn't expected official business to happen right after Stacy and Emmett's wedding.

App cleared his throat and pushed back his thin-as-a-beanpole shoulders. He started to speak, then paused... maybe for effect but it was time enough for Chance to intervene and stop them. He didn't though. A month ago, before Randy's death, he wouldn't have let them get started. Today, he kept his mouth shut.

"We are officially offering you the position as our preacher."

Cole was watching him, no twinkle in his usually laughing eyes. Chance was honestly confused. Why hadn't he just told them no?

The annex door suddenly flew open and Norma Sue came barreling out with her hands in the air. "Move out of the way, boys, a baby's comin' through!"

Behind her Clint Matlock was supporting Lacy as she walked. And behind them was everyone else. Lacy was grinning and grimacing simultaneously as she moved the way only pregnant women could do. Her hand was on her rounded belly and she leaned back into the support of Clint's arm.

Clint looked about as shaken as Chance had ever seen him. Then again, it was that I'm-about-to-be-a-daddy look. It was chock-full of the realization of the responsibility that was about to hit his shoulders.

Chance wasn't about to be a daddy but he knew that feeling. As a preacher he felt it for his cowboy congregation all the time. He'd walked away for a little while but he still felt it.

"I should have known the baby was going to take after his momma," Clint said as he passed them. "She's always full of surprises."

"And you know you love it—ow!" Lacy's laugh cut to a grunt.

"Y'all better stop talking and hoof it on to this here car," Norma Sue bellowed from the middle of the parking lot.

Esther Mae wore a huge red hat with a Christmas flower on it. She whipped it off, exposing her flaming-red hair, and began fanning Lacy as she trotted along beside her. "You just hold your horses, Norma Sue. We will get there when we get there. Lacy doesn't need to have this baby on the church parking lot!"

There was a flurry of advice as everyone spread out

in an arch, as if the wave of their energy would get Clint and Lacy to the car sooner.

"Here, I'm going to carry you," Clint said, and gently swept Lacy into his arms.

"But walking is better!"

"Lacy—I'm carrying you," Clint growled.

The petite blonde didn't give him any other protest.

"Lacy," Sheri, her best friend snapped as she hurried to keep up with Clint. "Do not have that baby in the car. Do you understand? You love that ol' thing but this baby does not need to come into this world in the backseat of an Elvis throwback!"

Lacy chuckled. "I'll do my best."

Chance had fallen into step with Lynn as she passed by him. She looked up at him with dancing eyes.

"This is so exciting," she said. "Lacy's having a baby!"

They reached Lacy's 1958 pink Caddy. Norma Sue was holding open the door and Clint eased Lacy into the seat.

Grinning, he jogged around and doubled up as he crawled behind the wheel. "I'll see y'all in a minute."

"We'll be hot on your trail," Sam said, putting his arm around Adela's shoulders.

"We are praying." Adela patted Clint's shoulder before he pulled the door shut and gassed it.

In a flurry of movement, everyone headed toward their vehicles.

"Are they safe in that crazy car?" Chance asked, still watching the pink monstrosity of a car's big fin taillights disappear into the dusky evening.

Lynn chuckled. "That car's in great shape. Lacy brings it to all the weddings because she likes the nostalgia of it. Clint enjoys his wife's quirks so he goes along with it. I think he'd have rather had the truck on this occasion though. He looked so nervous."

Chance agreed. "It's understandable."

"They goin' to the hospital to pick up their baby?" Gavin asked as he and Jack came running up from the back of the church.

"They sure are," Lynn said.

"This place is growin'!" Jack exclaimed, then paused. "We need to go to the hospital and pick us up a baby. They're funny."

Chance laughed at the alarmed look on Lynn's beautiful face. "Would y'all like to go to the hospital and wait for the baby to be born?"

"You mean we got to wait on it?" Gavin looked perplexed.

"I'm afraid so." Lynn smiled at Chance and his heart almost tripped over itself with the thrill of it.

"Lynn," Dottie called from the group where she was chatting. "If you want to go to the hospital I'll take the boys home with me. We're keeping Bryce for Stacy— Brady and I can't go anyway. Nive is going to stay and help me."

"I'll drive you," Chance offered.

"No, I can—"

"That would be great," Dottie said, interrupting Lynn before she could say no. "Lynn, you go now. With Chance. There is no sense you driving there yourself when he's offering."

"But," she started, then looked resigned to the idea. "You're right. Thanks for the offer, Chance."

If he hadn't figured out before that she was avoiding him he would have figured it out now. They said goodbye to the boys and had to repeat to them that only Lacy would be bringing home a baby.

Chance planned on finding out why Lynn didn't want to be around him. He was glad she was riding with him—even if it had taken Dottie's intervention. And not just because he wanted to spend time with her. He needed advice, a sounding board, and though he had three cousins whom he valued considerably…it was Lynn, despite her reluctance to be here with him, whose advice he wanted.

Lacy Brown Matlock gave birth to a nine-pound three-ounce baby boy twenty minutes after Clint fish-tailed into the Ranger hospital emergency entrance. Leave it to Lacy to ignore the ultrasound's prediction!

The waiting room was full. The nurses and doctors had grown accustomed to Mule Hollow showing up in force for the birth of their babies.

Lynn smiled through the glass. "He's beautiful."

"I don't see how you can tell with his face all scrunched up like that," Chance teased. He was standing beside her. The drive to the hospital had been strained. They'd talked about the wedding and the baby and also about the boys wanting her to bring home a baby. She'd chuckled about that but changed the subject quickly when she started wondering if Chance wanted children.

"He looks just like Clint," Norma Sue said. "He won't like being called beautiful."

"But he is," Esther Mae cooed. Her face almost touched the glass as she peered at baby Matlock.

Lynn was so happy for Clint and Lacy but her mind kept going to Chance. *He's the man you can trust.*

The words wouldn't leave her.

"You sure are quiet," Chance said when they finally headed toward the truck.

It was nine o'clock and a northern wind was whipping the pink skirt of her bridesmaid dress around her knees as Lynn walked toward the truck. "I'm sorry. I just have a lot on my mind."

"There's a drive-in up the road. Do you want to stop and get a soda? I'm a good listener and I need to talk to you about something, too."

He opened her door for her and took her elbow as she stepped up and sat in the high seat. Her pulse was racing as she found herself eye-to-eye with him. "That sounds great," she managed. They were in the middle of the hospital parking lot sitting directly beneath a safety light but it didn't matter. She lifted her hand and touched his jaw. His eyes flared in surprise at her touch. "You did an awesome thing today, marrying Stacy and Emmett. Thank you."

"I'm glad I did. It meant a lot to me, too." He placed his hand over hers, pulled it away from his jaw and kissed the back of her hand. "Thank you for pressing me to do it."

The touch of his lips very nearly brought tears to her eyes. The gesture was so sweet. She nodded—it was all she could do. Thankfully he took a breath, backed up and closed the door with a smile. *Get hold of yourself, woman!* She watched as he hurried around the truck. By the time he climbed in, at least she was no longer thinking about throwing herself into his arms.

Chapter Eighteen

Chance pulled into a drive-in spot and, after they'd decided what they wanted to drink, he pushed the button on the microphone. "When I'm on the road I eat at more of these places than I want to think about. It's not something about my work that I enjoy."

Lynn tilted her head to the side. "We didn't have to stop."

He cocked a brow. "I didn't say I wasn't enjoying it right now."

She smiled, despite the thoughts in her head. The thoughts of how she enjoyed being with him. Of how she knew in her heart that she could trust him. And the thought that had her insides so tied up that she'd almost not been able to concentrate on the amazing new baby that had just come into the world.... She was falling in love with Chance.

Falling might not be the right word but it was the only one she was willing to acknowledge. *Fallen* was too—she just couldn't accept that it had actually happened. The idea put her in shock. Falling in love was still controllable. She could stop it.

How was this all clashing around inside her while she was sitting calmly at the drive-in with Chance with fifties music playing in the background?

"Do you want to talk about why you're so quiet and why you were avoiding me after the ceremony?"

"No."

"You sure gave that a lot of thought." The girl brought their drinks and he was distracted momentarily while he paid her.

Lynn took the moment to talk herself off the ledge. No, she wasn't going to tell the man that she was quiet because she'd realized she'd fallen in love when he'd pronounced Stacy and Emmett man and wife.... *Fallen*—she'd just admitted it to herself. She closed her eyes and tried to breathe. Tried to backtrack and replace *fallen* with *falling*.

But it was hopeless. She knew that she'd used the right word. She had fallen for him but it was hopeless nonetheless. It didn't change anything.... It didn't.

He handed her the drink and watched as she took a long sip through the straw. "You said you had something you needed to talk to me about," she said, hoping to take the focus away from her.

His gaze narrowed, telling her she wasn't fooling him. He set his drink in the cup holder without taking a drink. "I've been officially asked to be the preacher at the church."

"You told them no, didn't you."

His brows dipped. "You didn't hesitate on that."

"No. I didn't. You did a great job but, unlike everyone else trying to put you in the pulpit, I believe you already have yours."

"So I guess you're still holding it against me that I talked about sweat in my sermon."

She wasn't finding much funny right now so didn't laugh. "I never held that against you. I just think your heart is in the arena with your riders. You don't need to give that up because you lost one."

Chance looked troubled. She realized then that he'd been troubled all along—it had just been hidden beneath a thin surface. "What if I have other reasons for wanting to stick around Mule Hollow?"

"My Girl" was playing in the background as he set steady green eyes on her. A shiver of awareness coursed over her and she could barely breathe with the knowledge of what he was thinking…. Surely she was wrong.

"You love the rodeo circuit and preaching. They need you." She set her drink in the holder. "And my boys need me. We'd better get back."

She pulled her eyes away from him but could feel his gaze on her as she put her seat belt back on. The inside of the truck was closing in quickly. She willed her emotions to calm and her good sense to rule. She was not looking for love. She was not looking for a wedding.

She and her boys were fine.

Chance drove. He pressed his boot to the gas pedal and glued his eyes on the road ahead of him. He'd almost told Lynn he wanted to stick around Mule Hollow because of her. And her boys. He'd almost told her that…he loved her. At the drive-in soda stop, no less.

The look in her eyes and her reaction told him she wasn't ready to hear him. He hadn't known until standing beside her looking at the baby that he was ready to say anything. The truth had come calmly over him, with a sense so sure and strong that it reminded him of the day he'd committed his life to the Lord. There had been no turmoil in that moment. It was as if God had been standing beside him that day and simply asked him, "Do you love me?" Chance had known the answer was yes right then. Before that moment, he'd been fighting a battle over living for God or being caught up in the world. But on that day he'd known he was forever changed. Standing beside Lynn he'd known that same peace and clarity. He loved her. He wasn't certain what the next step was, but that didn't change the fact that he loved her.

He loved Lynn Perry. It was a beautiful thing.

"Are you all right?" he asked after they'd ridden fifteen miles in silence. He wanted to pull the truck over and tell her how he felt but he knew now wasn't the time. He was worried about her.

"I'm fine. But Chance, you shouldn't make a decision like this suddenly. You told me how much it means to you to be there for those cowboys on the road. I'd hate to see you make a mistake."

"Why don't you think I could be happy at the church?"

"I guess I don't know that."

"How do you feel about us?" The question came out before he could stop it. He glanced at her. She looked stressed at his question. Her hands were clasped in her lap and her lips were pressed tightly together as she stared straight ahead.

She didn't answer for at least a mile. He couldn't say anything. He was tied up like a ball of yarn inside.

"Chance, I didn't—"

"Hold on," he said, knowing he had to stop her. He

pressed the brake and moved the truck to a shuddering stop on the edge of the road. They were within fifteen miles of Dottie and Brady's house and there was no way he wasn't finishing this conversation. Or letting her answer too quickly.

He put the truck in park, opened his door and got out. He could feel her watching him as he stomped around the front of the truck. He opened her door, reached around her and unsnapped her seat belt.

"Chance, what are you doing?"

He stared straight into her eyes, took her hands and tugged her out of the truck. He gently cupped her face in his hands and held her still as he searched her eyes for any sign of the same feelings that were raging through him. He lowered his head and, when she didn't protest, he touched his lips to hers.

His heart was lost for certain in that moment. There was no turning back for him. He thought back to his prayers with Emmett and had a new understanding. He knew that he would wait for Lynn Perry's heart to heal and pray for her to love and trust him for as long as it took. To his surprise she melted against him and returned his kiss in a sweet, hesitant response. Hope filled him. She wasn't averse to him. She hadn't slapped him or pushed him away. She'd kissed him.

Joy filled his soul.

"You snuck up on me, Lynn," he said, moving his hands to her shoulders as he held her close and spoke against her ear. "I came home to be alone and to search my heart for answers from God and, instead of letting me be alone, God put you in my pathway. I love you, Lynn. I've been falling for you from the first moment we met."

Her hands dug into his back at his words and she stiffened in his arms. He could feel her heart pounding and could sense the strain that his words put on her. Was it fear? Was it that she couldn't trust him? Either way, it stung. "I'm not your ex-husband, honey. You don't have anything to fear from me. I would never hurt you or your boys. You can trust me."

She took a deep breath. "I don't know how to deal with this, Chance. I just don't know."

Her words were so full of angst that a helpless feeling washed over him and he asked God to intervene. "You can pray and we can take this one step and one day at a time."

She pushed back from him. "I care for you, Chance. There is no denying that. I love the way you are with my boys. I love the heart that you have for others and their relationship to the Lord. You are a wonderful man and I am so blessed these last few weeks knowing you and all the help you've given me."

The man in him wanted her to return his love instantly. But he knew she had issues from her past that were holding her back. She'd been honest from the beginning that she had a problem with trust. He'd been forewarned. "Then there is hope for me."

"I can't promise you anything. I'm afraid you'll be hurt—"

"The only way I'm going to be hurt is if you tell me right now that there is no hope for us."

Her eyes were bright and her lips trembled. "I want there to be hope."

Joy as bright as sunlight split a shaft straight through him. "You can't even imagine how happy that makes me." He ran his fingertips along her jaw, loving the feel of her. "Let's take it nice and easy, one day at a time." When she nodded, he closed his eyes and thanked God. Opening them, he found her watching him. Slowly he touched his lips to hers, relishing the sweet scent of her…. His longing to hear that she loved him intensified. This was what it was all about. Finding someone to share his life with was the best blessing.

"So how's everything going?"

Lynn looked up from working on the church bulletin to see Lacy walk in holding a baby carrier.

"Lacy, you're out and about!" she exclaimed, coming out of her chair to hug Lacy. "I have to see Tate."

Lacy gently pulled the baby blanket away and exposed the infant's face. He was sleeping soundly. "Isn't that the cutest kiddo you've ever seen?"

"He is so cute. I like his name, too. I was surprised when you didn't name him Elvis."

Lacy smiled. "I love his music, and his taste in cars. But I wanted my baby to have his own name. Be his own man. Of course if God could give him a voice like Elvis I wouldn't complain."

Lynn itched to pick him up but didn't ask. She knew he'd be held too much as it was. Instead she sat back down. "What are you doing out?"

"Clint told me to stay home but I just can't. I thought I'd come bring this thank-you card by so you could put it in the bulletin."

"Sure I can." She took the card and opened it to read.

"So I hear you and Chance are an item."

Lynn's head whipped up. "An item?"

"Calm down, don't throw your neck out," Lacy chirped. "I was down at the diner with Clint and little

Tater—yeah, App, Stanley and Sam have already nick-named him Tater Man! Boy, did I have that coming."

Lynn laughed. "You walked right into that, didn't you."

"Did I ever. That boy is going to grow up get-ting called everything from Tater Man to Tater Tot. I thought about naming him Cas but realized he'd get called things like Castor Oil or something. Anyway, I heard Cole and Seth saying Chance had been over at your house almost every day this week. Girlfriend, that makes you an item in our books."

"Oh, well, I cooked and he helped the boys repair my front porch. And, well, he's alone and so he helped us decorate the tree—"

"And in there somewhere did you happen to kiss the cowboy?"

Lynn swallowed hard and met Lacy's twinkling eyes. "Lacy!"

"Hey, come on, Lynn, tell me you are stepping out. Tell me you are taking courage and moving forward with this handsome hunk of man God has put in your path."

"I'm trying."

Lacy sat on the edge of her seat and tapped her plum-colored nails on the desk for a second as her mind whirled behind her electric-blue eyes. "You have been an inspiration to me ever since you stepped off of that bus two years ago. You have fought hard to help your-self, the women who came with you and everyone who has come through those shelter doors. And yet you are afraid. I've been praying you let God set you free."

Lynn stood up and paced to the tiny window. She stared out toward the swings where her boys would normally be playing while she worked on the bulletin. Today they were riding horses with Chance. They were thrilled. She was in deep, and happier than she could ever remember, but she couldn't shake her fear.

"I'm frightened, Lacy."

"Of what?"

"Myself."

Lacy was startled. "I don't understand."

"I don't know how to take the step to the next level. I've reached a comfortable place in my life and, as wonderful as Chance is, I'm terrified I'm going to break his heart."

"Don't break it. Simple as that. Do you love the man?"

Lynn knew she did but there was more to it than that. "I loved Drew, too."

Lacy had stopped drumming her nails on the desk and now she tapped only her index finger methodically like a clock. Lynn could almost see her mind ticking along to the beat.

"You don't trust yourself, that's what you mean?"

Lynn nodded. "I'm comfortable finally. I'm not afraid as long as I'm not thinking about love and marriage. Every time I look at Chance and think about taking that step I freeze up."

"Then chill and give it time. God is the great healer. I'm sure Chance totally understands this. Has he talked about marriage yet?"

"No. I'm trying to talk him into going back on the rodeo circuit."

"So you're the one keeping him out of this office. Does App know this?" Lacy teased.

"I just want him to be happy and I'm afraid this isn't right for him."

Lacy stood up and plopped a hand on her hip. "I'll pray for you, sister, but why don't you stop worrying about what is right for Chance. He's a big boy, I bet he can figure that out…. You just concentrate on what's right for you, and God's going to take you straight through this to blue skies if you let Him."

Blue skies, clear pastures. Lynn sure wished one of the two would show up. And soon. She'd been having a wonderful and horrible week at the same time. And the worst part was that Gavin and Jack could get hurt if she didn't come to some sort of decision soon about what to do with her life.

"Are you going to the ball tomorrow night?" Lacy asked, lifting the baby carrier.

"Yes, Chance is taking me."

"You go, girl. Go have a good time and stop worrying. God's got this!"

Lynn herded the boys into the car after Lacy left the church and they headed toward the shelter. She'd promised Sandra she'd come by this afternoon. Despite their conversations about what Sandra had done right, she wasn't doing well. Guilt was eating at her. The therapist was working with her, too, but Dottie said she'd withdrawn even more over the last day.

Dear Lord, Lynn prayed as she drove, *give me the words that will help ease Sandra's pain. That will help her understand that she's done the right thing in getting out of the dangerous, abusive situation she was in…for her sake and her child's sake.*

She ended with a prayer for God's will and thought

about His place in her own life. Was she allowing God to have His will? Loving and trusting were intertwined in marriage. In her mind there was no way to have one without the other. Only her problem wasn't trusting Chance—how could she not? She didn't trust herself.

When she arrived at the shelter she knew immediately that something wasn't right. Brady's patrol vehicle was parked in front along with Deputy Zane Cantrell's. Dottie was in the yard talking to them.

"Hey, Mr. Brady, hey, Mr. Zane!" the boys called as they raced over and got big hugs from both men. Lynn's heart swelled at the sight.

"What's going on?" she asked as soon as the boys went to play on the swings.

Dottie was pale. "Sandra's gone. She called her husband and told him where she was. He showed up and she and Margaret left with him."

"No," Lynn gasped, looking at Brady and Zane as if believing they would tell her that Dottie was wrong. "But you should have stopped her."

Brady's serious gaze was steady. "She never filed charges and she left of her own free will. You know our hands are tied."

It was true, but Lynn wanted with all her heart to go after Sandra. To beg her to listen. To beg her to accept that the situation she was in wasn't going to get any better.

But it was too late.

Too late.

Chapter Nineteen

"And may I say you are looking particularly lovely tonight." Chance was on top of the world. He'd spent most of his week working around Lynn's house. He'd arrived early, before she left for the candy store, so the boys were able to sleep in and not be hauled out of bed and carried to the shelter for the day. He'd enjoyed them tagging along with him when they woke. They were fascinated with tools, hammers especially, and the front porch was better for it. They'd helped him replace the wood and were now eyeing the old barn with great interest. He'd also taken them riding at the ranch a couple of times and they'd been thrilled.

To give Lynn some space, he'd worked cattle two days on the ranch but had felt bad that he hadn't been there for the boys.

Lynn had told him over and over again not to feel bad about not being there because she understood he had his own business to take care of. He'd chalked that and a few other things up to her not wanting to impose on him. He considered his time with her and the boys as time well spent. Time well enjoyed. Time to cherish.

He hoped she felt the same. Especially after Sandra had left the shelter. The poor woman's decision to go back with her husband had devastated Lynn and she'd been thinking about it a lot. He had tried to talk to her about it—even explained that Lynn couldn't make Sandra's choices for her...no matter how much she wanted to.

He had niggling worries that Sandra's leaving was affecting Lynn on a deeper level than he could reach.

He hoped to help his case tonight and was glad that the weather was cooperating. The stars were like diamonds sparkling in the huge, dark sky as he'd walked to her door and knocked.

Looking at her, his heart lunged into his throat and shut off his air supply. It was a wonder he was able to tease her with his greeting.

She was smiling at him but in her eyes he saw the same tension that had concerned him all week. Even before Sandra had left, that edge in Lynn's eyes had him worrying that she was putting up a brave front before she broke and ran. It had him on his knees every night asking God to let her trust him.

"Hey, don't look at me like that," he said, determined to keep his voice light. "You do look lovely tonight."

She looked down at the jeans, boots and red sweater she wore. "I'll take your word for it then."

He leaned against the door frame and punched his hat off his forehead then gave her his best Turner smile. "Believe me, my word is good," he drawled nice and slow, even though he wanted to growl in frustration. No matter how good the week had been, her trust issues were hanging in the balance—in that look in the edge of her eyes. Frustrated by his lack of patience he gave up the nonchalant pose and straightened. His nerves were humming tonight. "Where are the boys?"

"Dottie picked them up on her way back from town."

He was disappointed. "We could have taken them."

"It's all right. Dottie didn't mind."

"It wouldn't have been a bother." Nothing about her or her boys was a bother to him. "I enjoy seeing them."

She nodded but instead of saying anything she picked up her purse from the hall table and pulled the door shut. "I guess we better go."

He nodded though the way she'd said the words settled in his gut like lead. Something wasn't right.

The community center was packed by the time they arrived. Lynn had been feeling downhearted all afternoon and felt guilty that she'd basically shot down Chance's good mood. It was mean and selfish and yet she'd done it anyway. She knew it was because of the pressure from the week. She was worried for Sandra and Margaret and heartbroken that Sandra had chosen to go back to her husband. But she above everyone else understood how mixed up Sandra's mind and heart were at the moment. Lynn had thanked God several times since yesterday that He had given her the strength to break free of Drew.

But with every second Chance spent with her boys the pressure built. Could she go back into a relationship again? Could she be totally free from the scars left from her marriage? She had to make a decision and she had to make it now. The potential for her boys' hearts getting broken was escalating and, no matter what Lacy or anyone else said, sitting back and just letting God handle it was not working for her.

She'd done that before—true, the situation had been different. Drew had been violent and manipulative while Chance was wonderful and loving. But if she couldn't give her heart over to trusting and fully loving Chance, she was going to have to pull away before everyone got hurt. With Drew she was the one who had finally made the break. Not God. And this relationship with Chance was on her shoulders, too.

Music was playing in the background. Mule Hollow's cowboys had talent. There were several who could sing like Nashville gold, and as Lynn and Chance entered the building Bob Jacobs was singing a Tim McGraw love song. Love songs…she was in trouble.

The room was decorated with Christmas lights strung about the ceiling. Garlands of colorful lights hung around the doorways. On the small stage they'd set a metal horse trough and filled it with Christmas presents. Beside the trough was a brightly decorated Christmas tree.

"This looks great," Chance said as they entered.

"It does," Lynn murmured, very aware of his hand resting between her shoulder blades. She fought to appear collected.

"Y'all came!" Esther Mae exclaimed from a table near the door. "Come over here and sign your names. We want a record of all who attended. That way next year we can look back and see how many of the couples who came tonight ended up getting married."

She smiled and looked from Chance to Lynn.

Lynn's stomach hurt. Chance gave her a humorous wink that Esther Mae was thrilled to see.

"Y'all make the cutest couple. Babies would be so sweet."

"Hang on, Esther Mae," Chance said, coming to the rescue. "Don't get too far ahead of the plan. I'm just thankful tonight that Lynn came with me at all."

Lynn smiled and touched his arm. "I've got two already," she said to anyone listening. She felt defensive.

"And they're two good ones to have," Chance said, giving her a look that said he understood. "It's good to see you, Esther Mae. We'll get out of your way so the next ones can sign up."

The bouncy redhead waved them off. "Chance, you be sure and dance with Lynn," she called as they were mixing into the crowd.

"I'm planning on doing just that," he said in Lynn's ear as he leaned in and spoke only to her. "You doing okay? You look upset."

The man was too perceptive. "I'm fine, just feeling stressed."

He draped his arm across her shoulders and gently pulled her into the crook of his side. She had the urge to rest her head against his shoulder but she didn't.

"Don't stress, Lynn. Just relax and enjoy the time here with our friends. Don't let Esther Mae upset you. She didn't mean to put too much pressure on you."

That made her laugh. He did, too.

"Okay, so I take that back. She meant it but she didn't mean it to make you feel bad. She meant it out of love and concern for you, and for me, for that matter."

Lynn took a deep breath and momentarily enjoyed being so close to him. There had been times during the week that he'd kissed her when the boys weren't around. And he'd kissed her before he'd left each night. And each time she'd felt like she could kiss him for the rest of her life. She'd felt a longing for more, for the loving relationship, physically and emotionally, that God meant for a married husband and wife to have. She'd missed out on the true relationship that God had intended a marriage to be…. She wanted it.

But there was the risk involved. The heartache. The disillusionment. Depressed, she tried to force the thoughts from her mind.

"Come on, what you need is a little two-step." Chance grinned and swept her out onto the dance floor. "You know, my grandmother called this exercise, not dancing."

Lynn would have laughed but she was trying to concentrate on getting the steps right. She hadn't danced in years. Not since she was in high school. Chance was careful to keep a respectable distance between them as he held her hand in his and kept his arm draped across her shoulders. Cole and Susan danced past them, enjoying the song and time together. Stacy was on the dance floor with Emmett, having returned from their honeymoon at the beginning of the week.

Lynn should have relaxed. She told herself to breathe deep and relax. To enjoy the moment and the prospect of the future she and Chance could have…but Drew's face and all the manipulation that he'd put her though slammed into her with such force that she couldn't even hear the music any longer. Her past was the past, but it clung to her like dirt. She'd hoped loving Chance would wipe it away but it was still there. Thoughts of all she'd been through with Drew sucked the enjoyment out of moments like this.

"Lynn, you're crying," Chance said, looking closely at her. His eyes were so concerned.

"No," she said, but knew it wasn't true as she blinked

hard and fought off tears welling in her eyes. She had never been so thankful for low lighting in all her life. "I'm sorry, Chance."

He dipped his head as he slowed their two-step and met her gaze. "Don't be sorry, but I think maybe we need to go outside and talk about this."

She nodded, afraid to speak. Afraid of crying and just as afraid of what she knew she was going to say.

Chance had a bad feeling.

As soon as they'd gone outside Lynn had told him she wanted to go home. He'd said sure, asked if she felt bad, and she'd said she just needed to go home. She'd refused to say anything the entire six miles from town. His heart felt heavy for her. She was fighting demons from her past, he was certain. *Dear Lord,* he prayed, *give me the words to help free her from the wrong that has been done to her.*

The Christmas lights were on, cheerily welcoming them to her home. He half expected the boys to run out of the house and throw themselves at his legs like they loved to do, but they weren't home. He'd started to go get them but she'd said no. She'd simply wanted to go home and after that she'd been silent.

His heart was aching and fear gripped him as he parked. He started to get out but she placed her hand on his arm and stopped him.

"Chance. Wait. I'm so sorry, but this isn't going to work."

"Lynn. Give it time. I love you and I believe—no, I *know* you love me. I want to marry you and have a future with you. It can be wonderful—"

"It's not that simple, Chance."

She'd been on the verge of tears at the ball but now she was calm. Her voice was steady and her beautiful midnight eyes as clear and bright as a night sky lit by a full moon. It was that calmness that scared him the most.

"I can't, Chance. I just can't do this. You have a life, too, and it's out there on the rodeo circuit. Not here tied down." She opened her door.

"Lynn, don't do this. I'm not going to get out now, because I know you need time to think. But pray about it—"

She nodded and as she closed the door he saw a tear run down her cheek. He couldn't take it. He pushed open the door and was storming around the truck in seconds. He'd let Randy go the wrong direction because he hadn't taken action. He would not do that with Lynn.

She was standing in the headlight beam wiping tears from her eyes when he reached her. He took her by the arms. "I can't force you to do something you don't want to do. Or that you can't do. I can't force you to trust me. I can't take your past away. Or get rid of your emotional or physical scars. I couldn't make Randy's choice for him. You couldn't make Sandra's choice for her. There are some things we are not in control of, but this I know... I can love you. I can and will protect you, from here on out." He pulled her into his embrace but she pulled away.

"I don't want a man to have to protect me. I'm going to protect myself."

"So that's what this is. You are protecting yourself. From me?"

"From anyone."

"From me." He clarified. It was obvious what she meant. "I would never hurt you."

"I know," she said.

"Then what is this?"

She took a deep breath. "This is me protecting myself."

Chance took a step back. "No. This is you taking the easy way out. God never promised we wouldn't have trouble. As a matter of fact, in His word He says, 'In this life you will have trouble.' You are trying too hard to stay safe. You have to trust God at some point." Chance spun and stalked to his truck. She had to come to him of her own choice. He'd just told her she needed to trust the Lord, and he needed to do the same thing.

But as he got into his truck, it took every ounce of his willpower to hold himself back.

As he drove away he knew she was wrong—his life wasn't on the rodeo circuit. It was here with her and her boys and somehow, some way, he was going to prove it to her.

Chapter Twenty

"Momma, where is Chance?" Gavin asked. It was Christmas Eve night and she was tucking them into their beds.

"He was supposed to be here for baby Jesus' birthday," Jack said.

Both boys were tucked in and staring up at her with their wide eyes. They'd been asking about Chance for the last two days. Ever since Dottie had brought them home the morning after the ball they'd been confused.

She'd waited too long to figure out that the best way to protect them was to play it safe. Chance disagreed with her but she couldn't help that. In her mind she'd waited too long and now she knew this breakup was going to hurt them. But it wouldn't hurt as bad as it could have if she'd kept on seeing Chance and things hadn't worked out. No. Despite the fact that it was going to hurt them now she knew it was better this way. Her own heart—well, she couldn't think about that.

The thought of actually crossing the line into giving control of her life over to someone else again scared her to death. Yes, Rose and Stacy had moved on. But everyone dealt with abuse and heartache in different ways. She'd thought she was the strongest of all the women when she'd boarded the bus and headed to Mule Hollow. Well, she wasn't. She couldn't resolve her feelings about the past and she couldn't move forward into a relationship, no matter how desperately she wanted it to work.

But still, she hated to tell Gavin and Jack that Chance wouldn't be coming around anymore. And she couldn't bring herself to tell them now, on the eve of Christmas. But what else could she do? She'd walked right into this.

She sat on the edge of Jack's bed, which was a mere arm's length from Gavin's. "Chance isn't going to be here in the morning," she said gently and saw their expressions fall instantly.

"But why?" Jack asked.

Gavin sat up. "He promised."

Because I can't let him be here.

"But Santa Claus is coming and we're gonna read the story of baby Jesus 'cause that's what Christmas is really about," Jack said solemnly.

She smoothed his hair and kissed the top of his head. Then she moved to Gavin's bed and hugged him. "Come on, lie back down. We'll talk more in the morning but right now you two need to go to sleep."

"He's gonna come," Gavin said. "He said a man's word was his bond."

"Yeah," Jack said, bolting upright. "His integ-itchy means everything. God wants us to grow up to be that."

Lynn's stomach twisted and her heart felt heavier than it already was, which was hard to believe. "It sounds like you've been having lots of interesting conversations this week."

Both boys' eyes were solemn. "We want Chance to be our daddy, Momma," Gavin said.

"We done asked God for him," Jack said.

Lynn swallowed the lump in her throat, felt the scald of tears fighting for release and the burn in her heart—she wanted this for them, too. She wanted Chance but... she had to make the right choice.

"Let's say our prayers, guys, and then get some sleep. Tomorrow will be a good day." She pushed other thoughts from her head and concentrated on the celebration of Jesus' birth.

Both boys closed their eyes and prayed for Chance to be their daddy.

Lynn hardly slept. She lay down but her heart was heavy and her thoughts were full. She'd missed Chance so much since sending him away. She pulled her Bible into her lap and stared at the verse that jumped out at her. Jeremiah 29:11, "'For I know the plans I have for you,' declares the Lord. 'Plans to prosper you and not to harm you, plans to give you hope and a future.'" It was the life verse of the shelter. It was a verse she grasped with all her heart. But she'd believed she was seeing her future here in this house with her boys. And then Chance entered the picture, and all the pain of her past was stirred up and the clarity she'd thought she'd found was muddied up as thick as riverbed sludge.

She'd prayed for God to give her peace to help her through this, and she'd yet to find any relief. Sending Chance away had only made it worse.

And now she realized he'd been teaching her boys all week things a man should be. He not only had been teaching them through his actions but also through his words. A man of integrity. That's what he was. And she'd turned him away.

* * *

It was five o'clock when something startled her and her Bible slid off her lap beside her. She glanced at the clock and realized that she had dozed off at some point.

"Lynn."

A tapping sound on her window had her bolting straight up, and she was sure she heard Chance calling her name. What?

Scrambling out of bed she hurried to the window. She yanked her housecoat on over her red flannel pajamas and peeked through the curtain. Sure enough, standing in the pale morning darkness was Chance. Tiny sat at his feet looking at him adoringly.

When Chance saw Lynn he smiled. "Can we talk?" he asked.

She nodded, dropped the curtain and almost broke her neck rushing to the back door. *He was here!*

She unlatched the door and hurried out onto the small porch. Chance stood there waiting, strong and steady.

"You came." Her words were breathless.

He nodded, and looked slightly confused by her greeting. "Lynn, I love you. It's been killing me to keep away from you and the boys, but I'm doing it because you asked me to. But I gave them my word, so I have to ask you if I can show up here in a little while."

He'd come. The words kept ringing in her heart and head. *He came. He kept his word to her sons. He was asking her permission. He loved her...he loved them.*

She couldn't speak. So much was in her heart. So much told her this wouldn't work. So much told her it would.

Chance stepped onto the porch but didn't touch her. "Lynn, I can't stand this. You love me." There was a fierceness in his words that dared her to deny it was true. "I've been praying for you. I know trust is hard for you, but can't you please see that I'll never harm you? I want to be your champion. I want to protect you, not to harm you."

God's words echoed in her head. *I have plans for you, Lynn Perry. Plans to prosper you. Not to harm you. Plans to give you, Lynn Perry—you—hope and a future.*

Chance dropped to his knee and took her hand, and her heart stopped beating. "I'm asking you to marry me, Lynn. I'm laying my heart out here so that there is no mistaking what my intentions are. I love you. I love your boys and I love your dog. I love the whole package. I keep thinking I didn't give Randy my everything."

"Oh, Chance."

"I keep thinking I could have done more.... I kept thinking that God should have given me more time. Another chance to get through to him. And then it hit me last night that He did. When Randy asked me to stand at the gate with him, that was my chance. That was a gift from God for me to offer Randy salvation once more. God gave me what I've been grieving about all this time. I just lost it in my confusion. Randy didn't take his last shot at accepting Jesus. I have to rest easy and be at peace with that. But I can't rest easy about us. Not until I give it my all. I am not going to let this be until you know that you mean everything to me. If I could have conveyed to Randy that God loved him even more than I love you, then he'd have seen the splendor of God's love. So I'm putting it all out here. I love you."

His deep voice rasped with emotion. Lynn couldn't breathe.

"Today is the beginning of our hope as a people— this is the morning we celebrate God's Son being born.

He loved us so much.... I love you, Lynn. I'll take it slow and patiently."

Lynn was crying. Her heart cracked wide open as he poured his soul out to her. All her defenses were wiped away as she cupped his upturned face, knowing without doubt that with God and Chance beside her she could conquer the fears, the doubts and the leftover hang-ups of her past. Tears blurred her vision as she bent and kissed him. "I love you, Chance. I love you so much."

He kissed her and rose to his feet as he did so, pulling her close.

"*Tiny!*" two small voices squealed from inside the house. Lynn spun and she and Chance hurried inside to see what was wrong. She'd left the door open and Tiny had taken it as an invitation. The horse of a dog was half crouching and looked as if he'd stopped mid-stride, having been found out by Gavin and Jack. He had a big ball of red flannel fuzz she'd cleaned out of the dryer's lint catcher billowing out of his mouth. He was looking up at them all with guilty eyes.

Lynn hurried forward and gently took the lint from his mouth. "Give me that, young man, before you choke on it."

He opened his mouth obediently and gave over his loot, which he'd retrieved from a small trash can beside the dryer.

"Chance," the boys squealed again, as they realized he'd stepped into the kitchen behind her. In unison they exclaimed, "You came!" and launched themselves at him.

Laughing, he caught them and swept them up, one in each arm. "I told you I would, didn't I?" he asked, looking from one to the other.

Lynn had never seen a more beautiful sight than her boys gazing at him with looks so full of love and admiration that it made her heart sing. This was what it was all about. This was the desire of her heart.

"Don't cry, Momma," Jack said, reaching a hand out to her. "You can hug us, too."

Gavin reached out to her, too, and Chance crossed the gap between them and instantly she was engulfed into the center of the group hug. No. The family hug...

Chance kissed her gently and both boys squealed, nearly breaking her eardrums.

"Are you gonna be our daddy?" Gavin asked.

"Yeah," Jack said. "We didn't put you on our list for Santa Claus. We asked God fer you."

Chance gave her his slow, cocky grin. "That depends on your momma. What do you say, Lynn?"

"Say yes, Momma," Gavin whispered, his heart in his eyes.

Jack touched her cheek, his dark brows dipped over serious, imploring eyes. "Yes, Momma. Ain'tcha in love with 'im?"

Chance hiked a brow. "I like the way you boys think. But guys, your momma needs more time."

"No!" she exclaimed, and all three guys' expressions crashed. "I mean, no, I don't need more time. Yes, I love you and I'll marry you."

Both boys let out earsplitting yells of joy and Lynn knew, looking into Chance's beautiful, green eyes so full of love, that her life—and her hearing—would never be the same again.

"Now, can we go get a baby at the hospital?" Gavin asked, breaking the moment.

"Yeah," Jack agreed. "We asked Mr. Applegate why we couldn't have a baby like Tater and he said once y'all was married that the hospital would give us one."

Gavin grinned. "Tater's good. Miss Lacy said he don't cry none. So can we have one like him?"

Chance looked from one child to the next, then grinned, his eyes teasing. "Hey, I'm great with that. But let's get to the wedding first."

Lynn couldn't help it—she laughed. "I agree."

Chance set the boys down. "Guys, how about me and your momma talk dates for our wedding and then we'll meet y'all at the Christmas tree."

They nodded then raced toward the living room singing, "We're gettin' a tater tot, we're gettin' a tater tot!"

"I hope you know what you're doing!" Lynn said, as he wrapped his arms around her waist and hauled her close, nuzzling her ear and sending her stomach into a spin and her nerves tingling.

"I know exactly what I'm doing. I'm planning on spending the rest of my life loving you."

"Good, I'm all in." She kissed him, slow and tenderly, and for the first time in a very long time she stepped out of the yaupon thicket and into clear pastures. It was a beautiful sight to behold.

Taking her hand, Chance led her toward the living room where their boys were waiting. "But just so you know," Lynn said, feeling lighthearted. "We are not naming our baby Tater Tot."

Chance winked at her. "That's okay, Lacy and Clint have dibs on that. Me personally, I like the ring of Spud Turner better.... Sounds like a rodeo champ to me."

Lynn laughed over the sound of her boys' happy chatter. "Oh, Chance," she said. "What a wonderful, wonderful life we are going to have—but if you think you are putting my boys on a bull you can forget about it."

"Darlin', we are in total agreement on all counts."

She laughed. "Not on all counts. Spud? Nope, we are not naming our child Spud."

"Then how about Idaho? That sounds good for the rodeo, too."

She laughed again. "Give it up, Chance."

At the word *rodeo* both boys stopped ogling their presents and spun. "We goin' to the rodeo?"

"Sure we are," Chance answered. "But not today. Right now we are going to sit down and I'm going to read to y'all about baby Jesus' birth like I promised."

"That sounds *good*," Jack cooed, and scrambled up close to Chance as he sat down on Lynn's couch. Lynn smiled contently and thanked God once more for the blessings she'd been given. And she knew she was done holding on to her past.

Gavin grabbed his Bible storybook that he'd set on the coffee table in anticipation of Chance coming over, and then he crawled up to sit on Chance's other side. He handed over the book and then looked thoughtful.

"You think God thought about naming baby Jesus Tater?"

"I bet he did," Jack drawled. "It's a real good name. I like it!"

Lynn met Chance's dancing gaze over the top of Gavin's head and chuckled. "Are you sure you're ready for this? For us?"

Chance sobered. "Darlin', I've been ready my whole life for y'all."

* * * * *

Dear Reader,

Thank you for choosing to spend time with me and the Mule Hollow gang! I hope, as I always do, that you were able to put your feet up and relax while you visited my little town!

I loved writing the Men of Mule Hollow trilogy featuring the Turner men, and I couldn't wait all year long to get to Chance's book. Writing about a rodeo preacher appealed to me, and I could see Chance Turner was a cowboy preacher with a heart for God, winning souls of the rodeo cowboys to the Lord. But as always, I wondered what would shake him up…what would happen if circumstances changed and that way of life was taken from him. And also, what would happen when the right woman came along? Of course when questions like that hit my brain it means I have to write the story to get the answers. I hope you've enjoyed reading it as much as I did creating it.

As always, I love hearing from readers. You can reach me through my website, debraclopton.com, my Facebook page or at PO Box 1125, Madisonville, Texas 77864.

Until next time, live, laugh and seek God with all your hearts.

Debra Clopton

We hope you enjoyed reading
this special collection.

If you liked reading these stories,
then you will love **Love Inspired**® books!

You believe hearts can heal. **Love Inspired**
stories show that faith, forgiveness and hope
have the power to lift spirits and change
lives—always.

Enjoy six new stories from
Love Inspired every month!

Available wherever books and
ebooks are sold.

Love Inspired

**Uplifting romances of faith,
forgiveness and hope.**

SPECIAL EXCERPT FROM

Love Inspired®

*When an Amish bachelor suddenly must care for a baby,
will his beautiful next-door neighbor rush to his aid?*

Read on for a sneak preview of
THE AMISH MIDWIFE,
the final book in the brand-new trilogy
LANCASTER COURTSHIPS

"I know I can't raise a baby. I can't! You know what to do.
You take her! You raise her." Joseph thrust Leah toward
Anne. The baby started crying.

"Don't say that. She is your niece, your blood. You
will find the strength you need to care for her."

"She needs more than my strength. She needs a
mother's love. I can't give her that."

Joseph had no idea what a precious gift he was trying
to give away. He didn't understand the grief he would feel
when his panic subsided. She had to make him see that.

Anne stared into his eyes. "I can help you, Joseph,
but I can't raise Leah for you. Your sister Fannie has
wounded you deeply, but she must have enormous faith
in you. Think about it. She could have given her child
away. She didn't. She wanted Leah to be raised by you,
in our Amish ways. Don't you see that?"

He rubbed a hand over his face. "I don't know what
to think."

"You haven't had much sleep in the past four days.
If you truly feel you can't raise Leah, you must go to
Bishop Andy. He will know what to do."

"He will tell me it is my duty to raise her. Did you mean it when you said you would help me?" His voice held a desperate edge.

"Of course. Before you make any rash decisions, let's see if we can get this fussy child to eat something. Nothing wears on the nerves faster than a crying *bubbel* that can't be consoled."

She took the baby from him.

He raked his hands through his thick blond hair again. "I must milk my goats and get them fed."

"That's fine, Joseph. Go and do what you must. Leah can stay with me until you're done."

"*Danki*, Anne Stoltzfus. You have proven you are a good neighbor. Something I have not been to you." He went out the door with hunched shoulders, as if he carried the weight of the world upon them.

Anne looked down at little Leah with a smile. "He'd better come back for you. I know where he lives."

Don't miss
THE AMISH MIDWIFE
by USA TODAY *bestselling author Patricia Davids.*
Available November 2015 wherever
Love Inspired® books and ebooks are sold.

Turn your love of reading into rewards you'll love with
Harlequin My Rewards

**Join for FREE today at
www.HarlequinMyRewards.com**

Earn **FREE BOOKS** of your choice.

Experience **EXCLUSIVE OFFERS** and contests.

Enjoy **BOOK RECOMMENDATIONS**
selected just for you.

PLUS! Sign up now
and get **500** points
right away!

Earn **FREE** REWARDS
HarlequinMyRewards.com
Join Today!

MYR16R

Praise for Debra Clopton and her novels

"A touching story about accepting that God knows what's best, even when it's beyond human understanding."
—*RT Book Reviews* on *Her Forever Cowboy*

"Familiar faces give this story a homey feeling."
—*RT Book Reviews* on *Yuletide Cowboy*

"Debra Clopton's *The Trouble with Lacy Brown* superbly combines humor, romance and action."
—*RT Book Reviews*

"*And Baby Makes Five* is a hilarious story about finding love."
—*RT Book Reviews*